Summer
with the
Country Village
Vet

Zara Stoneley

A division of HarperCollins*Publishers*
www.harpercollins.co.uk

Harper*Impulse* an imprint of
HarperCollins*Publishers*
The News Building
1 London Bridge Street
London SE1 9GF

www.harpercollins.co.uk

This paperback edition 2017

First published in Great Britain in ebook format
by HarperCollins*Publishers* 2017

A catalogue record for this book
is available from the British Library

ISBN: 9780008237974

This novel is entirely a work of fiction.
The names, characters and incidents portrayed in it are
the work of the author's imagination. Any resemblance to
actual persons, living or dead, events or localities is
entirely coincidental.

Set in Birka by Palimpsest Book Production Limited,
Falkirk, Stirlingshire

Printed and bound in Great Britain

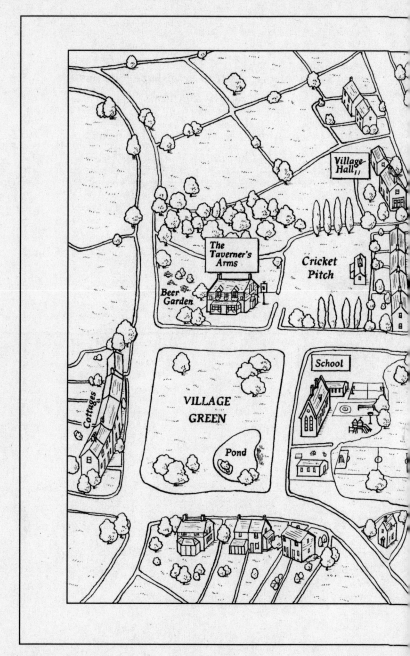

'It takes a big heart to help shape little minds'
Author unknown

To Anne, a teacher with a big heart.

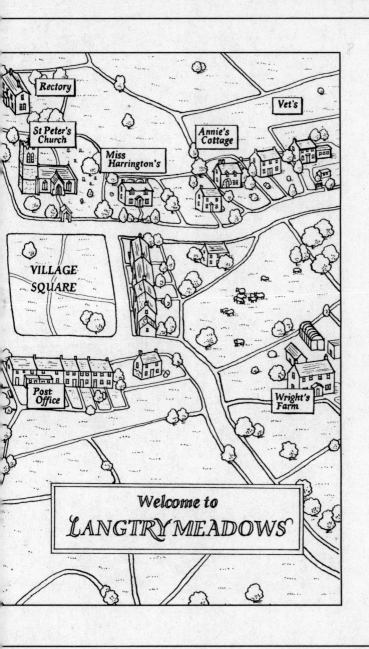

Rectory

Vet's

St Peter's
Church

Annie's
Cottage

Miss
Harrington's

VILLAGE
SQUARE

Post
Office

Wright's
Farm

Welcome to
LANGTRY MEADOWS

Prologue

Three little words with the power to take her straight back to her childhood.

Termination of employment.

Lucy Jacobs stared at the words which were shouting out so much more. Failure. Not good enough. You don't belong here. And she was suddenly that small, abandoned child in the playground again. Unwanted. Unloved. Alone.

Swallowing down the sharp tang of bile, she blinked to clear her vision. Smoothed out the piece of paper with trembling fingers that didn't seem to belong to her. Nothing seemed to belong to her, everything was disjointed, unreal. Even the weak, distant voice that she vaguely recognised as her own.

'No.' Taking a deep breath, she shook her head to dismiss the image. She wasn't a scared child. She was a grown woman now. 'This is a mistake.' Slowly the world came back into focus, even though her stomach still felt empty. Hollow. 'This has got to be a mistake. You're kidding me?' Her words echoed into the uncomfortable stillness of the room.

The man opposite gave the slightest shake of his head, as though it was a silly question.

She'd never liked this room, or more to the point she'd never liked *him*.

Nobody got sacked on a school inset day. Did they?

She blinked hard, trying to ignore the way her eyes smarted and transferred her gaze to the carefully regimented line of pens, before forcing herself to look back up at *him*. David Lawson. The headmaster of Starbaston Primary School.

Not looking at him would be admitting defeat.

He looked back at her through cold reptilian eyes and still didn't say a word.

'But I've just finished my new classroom display!' It was a stupid thing to say, but the only logical thought that was penetrating her fuzzy brain. 'Ready for tomorrow.' Tomorrow, the first day of term.

He finally shifted in his seat, his lips thinned and he stared at her disapprovingly. Then sighed. 'You always do plan well ahead, don't you?'

He said it as though it was a failing. Lucy felt her back straighten and her eyes narrowed, forcing the tears back where they belonged.

The fingers of dread that had been curling themselves into a hard lump in her chest were replaced with indignation. How dare he! The display was a triumph.

Last year's fluffy lambs and cute rabbits had led to a cotton wool and glue fiasco she never wanted to repeat. How was she supposed to know that a six year old would come up with the idea of dipping the rabbit tails into the green paint pot intended for spring grass and stick the resultant giant bogey up his nose, and every other boy in the class would copy him? No doubt when she was old and grey the smarty pants would be a great leader, probably of some union that would bring the government to its knees, or more frighteningly he could become prime minister.

She'd learned from her mistake, and this year she'd been clever. With the help of Sarah, her never tiring classroom assistant, she'd cut a flower out for every single child and gone for the theme of April showers and May flowers. They had spent most of the day stapling the petals up on the boards, awaiting the children's smiley self-portraits to be added in the centre over the next couple of weeks.

It had been hard work. It had been a total waste of time.

She stared at the headmaster, wishing she could wiggle her nose and make him disappear. He peered back over his glasses at her, and steepled his fingers, in much the same way he did when he was faced with a Year 6 girl who thought school rules about make-up (or more precisely the lack of it) couldn't possibly apply to the top class, or Mrs Ogden who'd said if her Storm wanted to have white hair and pierced ears what did it have to do with him?

The head didn't understand X-Men, he didn't understand the society he was living in, or the staff who worked so hard to give the children a chance to live a better life. He understood balance sheets, not feelings and aspirations.

'As you know,' he paused, politician style, circled his thumbs – which right now she had a childish urge to grab hold of and bend back – 'we did request offers for voluntary redundancy earlier in the year, but nobody,' the thumbs stopped

3

moving, and he studied her as though she was at fault, 'came forward, and so unfortunately...'

'But you can't ... I mean, why me?' She crossed her arms and frowned. 'I need this job, I've just bought new curtains.' Gorgeous, shimmery, floaty new curtains. And it was more than curtains: she'd bought a whole house. A house that had stretched her to the financial limit, but given her the greatest feeling of satisfaction (apart from getting all of Year 2 to sit on their bottoms and listen at the same time) ever. Ever.

'The Ofsted inspector labelled my lesson outstanding.' She made a valuable contribution, she worked hard.

This just couldn't be happening.

'You can't sack me.'

He tutted. Actually tutted, and looked affronted. 'We,' that flaming 'we' again, as though it meant he wasn't responsible, 'aren't sacking you, Lucy.' He paused again, politician style. 'You are being offered an excellent redundancy package.'

'Well that's different then.' He nodded, missing the sarcasm. 'So offered means I can turn it down?' She wanted to launch herself across his tidy desk and strangle him with his fake silk tie. It might be a sackable offence, but that didn't matter now. Did it?

He carried on smoothly, oblivious of her evil intent. 'No, I'm sorry it doesn't. As I've just explained, we did ask for volunteers, and as nobody put themselves forward we have had to make a decision. We've followed the correct procedure.' There was an unspoken 'so don't even think about challenging the decision'.

'I don't care about procedures.' It was getting close to a toss-up between losing her temper and shouting, or bursting into tears. She bit down on her lip hard. No way was she going to give him the satisfaction of seeing her collapse into a mushy mess. That would be the ultimate humiliation. Even beating the getting sacked in the first place bit. 'I've got a mortgage.'

He sighed as though she was being unreasonable. 'I am sorry, Lucy. We do understand, we all have commitments, but unfortunately we,' why did he keep blaming 'we' when it was very clearly his decision? He never had liked her, 'have to make cuts. It's inescapable. As you know education has been hit as hard as anybody.' She caught herself nodding in agreement, and froze back into position. 'We have tried to do this as fairly as possible, and as the most recent addition to the staffing at the school, then I'm afraid you were the—'

'But what about Ruth?' It came blurting out of her mouth before she could stop herself. She really didn't want to point the finger at anybody else, but this was her future at stake.

'We need to balance the accounts Miss Jacobs,' oh God, he'd reverted to calling her Miss, there was no way out of this, 'and as Ruth is very much a junior member of staff, her salary is, how do I put this? Commensurate with her experience.' He put his hands flat on the desk and leaned back, mission accomplished. She'd never particularly liked David Lawson, with his slightly pompous air, and sarcastic comments if anybody dared interrupt his staff meetings to offer constructive criticism, but now there was something stirring inside her that was close to loathing.

'And my experience doesn't count for anything? You employed me because—'

'It's a fine balancing act, my dear.' Now he'd moved on to

patronising, which he probably thought was consoling. 'It's complicated.'

'Try me.'

'The finances of the school are not something you should concern yourself with, Lucy.' He shook his head. Back to calling her Lucy and adopting his avuncular uncle act.

Obviously, she was smart enough to take responsibility for developing the young minds that would be tomorrow's leaders, scientists and all round wonderful people, but he did not consider she had the mental capacity to understand the balance sheet of a primary school. Despite the fact she had a maths degree.

'Now, you are bound to be upset and need to let this sink in, so to avoid any unpleasantness I had somebody clear your belongings from your classroom. There's a box at reception, I'm sure everything is in there, but if there's anything missing please do call Elaine and she will arrange delivery.' He stood up, smiled like a hyena about to pounce, and held out a hand. Which she automatically shook, then realised she'd conceded defeat. 'I do wish you well Lucy, you've done an excellent job with your little people and another school will benefit hugely from our loss.' He withdrew the hand, obviously relieved that his ordeal was over, and hers had just begun. He'd handed over the baton. 'And here is a letter with the terms of your redundancy, I'm sure you'll find it all in order. Close the door on the way out will you please.'

He'd already sat down again, his head dipped to study the papers on his desk so that he could avoid her. She'd been dismissed.

Lucy stood up and was shocked to realise her legs were trembling. Her whole body was quaking. She fumbled with the door handle, tears bubbling up and blurring her vision, her stomach churning like the sea in a storm. This wasn't her. She didn't do wobbly and tears in public.

She felt sick.

Lucy put the surprisingly small box, which represented two years of tears, tantrums and triumphs (usually the pupils, occasionally hers) at Starbaston Primary School on the kitchen table. She could scream loudly and set next doors dog off barking, or she could make a cup of tea.

The bright, modern kitchen had, until now, given her only pleasure, but now she felt flat as she switched the fast-boil kettle on and dropped a tea bag into the 'Best Teacher' mug that Madison, a Year 2 pupil, had presented to her last Christmas.

She stared out at the small but immaculate patch of garden, *her* patch with not a weed in sight, and the hollow emptiness inside her grew.

Around the edges of the neat square of grass, the crocus shouted out a bright splash of colour, goading the pale nodding heads of the snowdrops. Soon the daffodils would appear, and she'd already bought sweet pea seeds to sow with her class (the only flowers many of them would see close up) so that she could bring a few of the seedlings home and brighten up the fence that separated her garden from her neighbours.

She'd had it all planned out. She'd had her whole life planned out.

Tea slopped out of her mug as she stirred it mindlessly, the events of the last year spiralling on fast-forward in her mind, and bringing a rush of tears to her eyes.

They brimmed over and she scrubbed away angrily at them with the heel of her hand. Tea and sympathy was one thing, tea and self-pity was altogether different. Pathetic. She needed to get a grip. This was just a blip, things like this made you stronger, more determined. The failures were what made you who you were; the only people who didn't fail were the ones that never did anything.

The garden blurred as she wrapped her hands round the mug and took a deep breath, willing the lump in her throat to go away. If she hadn't moved to Starbaston, if she'd just settled for her old, mundane job with no job prospects she wouldn't be jobless. But she would never have been able to buy her home either.

Buying this house had been the biggest, best, scariest thing she'd ever done. She'd only been teaching at Starbaston for a year when they'd given her the promotion they'd hinted about at the interview. She'd got home from work, re-read the letter about twenty times, let out a whoop and started looking at the estate agents. Not that she didn't already have a good idea of the houses for sale in the area.

She'd scrimped and saved ever since she'd graduated, well even as a student, rarely going out and only buying clothes that she really needed, determined to have enough money for a deposit on a small house in her bank account ready for the day that her income level meant she could take the plunge. And she knew exactly what she wanted, and had a pretty good idea of the size of salary she needed to afford it. It would be hers. Nobody would be able to take it away. She'd never again feel like she didn't belong.

Her friends had laughed, but Lucy knew it was the right thing for her. She'd been eight years old when life as she knew it had been ripped into shreds. When her and Mum had moved from their comfortable village home into a scruffy rented terraced house with peeling paint and neighbours who peed on the fence. She'd lost everything: her dad, her dog, her lovely room, even her best friend. She was a nobody; nobody wanted her, and she didn't belong anywhere.

She'd wanted her home back. She'd wanted her mother how she used to be – always there when she needed her, in the playground each day with a smile when she came out of school. She'd wanted her dog, Sandy, to play with. She'd wanted her room with all her books and toys, her garden with the swing she'd sit on for hours. She'd wanted her friend Amy to sit with her under the big tree in the school playground. She'd even wanted her dad back, even though he could be cross if she made a mess, and insisted she practise the piano every day.

Instead she'd been alone.

Her mother always out, working all hours in dead-end jobs trying to make ends meet, and never having time to tidy or clean the embarrassingly messy house. She'd kept her own room tidy, because Dad liked tidy, and maybe he'd come to see them if she kept it nice. She'd dreamed that one day he would, and he'd take them home and everything would go back to normal.

He never came. Gran told her to forget him; he'd remarried. Her lovely bedroom belonged to somebody else now, and there was no going back.

Amy never replied to her letters – her mother probably wouldn't have let her visit their scruffy new home anyway. And the kids at her new school laughed at the way she spoke and wouldn't let her join in with their games, turning their backs on her if she ever dared pluck up the courage to edge her way over to them. She gave up in the end.

Life got better when she moved to high school and found friends. In the big impersonal city school she felt less alone, there were more people like her – struggling to find a place to belong.

But she still lived on the roughest estate, in the scruffiest house. And she promised herself that one day she would have a decent job, and a house of her own. A clean tidy home, on a clean tidy estate where she felt in control, a home that nobody could take away from her.

And the sacrifices had seemed worth it. Until now.

How could this have happened to her? She'd done every-thing right, she'd worked hard, she'd had a plan – and had been discarded, thrown out because she was *too* qualified. *Too* expensive.

She wiped the fresh tears away angrily. Except this time it was different. She was in control, she wasn't some kid who had no say in the matter, and she *did* belong here. She did.

She fished into the box that represented her time at Starbaston and pulled out a pen pot (empty), a packet of 'star pupil' stickers, a box of tissues, a spare pair of tights, an assortment of plasters, notepad and then spotted a slip of paper. Which had been placed so the eagle-eyes of the headmaster's secretary didn't spot it.

'Can't believe they did this to you, don't know how I'll cope without you Miss Crackers. Love Sarah x'

The lump in her throat caught her unawares and Lucy crumpled up the note in her fist and hung on to it. It had been one of their many jokes, she was Miss Cream Crackers after little Jack, he of the hand-me-down uniform and mother with four inch heels and a scary cleavage, had declared on her first day at the school that 'he could only eat them Jacobs cracker things with a lot of butter spread on them or they made him cough' and did she make them when she got home from school?

Jokes got them through the day.

She didn't know how she was going to cope either. The feeling inside her wasn't just upset, it was more like grief, as though a chunk of her hopes, her future, had been torn from her heart.

The cup of tea wasn't making her feel better. Halfway through her drink the feeling of grief had subsided, but it had been replaced with something worse.

She thought that she'd left the waves of panic behind – along with the spots, teenage crushes and worries that she'd never have friends or sex – but now they started to claw at her chest. She closed her eyes.

She just had to breathe. Steadily. In, out, the world would stop rocking, her heart wouldn't explode, she wasn't going to die. Everything would be fine.

She would think about this logically. Sensibly. With her eyes shut.

The redundancy money would cover the bills for a while, but she urgently needed to find another job before it ran out. There was no way she was ever, ever, going to go back to living in that horrible neighbourhood she'd been brought up in. It hadn't been her mother's fault that she hadn't time to keep on top of the house or garden, and that they could never afford anything new, but Lucy wanted her life to be different.

Putting her mug of tea on the table, she flipped open her laptop. She wasn't going to mess around, or waste another second.

She'd show David bloody Lawson. She'd get another job, a better job, a job where the headmaster wasn't a self-satisfied arse who didn't give a monkeys about his staff or his pupils. Blinking away the mist of unshed tears she typed two words into the browser 'teaching vacancies', and hit the enter key with an angry jab.

Lucy opened her eyes with a start. It was dark. One cheek was damp and plastered to her keyboard. She probably had an imprint of the keys on her face. She sat up slowly and blinked.

The outside security light, which must have woken her up, went off and plunged the kitchen into darkness.

She sighed and stood up, wincing as a pain shot between her shoulder blades. Her back felt stiff as a board, she had a horrible dry taste in her mouth and her hair was sticky against her cheek from either dribble or tears. Or both. So, life was going well. She'd only been jobless for a few hours and look at the state of her.

So much for the no tears strategy, she'd failed there as well. But did crying in your sleep count?

This would look better in the morning. It had to. Before falling asleep she'd looked at every conceivable (and inconceivable) teaching vacancy website and come up with a big fat zero. The trouble was, teachers were being laid off faster than they were being taken on. And even supply jobs were thin on the ground, as an increasingly large number of people (many with more experience than she had) competed for them.

She looked into the biscuit tin. My God, had she really emptied it, eaten every single one, even the broken bits? She was going to be fat as well as jobless.

Tomorrow. Tomorrow would be better. She'd be thinking clearly. She'd find a new job. She'd be back on track.

Chapter 1

Lucy slowed the car to a halt. Did the satnav really want her to turn down this road?

Turn left. Yep, it did. *Turn left.*

'Okay I heard, but you're kidding me?' The stern voice didn't reply, but her phone did. It buzzed. Maybe it was a last minute reprieve, the agency with a much better job offer back in civilisation.

She picked the mobile up. No reprieve, more a reminder of her old job, the challenges that came with working in a city centre school.

The life she loved.

She suppressed the groan, and smiled. Didn't they say the positivity of a smile was reflected in your voice?

'Hi Sarah.' She really didn't have time to chat, but she knew what the classroom assistant from Starbaston was like. Persistence was her middle name. If she didn't answer now she'd be getting another call mid interview.

'How are you doing, babe?' Sarah's normal sing-song happy tone was tinged with concern. Okay, so maybe her megawatt smile wasn't having the desired effect.

'Fine, fine.'

'Really? Then why haven't you rung?'

'Well no, well yes.' Fine was relative after all. 'I've got an interview, in fact I'm just on my way.'

'That's fab.' Her words hung in the silence. 'Isn't it?'

'I think I'm lost.'

'You always were crap at following directions, babe. Why aren't you using that satnav you got?'

'I am.'

Sarah giggled. 'And you put the right place in and everything?'

'I put the right place in and everything. It keeps telling me I need to turn left here for Langtry Meadows and it's this tiny lane.'

'Where? Lang what?'

'Exactly.' The back of beyond. 'Some village not even my satnav has heard of. Oh God, I'm throwing what's left of my life away.'

'No, you're not, you're making a new one, a better one. Away from this stink hole and loser Lawson.'

'But I don't need a new one.' She'd quite liked the life she already had. New house, nice car, job.

'Yes, you do, Lucy. The old one's gone.' That was telling her.

'Thanks for reminding me.'

'You know what I mean, Loo. There's something better out there. Believe me,' she sighed dramatically, 'lots of better things.' But Sarah didn't have a mortgage to pay, bills. She lived with her mum. 'You're the one that always tells me everything happens for a reason. I miss you, you idiot, but you're better off somewhere else.'

16

'I know I am Sarah.' She gazed through the car windscreen. Right now all she could see were fields and it was making her feel uneasy. Not a lump of concrete, or even person, in sight. 'But maybe not buried up to my armpits in cows.' She had passed plenty of cows, and was pretty confident there'd be some in Langtry Meadows – if she ever found the place.

'Better than being buried in this shit. We'll be back in special measures while twat face is still busy working out which politician to invite over for dinner next.'

'Should you call your boss twat face?' Just talking to Sarah made her feel more positive.

'You will never guess what he's just spent a huge chunk of our bloody budget on.'

'Probably not.' Lucy glanced at her watch. 'Not teaching staff, that's for sure.' She needed to get to this interview, seeing as it was actually the only thing between her and eating nothing but baked beans for a very long time.

'A metal detector.'

'What, for the kids to look for money?' The parents would be battling to borrow it every weekend.

'No, you idiot, a scanner type thing to check them on the way into school.'

'You cannot be serious? Okay Starbaston is a bit rough, but the kids are still more into flicking paper planes than knives.' She paused. 'They're kids, innocent.' Well maybe not all that innocent. But...

'But he doesn't know that, does he? He's a wanker. The man buys a frigging metal detector. In a primary school when he won't even give us any more money for tissue paper and glue.'

'Or teachers.' Lucy couldn't help adding that, and sounding bitter.

'Aww babe, I know, he's an arse. But that's what I mean, there just has to be somewhere better than this.'

'I know.' Lucy sighed. 'But am I ready to be buried in the countryside? I'm not brain dead, just redundant.'

Sarah giggled. 'So it's a proper village, in the countryside and everything?'

'In the countryside and everything, I think.' It looked very countryside from the picture on the website. 'If I ever find it.'

'You can join the WI and bake cakes.'

'How old do you think I am you cheeky cow? Anyhow I can't bake to save my life, watching Great British Bake Off is the nearest I get to making a cake, I kill every plant I touch—'

'Apart from cress heads.'

'Apart from cress heads,' she was good at that, she could grow cress in an eggshell or on scratchy green paper towels as well as any five year old, 'and the only time I tried to knit I ended up cross-eyed with my needles knotted together.' She'd thrown the whole lot in the bin and wondered how on earth she'd ever thought yarn-bombing was a sensible thing.

'So you're not doing an escape to the country, then Loo?'

'I'll be planning my escape out. I'm glad you're finding this so hilarious.' It was cheering her up though. 'Anyhow I haven't got the job yet, I'm just going for an interview.'

'You'll get it, they'll snap you up. You go girl.'

'And it is just a cover job for next half-term, so you can stop imagining me in a headscarf and wellies.'

'Spoilsport. You never know, you might meet some phwoar

farmer and want to make babies with him and breed cows and stuff.'

'Sod off Sarah.' She was grinning, she knew she was. 'Thanks though. I love you.'

'Love you too, babe. Let me know how it goes.'

'Sarah?'

'Yeah?'

'Don't tell Lawson about this.' Not that he'd even remember who she was.

Welcome to Langtry Meadows. Lucy breathed a sigh of relief as she passed the sign, and checked her watch again. She'd made it, with ten minutes to spare.

Not that it looked exactly promising. So this was it. Fields to the left, fields to the right, oh and hedges. And more fields. Shades of green she'd forgotten existed. Oh yeah, and cows.

No. Be positive. She was having a new adventure. A nice, restful temporary job while she recharged her batteries, jiggled her life plan a bit, before taking the next step.

She'd served her apprenticeship, sailed through her Newly Qualified Teacher year, been promoted and was soaring up the ranks heading for Senior Leadership Team and eventually Head and this was all just a blip.

David Lawson would have never had her on his leadership team, he hated her. So she'd had a lucky break.

A holiday in the sticks. Yep, that was how she'd have to look at it. A holiday. A six week break filled with spring flowers and chubby-faced village children.

As the road narrowed she slowed down and felt some of

the tension ease away. She had to admit that the second she'd entered the village even the hedgerows seemed prettier. The green was broken up with frothy white hawthorn blossom, and the grassy verges were sprinkled with yellow, pink and violet flowers. Something inside her lifted, and all of a sudden she felt more positive.

The road narrowed slightly more, if that was possible, and then curled round to the left. She held her breath as she rounded it, gripping the steering wheel, half expecting to collide with a tractor coming the other way. But what hit her was something quite different.

Lucy leant forward until her chin was practically balanced on the steering wheel, and stared at the scene ahead.

She'd been following the winding country lane, concentrating on the road, for what seemed like miles, and now all of a sudden *this* had opened out in front of her, bringing an unexpected lump to her throat.

The perfect picture-postcard village green.

Ahead the road forked to the right and left, cupping the pond, green and cascading willow tree in a gentle embrace. Drawing up at the side of the road, she pulled the handbrake on and got out of her Mini, stretching out the kinks that had settled into her back and shoulders.

Right now it didn't seem to matter that she didn't actually want to work in the countryside. She felt like she'd slipped Alice-in-Wonderland style from her own busy life, into a different world. Except in her case it was like being thrown back to her childhood. The good bit, before it had all gone so disastrously wrong.

The happy times were just a cloudy, indistinct memory though, buried under the weight of unhappiness. And now she'd been forced back, into the type of world she'd happily avoided until now.

The narrow lanes, with high hedges and dappled shade had demanded a level of concentration which didn't mix well with the jitters that had been building in the pit of her stomach, and if she hadn't been so doggedly determined to make this work she would have ignored her satnav and done an abrupt U-turn back to the safety of the city. But she hadn't, and now she wasn't quite sure if she was happy, or wanted to curl up and cry.

She'd done a very efficient job of blanking out her early childhood and the village she'd grown up in. And now this blast from the past had knocked the wind out of her sails even more effectively than redundancy had.

When they'd moved she'd missed her home, not the village. All her friends had gradually drifted away, apart from Amy, leaving her marooned on an island made for one. They'd stopped inviting her to their parties. Dad had said she was like her mum – a city girl – and would never fit in properly, but he'd make sure she was okay. Then he'd abandoned her too.

She bit down on her lip. The week they'd left the village of Stoneyvale had been the worst of her life. She'd thought that being the only girl in the class not invited to Heather's party had been bad. She'd run all the way home from school, then rushed up to her bedroom with Sandy, shut the door and cried into his fur until her face was all blotchy. But then it got worse. Two days later Sandy had gone, and her mother had taken her to a new, horrible place.

She could still remember that feeling in the playground. The pain in her stomach, the ache in her throat. Knowing that Dad was right. Everybody hated her.

There was a giggle and Lucy blinked, dragging her thoughts back to the present. A little girl, her arms wide like a windmill was chasing a duck across the green. A woman was watching her, and even at this distance Lucy could sense the proud smile on her face. It could have been her, once, with her own mum. Before things had changed.

Now, this gentle reminder of how it had once been was hurting far more than the gruesome thoughts that often interrupted her sleep.

She didn't want to go back to not belonging. To being the odd one out. She wanted to be that little girl again, happy, secure.

The view misted over before her eyes and Lucy wiped her arm angrily across her face to get rid of the threatening tears, gulping down the upset that was bubbling up in her throat.

Okay, maybe it wasn't as simple as the picture she'd painted for Sarah, the story she'd sold herself. Working in a village wasn't on her life plan for a purpose, and it wasn't just down to promotion opportunities. It was down to control. Being able to live the life she wanted. Going forward not back. Not feeling shunned by a close community that didn't like outsiders.

The old familiar feeling of panic started to snake up from her stomach, wrap itself around her heart and throat, making it hard to breath. This was *not* the village she had been brought up in. She clenched her fists and tried to stop the trembling that was attacking her whole body. She'd gone from calm and admiring the view, to feeling agitated and out of control in seconds, which was why she never looked to the past. She had to get a grip.

All villages weren't full of small-minded petty people. They didn't all hate people they'd decided weren't good enough, didn't belong. Places like this could be restful, pleasant, not bathed in an undercurrent of foreboding. She closed her eyes, counted slowly, willing herself down. Her mother had always been on edge back then, just before they left, expecting the worst, and that fear had grabbed hold of her as well. Leaked into the corners of her life.

She'd never found out what that worst was, but whenever she thought of country life she thought of that. Unease.

Lucy wanted to jump back into her car, head back to her nice safe home and the life she'd made for herself. The anonymity of city life. But she couldn't. It wasn't an option right now.

She took a deep breath. It *would* be an option one day soon. This was just a temporary solution until she got life back on track. Which she would do. She wasn't her mother.

This was so not why she'd qualified as a teacher though. She never wanted to relive her old idyllic life, the nice part before it all imploded. Before her dad had decided they weren't good enough and discarded them, thrown them onto the rubbish heap. Just like her so called friends had done. Just like David Lawson had done.

She hadn't deserved it as a kid, and she didn't deserve it now.

Oh God, she was being ridiculous. Sense of foreboding my foot. She'd been reading far too many scary books, it was no wonder the panic attacks were coming back. She was in a perfectly nice, tranquil village where the worst that could happen was she'd get bored to death.

The loud quack made her jump. Or she might get pecked to death. A very indignant mallard looked up at her. 'Well, I haven't got any bread if that's what you're after.'

The duck tipped his head on one side, then blinked in disbelief before raising himself as high as he could, on surprisingly long legs, and shook his feathers vigorously. He settled back down onto the grass and for a moment she did feel like that long forgotten happy child again. She was sorely tempted to kick her shoes off and step onto the thick inviting carpet of green grass, to stroll over and sit beneath the soft dappled shade of the weeping willow and watch the ducks. Which was far better than collapsing in a pathetic, bubbling heap. But she couldn't do that either. Not now.

Instead she let her gaze drift over the haphazard array of cottages, and settle on the large building at the top end of the green. Even at this distance she could tell it was a pub, which meant ... she looked to the right and spotted it. An old red-brick building which was instantly recognisable as the picture on the website. Langtry Meadows Primary School.

It was nothing like the old school she vaguely remembered

attending. She wiped her sweaty palms on her skirt, ignoring the slight tremble in her fingers, and took a deep breath. She could do this. It was just a job. She belonged here as much as the next person, she was a teacher now, not the child who couldn't live up to her father's expectations.

His words echoed in her ears, as though he was there. She couldn't escape them. 'It's not real, Lucy. Nobody cares about you,' he'd given a small sad smile, 'they only bother with you because I'm your father. If I wasn't here you'd see how useless you really are, just like your mother.'

She hadn't believed him at first. But it turned out he'd been right. Her dad was always right. After they'd moved, not even her best friend Amy had said goodbye, or replied to Lucy's letters, or come to see them in their new home. But neither had Dad. It was as if she'd never existed.

She closed her eyes and took an involuntary step backwards. Away from the green, the memories.

'Hey!'

Lucy clasped her hand to her chest and spun round at the harsh male tone. It couldn't be her father, not here.

'Move.'

He was bigger than her father. Taller, stronger, and even as her brain was telling her to fight off the hand that was reaching out towards her, he was rugby tackling her, taking her with him. Sending her off balance. She flapped her arms wildly, and was pretty sure from the grunt in her ear and the sharp pain in her wrist that she'd smacked him across the head as they staggered back locked together.

'What the—?' There was a loud clang and she shrank back

against him as a large horse (how the hell had she not heard that coming?), galloped past so close to her car that the stirrup iron caught the wing mirror of her car. She was dimly aware of the rider grappling with the reins, of a shouted apology, a whoosh of air and brief whiff of sweating horse.

Then nothing.

Lucy clung on to the arm that was wrapped around her. Her knees were trembling, in fact her whole body was shaking in sympathy with the pounding rhythm of her speeding heart-beat. She'd hated horses ever since her father had insisted she should learn to ride. They were so big. So scary. So many feet and big teeth. They could kill you and not notice. This one nearly had.

'Ouch.'

She suddenly realised she was digging her nails into the strong forearm, gripping on for dear life. And she was leaning against the safety of the firm body behind her as if she knew him. Which was kind of awkward.

Oh God, that warm breath against her neck was doing weird things to her. She closed her eyes, which made things worse as all her senses seemed to home in on his slightly woody scent, on the fact that the well-muscled arm was part of a very firm body. It was obviously delayed shock that was making her this hyper-aware.

'Christ you've got a good left hook.' She twisted, glanced up. Mistake. Dark, concerned brown eyes were looking down straight into hers as his lips practically brushed against her cheek. Full, dry lips.

He rubbed the side of his head with his free hand, a rueful

smile tugging at the corners of his generous, very-kissable, mouth.

They were practically in a clinch, well the closest she'd been to a clinch for quite some time. Oh hell. She swung back to face the front, before he realised just how close she was to actually kissing him.

She was pretty sure she made a kind of squeaky noise, and she was more than sure that she'd shoved her bum into his crotch so they were now spooned in the kind of post-sex intimate position that you just didn't do with clothes on. Or in broad daylight with a stranger.

He froze, then leapt away from her as though he'd been stung – almost throwing her off balance again.

'Sorry.' His tone was nearly as clipped as his action, and when she half-turned he was studying a spot about six inches above the top of her head. 'You were in its path. Bolting horses can run blind.'

Wow, he *was* tall, dizzyingly tall, and solid looking.

'Oh.' Suddenly light headed she bent over and rested her hands on her knees, and was shocked when he squatted down and peered up at her, studying her intently as he threaded his fingers through his mussed up hair.

'Are you okay? Do you need to sit down?'

She blinked at the soft tone which was in total contrast to the brusque edge she'd heard seconds before.

'Fine, I just need to get my breath.' She tried to smile. 'I'm not used to being almost run down by galloping horses.' Or being grabbed by strong, attractive men. There was a bit of a shortage of them in city centre primary schools. Sexy men, and horses. Not that he was responsible for her current light headedness – that had to be the danger, the nearly being killed. The thrill ... No, not thrill. Danger. Adrenaline – that was the word she was looking for.

'Don't apologise. I would have a sit down if I were you, shock can have a strange effect.'

Something was having a strange effect, but she had a horrible feeling it was more to do with finding herself pressed against the groin of a man, than the risk of a trail of hoof prints being left across her body.

'You look pale.'

She felt pale. Avoiding his gaze she glanced downwards. Bloody hell, his blood supply seemed to have redirected round his body again and headed southwards, right into the spot she'd been nestled against. She looked back up guiltily, straight into his eyes. Mistake. Maybe she was better shutting her eyes, concentrating on her own blood flow which seemed to be located solely in her heart which was still hammering away ten to the dozen.

He wasn't reacting to her, it was a male thing. Danger turned her into a wobbly blancmange, and men into, well into, well it could just turn them on.

'Hey.'

He was still waiting for a reply, and probably worried she was going to keel over on him. 'I'm fine. Thank you.' She studied his feet. Much safer than looking at his groin, or into his eyes.

'Good.' He stuck his hands into his pockets. He knew. The earth just had to swallow her up, whisk her away. 'Great, well if you're sure you're okay, I'll be off.' He stepped back almost nervously. 'Work to do.' He was doing his best to edge past her, squeeze between her and the car. She stepped back, feeling awkward. 'Sorry about grabbing...'

'No problem, thanks for...'

'Sure.' And he spun on his heel, and was off before she could say another word.

Lucy sank down against the bonnet of her car and watched as he set off down the road, his long legs swallowing up the ground as though he couldn't get away quickly enough. Wow. Nobody on Emmerdale looked like that, or on The Yorkshire Vet, or on Countryfile. Not that she really watched programmes like that. Home makeover programmes were more her thing.

She glanced at her watch out of habit. 'Bloody hell.' She'd almost forgotten what she was doing here, she was going to be late for her interview. She was never late for anything. Ducking back into her little car she started up the engine and pulled out. Following the left hand fork, she passed the Taverner's Arms, and then pulled up outside the school that lay just beyond it.

Smoothing her hair down with a slightly shaky hand, she tucked the loose tendrils behind her ears. All she had to do was remember to breathe and be natural, confident. Everything she wasn't feeling.

But she could do this with her eyes shut. She knew she could. Teaching in a small village school had to be easy after the day-to-day battles she'd fought in a failing city centre one.

It was fine, if she didn't get this job there would be others.

Lucy had applied for the temporary cover position at Langtry Meadows out of a sense of desperation. She'd actually wondered how the hell she was going to be convincing in an interview. One, she didn't want to work in a village, two she wanted to work within commuting distance of her home, and three she was over qualified for the post. But as she got out of her car and gazed in awe at the pretty primary school she realised she actually wanted this job. Maybe if she could do this, she could banish her past forever. Not just hide the hurt, but beat it down. Face up to it, and prove it no longer had a hold over her.

Which made it all the more nerve-wracking. She couldn't ever remember feeling quite this nervous, but that was probably because all of a sudden she knew it mattered. Really mattered.

Colourful stepping stones marked a path across the playground, leading up to a doorway which had 'Boys' etched into the arched brickwork above. She stared up at it – wondering if she'd somehow been transported back in time – when a young woman, with cropped trousers, a floaty blouse and paint covered hands appeared on the step.

'Hi there! You must be Lucy.' The woman smiled. 'Come in, come in. Oh, don't worry about that.' She'd followed Lucy's gaze. 'This school was built back in the days when they thought pre-marital hand-touching was a sin, we've got a girl's entrance over there.' She pointed to another entrance at the other end of the playground. 'We use that for open days, and everybody dives in through this one the rest of the time. You'll have to excuse me, I've been helping Reception Class with finger-painting.' She wriggled red and yellow fingers, and Lucy felt some of the flutters disperse. Just some. 'Mrs Potts is about somewhere, she'll show you round while I get myself cleaned up. Good journey?'

She paused for breath and Lucy smiled back.

'Great thanks.' Better not to mention the wrong turnings.

'I'm hopeless, I always get lost even with a satnav. I'm Jill by the way, classroom assistant and chief bottom wiper. I won't shake hands – not with fingers like this. If you sign in there and grab a visitor's badge I'll find Liz, she's probably gone to buy some biscuits. Best part of an interview day,' she grinned, 'candidates have biscuits and we get to finish them off, we usually get bourbons and cream custards, much better than the normal digestive biscuits. Ah, here she is, I'll leave you in her capable hands, and get back to painting caterpillar pictures. Catch you later.'

Liz Potts was frighteningly capable. After checking that Lucy had signed herself in properly, and had made a note of her car registration correctly, she gathered up her bunch of keys and set off on the introductory tour of the school at a speed totally at odds with her appearance. She reminded Lucy of Mrs Tiggy-Winkle. Which could have been down to her rather rounded appearance, sharp nose, and tiny feet. Or the speed they were scuttling down the corridors at.

Lucy was being whisked through the school with a ruthless efficiency, and a nod to left and right at various classrooms which Mrs Potts seemed to consider superfluous to teaching.

'Reception and Class 1 here on the right ... and the dining

room is there … this is our little library … Class 2 here, rather a big intake, it must have been a bad winter.'

'Sorry?' Lucy craned her neck, trying to peek inside at the children who seemed remarkably engrossed in their work.

'Snow, a hard winter always results in a flurry of autumn births don't you find?'

It had never occurred to Lucy, but there again there was probably less to do here than in the middle of Birmingham, which very rarely saw snow anyway.

The corridors seemed eerily quiet compared to what she'd been used to at her previous school, although that could have been partly down to the fact that it had been a modern build with thin partition walls and echoing areas between them – whereas this was a delightfully solid looking brick built affair that appeared to have been part of the village for years.

'Er, yes, well.' Easier to change the subject. 'Do you have a Wi-Fi connection throughout the school?'

'Wi-Fi?' Mrs Potts actually paused, very briefly, so that an unprepared Lucy had to swerve, before they picked up speed again. She was more than used to chasing round after young children, and dashing round a classroom to avoid catastrophe, but it was the sheer determination of the woman as she darted down the corridors that had caught her by surprise.

'You've got wireless throughout the school? An internet connection?' Flat shoes were obviously going to be a necessity here, if she took the five week cover position.

'Oh good heavens no, dear.' Mrs Potts pursed her lips and shook her head dismissively. 'That isn't how we do things here.'

Oh hell, she'd been right. They probably wouldn't even have interactive whiteboards. It would be old-fashioned style teaching, which was about as progressive as old fashioned granny knickers and string vests.

'We've got chickens.'

Lucy came to a stop, then she had to dash after her tour guide who was steaming ahead, had flung a door open and as far as Lucy was concerned might well dive through it and disappear. 'Chickens?' God, she was out of breath, this was worse than Sports Day.

'And a wonderful vegetable patch. Come along dear, I'll show you.' Mrs Potts glanced at her watch, her pace never faltering. 'We are rather pushed for time as the children are waiting to interview you, they've been preparing all week.'

Lucy frowned, this all seemed rather over the top for a temporary post, in fact it was exactly what she expected in an interview for a permanent position. It seemed that the school took its staffing very seriously indeed. Mrs Potts had picked up speed, marching across the playground with Lucy running to keep up, to where a small patch of rather worn grass was fenced off, with what had to be a wooden chicken coop inside. 'We do have computers in the classroom plugged in,' she gave Lucy a stern look which suggested she didn't approve, 'for teaching purposes, but they can't learn about responsibility by looking at those, can they? Now if the monitors for the day forget to shut the hens up at night, they won't repeat that mistake again, will they?'

'Won't they?' Lucy stared at the small wooden building, and a rather scraggy chicken gave her a beady once-over then proceeded to peck at the dirt.

'Of course not.' Mrs Potts looked at her as though she was a simpleton. 'The fox will get them, won't it?' She made a cut throat gesture that looked slightly sinister, as she headed back across the playground and Lucy scurried after her.

'It will?' The sense that she'd entered some kind of tranquil backwater where life was idyllic started to disperse.

The drive up the M6 motorway had left her frustrated and tense (sure that she would be late, and she was never late), and then she'd lost her way twice which had left her with sweating palms and the start of a headache, but the moment she'd entered the village the stress had started to ebb away and as her shoulders had relaxed she'd eased back on the accelerator and started to appreciate the pretty flower strewn hedgerows.

By the time she'd reached the well-kept village green with its swathes of bright dancing daffodils the pounding in her temples had stopped. Momentarily.

Until she'd taken an unwanted tumble back to her child-hood, before being unceremoniously tossed to the curb by a very big man. With a firm grip, tousled hair and gorgeous eyes. Oh hell, now all she needed was for him to be one of the parents and word would soon get round that she was up for a grope with any passing strangers. Not that she'd actually kissed him. Luckily. But she had rubbed herself against him. And wriggled against his crotch.

What the hell was she was letting herself in for?

'It certainly will. Foxes can be relied on.' They ground to a halt, and Lucy nearly cannoned into her. 'Believe me, the children only make that mistake once. And we have the vegetable patch of course.' Mrs Potts was on the move again. Of course. At Lucy's previous school they'd settled for egg shell men with cress hair, and a sunflower growing competition. And her sweet peas. Something caught in her throat at the thought of the seeds in their packets waiting to delight her class who had very little colour in their lives – apart from Pokemon and Marvel heroes.

'Picking their own beans is far more rewarding than a gold star on a chart, and if the slugs or rabbits eat their lettuces well there's a lesson or two to be learned, isn't there? Oh now would you look at the time! Come on, chop, chop, we've got a lot to fit in today.'

It was no wonder the staff were happy to be treated to an extra portion of biscuits, working here would burn more calories than a double dose of Zumba followed by a Spin class.

Chapter 2

'We don't normally take on temporary staff, but we're in rather a difficult situation, and you do seem ideal for the job. We need somebody who will fit in, and I'm sure I speak for everybody else when I say I think you'll slot right into life at Langtry Meadows Primary School.' Timothy Parry, the head teacher looked round the table for confirmation.

A bearded governor leant forward – his forearms on the desk and an earnest expression on his face – then suddenly smiled, showing a chipped tooth. 'The children loved you. Always a good sign, that is.'

Lucy wasn't sure 'loved' was the right word. Her second worst nightmare scenario (after being sacked) had to be a lesson where a child turned out his pocket to reveal an astoundingly large amount of soil and worms. The child in question, a chubby farmer's son called Ted with bright blue eyes and a pudding-bowl haircut had then tried to present her with the longest worm he had, 'to match her long hair.' He'd stretched it out so that it dangled ever closer to her head. Assuring him that the other applicants would be devastated if she accepted, she'd persuaded him to deposit the wriggling but rapidly drying out creature into a jar, for release into the wild at break-time.

'I'm Jim Stafford. I've seen more interviews than you've had hot dinners my dear, and I'm telling you, you're spot on.' The governor leaned forward even further and tapped the back of her hand, dropping his voice to a conspiratorial level. 'Ted Wright's father used to be the Head of Governors and he takes it very much to heart does our Edward if anybody upsets his little Teddy.'

Ahh, so that explained that one. Diplomatic relationships with parents was an essential part of the job that unfortunately had been barely touched on during her teacher training, and she'd had to learn fast.

Timothy coughed, politely regaining control. 'Edward would normally be here himself, but I'm afraid he had other commitments.'

'Sheep.' Jim tapped the side of his nose knowingly.

'Sheep?'

'Lambing time love.' He nodded wisely. 'Busy time is spring.'

'A masterstroke to slip in the animal welfare implications, as well as showing such equanimity to your fellow applicants.' A thin, well-dressed woman with her hair scraped back into a severe bun chipped in, steering them back onto the matter at hand. Lucy had a vague idea that she'd been introduced as the former deputy-head, '*now retired, but very active in the community*'. 'One of our interviewees abandoned his post after Daisy produced a frog from her pocket.' There was a disapproving tut lurking just behind the thin lips. 'What does he expect in the countryside? Honestly!'

The nearest to wildlife Lucy had seen in the classroom at her previous school had been head lice, at least frogs didn't make her want to scratch her head in sympathy – which the sight of nits always had.

The interview with the school council, the pupils, had been the most astounding part of this whole process. At all her previous interviews, the children had asked well-thought out (and no doubt prompted) questions about positive reinforcement and community spirit – the children at this school had been more interested in her reaction to frogs, whether she agreed with Alice's dad that 'those buggers sat behind desks had no right to tell him when he could cut the sodding hedges', and what she thought about the country pong in the air following the liberal slurry spraying over the weekend.

It had taken all of Lucy's self-control to stay in her seat, and to resist putting a peg on her nose. She was not a country girl; she didn't like mess, unpleasant smells, or any kind of large livestock in the immediate vicinity. She really had never ever considered when hedges were cut (but maybe the 'buggers' had the bird's welfare at heart?) and she really did wonder what she was letting herself in for. But now that she'd got over the initial shock of being cast back to her childhood, and been able to rationalise that it wasn't the same after all, she'd been able to admit to herself that the village was really the most gorgeous place. Ideal for a week's chilling out kind of holiday, but what working here would be like could be a different matter altogether.

Except it was simple. She was saving her house, her future.

She had to concentrate on that. This was a short term solution, for a few weeks cover. It would be good for her, help her lay some ghosts to rest, and then she was sure something more suitable would turn up. All would be well. She'd be back on track.

'Oh no, what a shame.' She dredged a weak smile up, thinking herself lucky that she'd only had to cope with worms, and tried to remember which one Daisy was.

'That lass is just like her dad.' Jim chuckled. 'I remember when he brought his ferret in to school, took it out in the middle of the 11 plus exam. Teacher was as calm as you like, whisked it away and stuck it in a cardboard box. Shame of it was that the bugger had eaten his way out by the time we'd finished, whole school had to join in the search.'

Quoting health and safety rules probably wasn't the right response. 'Well children will be children.' She crossed her fingers under the desk, hoping that if she got this job neither frog nor ferret would find its way into her classroom.

Luckily the head teacher shuffled the papers on his desk and coughed, to regain control of the meeting. 'They certainly will. Well I'm sure I speak for everybody when I say we'd be delighted if you could start as soon as possible, Miss Jacobs, or may we call you Lucy?' He was totally unlike any of the head teachers she'd come across in the city: older, kinder, owner of a bow-tie, a very well-worn tweed jacket with actual elbow patches the likes of which she had only ever seen on TV before, and he hadn't mentioned account balancing or issued a single rule about the use of blu-tac or staple guns. And she was pretty sure that the only type of metal-detector would be the handheld type for use on the school field, in search of ancient coins rather than knives and knuckle dusters. 'Your references are excellent, and I really feel you could bring new vitality to our little school whilst maintaining a positive and kind outlook. Now we mentioned to the agency the first day of next term, after the Spring break. Would that suit? Does that give you time? Monday is a teacher training day, so we quite understand if you can't start until Tuesday.'

Relief flooded through Lucy, who hadn't realised quite how tense she'd been. It would mean she'd only been jobless for a half-term, and so far she'd been able to juggle her finances without eating too deeply into the redundancy money.

'The first day of term sounds excellent, Monday is fine, and please do call me Lucy. I'll have to find somewhere to stay though.' She frowned, that bit did concern her. From what she'd seen it was a fairly small village and she hadn't spotted a single 'Room for Rent' or even a 'To Let' sign. 'I need to look for a small hotel,' she cringed inwardly as she said the words, 'or see if there are any rooms to let.' She really did need somewhere impossibly cheap or she'd be struggling to pay her mortgage and buy food as well. Bye bye fruit smoothies and hello boil in the pot noodles.

'Ahh yes, you live well out of our area don't you? We're honoured you chose our school Lucy, it's not many teachers will uproot themselves, and don't worry about finding a place to stay. I'm sure we can help, Jim?'

'I know just the place.'

She looked at the governor in surprise. 'You do?'

'I do. Come on, you gather your stuff up love,' relieved of

his governor's role Jim relaxed visibly and his careful diction was replaced with a gruff rumble, 'and I'll take you to meet my sister Annie.'

'Oh,' the head held his hand up, 'do introduce Lucy to Charlie Davenport if you see him, her first challenge can be persuading that young man to come in and chat to the children. He's been surprisingly adept at avoiding me,' he winked at her, 'you, my dear, can be our secret weapon.'

Annie was as round and cuddly as Jim was tall and stringy, had a mass of greying curls held back by two clips adorned with big red flowers, and was wearing a flowery t-shirt that seemed to be fighting a losing battle to keep her bosom under control. She was sitting behind the counter in the village post-office-cum-general-store, filling in a Sudoku puzzle which appeared to have more crossing-outs than numbers.

'Well now isn't this a nice surprise. I was just thinking there'd been a mass evacuation and nobody had told me.' She gave Jim a hug and smiled at Lucy.

'Annie, this is Miss Jacobs, Lucy. She's filling in for little Becky and,' Jim paused theatrically, 'looking for somewhere to stay.'

'Oh my goodness,' Annie clapped her hands together and beamed as though she'd just found out she'd picked the winning numbers in the lottery, 'now isn't that a stroke of luck? Chocolate éclair or egg custard, love?' She pointed at the display of cakes. 'There'll be a new lot in tomorrow so these need eating up. Sit down, sit down. I'll make us a nice cup of tea and we can have a chat, been run off my feet I have.'

Jim rolled his eyes and gestured to Lucy to sit down on one of the stools behind the counter. 'Annie is off to the Caribbean, not that I understand why.'

'Well you wouldn't, would you Jim? He's a real home bird is my brother, about as adventurous as a goldfish in a bowl aren't you love?' She passed Lucy a mug of tea, and put her own on the counter so that she could concentrate on her cake which was oozing cream faster than she could scoop it up. 'Well love,' she patted Lucy's knee with her free hand, 'me and my husband have always wanted to go travelling, and we promised ourselves that once the kids finished university we'd be off. So we are.' She smiled, a broad beam of a smile. 'I've been looking for somebody to look after the house and not had any luck up until now, and all the tickets are booked and everything. It's my last day behind this counter, then we've a few days of packing and Bob's your uncle.'

At least, Lucy thought, as she tackled her egg custard, she wasn't expected to speak.

'We're planning a year away, although it could be longer if I get my way, how long will you be here, duck?'

'Oh I'm sorry. I'm only planning on the half term, it's only a temporary position.' Lucy tried not to spit out pastry crumbs. 'In fact,' she wasn't quite sure what to say with Jim the governor listening in, 'I do love my own home and I'm hoping a local job comes up soon.'

There was a bit of a splutter from Jim's direction.

'But Langtry Meadows is wonderful,' she added hastily.

'I reckon you won't want to leave once you get to know the kids.' Lucy watched transfixed as half the cake disappeared into Jim's mouth, and was swallowed in an instant. 'They're a grand bunch, and the village isn't bad either.' He looked pointedly at his sister. 'Even if some people do have some strange notions. So, that's settled then, you'll move into our Annie's house and look after things?'

Things? That seemed a strange way of putting it.

'Well if that's okay, I mean I suppose you do really want somebody longer term? And er, how much is the rent, it's just...'

'Oh no that sounds splendid, we won't be charging much rent love because it really is a big relief off our minds knowing everything will be looked after properly.'

Everything?

'It was quite a worry at first, wondering how we'd manage because I'm not really into rehoming, and then Jim here came up with the idea of house-sitting. Not a total dollop are you love?' she grinned affectionately at her brother, who looked quite pleased with himself. 'And now you've come up trumps again, finding young Lucy for us. You stay as long as you want my dear, and don't you worry about what you can afford, we'll work something out.'

'Sorry, rehoming? House-sitting? I thought you were renting out...'

'Oh yes love, don't you worry. The house is all yours. There's a bit of a condition attached though, which is why we're only asking for you to settle the bills and keep on top of the garden.'

She could do gardens, no problem at all.

'We need you to look after the animals, but I can tell that won't be a problem to somebody so organised, you look so efficient dear, and a school teacher is perfect. If you can cope with those kids, then my lot will be a walk in the park. More tea?'

Lucy put her hand over the top of the mug. 'I'm sorry, you've lost me. I've no problem at all with a bit of gardening, I'm more than happy to do that and pay the bills, keep everywhere tidy, but animals?' She'd never even had time to look after a hamster, let alone 'animals' whatever that meant.

'Oh, didn't our Jim explain?' She tutted at her brother. 'There's the cat, Tigger, then we've got a few chucks, they're no trouble at all, and Pork-Chop the pig of course.'

Of course. And what the hell were 'chucks'?

'He does like a bit of company and a walk round the green now and then but he's no bother at all if he's got his harness on, oh and little Mischief.'

'Mischief?'

'The pony, love, I mean once the kids outgrew him we couldn't just sell him could we? Is that it Jim?' She frowned, doing a mental check of her menagerie. 'Oh and Gertie, silly goose me,' she guffawed at her own joke, 'how could I forget her? Right then, I'm so glad that's settled, a weight off my mind.' She licked cream off her finger. 'I'd take you up there and show you round, but I can't get away until 5pm. Jim can take you for a quick shifty, can't you, dear?'

'I certainly can, and our dear headmaster asked if I could introduce her to young Charlie, let her try out her skills of persuasion, so we can pop in there too.'

Annie chuckled, a rolling sound that seemed to come from the very centre of her. 'He's not daft our Timothy. Good luck with that then dear, I'm sure you stand more chance than all those other old codgers, though I think he even managed to duck out when they sent Jill. Always did have a stubborn streak in him, that one.'

'I'm sorry, who is this Charlie, and why do I have to talk to him?' Lucy looked from Annie to her brother Jim. It was all very well being labelled the headmaster's 'secret weapon', but so far she hadn't a clue who this man, that she was supposed to be persuading to come into school, was. Maybe he was a famous author, an artist, a great and shy inventor?

'Charlie Davenport.' Annie nodded as though that said it all.

'The new veterinary surgeon.' Jim chipped in.

'Well you say new love, but he's no stranger is he?' She smiled at Lucy, 'Charlie grew up here in Langtry Meadows, lovely little kid he was, bright as a button and cheeky with it. His dad used to be a partner in the practice, then he took early retirement and they moved away. Lovely to see young Charlie back again,' she paused, 'although he doesn't seem that sure himself, if you know what I mean.'

Lucy wasn't sure she did.

'Old Eric has always come into school once a year without fail to give the kids a bit of a talk and they love it, but this fella's been a bit elusive.' Jim carried on as though he hadn't been interrupted.

'Eric?'

'Aye, Eric. He's the vet that runs the place but he had a bit of a mishap so Charlie's helping out. He's a nice enough chap, but tricky to pin down, so we're relying on you and,' he coughed, 'your ahem feminine wiles if I'm allowed to say that in this day and age.'

Lucy stared, not quite sure what she should say, and Annie recognising the look of panic changed tack before her house-sitter had a chance to scarper. 'Well now, look at us chattering away and not letting you get a word in. So, what's a wonderful young lady like you doing looking for a new job? I'm surprised anybody would let you go.'

'I've been made redundant actually.' It was the first time she'd said the words out loud. She'd purposefully skated round the issue when talking to her mother, but now it didn't seem quite such a terrible admission.

'Oh the fools, I can tell just by looking that you're a wonderful teacher. You've got a way with you, hasn't she Jim?'

'You aren't wrong Annie. She has. Kids loved her, and even Liz Potts couldn't find fault.'

'Well if Liz can't find anything to complain about then that says it all.' Annie seemed to take that as conclusive proof, and it gave Lucy a desperately needed boost. Up until now she'd thought of herself as fairly self-confident, but the whole business at Starbaston School had knocked her more than she'd dare admit even to herself.

'I did love it at my old school, it wasn't easy but it was very satisfying. It was put in special measures by Ofsted just before I was taken on, and we all worked so hard to turn it around.'

'I'm sure you did, dear.'

'We put new plans in place, and worked to make the class-rooms brighter. When the Ofsted inspector came back she was amazed at the transformation.' Lucy didn't like to boast, but she'd been proud of what they'd achieved with hard work and the way all the staff had pulled together after a few changes. 'She said she'd never seen such a turn-around in such a short space of time. It was worth all the late evenings at school, and all the weekends we spent putting together a new strategy and lesson plans that took into account the capabilities of all the children. I mean, they're such a mixed bunch and it's really important we do our best for all of them, isn't it?'

'Now I don't want you to take this the wrong way, lovey.' Annie was looking at her in a disturbingly measured way. She put down her mug of tea. 'But it sounds to me like you've been taking it all a bit too seriously, a girl your age needs to lighten up and have a bit of fun.' She held up a hand to still Lucy's objections. 'There's more to life than spending evenings in a classroom. Now I can tell you love your job, but nobody on their deathbed ever said they wished they'd spent more time at work, did they?'

Lucy stared at her. Maybe it did sound all a bit boring, and work, work, work. But that was just how it was. Annie looked back, her gaze never wavering.

'Well *you* won't, will you sis?' Jim broke the uncomfortable silence.

'I certainly won't, it's all about balance.' She put her hands on the counter and levered herself up. 'Ahh well, no rest for the wicked. Lovely to meet you Lucy, now Jim'll have all your details won't he? What with him being a governor and all, I'll sort out the keys with him and then you can move in the weekend before you start, can't you? We'll be gone before you get here, but don't you go worrying about that,' Lucy hadn't been about to, 'we'll sort something out. Such a shame you're not staying for longer, love, but beggars can't be choosers can they? Now what did I do with that newspaper?'

Annie's cottage was a few minutes' walk from the school and as different to Lucy's modern, new-build semi-detached house as was possible.

Where she had an immaculately tended front lawn and moss-free block paved driveway, this was a riotous array of spring colour – plants competing for space as they tumbled over each other (and the narrow uneven cobbled path) in disarray. Her fingers itched for pruning shears and a ball of string, but she had the feeling that taming this front garden would be like maintaining the Forth Bridge.

Lucy forced her gaze beyond the garden, to the cottage that lay in its midst. From a distance it had looked picture perfect, but now they were closer she could see that the paint was flaking from the window frames and the thatch was looking rather old-man thin in places. It still looked incredibly sweet though, despite the fact that she was sure there would be draughts from the single glazed window and no doubt inside it would be a higgledy-piggledy mess that was nothing like the tidy order she loved. She could imagine the flowery and cracked mismatched pottery, and the worn chairs that no doubt showed traces of cat hair. But a change was always as good as a rest, and looking on the bright side it really could be quite an idyllic spot if the sun shone.

'Think it will suit then?'

'It's lovely, Jim.'

He grinned, showing off the chipped crooked tooth.

'Shall we go in and...?' She reached for the gate latch and had only opened it a fraction when an enormous white bird came hurtling round the corner of the house. 'Bloody hell.' Slamming it shut she jumped back, nearly colliding with Jim.

'That'll be Gertie.' He nodded.

The bird flapped its wings indignantly sending flower petals in all directions and stuck a bright orange, sharply pointed beak in their direction.

'Gertie?' She was pretty sure she'd gone nearly as pale as the bird which had fixed her with a very black, beady glare.

'Aye. Gertie the goose.' Jim had barely flinched. He tapped his watch pointedly. 'I'd show you round, but I've got business to attend to.'

Hmm she bet he had.

'All you need to do is wear our Annie's boots for a few days and little Gertie will be putty in your hands. Imprinted on those she is.'

Little? In what world could you describe this goose as little? 'Imprinted?'

'Aye, imprinted.' He looked at her as though she was an underachieving student. 'First thing it saw when it hatched was those bloody bright pink wellingtons that our Annie likes to parade about in, poor bugger thinks they're its mother.' He guffawed and Lucy felt herself drawn to this big, friendly man, who the moment he'd left the school had dropped his governor's hat (and voice) and become Annie's brother with a slight country burr. 'Well now, you can meet the rest of the menagerie when you move in if that's okay with you? Annie will leave full instructions and I'm always on hand if you need me. Well, I'll love you and leave you if that's alright?'

'Of course, yes, I'm sure you have things to do. It's very kind of you to show me round, and I'll see you when I move in then?'

'My pleasure, Lucy. Oh, and you've got the vets practically next door,' he pointed over her shoulder. 'Old Eric had himself a bit of a run in with some cows and he's laid up for a while, but our Charlie seems to be shaping up well enough, chip off the old block. His dad was a good man, popular. The lad's a bit of a dark horse these days mind, keeps himself to himself,' Lucy thought that could be a problem for anybody here, 'but I'm sure you'll soon win him over,' he winked, it was the second wink of the day which was a bit worrying, 'you'll be getting plenty of opportunity.'

'I will?'

'Oh aye, our Annie is always in and out, I reckon she keeps that practice going. Although since our Charlie came back I've heard from Sal that bookings have soared.'

'Really?' She didn't know what to say to that.

'Just like his dad, he is. You'll see.' He tapped the side of his nose and chuckled in a most un-Jim like way, reminding her of Annie. 'So any problems he's on the doorstep, though I'm sure you'll cope. Now would you credit it,' he paused, and it seemed he'd completely forgotten that he was in a hurry, 'there's the man himself. No time like the present, let's introduce you to Charlie and you can ask him to do that school visit.'

Before Lucy had a chance to object, Jim had her elbow and was guiding her down the lane and across the small car park that fronted the veterinary surgery.

Protruding from the boot of a hatchback car was a very long pair of legs encased in brown trousers, and what she had to admit was quite a trim rear. Not that she was looking.

Jim coughed loudly, and Charlie straightened abruptly, banging his head with a clunk on the tailgate, which trembled, rose up then bounced back down giving him another wallop for good measure. Lucy flinched. He swore. Not in the loud, clutching-her-head way she would have done, but in a much more teeth-clenched, restrained manner.

He backed out slowly, then he straightened up and she knew before he'd even turned round. How could she not recognise that arse?

It was him.

A pair of brown, familiar eyes stared straight into hers. Definitely him.

His hand instinctively went up to the side of his head, just as she wrapped her own hand round the wrist she'd used to whack him. Well not *used* to whack him. That suggested intent, and she'd never intended anything. It hadn't even been self-defence, her brain had barely registered she was under attack until she'd been in his arms. She gulped. Clutched against his firm body.

'You!'

He didn't sound pleased. Not that she could blame him, knock 'em dead wasn't supposed to mean literally, and so far it was looking like she'd been aiming to give him concussion.

And she hadn't been trying to knock him dead in any sense actually.

Not that he wasn't attractive. Very. To the point that she'd nearly snogged him. Oh God. The heat rushed to her face. She had to say something. Stop gawping.

'You're not, you can't be...' This could not be Charlie Davenport, the vet. The man she was going to be seeing a lot of. The man she'd gyrated against in full view of the rest of the village (well anybody who might have strayed onto the green, or been peeping round net curtains) before they'd even been introduced. The man Jim wanted her to use her feminine wiles against. Wiles she was pretty sure she didn't possess. Not that she'd ever use them in that way.

This was bad. This was embarrassing. This explained a lot.

He was the village heart-throb. If he made a habit of rugby-tackling every woman he came across it was no bloody wonder. No, that wasn't fair. He'd been saving her.

'Charlie,' Jim butted into her thoughts, probably a good thing, 'let me introduce our new teacher, Lucy. Lucy Jacobs. And Lucy this is Charlie Davenport.' He frowned, looking from one to the other of them, obviously realising at last that she hadn't been struck dumb by his awesomeness, there was more to it than that. 'Have you already met then? I thought you said...'

'Not really, well yes, well we've not been introduced.' This wasn't going well. 'I didn't know this was Charlie, he er, rescued me earlier today.'

Jim chuckled and she stared at the ground, hoping a handy chasm would open up and she'd fall in. It didn't so she risked glancing back up. 'Told you he was popular, rescued you my foot.' He obviously thought this was hilarious. 'What did you do then lad? Sweep the young lass off her feet? Not that I'd blame you. I'd have done the same myself a few years ago.'

This was getting worse by the second. And she'd accepted a job here. She had to be mad.

'I didn't really do anything.' She watched mesmerised as Charlie threaded long fingers through his dark curly hair and tentatively rubbed the spot that had been in collision with his car. 'That horse of Holly's bolted again, and, er Lucy was in their path. I just nudged her out of the way.'

Their gazes met, a slight quirk of humour tugged at the corner of his mouth. The feel of his solid, warm hand at her waist seemed to be imprinted into her body. She could feel it now, smell the smoky, earthiness of his scent. It was almost intimate. She folded her arms around her body to stop the shiver of awareness, then realised she was being defensive and dropped them to her sides. Stared at his left ear, which was much safer than looking into his eyes or at that sexy mouth.

'Ah, thought I heard a bit of a clattering through the square earlier on, them cobbles don't half ring when she belts over them.' Jim smiled broadly. 'Well you two will be seeing a lot more of each other, I'm sure.'

Charlie looked warily from Lucy to Jim, then back again. 'Nice, to erm meet you properly, Lucy. Welcome to Langtry Meadows.' He held out a hand, there was the briefest touch of warm fingers then it was back safely in his pocket. 'Sorry Jim, but I'm in rather a hu—'

'Now then, not so fast lad, our Lucy has a favour to ask,

haven't you Lucy?' Jim prodded her in the ribs. She'd always thought *she* was pretty direct, but Jim would beat her hands down any day.

'Well I'm sure it can wait if Mr Davenport is busy.'

'No time like the present, if you don't mind me saying.' Jim folded his arms as though he was here for as long as it took, then jerked his head in Charlie's direction. 'Go on, ask him, lass.'

She did mind him saying. But it seemed rude to say so, and there really wasn't any harm in sorting it out here and now. That would be something to tick of the list, even if it was a minor accomplishment. 'We can discuss it properly when I've moved in, but, well we, I, well I understand the practice sends somebody in to the school to chat to the children at this time of year.'

'And?' He was looking at her blankly.

'Well, if we could arrange a day?'

He frowned.

'Early next term? For you to come...'

'Oh, no.' He held a hand up, a barrier between them, and if she hadn't been so aware of him she wouldn't have noticed the slight tremble. He shoved the hand back in his pocket. 'Sorry, that's Eric's domain, I'm afraid I—'

'Oh well fine, we can wait...'

'They look forward to it.' Jim rubbed his beard and gave the vet his 'governor's look'.

'I'm sure as soon as Eric returns to work...'

'Aye, I'm sure he will, he's a generous man is Eric.' He gave the vet a pointed look. 'But Spring's the time we like to do it, and,' his eyes narrowed, 'after Easter, I'm sure your old man would expect you to do the right thing.'

Charlie's lips tightened, along with his jaw and Lucy was pretty sure he was gritting his teeth to stop himself saying anything. He folded his arms. Showdown in the car park, maybe this wasn't going to be such a minor accomplishment after all.

She would have quite liked to have told Jim to be quiet. 'Maybe if you leave us to chat?'

'Ah, yes.' He grinned and winked. 'Whatever you say, I'll leave you two youngsters to it then.'

The heat rushed to Lucy's face, and she was just about to launch into an explanation when the vet held up a hand.

'Look I am sorry, but before you start, the answer is no.' He glanced at his watch pointedly. 'I've got an emergency call to tend to.'

'We could walk and talk?' She was curious as much as anything, he'd recovered now but his reaction had been weird to say the least.

'I'm driving.' Obviously. He threw his bag into the back of the car and closed the door firmly. 'Nothing personal. Nice to meet you, I hope you enjoy it at the school, Miss er.'

'It's just that Jim, well the school, well I, well we just wanted you to spare an hour to talk to a group of kids?' He was opening the driver's door, any minute now he'd be driving off. 'Please, could we at least have a chat about it?' She wasn't quite sure why it was so important to the school, or why it was such a problem to the vet, but she at least had to try. Failing at the first task she'd been given wasn't a good start.

And he'd looked shocked, mildly horrified, at the thought of going into school, which seemed off when he appeared so level-headed and adrenaline-free. Bolting horses seemed to be a daily hazard, so why would a group of kids pose such a threat?

'This really is a matter of life and death.' His tone was firm, she could quite imagine him using it when a dog was misbehaving. Before she could say another word he'd started up the car engine, and was easing the door shut so that she had to skip out of the way, or get squashed. For a second his gaze met hers through the glass, and she sensed a genuine regret, then he put the car into gear and looked away.

Jim sidled up as the vet's car, and her opportunity to fulfil her first task, slipped away.

'Ah well, I told you he was a tricky one, slippery as an eel, but I'm sure you'll sort it.' He winked. 'A woman with your resources.'

'But he really doesn't seem to—'

'You'll talk him round.'

She wasn't sure she *wanted* to talk him round, his response had been so genuine it almost seemed wrong to ask. 'Isn't there anybody else? Another vet?' If the man didn't want to do it then surely there was somebody else who could do it?

'Only the one in the next village, and we won't be asking him now, will we?'

'We won't?' Oh God, even Jim was showing a steely side, another stubborn male.

'Over my dead body, and those of most of the other governor's.' He rubbed his hands together as though that settled the matter. 'We're relying on you my dear. Right, I better not keep you, got a fair drive haven't you?'

Lucy nodded. Hoping the journey home would be less eventful than the one here. At least she was heading back knowing she had a job, even if it was only for a few weeks.

'I'm sure you'll love it here, fit right in you will.' He smiled and just as she was putting her hand out to shake, he clapped both hands on her upper arms which she guessed was one step down from a hug.

She watched him stride off down the lane, then gazed back at the cottage that was going to be her temporary home.

It *would* be a long drive back. In fact her home seemed on a different planet to this little village.

She deserved a celebratory glass of wine. Even if it was a temporary, very unsuitable, job. Lucy closed her front door, kicked her shoes off and headed straight for the kitchen and the chilled bottle of Pinot Grigio that was calling her name.

Sitting down at the kitchen table, she pulled her laptop from her bag.

It only took a couple of minutes to write an email to the agency, confirming that she had been offered the position, that it was for a half term only, and that she'd be looking for something more local (and ideally a permanent position) if possible when she completed the contract. The out-of-office reply, stating the hours the agency were open pinged straight back into her inbox.

Then she sent a text to Sarah telling her she'd got the job, that there were no phwoar farmers, just a very grumpy vet that was more Doc Martin than James Herriot (Sarah didn't need to know about the nearly-kiss or the mesmerising eyes), a headmaster who actually seemed to like children, and chickens.

Lucy headed upstairs. She'd have a nice shower first, then pour herself that drink. The job might not be her dream position, but it did mean that she had money to pay the mortgage. With the low rent that Annie was asking for, and the higher salary as it was a short-term contract, with luck she'd even be able to put some money aside in her savings account. And it might actually be quite pleasant spending a few weeks in the lovely little village – quite a change from the hustle and bustle she was used to in the much larger school.

The children had all seemed bright and inquisitive, and the classes were small so she wouldn't miss having a dedicated classroom assistant. It was going to be so much fun. A little shiver ran down her spine as the excitement she'd been fighting kicked in. She couldn't wait. Even the goose would be an interesting challenge, she just had a horrible feeling that her immaculate clothes would need throwing away when she got back to civilisation. Cat hairs were notoriously difficult to remove, and she just knew the animal smell would linger on.

She switched off the shower and wrapped her hair up in a towel.

There was just one more thing she had to do though before she started to plan her move. And now she had at least got work lined up she could put a positive spin on this.

Wine glass in hand she picked up her mobile.

'Mum, I've got a new job.'

'Oh how lovely.' There was a pause. 'But I thought you loved the one you had, darling?'

'There's been a re-organisation, but this one's in a gorgeous village school.'

'Village?'

'It's sweet.'

'And it's not too far to drive each day? You work such long hours as it is, without a long journey on top of it.'

'Well no, I mean yes, it is too far to drive. I'm going to rent a place there for now. It's only for a while, and I've found a lovely cottage where the owner has pets she needs looking after so the rent is really reasonable.'

'So you've got your own house *and* a place to rent? Can you afford that dear?'

She could almost see her mum's worried frown. 'Yes Mum, it's just short term.'

'But I thought you were too busy to have a pet, darling? And didn't you say you liked keeping the house neat and tidy? When I came over with your Aunt Steph you made her tie Bono to a tree at the bottom of the garden.'

Lucy rolled her eyes as the memory of Bono, a very shaggy bearded collie who'd just been for an unscheduled dip in the canal, came to mind. 'I had just bought a new cream carpet, Mum.'

'That's the trouble with these modern plain carpets, you need a pattern dear, hides a multitude of sins.'

Maybe that's what her busy job had done, hidden the cracks in her life, but she didn't want to ponder on that one. What was the point? 'I like plain.' Keep it simple. 'Anyway, this job will be different, I don't need to commute.'

'And I hope you won't need to be working those long hours any more. When I was your age...'

Lucy gritted her teeth, but some part of the retort she was biting back must have escaped and travelled over the airwaves. Her mum might not have worked long hours at her age, but she'd made up for it later on in life. Surely it was better to put all the effort in now? To be independent and secure.

'Well yes I suppose times have changed.' She could imagine her mother's pursed lips. 'But you work too hard, being a teacher used to be a nice job for a girl and now it's all rushing round and paperwork. I always wanted an easier life for you, love.'

'All jobs are like that, it's about accountability.' And Ofsted.

'Well that is nice anyway dear,' she could tell her mother was about to brush over that. 'It'll be nice for you to get out of the city for a bit. You did have fun when you were little in Stoneyvale, do you remember?'

'It was horrible. I hated it.' The words were out before she could stop them.

'Oh, Lucy.' Lucy felt a pang of guilt at the regret in her mother's voice. 'You didn't hate it. There were some good times, I used to love our time feeding the ducks, and picking you up from school. It was a pretty place, even if life wasn't quite as perfect as I'd hoped.' She sighed. 'You were such a happy toddler.'

'Yeah, and then I grew up.' And life had been turned upside down, and all her friends turned out to be nasty, small-minded people who only cared about themselves.

61

'It wasn't all bad, Lucy.'

'Mum, I didn't belong there, I didn't have any friends.'

'Oh you did, darling. It was just, after your party when your father got a bit cross I think some of their parents thought it better if they didn't come round to play. He just didn't like...'

'The mess, yeah I know.' She'd blocked that party out of her mind. Dad had been so cross to come home and find sticky finger marks on the table, and cake crumbs on the sofa. He hadn't shouted like some of the other dads did, he'd just laid the law down very softly. Even as a child she'd sensed the slight menace, the uncomfortable air as her mother had wiped her tears and shooed her up to her room. She hadn't thought about it before, but that was probably when it had all started to go wrong. When children stopped coming round to play in their garden. When all the party invites started to dry up.

'He never really wanted me to have people round, did he?'

'Well no,' there was a crackle and silence, and she wasn't sure if it was a bad line. She hated silence, silence at home had always meant bad things, so she'd grown up wanting what some people would think of as chaos.

'Mum, are you still there?'

'I am. But you still had friends, didn't you dear?' There was a hopeful note to her mother's tone which she didn't want to kill. So she didn't say anything. 'You saw the others at school. There was lovely little Amy, and...'

'Exactly.' She sighed. 'Just lovely little Amy, and even that was an act.'

'Lucy, it wasn't you, your dad...'

'Forget it, Mum. I have. Langtry Meadows isn't Stoneyvale,

and I'm only there for a few weeks, I like working in the city.'
She did. It was less claustrophobic, more impersonal. Where
people came and went, where nobody was an outsider.

'Anyway,' her mother's voice regained its normal no-nonsense
brisk edge, the 'let's make the most of life' tone. 'A bit of
country air will do you good, you've been looking a bit peaky
lately. A change is as good as a rest, as they say.'

Lucy chatted to her mum for a bit longer then pressed the
end call button and stared at her phone, suddenly wishing
that she hadn't told her mum to forget it.

She hadn't, she couldn't.

There were questions that had peeked their heads over the
self-protective barrier she'd built around herself as she'd driven
home. Questions about her dad she'd never dared ask.
Questions that the absolute peace and quiet of Langtry
Meadows had poked out of their slumber at the back of her
mind. Questions about the almost obsessive tidiness that her
father had insisted on.

It hadn't hit her until today just how different their new
life had been. As though her mum had been determined to
wipe every last trace of Stoneyvale out of her system.

But maybe it was time she tried to move on. To shift the
ache that had settled in the centre of her chest once and for
all.

Chapter 3

Charlie stared at the small white van. Whoever had parked, or should that be abandoned it, at such a crazy angle, couldn't have done a better job of blocking him out if they'd tried.

He was knackered. All he wanted was half an hour's peace with his feet up and a cup of coffee before his patients for the day started to arrive – and some delivery man had decided there was nothing wrong with blocking the entrance to his surgery.

His day had started at 5 a.m, a farm dog had been run over, and despite battling with every bit of experience and knowledge he had, they'd lost it. However long he did the job, he hated that bit.

Losing a battle to save a life that was ending far too early always left him feeling he'd failed. Owners that understood and thanked him destroyed him even more. They shouldn't have to be thanking somebody for losing the battle, and along with the sour taste in his mouth there was always the curdling doubt in the pit of his stomach. What if he'd missed something obvious? What if he'd acted quicker?

The farmer had offered sweet tea, and a bacon sandwich, apologising for calling him out at such an ungodly hour. He'd not wanted to churn out the same old words – for the best, not suffering now – but he had because he didn't know what else to say.

He clambered out of his car, feeling drained, and marched towards the van. One of the benefits of living in a village was the lack of road rage, nobody was ever in that much of a hurry. The worst that could happen was that you had to follow a herd of cows down a lane as they ambled from field to farm, which he had found slightly frustrating the first week he'd been back here, then he'd realised he just had to go with the flow. In fact, he walked now whenever he could – but most farms visits meant taking the car.

'I can't get in my car park.' He rounded the open door, just as a girl backed out at speed, dragging a large cardboard box with her. Without thinking he grabbed her waist with one hand, and the van door with the other to stop them toppling.

She glanced up.

Oh shit, he'd been here before. In a tight clinch. Her soft lips were slightly parted, eyes wide staring straight into his own, his hands were only inches from her breasts. And he had an almost uncontrollable urge to kiss her.

Again.

It was the girl he'd nearly flattened by the village green. The teacher.

The one who'd asked him to go into school. The one who'd irrationally sprung to mind every time he walked past the village school – wondering when she'd be back.

Last time he'd had his hands on her he could have blamed the surge of adrenaline for the way his body had reacted, but he'd have been lying to himself because it was doing exactly the same this time round.

The smell of her perfume, the brush of her soft skin against his cheek, and the gently quivering body pressed against his had turned him on something rotten. And she'd known. From what he remembered he'd solved the problem last time by practically throwing her back into the road. And now he was staring at her like a simpleton. Which he could, being logical, put down to lack of sleep, and emotional upset.

She blinked, and pulled herself together before he could. 'Oh hi, it's you. We must stop meeting like this.' She looked down pointedly and he realised he still had hold of her.

'Sorry, er I'm not in the habit of...' He let go, waved his hands in the air, glanced down to save the embarrassment of looking her straight in the eye. 'Good God, what are those?'

Bright pink wellingtons, which were more than just bright, they were positively glowing. They were ridiculous, but they suited her, in a cute kind of way. Oh God, what was he thinking? Cute? Where had that come from? He didn't even call day old kittens cute.

He glanced back up and she was grinning. She lifted a foot. 'These? Awesome aren't they? They're my secret weapon. If I don't wear them I'm in trouble. Serious GBH type of trouble.' She wrinkled her nose. How had he missed her slightly upturned nose last time they'd met?

He swallowed, trying to ignore the way the rest of her body had jiggled, and the dancing light in her eyes. It had obviously been far too long since he'd had a soft female form pressed against his (apart from hers). Maybe his self-imposed ban was a mistake, it was turning him into a horny old man.

'They're Annie's actually.' For a moment he was confused, then focussed back on the wellingtons again. That figured, yep now she mentioned it he had seen Annie parading round the village in them. But on Annie they looked quite different. Unremarkable. 'Her goose Gertie is imprinted on them, and without these I'd be mincemeat. Imprinting, you know they were the first thing...'

'I do know what imprinting is.'

A flush tinged her cheekbones. Now what had made him shoot her down like that? He was being a patronising git now. Why couldn't he just be friendly? But it was just, he hadn't felt this drawn to somebody for a long, long time, not since he'd met Josie. Not since the most precious person in his life had appeared, not since he'd fallen madly, wildly, in love in a way he hadn't thought existed ... and this was his way of making sure it didn't happen again. He blinked, and tried to concentrate on what she was saying.

'Ah yes, of course, you're a vet. Well at the moment these are a lifesaver, talking of which,' she avoided his eye, 'thanks for er, saving me the other week, when I came for my interview.'

'No problem. Look I don't want to be rude, but I really do need to get in, I've got work to do. If you could just straighten it up, move over a bit.'

'Oh, right, sure. Isn't it a bit early for work?' She looked at her watch. 'I'd never normally get up at this time, but I knew it would take me hours to move all my stuff into Annie's, and I didn't think I'd be in anybody's way. Or do you all get up at the crack of dawn round here?' Her eyes were twinkling, and he could have sworn she was teasing now.

'I prefer a lie in to be honest, but when there's an emergency.' He shrugged.

'Oh no. Was everything okay?' She'd stopped smiling.

'Not really.' He sighed. 'Look I need a coffee,' he'd been a git, surely he could at least have some manners and be a bit welcoming, 'fancy one?'

'You've no idea how good that sounds, I feel like I've done a day's work already. I'll pull the van up a bit so you can get in.'

'So,' Lucy wrapped her hands round the mug of coffee and stared at him, her head on one side. 'You're only here temporarily, like me?'

'I'm hoping so.'

Her eyes widened. 'The place is that bad?'

He grinned, he couldn't help it. 'No, it's not bad, but coming back here wasn't part of my life plan.'

She leant forward conspiratorially. 'Don't tell anybody, but it wasn't on mine either. So, where are you heading next?'

'Now that is the million dollar question.' He'd already been doing what he wanted, and when he lost that, for a while he felt like he'd lost everything. 'Well, when I sold my town centre veterinary practice I had a vague idea of taking a few months off, before setting up somewhere else, faraway. Like Australia.'

'Oh.' She looked slightly shocked. 'Major deviation from the plan then. So, what made you come back here?'

'Family pressure.' He gave a wry smile. 'I hadn't made any firm plans, and my dad cornered me. He told me about Eric, I thought it would be pretty selfish to refuse. Dad and Eric were big buddies.'

'Ahh.'

'He said he was in a real mess, could be off work for months. As Dad pointed out I do know Langtry Meadows and the people, and about running a practice of my own. It was hard to say no.' But that had just been the beginning of the charm offensive. '*You'd just be able to walk in and get straight down to it,*' his father had said. '*This isn't charity, Charles. The man needs support, and he'd much rather hand the reins over to somebody he knows, than pull in some random Tom, Dick or Harriet vet from an agency. Go and see him. He's still in hospital.*' And even as he'd tried to object, he knew he hadn't really got any choice.

'I bet your dad was pleased, and it sounds like you're popular in the village.'

'He was, and so was my mother, she didn't like the idea of me at a loose end, or going to Australia.' He knew they cared. But he really hadn't planned on this, creeping back to the village with his tail between his legs, admitting he'd failed – had lost it all. 'I wasn't actually at a loose end,' they swapped an understanding look, 'I was considering my options. But you know what mothers can be like.' He paused, took a gulp of his coffee. 'I think this is actually more of a trip down memory lane for Dad than me, he misses the place. Started to ramble on, asked me if I remembered the time when Ed Wright had chicken pox and was convinced he had foot and mouth. He said the little idiot was sure they were going to throw him in a pit and cover him with lime, he disappeared up the fields and hid. The whole village had to go out searching for him.'

Lucy giggled, which sent a shiver down his spine. 'And did you remember?'

'Did I hell!' He'd let his father reminisce, let the words flow over him, and wondered how on earth he'd ended up losing everything he'd worked for. One day he'd got his bright, shiny, efficient town centre practice handling referrals and money-no-object operations, and the next he had somehow agreed to bury himself back in Langtry Meadows in a tiny, old-fashioned veterinary practice.

'But you're happy you came back?'

'Well I haven't really thought about it,' he paused, 'but yes, yes it's a nice place and who needs time off work anyway when you can be dragged out of bed at 4 a.m. and stick your arm up a cow's rear?'

She was laughing again. He didn't know why, but he seemed to be trying to amuse her. And he seemed to be rambling on, it was far too easy to talk to her. Any second now and he'd be spilling all his sordid secrets.

'True, and in Australia you'd miss the mud and frosty mornings.'

'Would I?' Langtry Meadows was perfect in many ways though, well one big way. It was miles from his old stomping ground and the practice he'd run with his ex-wife. Miles from any reminders that the cosy life he'd thought they'd built up had existed only in his imagination. Even miles from his

71

suffocatingly concerned family who'd moved from the village to somewhere 'more convenient' when his father retired. 'What about you?' He needed to head the conversation in another direction. 'Are you looking forward to working here?'

'Oh yes, well I think so. I mean it wasn't what I'd planned on doing, but everybody seems lovely, and it's such a gorgeous place. To be honest, I didn't really have any option.' She hesitated. 'Look, sorry for pestering about the school visit thing last time we met.' She looked apologetic now, rather than demanding. 'I didn't mean to be pushy, I just had Jim prodding me in the back. It's the first thing they've asked me to do, and I don't like to fail.'

There was a question in her voice. 'Look, I'm sorry too if we got off on the wrong foot.' He couldn't help but glance down at the pink wellies again. 'But it's really not something I can help with.'

She was looking at him, like a spaniel deprived of its ball. Can't or won't, said the look – she was too kind to voice it. He was doing his best to avoid eye contact, but still felt a heel. He couldn't though, just the thought of standing in front of those hopeful, innocent faces made him come over hot, then cold. He wasn't the only loser in this mess he'd made of his life, and that was the bit that made him feel totally useless. Helpless.

Her gaze hadn't wavered. 'It's just I've got my hands full with the surgery.' To her it was just a simple request. But it was asking him to expose his heart, to lay himself open to yet more hurt and he wasn't ready. He couldn't do it yet – and certainly not in front of the watching eyes of the whole village.

Teenagers he could have coped with, the WI, the teachers. Just not a class full of primary school kids, expectant smiling faces. Kids that were at that age when they trusted adults, thought they could solve every problem in the world. He closed his eyes for a second, and the image that snuck its way into every dream, every nightmare, was there. A giggling little girl. Auburn curls soft as clouds around her angelic face. Large brown eyes gazing straight into his. Innocent, unknowing. Trusting.

He couldn't do it.

'They don't bite. Not like some of your patients.' Her lips curved into a seductive smile, but he was pretty sure she was just trying to lighten the mood, not drag him off to bed – that was wishful thinking on his side.

'No.' He swallowed down the clawing pain in his throat and hoped to God he looked more normal than he felt. 'It's just,' what was he supposed to say? 'This place can feel a bit claustrophobic.'

'Villages can.' Those two words had an unexpected depth to them, she said that as though she knew.

'Everybody in each other's pockets and I would rather like to keep a professional distance.' And that was the truth, up to a point.

She nodded, looking thoughtful, then sighed. 'Yes, I can understand that.' And there was something in her eyes that convinced him she did. She was a bit of an outsider as well, and he had a feeling that despite all the smiles she wasn't entirely comfortable about being here. 'It's okay, don't worry I'll think of something.' She twisted her lips to one side as though she was thinking. 'But Jim swore blind that asking any other vet was out of bounds.'

'It is a bit of a no-no going to the other practice, you know what village politics can be like.' Now she was making it even more difficult. Understanding made him feel tetchy, and for some reason he couldn't quite fathom he felt almost like he was letting her down. Christ, he had enough problems with all the other people he felt he'd let down – and now he was doing it with a complete stranger. 'I'm sure you'll come up with something. I'm not here for long anyway, as soon as Eric is back on his feet I'll be off.' He couldn't do it, better to make that quite clear. 'I'm sorry, I really am.'

'No problem.' Her tone was light, but he still felt bad.

'It's just...' He hesitated, not quite wanting to leave it like that. But any discussions about how he should be involved in the village school were off the agenda. Some things he could do – being surrounded by young children he couldn't. Not yet. The health of the village pets was his responsibility, the kids weren't.

She was looking at him quizzically, as though she was expecting him to say more. Offer an explanation, at least finish his bloody sentence, which was perfectly reasonable. But this was why he shouldn't have come back here. Why he should have buggered off to Australia. He wouldn't have these bloody problems then, he didn't need to feel irrational guilt on top of everything else. And he couldn't explain.

The silence lengthened between them and he felt awkward. This was getting ridiculous. He was looking ridiculous.

He was just trying to come up with something to say when

she smiled, stood up. 'I better get back to moving boxes. Thanks for the coffee and chat, lovely to meet you properly.'

'You too.' And he was surprised just how much he meant it.

As she left the surgery, his positive mood seemed to go with her. Talking about his return to Langtry Meadows reminded him just why he'd had to move on. Rolling his shoulders, he tried to ease the tension that had instantly grabbed hold of his body.

He wandered into the recovery room, determined to shake his mood. Being busy always helped. Stroking the little black cat that was stretched out on its side in one of the cages, he instantly felt his blood pressure drop as the faintest of purrs rumbled through its chest. Charlie smiled as it raised its head slightly, asking for more.

He loved these quiet times, with a patient that had turned the corner. This was the good bit; this was what the job was all about. It didn't matter where in the world he was, animals were animals and moments like this made all the long hours and difficult decisions worthwhile.

'Ready to face the wrath of the Langtry Meadows women are you, Charlie?'

Charlie gave the cat one last rub behind the ear then glanced up at Sally, his receptionist, animal nurse and general answer to all his prayers.

Two months earlier he'd arrived at the Langtry Meadows Veterinary Centre expecting to be faced with the same officious, bossy receptionist he vaguely remembered from his childhood when he'd sneaked into the surgery to see the animals, borrow his dad's bag of tricks and pretend to be a vet – although that was pretty silly as she'd been considerably older than his father. He'd still been pleasantly surprised to meet the ever-friendly, and amazingly helpful Sally.

Her mid-length brown hair hung in straight, glossy sheets either side of her solemn face which lit up when she smiled, her large brown eyes as steady as a Labrador's and the frown lines on her forehead evident whenever she was concentrating. Within a few days Charlie had fallen in love with her, in a totally un-romantic way. She was efficient, kind and knew everybody in the village – which smoothed the path and allowed him to concentrate on the animals. Which was just how he liked it. Perfect.

Eric had played a masterstroke the day he had persuaded Sally to join the small veterinary practice, and Charlie hoped he realised it.

He rolled his eyes, and secured the catch of the cage. 'How many?'

'Only three so far.' Sally giggled. 'Don't worry, once you've been here a few months they'll lose interest, but we don't often get a hunky new man in the village.' She tipped her head on one side, 'and the fact that you've come back means the nosey old bags want to come and interrogate you as well.'

'I'd have thought they'd got more interesting things to think about.'

Sally laughed. 'You're the talk of the village shop, and the pub, and in the doctor's waiting room...'

'Shush.' He held a hand up to stop her. 'I don't think I want to know.' At least Lucy, the other newcomer in town, had the advantage that she had no history here, so there was no gossip to be had.

'Though if it's any consolation the magazines in the surgery are so old, and Dr Jones is so bloody slow, it's no wonder they've had to resort to talking about you. Last time I was in there the other hot topic of conversation was whether Jim Stafford was cheating at the last gooseberry show, apparently his were massive. Swollen out of all proportion.'

'Thanks, Sal, I feel much better now you've lowered my level of importance to an over-inflated soft fruit.' Jim had actually seemed quite protective of the cover teacher. Maybe he wasn't the only one who was affected by her light floral perfume and softly curved body. He shook his head to dismiss the thought. She wasn't even his type. She was more what you'd call athletic than womanly, and she was blonde, and a bit well, well he couldn't put his finger on it, but not his type. Definitely not his type.

He'd never been a player, but maybe that was the antidote he needed. Except not with her. A teacher. The prickle of sweat that sprang up on his brow left him feeling clammy. He really had to get a grip.

'Talking of soft fruit, Holly rang to say she wants that colt of hers castrated.'

He switched his brain back to concentrating on work, his saviour. 'Why doesn't she go to the large animal practice in the next village? Most of the farm clients go there, and they've got a great horse vet.'

'It's you they love.' Sally winked. 'And you're getting quite a reputation as the man to go to for,' she made a snipping gesture and he winced, 'snipping off testicles.'

Balls were what he felt like he'd been lacking himself lately. Agreeing to come back here, and admit he was a failure professionally as well as in his private life wasn't doing him any good at all, not that any of them knew about the private bit. Yet. She'd looked at him like she knew though, Lucy. And he'd nearly said more than he'd intended.

'I remembered this place as a quiet backwater, full of farmers with tight wallets who never visited a vet unless they had to.' If he was honest, he'd expected to be bored witless, and in need of a hobby.

'Ahh, you thought you could put your feet up, didn't you Charlie boy?' He hadn't actually wanted to put his feet up, keeping busy was what he needed now, but he'd never expected it to be this hectic. 'Thinking of taking up golf were you?' He shifted guiltily. 'Well in case you've missed it, most of your clients are females, and they don't tell their hubbies until the bill needs paying.'

'Well I wish they'd at least book appointments and not turn up at all times of day and night.' He'd got used to the way his town centre practice had run like clockwork, efficiency itself. Here, the waiting room was constantly busy, often between surgery hours when he was struggling to catch up on operations and paperwork. 'They seem to think I haven't got a life.'

Sally arched an eyebrow, obviously trying not to laugh.

'Okay, I haven't got a life. I admit it. But can't they at least take the farm animals up the road?'

'They're loyal to Langtry Meadows, Charlie. They want to support Eric, and anyway, there's been bad feeling between us and them, since they pulled that stunt at the county show.'

He held up a hand. 'I don't want to know.' He was going to keep a professional distance, not be dragged into village politics. 'But we had a trailer load of piglets the other day, and a very persistent man with a lamb in the back of his estate car.'

'They think it's quicker to come to you, than call you out. You have to admit they've got a point.'

'And since when did we have alpacas in the village? I'm sure it wasn't like this when Dad was here.'

When he thought about it though, his dad had been in and out on calls constantly, but he'd just taken it for granted. His mother had always been there for him, even if his father hadn't been. And he'd loved it when Dad had brought home a stray lamb, or a dog that needed careful monitoring and a warm spot by the Aga.

'I suppose I better make a start then.'

'Geriatric hamster, or the cat from hell first?'

He peered round the door, trying to see if he recognised anybody in the waiting room. 'It depends on who owns them.' Dealing with the animals was the easy bit, keeping some of the owners at arm's length was a different matter. 'Oh hell, Serena Stevens is in again,' he withdrew, and dropped his voice to a whisper, 'what is it this time?'

Sally giggled. 'She wants to discuss babies.'

The back of his neck went clammy, then common sense kicked in. He really should be able to handle any talk of babies and young children by now. 'Babies?' The word was raspy, and Sally gave him a strange look.

'Puppies! I don't think she'd risk seeing her own boobs droop. She rather thinks that Twinkle should experience motherhood before it's too late, she wants her to experience sexual thrill and maternal joy.' The sparkle of laughter was back in Sally's eyes. 'You should see your face! Anyway, don't worry, even if she is broody I don't think she's signed you up as sperm donor yet, and I've got your back, I won't let her get her wicked way with you.'

Some people lived their dreams vicariously through their children, Serena was intent on living it through her dog – a very sensitive long-haired Chihuahua who lived a life of luxury, mainly in one of Serena's large designer tote bags.

He was just wondering whether he could get away with referring her to another vet, on the grounds of his complete lack of understanding when it came to such delicate matters, when the buzzer on the door announced another customer.

Holding the door open, and peering in was a girl in jodhpurs. 'Soz to bother you, it's just that Jasper's caught himself. You couldn't whip a quick stitch in could you?'

Jasper was a horse. The same horse that was often seen bolting through Langtry Meadows, the animal that had been responsible for his very unconventional introduction to the new primary school teacher, the thought of which made him come over all hot and bothered again.

He took a deep breath and looked at Holly. She smiled back in a winning way. She was the capable, unflustered type, so he knew 'a quick stitch' could be shorthand for 'he's bleeding all over the car park and could drop dead if you don't hurry up'.

He was ashamed to realise though that even stitching up a hyper-horse was actually far preferable to discussing sex with the immaculately groomed Serena.

'Of course we can have a look, Holly. How are you?' Sally was already tapping away at her computer and Charlie saw a busy day ahead. 'What's he done now?'

'Overreach, the silly sod. If he concentrated on what he was doing instead of being so bloody nosey then he'd know where his feet were.'

Ahh, not so bad then, the downside being that he was going to be stitching an area well within kicking range.

'Typical male.' Sally smiled.

'Thank you for your continued efforts to keep my feet firmly on the ground.'

'You're welcome, Mr Davenport.' She looked back in Holly's direction. 'Are you still up for drinks tomorrow night?'

'Sure am. Eek, stop it Jasper.' She was yanked backward, the door clanging shut behind her and they heard a clatter of hooves on the tarmac. Two of the customers got up and tried to peer through the window.

'I'll put the kettle on shall I ladies? I'm sure you won't mind waiting a few minutes while Charlie sorts this urgent case out?' Sally scanned the waiting room with a professional eye. 'You can watch him in action of course.' Serena glanced at her watch and made reassuring cooing noises at Twinkle who was growling in indignation.

'Of course not, I do like to see a man in action.' The owner of the cantankerous cat, who'd also got a cantankerous husband always loved an excuse to stay out of the house as long as possible.

Serena gazed admiringly. 'You've got such sensitive hands, you really shouldn't have to deal with such big, dangerous animals.'

Charlie stared blankly at the computer screen. Being cornered by a herd of rampaging bullocks was a safer bet than Serena and her Chihuahua.

'Oh no, no, not at all, do you want a hand with the coffee?' A slim woman in her thirties, who Charlie had never seen before, stroked a hand over her son's head and looked down at the box he was clutching. This had to be the geriatric hamster, and from the look of discomfort on the woman's face she was obviously expecting the worst – and was more than happy to put the moment of judgement off. The trouble with hamsters, Charlie knew, was that with a life span of rarely more than three years they had a habit of leaving grieving children in their wake. 'Do you want to sit here with Mario, Harry?' Harry nodded, and shooting Charlie a distrustful look clutched the box even tighter.

Another clatter of horseshoes on tarmac reminded Charlie that Jasper wasn't going to be an easy customer. With a sigh he went into the operating room and sneaked out through the back door to examine his patient.

As he bent closer to make a preliminary check of the wound, Charlie was suddenly excruciatingly aware of a pair of bright pink wellingtons, which he could see out of the corner of his eye as Lucy edged closer. He was used to being observed, but this felt different, it was as though he was still back at college – trying to impress. He had to get a grip, this was ridiculous. What did it matter if she thought he was some uncooperative, incompetent idiot?

'Is that the horse that tried to flatten me when I came for interview?' She'd moved in so close he could smell her perfume again, which was far too disconcerting.

'Oh you're kidding?' Holly put a hand to her mouth. 'Oh God, was it you in that cute little car by the pond?'

'It was.' Lucy stepped back abruptly as Jasper attempted a pirouette, and joined the rest of his clients who, keen for entertainment, had drifted out from the waiting room and were now lined up at a safe distance.

'We'd just gone past those damned alpacas and one stuck its head through the fence and made faces at him, you don't like those weird things do you honey?' She kissed the end of Jasper's nose and he threw his head in the air.

'Let's face it Holly, he doesn't like much at all does he?' commented Sally, who was standing nearby with a tray of sterilised equipment.

'Is he okay with a hosepipe?' Charlie had to concentrate on the job.

'Oh yeah, sure, he's bombproof.'

The bombproof animal whizzed around her and Holly hung on to his bridle as Charlie very slowly unwound the hosepipe.

The audience were to be disappointed. After a good clean up it was obvious that no stitching was required, and the amount of blood was due to the size of animal and location of wound rather than any serious problem.

'That looks fine, Holly. I'll just grab a twitch then we can tidy up that flap of skin.'

'Oh he'll be fine, I'll hold his nose. He's a gem, aren't you?' Holly kissed the 'gem' on the end of his nose and Charlie could see the whites of his eyes, as he shot him a warning look, followed up by a stamp on the ground in case the vet was in any doubt.

Charlie narrowed his eyes and studied the target, wondering just how quickly he could snip the skin off and dive to the side. At veterinary school he'd been told that commando style rolls could be seen as unprofessional, but he'd always thought that they had a place. Especially when the alternative was a horse's hoof up your backside. He sneaked a glance up at Lucy, who was watching intently, and wondered if he really wanted to strike another self-inflicted blow at his manhood.

'He hates a twitch, it makes him nervous.'

Snipping flaps of skin off un-anaesthetised equines made Charlie nervous.

Not giving himself time to think, he dived in and snipped decisively and was back on his feet before owner or animal had time to realise. There was a round of applause from his clients.

'Excellent.' Whatever you're doing, it pays to do it bloody quick, one of his tutors had told him, apart from surgery of course. 'I'll give him a shot of antibiotic, and if you can keep it clean...'

'Oh cheers, that's super. I would have done it myself, but I was passing and thought I might as well pop in rather than ride him all the way home and then find out it was worse than I thought.' She patted the horse. 'Fab, give my love to Eric if you see him, and put it on Dad's account will you Sal?'

Charlie would have liked to insist on payment now, as the small sign on the counter requested. The business had a serious cash-flow problem, which was largely due to well-heeled customers who didn't feel the need to pay until absolutely necessary, and thrifty farmers who argued over every penny and asked for a discount. Charlie had been shocked at Eric's relaxed attitude towards money, with the price of drugs he was surprised they hadn't gone bankrupt. It was yet another thing he really had to look into if he had time.

Smiling at Holly, he glanced towards the surgery and was disappointed to see Lucy had gone. Along with her van.

He sighed, feeling strangely deflated, and rolled his sleeves up. It was time to tackle a sex-starved Chihuahua and a cat that he just knew was out to get him.

'You look like you're ready for battle.' Sally grinned. 'Oh, and Charlie there's a message from Mr Gibson about the cricket, and the vicar's wife has rung again to ask about judging the village fete.' She peered at him over the top of her notepad. 'You do realise there's no escape, she will hunt you down?'

Charlie knew that the 'Eric would do it' argument was on the way, so he held up a hand to stop it. 'I know Eric prob-ably—'

'Well actually he refuses.'

'Really?' That stumped him.

'You will never guess the amazing excuses he's come up with every year, he manages to come up with something so brilliantly believable that she lets him off the hook.'

'Brilliant? Like what?'

'Oh no, Charlie, you've got to come up with your own.' The light in her eyes danced as she waved a finger at him. 'A man like you shouldn't have any problem at all.'

'You're laughing at me.'

'Probably.' She grinned, unabashed. 'Claws or clitoris first?'

Charlie cringed and shook his head. 'Very witty. I think a geriatric hamster is the safest bet, don't you?'

'Probably, it'll give you time to work out how to fight Serena off, she thinks you're so manly now.' She leaned forward confidentially. 'I heard her telling little Twinkle that you really are everything a man should be. I'm sensing church bells ringing and the need for a posh hat.'

'You'll be sensing something if you don't get back behind your desk and stop causing trouble, woman.'

Chapter 4

After a very busy surgery, followed by an eye-crossingly intricate operation inserting pins into a tiny Yorkshire terrier's leg, all Charlie wanted was to head for a pint at the Taverner's Arms.

'You've not forgotten you said you'd pop in and see Miss Harrington, have you Charlie?'

He glanced up as he peeled off the green scrubs he'd been operating in. 'The thought of Miss Harrington is what's kept me going all day.'

Eric had a very chaotic style of management, and the clients could be challenging to say the least, but in amongst the villagers were some real gems – like the slightly eccentric character of Miss Harrington. She didn't seem to have a first name, and she insisted on calling him Charles rather than Charlie, but despite the old-fashioned formality he always left her house feeling better than when he'd arrived. To her he was probably still the little boy in short trousers that she'd chastised if he rode his bike on the pavement.

'I'm looking forward to a quiet cup of tea and a slice of cake as I check over Molly's new litter of puppies.'

'You only go for the homemade cake.' Sally was hugging her ever present clipboard to her chest.

'I do. That parkin last week was unbelievable, and I heard a rumour she's got fresh cherry cake on offer.'

'You men are such simple creatures when it comes down to it, aren't you?'

He grinned and grabbed the few medical supplies he might need. 'See you in the morning?'

'You will.'

Shouting a farewell he threw his scrubs into the wash bin and strode out of the surgery. Then ground to a halt.

The van was back, and parked even more haphazardly than before – if that was possible. Lucy had obviously gone for another load, and now he couldn't get out.

'Hi!' She waved an arm enthusiastically as he walked over, before pulling a box out of the van, and once again he felt himself smiling automatically.

'You're er, blocking the driveway again.'

'Oh, sorry, I thought it might be okay now, seeing as you're done for the day.' She pointed at the sign. 'It says that the surgery has finished, and it was just easier here, it gives me more room.'

'Ahh right, it's just that consultation hours have finished, but I haven't.' He needed boundaries here. If he kept her at a professional distance then he could handle her – or more accurately not handle her. 'And I live above the shop, so it would help if you found somewhere else to park, it's just a bit cramped for space.'

She frowned, then dropped the box into a wheelbarrow,

which he hadn't noticed on the other side of the van, and pulled her hair through the ponytail a bit more securely.

'Oh, I didn't realise. But I won't be here much longer.'

'It is private property.' Why the hell had he said that? Now he just sounded like a pompous idiot.

'It is only for a short while.'

He was being unfair. She looked as frazzled as he felt. There were dark smudges under the dazzling blue eyes, and a pink flush of what could have been embarrassment or anger along the high cheekbones. All he had to do was be polite, and there was no harm in that, was there? 'I thought you had a Mini anyway, not a van.'

'I borrowed this to move my stuff.' He could sense she'd been about to say 'of course', and then bitten it off.

'With a wheelbarrow?'

'Well yes,' she frowned and folded her arms. 'Is that a problem as well?'

He could see it in her eyes, the challenge. The *is everything a problem to you, parking, wheelbarrows, coming into school?* Something inside him tightened defensively in response. 'I do need to get my car out.' He lifted his medical bag, as he glanced into the van which looked like it contained another twenty barrow loads of stuff.

'Ah, another emergency?'

She was talking to him as though he was an irritating six year old, and he could understand it. He was acting a bit like one. 'Exactly.' How the hell had they gone from the pleasant cup of coffee this morning, to this? But he knew the answer to that. He was lashing out.

'Sorry, but there really wasn't anywhere else to park.' She turned away, her voice slightly muffled as she dragged another box out of the van. 'I could pull up a bit so you could squeeze past, but there's only room for my car at the cottage.'

'Well it's not exactly Crewe station is it?'

'What's that supposed to mean?' She frowned, dropped the box and stuck her hands in her pockets.

'There isn't any traffic, you can park on the road in front of the house. Oh good heavens.' He knew he was being impatient and awkward with her, but he couldn't help himself. He leaned in and grabbed a suitcase out of the back of the van. 'Here, I'll help if you're not going to move this thing until you've emptied it.' It was a last ditch attempt to make up for all the negative energy he knew he was aiming straight at her.

'No you won't.' Lucy made a lunge for the case, and all of a sudden she was inches away from him. He dropped the case abruptly.

'Fine.' He held up his hands. 'I'll walk.' He took a step away, desperate to put some distance between them, trying to ignore the pretty blush that tinged her high cheekbones, the slightly open lips. A walk would calm him down. Walking wasn't a problem. Before she could say anything he grabbed his bag, and stepped back abruptly.

'I'm sorry.' She sighed. 'I should have at least asked.' She waved an arm to encompass all her stuff. 'I've just got a lot on.'

'I know.' His shoulders sagged. 'I'm sorry too. If there's anything I can do to help.'

'Not really, just maybe come up with an alternative suggestion for my vet visit to school?' She sounded tired.

She was like him – at the end of a long day, in a place she didn't feel comfortable. And he was being a shit. He didn't have any argument with her, just the fact that right now she was jarring a nerve with deadly accuracy, even though she didn't know it. The whole school question hung between them. 'I'm only a locum, doing cover, I really think it's up to Eric...' He could hear the defensive edge creeping back into his voice.

'I know, I know.' She sighed. 'One of my bad habits, refusing to take no for an answer. It's been a long day, and I've got so much to do, and I'm only doing cover too.' Her gaze caught his. 'To be honest I'm desperate, but I was only after a suggestion, I'm not trying to force your hand.' Her face softened, in much the same way he imagined it would when she had to deal with impending tantrums. 'But it is only a bunch of kids, they won't expect much. You might even enjoy it.'

'I wouldn't, I can assure you.' Standing in front of a hall full of smiling faces was the last thing he wanted to do. It would bring it all back. Remind him just what he'd lost.

'Still here, Charlie?' Sally's bike scrunched to a halt on the gravel beside them, and she wobbled, her hand on his shoulder. 'I'm surprised when you've got a slice of Madeira cake calling you.'

'I'm rather hemmed in.'

She laughed, and Lucy joined in.

'Not introducing us?'

'Sorry, Sal this is Miss Jacobs, Lucy, the new teacher at the primary school.'

'Cover teacher.' Lucy smiled, wiped her hand down her jeans and held it out to shake.

'Oh, so you're the one covering for Becky are you? I'm Sally by the way, I run the practice.' She winked at Charlie, and Lucy laughed.

'She's right, who am I to argue? Without Sally there's no way I could handle this weird practice, Langtry Meadows seems to run with its own set of rules.'

'I saw you watching Charlie's heroics with the horse earlier, isn't he manly?' Sally laughed as she squeezed his bicep. For a brief second Lucy's gaze clashed with his, then they both looked down, embarrassed.

'Oh, er, yes.' She cleared her throat. 'Pleased to meet you, Sally. I think you're just the person I need on my side.'

'Oh?'

'I've been trying to persuade him to come into school and talk to the children.'

'Good luck with that. I'm not surprised you resorted to blocking him into the car park!' Sally chuckled. 'I'll leave you two to it then. Lovely to meet you Lucy, catch you later.' Waving a hand, she let go of Charlie and with a wobble sailed off up the lane towards the centre of the village.

Lucy was looking at him. 'You really don't want to do it, do you?'

He sighed. 'To be completely honest I'd rather be trampled by a herd of wildebeest.'

'Oh my God, you don't get those here?'

He laughed. The tension that had somehow built between them, when he'd felt like she was asking him to do the impossible, ebbed away. It wasn't her fault, and anyhow at some point he'd have to get his act together. Stop hiding and start to live a normal life again. 'I'll think about it, but I can tell you now that I'm unlikely to change my mind.' He paused, feeling like he should give her more of an honest explanation. 'It's personal. I really do have a patient to attend to though, so I better get off. Good luck with the unpacking.'

'Thanks.'

He looked back into the gorgeous blue eyes and his feet didn't want to take him away. 'I can give you a quick guided tour of the village some time, if you like? Seeing as you won't let me help unload this stuff.'

'Thanks. That would be lovely.' The broad smile warmed up his insides, and he just knew he was grinning back. Why the hell had he said that? He had enough problems, he certainly didn't need to get involved with a slim, pretty girl with a cute pony tail and pink wellies. But she was nice. She was funny. And she was like him, out of her comfort zone, and being here was a temporary fix for both of them. They'd both be moving on soon, so what was the harm?

'Now then, Charles. Wash your hands and sit down with me and tell me all about your day. I do love our little chats.'

'So do I.' Charlie gave Molly the golden retriever a stroke, and straightened up. 'You're a clever girl, aren't you?' Her tail gave a lazy wag, then she looked up at the podgy puppy he was still holding. He lifted it up to his face, the soft, velvet fur warm against his skin. 'They really are lovely, I'd keep this one if I could.' He missed having a dog around, the undemanding, non-judgemental company. He missed a lot of things that he'd taken for granted up until a few weeks ago.

'Well if you'd settle down here, instead of gallivanting off.' Her tone was tart, and Charlie tried to repress the sigh.

The pup wriggled, so he concentrated on that and bent down to place it amongst the others. Molly turned her attention back to the five puppies, nudging them back into position. 'She's doing a wonderful job with those pups, Miss Harrington, they're all looking healthy and well fed.'

She gave him one of her stern looks, then let him change the direction of the conversation. 'She is, isn't she? Quite surprising considering her normal disreputable behaviour.' Miss Harrington smiled, obviously pleased with her dog, but unwilling to shower her with praise. 'She's much steadier than that collie I used to have though, did I tell you about the time she chased a squirrel up the apple tree? I have never, in all my days, seen a dog do that.' She shook her head as she looked down her long aristocratic nose at the retriever who flopped on her side with a contented groan. 'I do hope motherhood isn't going to turn this one into a bore though, there is so little of entertainment value happening in this village at present.'

'You did tell me.' Charlie headed for the spacious downstairs bathroom, where a new bar of soap, freshly washed hand towel and hand-cream had been laid out for him. He stood for a moment, studying his reflection in the mirror. Even to his own eyes he looked knackered and grumpy, no wonder the lovely Lucy hadn't wanted to take him up on his offer of helping her empty the van.

He closed his eyes, letting the total peace and quiet wash over him for a moment. Since he'd moved back here he'd just buried himself in work, the sure fire way of avoiding the rest of the village and their curiosity. But he knew deep down that he needed some time out, and maybe that was the instinct that had prompted him to offer to show Lucy round. They were both here temporarily, two people out of their comfort zone. Nothing wrong with sticking together. And it had absolutely nothing to do with the fact that she'd been in his arms twice already, and it had felt far more natural than it should have.

'Now then,' Miss Harrington was pouring tea as he sat down, then nudged the plate of cake in his direction, 'I am relying on you to fill me in on the gossip, young man.'

He took a large bite of cake and waited for her to embellish. Miss Harrington was more than capable of picking up on gossip, but seemed to like to hear it from all angles before making her mind up.

'What do you know about this young school teacher they've employed? I spotted you having a little chat, you seem very friendly. Pretty young thing, isn't she?'

He spluttered out cake crumbs, then recovered, wiping his mouth with a napkin.

'I hardly—'

She leaned forward, ignoring his interruption. 'I've got a feeling she thinks she's only here for a few weeks, but if I know Timothy Parry he's got other plans in mind.'

'He has?' There was a weird sensation in the pit of Charlie's stomach and he wasn't sure if it was foreboding, or something far more worrying. Like anticipation, pleasure.

'Oh yes. Well I wouldn't be at all surprised if little Becky decided to stay at home once she's had her baby. That husband of hers has a very good job. Pin money that teaching job is, pin money.' She tapped the side of her nose, and for a moment reminded Charlie of a vulture. Then she smiled, her eyes twinkling with merriment, and he shook his head to dismiss the unkind thought. 'Eat up, Charles, do have another piece or it will go to waste. Yes, that husband of hers would be far happier to see the girl chained to the kitchen sink.' She gave a disapproving grunt. 'Or entertaining his clients, and,' she paused melodramatically, 'Timothy wants some new blood in the school, somebody capable of fighting his battles and I think this new one could be just the girl, looks like she has some spirit, doesn't she?'

'Battles?' Charlie spoke through cake crumbs. 'I'm not sure about spirit, but she's definitely stubborn. And persistent.' And pretty.

'Battles.' She didn't elaborate. 'And he won't be there forever you know, I think he's planning his escape.'

'He is?' His mind was still half on the teacher, Lucy.

'Not that the governors or PTA have caught on yet, so you better keep that to yourself. No point in stirring things, is there? More tea?'

Charlie had no intention of stirring anything, but wasn't so sure Miss Harrington had the same pure intentions.

'Is she feisty? She looks like that pretty exterior could hide a firm backbone.'

'I really don't...' She obviously didn't want to drop the matter that easily. What was it about the women in this bloody village?

'I've got no time for these girls that just want to be wedded and bedded. Pregnancy and birth seems to kill your brain cells you know. One can't think straight for years.'

Charlie nodded, he could go along with that line of thought. If only he'd had this chat with Elsie Harrington seven years ago life might have been much more straightforward.

'Just look at Molly.'

He looked at the dog, who narrowed her eyes, the corners of her mouth turning up into a smile of apology.

'Befuddled aren't you, girl? What does young Sally think of the girl?'

He sighed. 'I haven't a clue, she's only just met her. Have you been spying on us, Miss Harrington?'

'I was looking out for you, you were a little late you know and I do like promptness.'

He decided not to point out the fact that it was impossible to see the surgery car park from her house.

'And,' she paused, so that he had no choice but to look up, 'you can't hide away forever Charles. You should tell somebody, talk. Maybe another person who's not sure she wants to be here is as good a person as any? You may have more in common than you think.' Her tone was soft, but too direct to ignore. 'I might be old Charles, but I do understand, believe me I do.'

'She's only spoken to me because she wants me to go into school and talk to the kids!'

'I know. It's a start.'

He decided to ignore the second part of the statement. 'Is this a new tactic from Tim Parry to get me to go in? Because if it is you can forget it, the answer is still no.'

'No it's not.' She looked affronted, but he had known her far too long to take that at face value. 'That girl is lonely and doesn't feel needed.'

He sighed. 'I can't help that, now can I? I'm only here for a few weeks, you know that as well as me. It's temporary, to help Eric out, and cash to bridge me over until...'

'Until you run away to Australia?'

That was about it, yes. He could lose himself in the vast-ness of a cattle station, so it wasn't all about him and his mistakes. So he would just be a small blip on the horizon. Invisible.

'You never struck me as a coward, Charles.' She straightened her skirt. 'You still don't. Now,' her voice took on its normal brisk edge, 'I'm sure you've heard enough from me, and are dying for a pint of beer. You can see yourself out, I trust?'

Chapter 5

'It would be a lot easier if you could talk.' Lucy stared into the cardboard box at the hen, which glared indignantly back.

The move to Langtry Meadows had actually gone more smoothly than she'd expected. She really wasn't a gypsy at heart at all, she liked her home comforts, liked what she knew – and this move was a step outside her comfort zone. But things had been going okay, and she'd been surprised to find that she was already feeling quite at home.

In fact, the inside of the cottage had been quite a revelation. It was as organised and tidy on the inside as it was wild and disorganised on the outside. The sense of order had wrapped itself round her in a comfortable hug, and Annie had even left a folder that answered almost every question she could have ever thought of, and many she couldn't. There was also a welcome box of food, and a lovely homemade cake.

From the day she'd moved in she'd been far too busy clipping back bushes and feeding Annie's menagerie to feel at a loose end or lonely at all. In fact, the way things were going she wouldn't have time to fully prepare everything that she wanted to for the first day of term on Monday.

All had been going well until she'd spotted the hen, which was behaving quite differently to all the others. Annie's folder didn't help at all.

She'd rung the veterinary surgery, hoping that the friendly looking Sally (as opposed to the grumpy looking Charlie) would be able to give her some advice. It wasn't that she didn't want to see Charlie, but they seemed to rub each other up the wrong way. One minute he seemed to be rescuing her (though she hadn't needed rescuing from the van, if he hadn't sneaked up like that there wouldn't have been a problem) and the next moment he couldn't get away fast enough.

Maybe that was his problem, that he actually didn't like her. Or maybe it was just because he seemed to have an aversion to children, so being around her was his worst nightmare.

Sally sounded as friendly and welcoming on the phone as she had in the car park though, which was instantly reassuring. 'Oh, pop in, it's a quiet time and much better to be safe than sorry. Annie practically lives down here when she's home. I'm sure there'll be a box, or a cat basket in the house to bring it in. If not we can lend you one.'

'What time are consultation hours? I thought it said on the board...'

'Oh don't worry about that. Friday afternoon is a quiet time, Charlie's not too busy. Come now.'

Which was why she was sitting in the empty waiting room with a hen on her knee, wondering just how irate Charlie Davenport was going to be when he realised she'd turned up outside his consultation hours. He really didn't seem keen on her anyway, there'd been an undercurrent when they'd met. He was going to like her even less now.

'Miss Jacobs?' He didn't sound cross, more preoccupied, and professional, which for some strange reason left her feeling slightly deflated.

The run in they'd had in the car park had been ridiculous though. I mean what was wrong with the man? What did he think she'd been doing with the van? It had seemed pretty obvious to her, and sensible. Parking on the road and causing an obstruction would have been stupid.

She'd bumped into him three times now, and two of those times she'd somehow ended up in his arms, then he'd looked like she was a massive inconvenience. The first time she'd been thrown back in the road like a hot potato, the second he'd backed off so quickly she might have had something contagious. He had offered to show her round the village, but *some time* obviously meant way into the future. But he wasn't really to blame, he'd offered on impulse to make up for not coming into school, then probably instantly regretted it, and it wasn't his fault she'd actually been quite looking forward to it (to an almost stalker-ish degree – did strolling past the surgery most days with a pig on a lead count as normal?).

She stood up and followed him through to the consulting room, hoping there was actually something wrong with the chicken, and she wasn't just using it as an excuse to come here. But it *was* walking in a funny way. Very funny, even for a chicken.

He was peering over his glasses at her, looking very serious.

Like he had in the car park. Hadn't even James Herriot had a sense of humour, a good bedside manner? Or was she thinking about somebody else?

His hair was more tousled than it had been when she'd seen him before, with a bit sticking up that her fingers were itching to straighten. She curled her fingers into fists to stop herself, he wasn't a child in her class, he was a grown man. A very grown man. His chin had a darker shadow than last time she'd seen him. Very Poldark. From the firmness of his chest last time he'd grabbed her, she'd say he'd probably look quite good stripped to the waist, swinging a stethoscope rather than a scythe.

Even the glasses made him look sexy. Oh God, since when had she fancied the studious type? She had to get out more.

Luckily he didn't seem to notice that she was mentally undressing him, tidying his hair or slowly removing his specs. He was more interested in the sorry looking chicken that seemed to have lost its cluck.

The hen melted into his hands as he took it out of the box, which wasn't at all how it had reacted when she'd put it in. There had been flapping and the threat of its sharp little beak. It glanced over at her reproachfully as it sank down on to the black, rubber topped table, as though to say *that's how you handle a hen*. She glared back with a silent *you'll be accompanying stuffing and roast potatoes soon if you're not careful.*

'Settling in okay?' Charlie interrupted their staring competition, and she wasn't sure if it was directed at the hen or her, as he was studying it so intently. The hen's head sank further into its shoulders. He glanced up, and she had a brief glimpse of his dark brown eyes before he looked away.

'Er, yes, thanks. Fine.'

'And what seems to be the problem?'

'Well nothing, oh sorry, the hen. She looks, er, well she's not happy, and she's been waddling like a penguin.' She put her arms out, about to do an impression when she realised she wasn't in school now and stopped abruptly.

He nodded, so she carried on with the speech she'd rehearsed while she'd been waiting, which was sounding pretty strange even to her own ears, but it was the best she could do. 'She's been, well squatting and, this might sound silly,' definitely not the time to demonstrate, 'it's as if she's consti-pated.' Staring at the chicken seemed the safest bet, but she risked a quick look up to see if he was laughing. He wasn't. He was still looking very professional. 'I'm afraid I don't really know much at all about hens, well any animals if I'm honest.'

'Well I'd say that's a pretty good description of an egg-bound chicken. Very succinct.'

She flushed, embarrassingly pleased at the praise, which made a change from being pushed out of the way as he rushed off to handle an emergency.

'Annie left feeding instructions?'

'She did.'

'And you've followed them?'

'To the letter.' She could feel herself bristling, if there was one thing she was good at it was following instructions.

'Plenty of water?'

'Plenty. Would you like to check?'

He didn't even bother looking at her, but carried on examining the hen. 'It feels like it's just a bit on the large side, if you can just hold...'

She must have looked horrified.

He picked the hen up in large capable hands, and it settled against his chest, practically cooing. She couldn't blame it, she'd felt quite safe and secure when he'd done the same to her ... oh hell, she'd promised herself she would not think about that again. 'I'll just take her through and get Sally to give me a hand, see if we can get it out. If that's okay?'

Well that brought her back down to earth. She wasn't exactly squeamish but there were limits to how far into this looking after livestock thing she was going to go. 'Fine. Good.' Holding a hen while a vet prised an over-sized egg out of its rear was not on her to-do list at all.

'Take a seat in the waiting room if you like, won't be long.'

The waiting room was bright and airy, modern and completely at odds with everything else in the village. There was a polite notice displayed prominently on the desk, next to Sally's computer, stating that payment for all treatment had to be made on the day. To the left was a neat notice board, with a photo of some adorable terrier puppies needing good homes, a missing cat poster, and a notice about the annual May Day celebrations. There were also posters about the need for annual vaccinations, and one with a very creepy looking picture of a tick. She diverted her gaze towards the display stand that had a variety of dog toys, along with brushes and combs, and a stack of convalescence cat food.

'All done! One much happier hen.'

She started guiltily. Sally was holding the hen, which did indeed look relieved.

'Here you go.' Charlie held up a very large, and slightly misshapen, egg. 'It's probably just a one-off, but if it happens again then we'll look at their diet.'

'So, it's nothing I've done?'

'No.' Sally grinned reassuringly as she put the hen back in the box, then nodded towards the May Day poster Lucy had been looking at. 'I'm counting on you to make sure the kids don't tie themselves in knots round the maypole this year, I swear Timothy lets them do it on purpose so he can sneak off for a pint.'

'Me?'

'Oh yes, hasn't the crafty devil told you yet?' She giggled.

'I'm beginning to wonder just how much he hasn't actually explained.' She looked pointedly at Charlie, who shook his head. But this time there was a hint of a smile.

'And before you ask again, the answer is still no, I'm not coming in to talk to the kids.' He paused. 'Sorry, if I was a bit brusque the other day though when you were with Jim, it's just it was a bit of a life and death thing, well I thought it was.'

'Life and death!' Sally rolled her eyes. 'Can you believe it? Serena rang to say little Twinkle was dying, and it just turned out she'd come into season! Oh gosh,' she put a hand over her mouth, 'I really shouldn't say things like that.'

'I only have two words to say.' Charlie raised an eyebrow.

'Client confidentiality.' They both chimed together, but Sally didn't look at all put out.

'We all know she's just trying to get her wicked way with you though, lure you over there. One day you'll arrive and she'll be in a negligee.'

'Who's to say it hasn't happened already?'

Lucy could have sworn there was the slightest hint of a blush spreading along Charlie's cheekbones as he spoke.

She was also slightly shocked to see this light-hearted side of Charlie, who was more relaxed in Sally's company than she could have imagined. Maybe there was something going on between them, and the moment he was alone (or with her) he'd revert to type.

'If it had happened, you'd be locked in your operating theatre and have battened down the hatches, Charlie Davenport.'

'You know me far too well, Sal.' He dropped the egg into Lucy's hand. 'I'm looking forward to May Day already.' His tone was grave, but there was the slightest hint of a humour in the crinkles that fanned out from his eyes.

Sally giggled. 'Never work with animals or children, isn't that what they say Charlie?'

'And that, Sally, is why I steer clear of the school. Animals on their own are no problem at all, it's the owners and the children that scare me.' He took a step back, towards the safety of the counter that divided his world from the public. 'You did the right thing bringing her in straight away, if you're worried at all, call.'

Sally leaned in as Lucy picked the box, and chicken, up. Her voice was low. 'You know what? I think you've got a chance of winning him over, you know. He's weakening.'

'He is?' He didn't exactly look weak to her.

'He is. Yet again, Timothy Parry plays a blinder. That man is smarter than he looks.'

Two days later on her first day at Langtry Meadows primary school, Lucy had to admit that head teacher Timothy Parry was indeed sharper than his unassuming manner suggested.

'Staff meeting in ten minutes ladies, and then we can all have a cup of tea and a biscuit.' He gazed at the classroom display, which she'd nearly finished putting up with the help of Jill. The classroom assistant was currently balanced on a chair, hanging on to the end of some colourful bunting with one hand, had a drawing pin in the other and a picture of a duck between her teeth. 'Splendid, all hands to the pump eh? Very good.'

She rolled her eyes at Lucy, who giggled.

'You'll love the May Day celebrations,' Jill's words were muffled by the duck which flapped up and down in her mouth as she spoke the words, 'it's great fun, the whole village turns out. And this bunting can stay up for the rest of the year if you like.' She fastened it into place and jumped off the chair. 'Still not persuaded Charlie boy to come in?' The duck was assaulted with the staple gun and the two girls stood back to admire their handiwork. 'He'll cave in eventually, men always do, anything for a quiet life.' She paused, 'although I'm surprised he's refused, he used to be pretty easy going.'

'You knew him before?'

'Oh yeah, he lived in the village until he went to Uni. He moved on to bigger, better things after he graduated, but still came back to see his parents. Now,' she adjusted the maypole which was looking a bit like the leaning tower of Pisa. 'We normally let the kids do pictures of themselves to pin them round the pole, but it's completely up to you?'

Lucy nodded, trying to concentrate on the job in hand, and stop wondering about Charlie and his aversion to the school. 'Sounds like a good plan to me, it'll help me get to grips with all the names. Although to be honest this should be easy compared to the class of thirty-five I had before.'

'You'll soon learn their quirks. It's the twins that are the tricky bit, they swap clothes.' Jill tapped her watch. 'I suppose we better head for the staff room, Tim comes across as a bit bumbling and easy-going, but he's a stickler for punctuality. It's a control thing.' She grinned. 'You have to hang on to the little things in this job, don't you?'

Lucy smiled back. 'You certainly do.' The atmosphere at the school was unlike any other she'd worked in. It was gentle, easy-paced (with the exception of Liz, who scurried around as though she was on fire) and she had no problem at all with sticking to an agenda and being punctual. Control was a word she quite liked herself.

Her classroom for the next half term was much brighter and lighter than she'd expected it to be, in such a small old building. Large windows on one side of the classroom let in the sun, and gave a view that would be hard to beat in any school. She reluctantly pulled the window shut and glanced across the field for one last time before following Jill out of the classroom.

Next time she came in here it would be chaos; excited

children fresh from their holidays, keen to test out their new teacher.

'Now one final point before we wrap up for the day.' Timothy looked around the staff room and beamed in Lucy's direction. 'As our temporary replacement for Becky, Lucy will of course be taking on most of her responsibilities. I'm sure that you will give her all the support she needs as we approach May Day, two weeks preparation is a bit on the tight side, but I have all confidence in her.'

There was a smattering of applause, and murmurs of approval. She glanced at Jill for some inkling of what was going on, and received a wink back.

'Liz will of course help with the equipment.' This was sounding scarier by the second. 'And Jill knows the erm, ropes, as it were.' He chuckled. 'Or should I say ribbons.'

Jill patted her hand reassuringly. 'Don't worry, you'll be fine. It goes wrong every year and nobody cares, they're far more interested in getting stuck into the Pimms and beer.'

'And what is 'it' exactly?' Lucy put down her pad of paper, and looked around at the staff who had given her a warm welcome, but were now looking suspiciously relieved.

'Dancing around the maypole of course,' Liz who was up on her feet collecting cups paused by Lucy, 'it goes up on the village green, but don't you go worrying about that, we use the post in the middle of the veterinary surgery car park to practise. There's plenty of space there, and Eric loves watching us, he's even been known to join in.'

'But Eric isn't here.' Lucy would have buried her head in

her hands if she hadn't had every eye in the staff room fixed on her. Eric might have loved it, but she had a horrible feeling that Charlie Davenport wouldn't approve at all. So much for their temporary truce.

'You look like you need a stiff drink!'

Lucy glanced up in surprise as the deep male voice reverberated across the playground and snapped her out of the mental battle she was fighting. Her brain had turned to spaghetti and she was still trying to untangle all the bits of information she'd picked up today, and work out how she was going to fit in all the extra tasks she seemed to have agreed to.

'You aren't kidding.' She felt the frown fade from her brow as she stepped through the school entrance, took a deep breath and looked at Charlie. 'The kids aren't even in yet and I'm beginning to wonder what I've let myself in for.'

'Really?' He looked amused.

'I love the teaching part, but it's all the paperwork and extra jobs that are a pain.'

'I know exactly what you mean, if I only had to treat animals my job would be a dream. Although,' he paused and she took the opportunity to study him a bit more closely. His open-necked polo shirt was tucked into chinos that hugged his muscular thighs, the normal dark shadow skimmed his jaw, but today his eyes seemed to shine. He looked happy, relaxed, which she was pretty sure was a first in her company. 'If you think you've had a tough day, you should have been in my shoes this morning. Never get stuck to a kitten is my advice.'

His eyes were more than shining, there was laughter dancing in them. He was gorgeous, irresistible.

'Stuck?' The word struggled to emerge from her dry throat, but he didn't seem to notice.

'Literally.' He nodded. 'I use glue to mend minor tears, and wasn't as careful as I should have been.'

'Really?' A smile tugged at her insides. 'You were actually stuck to a kitten?'

'Really. The owner nearly had to take me home as well as the cat.'

Now that might not be too much of a hardship.

'I daren't move in case I did more damage than I'd already repaired, and you have no idea how wriggly an indignant kitten can be. Luckily Sal was at hand to rescue me.' He grinned. 'Once she'd picked herself up off the floor and stopped laughing. So, beat that.'

She laughed, she couldn't help it. 'I admit defeat, no way can I beat that.' She paused, 'Yet. Give me a couple of weeks and it might be a different story, Timothy has already roped me into dancing round the maypole, which I know bugger all about.' She glanced sideways, but he didn't react, so she'd leave the whole invading his car park plan for now. It was nice, just chatting to him, and she didn't want to spoil things.

'Dancing round the maypole?' He raised an eyebrow and laughed, he was just being so nice and relaxed, showing a side of himself that was suddenly very welcome after the stresses of the day. The first day at a new job was always exhausting, and this was so different to anywhere she'd worked before.

'Well it's not me that's doing the actual dancing, it's the kids I'm expected to get doing it, which sounds a nightmare to me. And that's only the start of it, I'm only here doing cover, I really didn't expect...' She caught his eyes and he twinkled back. He was grinning. Actually grinning, a lovely smile that changed his whole face from handsome to quite devastating. Her knees were all wobbly, and she'd completely lost her train of thought.

'Only doing cover?' He raised an eyebrow and looked surprisingly wicked, it was the type of intimate look that you swapped on a shared pillow. Oh bugger, she felt her face heat up.

'Okay, okay. Stop laughing at me. We're in the same boat. Sorry, I promise not to try and persuade you to come in. I think you better give me some lessons on how to avoid getting roped into everything.'

'I'm beginning to think there's no escape.'

As they walked, Lucy felt the tensions of the day trickle from her body. It was so nice to have somebody to chat to, somebody who wasn't part of the school. Okay, he'd lived here once, but he wasn't a part of the tight knit community. He was like her, on the outside. And he was somebody who didn't know about her past failures, who wasn't going to judge. A friend. 'And I've already had three letters from parents complaining about my plans.'

'Plans?'

'Well I'd mentioned at my interview that I thought it would be nice to have the children start off the day with some exercises, it worked really well at my last school. It helped them switch off from the stuff going on at home, and get some of the high spirits out as well.' She sighed. 'Word seems to have got around.' That was the trouble with villages, tell one person something and news spread like wildfire. 'They're ganging up on me already. One of them was waiting for me when I arrived this morning!'

'They don't beat about the bush these farmers.'

'He said it wasn't the way they did it round here, I mean why? Why can't they try something new?'

'It's not the way we do things round here are words you'll hear a lot.' He winked. 'Don't mind them, they're friendly enough really, but you know what it's like in these small communities.'

'Oh I know that alright.' She glanced up and was surprised to find that as they'd walked and talked they'd got as far as the cobbled square. 'Sorry, I'm not keeping you, am I?'

'Nope, you're not keeping me, it was me hassling you. I thought I could show you round a bit, but it sounds like you've got a good idea of what's what without me. So, you have lived in a village like Langtry Meadows before? I thought you were a city girl.'

'I am a city girl. I was young when we left the village.'

'It must be strange for you coming to a little school like this.' His voice was soft, but she heard every word perfectly. It was as though her whole body was perfectly tuned into him. 'I couldn't wait to leave this place and set up a practice somewhere I was really needed.'

'A bit like me.' She shrugged. 'Nobody's an outsider in a city, everybody is struggling, there's a different new challenge every day. I found that out when I moved up to high school.'

'Not many new challenges in a place like this. Unless you grow up wanting to follow in your dad's footsteps milking cows and sowing seeds,' he gave a rueful smile, 'or taking over your dad's veterinary practice, then there's not much to do. I couldn't wait to escape the monotony.'

She couldn't help but smile. 'Milking cows and sowing seeds!'

'Although I'm sure that's what Miss Harrington would say life is all about, it's all about the food and new life. I was young and impulsive though, was sure there was a much bigger, more challenging world out there.' He was staring across the square, but she was pretty sure it was the past he was seeing, not the present. And all of a sudden she could see her own past. The child on the outside, or in her case the inside of a house – looking out at all the others having fun.

'I wanted to escape the loneliness, not boredom.' The words were out before she could stop them, and she looked down at her hands, but knew his gaze was on her.

'It's impossible to be alone in this place.'

'It was possible for me in Stoneyvale.'

'Why?' His tone was gentle, the single word simple enough. But she'd never really stopped to think, she'd been an only child, her and her mother had not been born there, her father said they weren't good enough, didn't belong…

'It was him.' She started as she realised she'd said the words out loud.

'Sorry?'

She could see it as clearly as if it was yesterday. 'My dad.

I don't think he actually wanted me to have any friends.' She shook her head as though she could shake the unwelcome thought out.

He'd hugged her close when things had gone wrong, always been on her side. He'd told her she didn't need anybody else. Not even her mother, who would let her down. She could still remember the look on her mother's face as she'd watched them. Dad said she was jealous, but even then Lucy had known it had been something else. Then she'd just felt unease, the feeling that something wasn't right. Now she recognised the wary stillness she'd seen in her mother, she'd been the rabbit frozen in the headlights. The prey about to flee.

She'd believed most things her father told her, but never that her mum would let her down. They'd been too close, the bond between mother and daughter too strong to break, too many happy memories, too many shared giggles and hugs. Too much love. And that had made him cross.

'Are you okay?' The bump of Charlie's shoulder against hers broke into her thoughts.

'Sure, I'm fi—'

'Oh hell.' She looked at Charlie in surprise as he grabbed her hand. 'Sorry, I've just spotted Maria Grainger and I just can't face any more testicles right now.'

Lucy blinked, then frowned. 'Isn't Mr Grainger the one that has the testicles?'

'Nope.' He tugged on her. 'Come on, quick, let's hide in the church.'

'Where I come from, churches are locked.'

'Not here.' He pushed the door with one hand, and drew

her in behind him. Close behind him, so that when he turned they were nearly nose to nose. 'Maria owns the alpaca farm up the road and seems to have an endless supply of youngsters that need castrating.' It was hard to concentrate on his words when he was this close. 'That's all I seem to be doing at the moment. You have no idea how disconcerting it is to cut the balls off an animal that's humming at you.'

She didn't. But she did know how disconcerting it was to be pressed against Charlie Davenport, and she was starting to have very ungodly thoughts. Not good in a church.

He was cute. Oh, what the heck was she thinking about? She'd be heading back to Birmingham soon, and the single life she was quite comfortable with – and he'd be off wherever he was going – he'd made it quite clear that he had no more intention of staying here than she did. It wasn't real attraction – just a meeting of minds, circumstances, stuff they had in common. The fact that he was so easy to talk to…

It was her mother she should be talking to though, not Charlie. She'd put it off far too long, hidden behind half-truths and excuses she'd given herself.

She looked up at Charlie and in the dimly lit church he looked even more solid, reassuring. She couldn't help herself. She brushed her lips against his dry, firm ones. Then, before he could say anything, before he could push her away or pull her closer, she squeezed past him and ran down the stone steps, across the cobbled square. Home.

Chapter 6

'You're really sure it won't be a problem?'

Sally smiled at Lucy who had her hair tumbled up into a bun on top of her head, and held in place with a pencil. Teachers always needed a pencil handy she supposed. 'Of course not, Eric always loved seeing the kiddies practising.'

'But Charlie...?' She seemed flustered, almost embarrassed about mentioning the vet. In fact, it was almost like she *wanted* Sally to say no and send them away.

'I won't tell if you don't.' She winked at Lucy, then turned her attention back to the client who was leaning against her counter. Matt Harwood was clutching his small dog, which seemed to diminish even further in size against his very broad chest. 'Take a seat, Matt. He won't keep you long.'

Lucy spotted the dog and stared aghast, she took a hasty step back as though she expected to catch a nasty disease from it. 'Oh my God, oh the poor thing. Will it be okay, will it recover?' She glanced up at Matt, who grinned.

Sally sighed, waiting for him to turn the Harwood charm on. He couldn't help it, the roguish grin flickered into action, dimples at the corners of his mouth, a fan of wrinkle lines around the blue eyes that all the girls wanted to fall into. Then he topped it by shifting the dog in his arms so that he could flex his very impressive pecs. Lucy's eyes opened a bit wider, and Sally waited for her to tumble under his spell.

But she didn't, she looked horrified. Genuinely shocked.

Sally was impressed, she had a feeling she could get to like this girl. Call her old-fashioned, but she much preferred the gentler charms of Matt's older and steadier brother James – who kept his body and his thoughts about the opposite sex under control.

'I bet that itches something rotten,' Lucy looked at Sally for confirmation, 'is it some kind of skin disease? Is it contagious?'

'No.' Sally grinned, and rested her forearms on the counter. 'Although her owner thinks he is, contagious that is.'

Lucy raised an eyebrow.

'Lucy, meet Matt Harwood, who thinks it's his duty to spread himself and his charms liberally through the village.'

Matt chuckled. 'That's a bit harsh, even by your standards, Sal.'

'But true. I thought I told you to sit down and stop hanging round my desk harassing my clients.'

'You're worse than a teacher.' He ruffled her hair, and if it had been anybody else she would have glared, but it was impossible to dislike Matt. So she swotted him back. 'Oh give us a kiss, Sal, I know you want to.'

'Behave. Years of knowing what you get up to has made me immune.'

'Come and sit with me.' He winked at Lucy as he headed

off to plonk himself on one of the far-too-small plastic chairs, the little dog perched on his knee. 'Away from Miss Bossy, and I'll tell you about Archie.'

'Well really I...' Lucy waved an arm in the direction of the car park, where Jill was keeping the kids busy attaching ribbons to the makeshift maypole. But Sally could see she was tempted, she'd taken a step after him.

'Leave her alone Matt, she's got the children with her,' she paused, 'all twelve of them.'

'You've got a dozen kids? Really?' He looked her up and down, his eyes wide. 'And you've got a figure like that still? Wow. High five to that.'

'Matt, stop flirting. She's the new teacher, covering for Becs, as if you didn't know!' She looked at Lucy. 'It's impossible to keep anything quiet in this place; they'll all know your tipple of choice and what you had for breakfast.'

'Phew.' Matt flicked imaginary sweat off from his brow melodramatically. The little dog lay down on his knee with a sigh.

Lucy had taken another involuntary step towards him, as though his magnetic field was sucking her in like it did with most women, and Sally was just about to issue a warning when she crouched down. 'Poor thing.' She put a tentative hand out to stroke one of the few bits of fur that Archie had.

'He's fine Lucy, he's a Chinese Crested Dog and that's how they're supposed to look, bald apart from the fluffy head, tail and feet, but you're right to feel sorry for him because he has to put up with Matt.'

Unperturbed, he winked at Lucy. 'Ignore her, she loves me really.'

'Only in the way you love a horrible little brother, and as we've known each other since primary school it's nearly the same thing.'

'He's my babe magnet, the girls love him almost as much as they love me. Meet Archie the Bald.' He waved the little dog's paws in the air. 'Archie, meet Lucy.'

'You're mad.' Sally turned to Lucy, who had backed off. 'He is, he's totally loopy. The man has a seriously bad sense of humour, I mean Archie-bald? Anybody would think he's a comedian not a farmer.'

'You're a farmer?'

'Don't worry, his brother Jamie looks like a proper farmer.' And acts like one, she could have added. And is unassuming, serious, but twice as gorgeous. She concentrated on the dog, sure that Matt would read her mind if she met his gaze. If he ever caught on to her guilty secret he'd never let her live it down. At least right now though his attention was on the very pretty newcomer.

'He's actually supposed to look like that?' Lucy still didn't seem to have got her head round the fact that the little dog was supposed to have bald, mottled skin with a few silky feathers here and there. At least it was distracting her from the owner, which had to be good. Sally tried not to grin as Matt upped the flirting – the dog was supposed to draw the ladies in, not *be* the attraction.

'He is,' Sally reassured her, 'and the dog is too.'

Lucy rolled her eyes, and giggled.

'Am I missing something?' Charlie's gruffer than normal tone cut straight across the laughter. Lucy jumped and went pink. Very pink. And studied her feet. Which was all very interesting.

'Archie's doing a bum shuffle again.' Matt grinned at Lucy, oblivious to Charlie's disapproving frown. 'Good luck with the dancing.' He winked. 'I'll come and give you a hand when I'm done here.'

'No you won't.' Sally didn't want Charlie in a bad mood all day, and she really didn't want Lucy who seemed quite lovely, to fall under Matt's spell before she realised what he was like. She hoped her voice had a note of finality in it as she pointed towards Charlie and his consulting room. 'In you go, Matt.' She smiled at Lucy and made an ushering-outside gesture, which Lucy took notice of and fled – before explanations became necessary.

There was something about the way Charlie watched the new school teacher. He'd never looked at any of his waiting-room groupies like that, he spent most of his time peering over his glasses at their pets and studiously avoiding looking them in the eye. But with Lucy it was almost like he couldn't resist looking at her, then felt awkward, and looked away like a guilty Labrador before anybody caught him in the act.

No way was she going to let Matt interfere. She leant on the counter. Or maybe she could encourage him just a tiny bit – as long as he didn't overstep the mark and decide Lucy was fair game to add to his trophy collection.

Sally had to admit that Matt was gorgeous: he was good-looking, fun, down-to-earth and flirty, but she was very glad she didn't fancy him. And she really did hope that Lucy wouldn't fall for his charms. One day, Matt no doubt would fall for and marry the girl of his dreams, and a lovely husband he'd make too. But he was leaving rather a lot of broken-hearts in his wake as he looked for her.

Sally propped the surgery door open, so she could hear the phone if it rang, and wandered out to watch Lucy at work. Give her an anxious cat any day, over a dozen excitable school children. Lucy seemed to be a natural though, she was patient but firm and the kids already seemed to have fallen in love with their new teacher.

Dancing around a pole, holding one end of a coloured ribbon, shouldn't have been that difficult even for a group of five to eleven year olds, but the mixed ages and heights (not to mention some very exuberant boys who liked to pretend they were doing an aerobatic display for the Red Devils) always made it a spectacle worth watching.

'Miss, Miss.' Sophie stopped abruptly, the girl behind collided with her, and the boy who should have danced between them improvised by doing an impromptu circle, then squealed and started dashing round and round them until Lucy stepped in and stopped his progress before he had the two girls cocooned in blue ribbon.

'Sophie?'

'My mam says that you should put sunscreen on us if we're outside.'

'It's quite cloudy today.'

'She said.' Sophie sat down, let go of her ribbon and stuck her lower lip out in rebellion.

'I will write you a letter home to explain, it is only April.'

'Can I have one Miss?'

'Me too Miss?'

'I don't want one, I'm not a cissy.' Billy wound the ribbon round his forehead and did a rain dance on the spot, complete with whooping and stamping.

'Joe's a cissy, he's got a pink ribbon. Joe's got a pink ribbon.'

Sally watched as Lucy calmed them down, untangled the ribbons, repositioned the children and restarted the music. The younger children were all lined up around them, clapping in time (or not) to the beat.

'What's going on?' Charlie had approached unnoticed, and sounded slightly irritated.

'I don't care.' Matt's treacle-smooth voice washed over it and he draped an arm over Sally's shoulder so that Archie licked her ear. 'I could stand and look at scenery like this all day.'

Charlie took his glasses off, and wiped the palm of his hand wearily over his eyes as though it would help him see more clearly. 'I thought this was our car park, not a playground. Don't they have their own place?'

'It's tradition.' Sally knew he wasn't hot on the tradition side of things when it involved him. 'Don't you remember? They always rehearse here because we've got a big space and a pole, and...'

'Don't tell me, Eric always let them?' It came out on a frustrated sigh.

'He does.' She tried not to smile too broadly, and linked her arm through his. 'And so did your dad. They won't be here long, they get bored easily or tie themselves in knots.'

'I'd quite like to see Miss Jacobs tied up in knots.' Matt grinned, and Charlie threw him a dirty look, which was the first time Sally had seen Charlie even vaguely unprofessional. This summer looked like it could be shaping up to kick out Langtry Meadows' sleepy 'Darling Buds of May' vibe, with the two new additions to village life. She really would have to pop over and have a chat with Miss Harrington and see what the wise old woman thought. Nothing escaped her notice.

'Go and do some muck spreading on your field Matthew.' She patted Archie, and gave Matt a gentle push, then let her hand slip from Charlie's arm. 'Come on Mr Davenport, let's go neuter that randy spaniel we've got in, a bit of snipping will make you feel much better.'

They watched as Matt made a detour on the way over to his Land Rover – stopping to whisper in Lucy's ear, blow a kiss at Jill and let the younger children pet his dog.

Lucy, she was pleased to see, just nodded politely. But that could have just been because she was in professional mode. She had blushed. Oh dear, a girl that blushed that easily was going to find life in this village a bit of a challenge to say the least.

After tidying up the consultation room, setting the sign to closed, straightening the chairs and mopping the floor, Sally switched the answer machine on and turned the lights off. She collected her bicycle from the back of the surgery then headed off up the lane, but found herself slowing as she neared Lucy's cottage. Propping her bicycle up against the fence and made her way up the cute pathway, and rapped on the door. It was opened immediately, by a rather surprised Lucy. 'I just thought I'd check you were getting on okay with the hens? My God, you've done wonders with the front garden, how on earth have you done it that quickly?'

Lucy smiled and opened the door wider. 'Come in, come in, oh I haven't done much yet really, I just attacked it with the shears. I love gardening and this place is amazing isn't it? The prettiest garden I've ever seen, it's already gorgeous with all the spring flowers and the winter jasmine, but I bet it looks even more wonderful in the summer.'

'It is, but it doesn't often look wonderful to be honest. Annie likes the wild look.'

'I had some time before term started so I thought I should show willing, she's letting me stay here for a pittance.'

'But you're looking after the place and the animals. That means far more than money to her.'

'I still feel I should.' Lucy tucked a strand of hair behind her ear. 'The hen's been fine. Do you want to see it?'

'Oh no, no. I'm not checking up on you, I just wanted to say hi really. And maybe if you fancied going for a drink sometime? Like tonight? I could introduce you to a few people.'

'That would be lovely, it's really kind, it's just,' Lucy waved behind her at the paperwork on the large pine kitchen table, 'I do have lots of lesson prep, and I'm only here a few weeks.'

'Just an hour or two? I mean it is a Friday evening. I thought the beauty of doing cover work was that you didn't have as much to do?'

Lucy hesitated.

'Even if you aren't here long, it does help if you know people, makes it easier. We're quite a quirky bunch.'

Lucy grinned. 'Like Matt and that dog?'

'That dog is unique in Langtry Meadows, he doesn't actually need it to attract attention but Matt is a terrible flirt and attention seeker, his brother James is much more normal.'

'How normal?' Lucy grinned and raised an eyebrow, and Sally felt the colour rush to her face. It was silly. She'd known both the brothers all her life. Matt was the same age as her, and James was a couple of years older. And he'd always seemed older and wiser.

Mature. He'd pulled Matt off her when their arguments over whose turn it was on the swing had turned to rough and tumble. He'd rescued her when Matt had pushed her into the village pond, and caught her pony when it had spooked as she'd ridden across their farm. He'd been the big brother she'd always longed for, and totally unlike Matt who was the little brother she definitely didn't want.

'Maybe he feels in his brother's shadow a bit, you know, needs to shout look at me?'

'Oh he's never been in James' shadow; James is the quiet sensible type.'

'Once you get labelled the noisy clown it's hard to shake it off, people play to it.'

'Like some of the kids dancing round the maypole today?'

Lucy rolled her eyes. 'I'm beginning to feel like I've been duped. The headmaster saw me coming didn't he? Mug,' she pointed to her forehead, 'pasted right across here. Oh, and thanks for diverting Charlie, he seems a bit grumpy whenever I mention the school.'

'He's having a tricky time, ignore him, he's lovely really.'

'Apart from when you corner him the first time you meet him and demand he comes to see kids when he obviously hates them, then block his car into his own car park when he's got an emergency, and then fill his car park with kids and coloured ribbons?' Lucy buried her head in her hands.

'Well you might have overloaded the poor man a bit. He does seem to prefer animals to people, but underneath it all he is lovely. Really. Are you sure you haven't got time for a quick drink?'

They both studied the pile of paperwork.

'I suppose I could do this tomorrow. It's prep for parent's evening really, I like to set up a spreadsheet then I can add notes as I get to know them.'

'I can do a far better job of filling you in on the families in Langtry Meadows than wading through a pile of school-work and past reports will. Honest.' She crossed her heart. 'And I can tell you just what you need to say whenever little Soph mentions her mum.'

'You're seriously tempting me now. Annie told me I need to live a little, do I look such a sad case?'

'Annie's right. I'm all for a bit of living, but you're not a completely lost cause.' She grinned. 'You just work too hard. Believe me, there's a lot to be said for lightening up. Come on, I'll tell you about before I worked for Eric.'

'Or, we could sit out in the garden and drink this?' Lucy opened the fridge and pulled out a bottle of white wine. 'From what I've heard it's heaving in the Taverner's Arms on a Friday night and you can't hear yourself speak.'

Sally laughed. 'You know what, you're even smarter than I

thought. I'm not going to stand any chance of interrogating you properly in there, am I?'

Lucy frowned.

'Kidding. Honest. Although Miss Harrington is dying to know more about you, she considers it her duty to know everything about everybody.'

'Really? Is that the old lady that lives in that lovely house near the church?'

'That's the one. And don't let appearances fool you; she's as sharp as they come. She's lovely too though, not out and out nosey for the sake of it like a lot of the buggers round here. She just likes to know where everybody fits.'

'A bit like me in my classroom. God,' Lucy rolled her eyes, 'I'm seriously thinking about dyeing the hair of one of the Hargreave twins so I can tell them apart, and I still can't work out whether it's a good idea to let Ted sit next to Daisy.' She uncorked the bottle and poured two glasses out.

'Why?'

'They spend all their time pulling livestock out of their pockets to see if they can outdo each other. I never had this problem in Birmingham, squashed spiders and nits were the nearest we got to wildlife.' She grimaced. 'The only worms were the unmentionable ones that came out of bottoms.'

'Eurgh stop it. The nit bit was bad enough, it sounds more like our surgery than a school, except we get more fleas.'

'I give in, no way can I beat you at the bugs game.'

'Glad to see you're sensible. So, what do you think of Langtry Meadows? Settling in okay?'

'Oh yes, it's lovely,' Lucy paused, 'but it is totally different, not just the worms. The kids are just more innocent for a start.'

'Aren't all six year olds innocent? Not that I'm an expert, give me a puppy any day.'

'Not really, some of them at my last school had tough lives. And since I've been here I haven't had a single parent come up to me and threaten to shove my snotty letter where the sun doesn't shine if I try and tell them how to bring up their kids.'

Sally flinched. 'Oh God, really, you used to get that?'

Lucy took a mouthful of wine and seemed to consciously sit up straighter, and lighten her tone. 'It's just so hard for some of them, and it's all concrete and car fumes. Lots of them have never seen a cow or sheep, and probably never will. Here they're just happier.' Lucy sighed. 'I do miss them though, the parents could be daft, but it was so rewarding when you got children that actually wanted to do their homework, they took pride in it even if they only had a mum who couldn't see the point of books.'

'It must be very different for you here.'

'It is.' She paused as if unsure whether to continue, then it came out in a rush. 'I was brought up in a village not much bigger than Langtry Meadows, but we moved when I was little. To be honest I can't remember much at all about it.' She shrugged. 'I just never imagined I'd move back out to a place like this I suppose.'

'Boring life in the sticks eh?'

'No, no, I don't mean that, it's gorgeous here and so peaceful. I just, well it was a funny time, I suppose I just shut that bit out of my mind and thought that moving on was all about a bigger school, better money, more of a challenge. Which meant a city school.'

'I've always been here. Apart from a brief, disastrous stint away.' She studied Lucy over the top of her glass, and tried not to be envious. The girl had done what she hadn't been able to – moved on. 'I was always rubbish at school, but I loved animals so being a veterinary nurse was the only thing I could do.'

'But you're doing what you love, you're good at it, brilliant. School exams aren't what's needed for every job. I bet you've had to work so hard to do what you do.'

'Well,' Sally shrugged, 'I have done all my vet nurse training, and learned to type properly. My mum was shocked when I did a book keeping course as well. But I sometimes wish I was more like you.'

'Me?' Lucy choked on her wine again. 'Wiping snotty noses and explaining why it's not acceptable to pull the legs off spiders?'

'No, oh no, I couldn't teach. I mean, do something different. I tried to leave Langtry Meadows and failed miserably.'

'Where did you go?'

Lucy actually looked interested. The first person who ever had. Her dad had just said 'now what would you want to do that for?' when she'd told her parents she'd applied for a job twenty miles away, and her mum had said 'I'll miss you so much, are you sure you really want to do it, darling? It just won't be the same there, town people are different, they don't even stop and say hello, don't have time. Who will you talk to? You won't have any friends.' As though she'd told her she was moving to Outer Mongolia, or outer space.

'I saw this job advertised at a veterinary hospital, you know the whole bigger, more challenging thing, but it was awful.' She'd failed, had to hand in her notice and come running home.

'Awful?' Lucy prompted.

'They were just so demanding, I was expected to work these really strange shifts and they were always asking me to do cover for people who were off. You could end up working nearly two weeks without a day off if you said yes, and if you said no,' she sighed, 'I did say no once or twice and it seemed fine, just a bit awkward. Then, I had my three month review and the buggers said they were going to extend my probationary period.'

'But they can't do that! You were doing your job properly weren't you?'

'I was, but Dad was ill and Mum doesn't drive so I needed time to come home to see them, and ferry him to hospital, so I couldn't work every day even if I'd wanted to.'

'But they must have understood?'

'Not that you could tell. I did love the job. There were all kinds of interesting cases because people got referred there. But they were so unfriendly. It was a real them and us thing, and the pay was rubbish as well. So, I wimped out and told them where to stick their shitty job. If you'll pardon the language.'

'They didn't deserve you. If you ask me you had a lucky escape.'

'I'm destined to be here forever and marry a farmer.'

Lucy's eyes were positively twinkling. 'And did you have any particular farmer in mind?'

'Well now you mention it...' Oh God, she was losing it, she had never ever told anybody about her crush on James Harwood. But since her return to Langtry Meadows she'd had a growing feeling that she really had to do something with her life – she had to speak out, be a bit more positive. It was easy at work. She had no problem at all telling the clients what she thought. But telling James how she felt? That was different altogether. What if he laughed? Well, he wouldn't laugh, he was far too nice. No, he might feel sorry for her, and that really would be the pits.

But Lucy seemed lovely, and kind, and non-judgemental.

'Go on, you can't leave me hanging. I need more!'

'Well, it's Matt's brother, Jamie.'

'Matt?' Lucy frowned. 'The one with the bald dog?'

'He's not at all like Matt. And he's got two lovely whippets.'

'Two lovely whippets?' Lucy giggled, and looked younger. Like she was finally relaxing. 'Is that a euphemism?'

'Sorry no, although it might be.' She'd been thinking about Jamie for years, and every bit of him was lovely, including his whippets. 'It's a bad habit associating people with animals, part and parcel of the job! The thing is though, about that crap job I had, it made me think it might not be so bad here after all. I mean I would like to do a bit more with my life before I turn into a wrinkly, but people do care. Well actually they care too much, there is so much gossip, but at least they do look out for you, and Charlie is great to work for.'

'He is?' Lucy looked genuinely surprised. 'He always seems a bit, well, grumpy and er, stern. He looks at me like I'm asking him to leap off a cliff, not talk to a few kids.'

Sally shrugged. 'I don't know what his problem is about the kids, but he is fine. Quite a few of the women hassle him, it's not often we get a sexy new man.'

'Sexy?' Lucy had an eyebrow arched.

'Oh come on, you have to admit he's sexy, a bit geeky maybe. But he is hot, even though I prefer somebody a bit chunkier.'

'Well, okay, he's nice enough.'

'Nice enough?'

She rolled her eyes. 'Okay, *very* nice. But he's not keen on me at all.'

'Oh I wouldn't say that.' Sally giggled and watched as colour tinged Lucy's cheekbones. 'He's a bit fussy about how stuff is done, but he's kind and considerate, and generous.'

'Generous?' Lucy spluttered into her glass. 'If you say so. He obviously hasn't shown that side of himself to me yet. He kicked up such a fuss when I parked the van across the driveway. But,' she paused, 'he did apologise for being a bit bad tempered.'

'See. He's nice.' Sally could see Lucy's brain working over-time.

She poured a generous measure of wine into the glasses. 'And he did let us practise in the car park. So,' she stared at Sally, 'it's just me trying to get him into school that's the problem?'

'Maybe.' Sally hadn't got a clue, but she was pretty sure that Charlie didn't dislike Lucy at all. In fact from where she was standing, it looked quite the opposite. 'He's like you, another hotshot. Local boy made good. He managed to escape this place once, although it's a shame he won't come back for good. His dad wanted him to and,' she grinned, 'he's very easy on the eye wouldn't you say?'

Lucy went pink again, and didn't give her a straight answer. 'I'm not a hotshot, and I can't say I've made good, but I did enjoy teaching where I was. I told myself I'd be able to get back to my home soon.'

'So you really don't want to stay? Oh God, what a shame, you and Charlie are the most exciting thing that's happened here in ages.'

'It is lovely here, and you are, but I have got my house and this is just temporary.' She frowned. 'Except everybody just seems to assume I'll be round for a while.'

'You're not wrong on that one.' It was certainly what Miss Harrington seemed to think. 'So why not stay, sell your house? If you like it here.'

'It's just, well I thought I'd left village life behind, I er,' she seemed to be struggling for the right thing to say. 'I love the challenge of city kids, it's different here, they don't need me the same.' She glanced at Sally, then back at her glass of wine. 'I don't belong here.'

'Oh that's rubbish, you're already the talk of the place,' she grinned at the look Lucy threw her, 'and for all the right reasons. And it's not such a bad place.' Sally was pretty sure she'd only wanted to escape to prove she could, not because she wanted to. 'And what about all that lonely in the city stuff?'

'I felt lonelier in a village to be honest.' Lucy swirled the wine in her glass. 'I suppose it's fine if you feel you belong, but being surrounded by a crowd who don't want you is worse than being on your own. The city primary school I went to was pretty rubbish as well, I actually found it easier once I got thrown into a big secondary school, I wasn't the odd one out any more. Then I loved it at Uni. There were no prying eyes, it was a fresh start. I wasn't the only one with a broken family.' She shrugged. 'Nobody judges in a city school, we're all struggling, all pulling together to make things better, and I guess I feel like I understand those kids, how they feel, I can make a real difference.'

'Oh.' Sally frowned. 'You can make a real difference here you know. This place needs new people, new ideas, and the kids need somebody who's got a different, well, vision of stuff.' She shrugged self-consciously. 'They need to be shown the world, the opportunities, all the stuff I was never told.'

'Oh.'

'And maybe times have changed a bit since you were a kid. Not that I'm saying you're old.' She laughed, trying to lighten Lucy's mood. 'But stuff is accepted more, villages aren't as close knit as they used to be, and probably not as judgemental. People like me need people like you, Luce.'

She glanced at her watch. She would have loved to suggest opening another bottle of wine, to have found out more about Lucy and why she wasn't that keen on country living. But it would have to wait for another time. 'Oh hell, is that the time? I've got to go and check up on a couple of cats that are in overnight. It's been great to chat, and if you're only staying a few weeks we've got to make sure you get a good night out in the Taverner's before you go. Quiz night in there is as competitive as it gets.' She put a hand on Lucy's arm. 'How about the four of us make a team up? You, me, Matt and Jamie?' She grinned. 'I know Matt would jump at the chance, although you have to promise me you won't kiss him.'

'Kiss him? Why would I…'

'That man has got so many notches on his bedpost it's fancier than a totem pole.'

Lucy laughed. 'Well I've nothing against a nice totem pole.'

'Lucy!'

'He's not exactly going to get the chance to break down my defences and my heart in just five weeks, is he?'

Chapter 7

The feet still hadn't moved. Lucy had noticed them the moment she sat down on the toilet seat and her mobile phone had buzzed.

She'd sworn she'd never, ever, text on the loo again – after the time her mobile had dived between her legs on a suicide mission and she'd had a choice of donning rubber gloves, or risking flushing it away. But she couldn't help it, she had to look. Once the quiz started she'd have to switch it off or risk being labelled a cheat.

She was glad she'd checked. It was a text from Sarah at Starbaston.

Twat face made me cover class 6. Jason relabelled Uranus on the wall chart as rectum and I never noticed, and Britney wanted to know why all the vampires aren't dead if moonlight is reflected sunlight. Send gin, I am broken. Sarah x

She tried not to giggle, as the feet outside shifted impatiently, and tapped a reply.

Britney has a point. Gin on way – if don't drink it all myself. Pub quiz! Catch you later. Loo x

Dropping the phone in her bag, she pulled the old fashioned

chain which gave a very satisfying clunk before whooshing a volume of water that definitely wasn't eco-friendly into the toilet bowl. At least out here they still knew how to flush their problems effectively away.

She flung the door open to find the owner of the shoes stood between her and the washbasins. A portly figure with her arms folded, looking like she meant business. The other cubicle was empty. She'd been ambushed.

She smiled and eased her way round the woman, racking her brains trying to remember who she was.

'Now then, dear. I know you mean well,' it had to be a parent, 'but you have to understand how things are done round here. If it's not broke then don't mend it is what I say, if you know what I mean?'

Lucy fought the urge to roll her eyes, and concentrated on washing her hands. One absolutely brilliant thing about teaching in a city was that the chances of bumping into a parent outside of school was practically zero. Life in a village was slightly different.

Much as she loved the children, she didn't really want to bump into them when she was loading her basket with wine in the post-office-cum-general-store (which had happened more than once), and she really, really didn't want to get ambushed by angry parents in the washroom at the pub.

'My Sophie,' oh God this was Sophie's mum, she'd heard *my mam says* enough times from the little girl – now she was going to get it from the woman herself. 'My Sophie says I'm supposed to help her do her sums, now don't get me wrong I've no objection to that, not that I've not got enough on my hands, but you've told her it all wrong.' Lucy added more soap, carried on scrubbing her spotless hands, sensing it was futile trying to get a word in when the woman was in full flow anyway. 'You're doing sums with them differently. Now I'm sure you're a very good teacher and all that, but there's a time and place for these new-fangled ways, and the way I learned worked fine—'

The woman wasn't going to stop for breath. 'Mrs Smith.'

'Oh call me Jane, duck. Everybody does.' Her arms were still folded, making her bulk practically impassable in the tiny room.

'Jane, er, do you mind if we chat about this at school, it's just Sally will be waiting...' Lucy squeezed past her towards the hand dryer.

'Oh I can come out and sit with you.'

She flung the door open. If she moved quickly enough, surely she could disappear into the crowd? The pub was packed, and noisy.

'Am I pleased to see you.' Lucy had only taken a couple of steps when her arm was grabbed. 'I've been looking all over, thought you'd done a runner as well.'

Lucy threw an apologetic look in Jane's direction, then frowned at Sally. 'What do you mean as well?'

'We've got a problem.' Sally hissed in her ear and dragged her off to one side. 'Sorry Jane, team tactics.' She gave a thumbs up to Jane, who scowled like a cat that had been deprived of its mouse, before marching off to her own team who were sat in a huddle by the bar.

'Tactics?'

'Team tactics, as in how the hell will we win without one.'

'You've lost me.' Lucy had been pretty pleased about being rescued from Jane Smith, but was now wondering whether she'd have been better hiding out in the loos.

'We've not lost you, we've lost Matt! The bugger has defected, look.' Sally pointed at the small table under the darts board, where Matt had one hand on his pint, and the other on Jill's shoulder. 'Jill said she'd lost two of her team, which meant they only had two left. She'd been hoping to rope you in, but Matt offered. He said them having three and us having three was fair.'

'Well, it is isn't it?'

'No it bloody isn't. He might look and play the dumb blond at times, but he can answer *all* the sports questions and a shit load of the music ones.'

'Oh.'

'And we're starting in five minutes, we're going to be annihilated.'

'So you've heard how bad I am?'

'Oh, I didn't mean that. But,' Sally paused, 'do you know anything about rugby?'

'Zilch.'

'Punk music?'

'Not a lot.'

'Hang on, I've just had an idea.' She spun Lucy round and steered her away from the bar, and she found herself thrust against a tall, sturdy man. She cricked her neck trying to look up. He looked bemused and vaguely familiar.

A face that was too like Matt's, the one with the peculiar

dog, for them to be anything but brothers. 'Oh, er, hi, you must be James?'

He looked down at her and grinned. 'I love you already!'

'Sorry?'

'Anybody who doesn't call me Matt's brother has to be alright.'

Sally giggled and let go of her, which meant she could separate herself from his broad chest and take a step back to a civilised distance.

'Call me Jamie though, only my mum calls me James. I'd shake hands but it seems a bit over the top after we've been pressed together like that.'

'Right.' Sally looked relieved that the two of them seemed to approve of each other. 'You two sit down and get to know each other. I'll be back in a second.'

The idea was Charlie, who Sally towed over to the table a couple of minutes later.

'Success!' She pushed him onto the bench next to Lucy with a triumphant smile. 'Shove up, we don't want the next table to be able to overhear all our answers.' She gave Charlie a pointed look, 'I'm expecting you to know everything.'

He shoved up. Until they were tightly sandwiched together. So tightly she could feel the ripple of thigh muscle as he leant forward to put his pint on the table.

'Team talk.' Sally motioned them inwards, and Lucy was pretty sure it was an excuse so she could get closer to Jamie. The girl had it bad.

The only trouble was it meant she was closer to all of them, including Charlie. Embarrassingly close. The last time she'd been this close to him was when she'd kissed him. She tried not to sneak a sideways look, but she couldn't help it. The brown gaze met her head on, he'd caught her out. Embarrassing. The only way was to brazen it out. 'Don't worry, I won't do it again.'

Sally glared, and Lucy felt like she'd been caught whispering in class.

'Can you two chat later? This is serious.' Then she paused and frowned. 'You won't do what again?'

Charlie tapped on the sheet of paper that had been provided for them to write their answers on. 'I thought you wanted a team talk?'

He, at least didn't seem too bothered, not like her. Maybe she'd imagined it, maybe she'd not actually kissed him. Or he hadn't realised she had. She sneaked another look at him, under her eyelashes while he was occupied with Sally. He couldn't have not realised. For a start he'd kept well away when she'd been in the surgery car park with the children, rehearsing for tomorrow, he'd not said a word to her.

'Oh my God, we're starting!' Sally had her pencil poised, and the whole pub had fallen silent, apart from the odd thunk as glasses were placed on the table, and the scrape of chairs being shifted on the stone floor as the competitive spirit kicked in and people huddled together to avoid being overheard.

Lucy hadn't got a clue with most of the questions, for some reason people always assumed she'd have an excellent general knowledge being a school teacher. But she hadn't. Unless you were talking about Ofsted regulations, or the school curriculum.

'Which year did Bob the Builder have a number one Christmas hit?'

All eyes swivelled in her direction, and Lucy shook her head. 'Sorry, haven't got a clue.'

'But it's a kid's thing, isn't it?'

'Starbaston kids were more about Pokémon and Power Rangers.'

Sally buried her head in her arms as Matt, over on the far table gave a whoop of delight.

'Next question.' Jim coughed and the crowd quietened again. 'Rugby league...'

'I need another drink.' Sally put the pencil down in despair.

'And this one is for all our pet lovers. How many claws does our domesticated moggy possess? Providing of course our veterinary in the corner hasn't removed any.' Jim chuckled.

Charlie laughed good-naturedly and watched as Sally, cheering up a bit, scribbled the answer down.

They just needed more animal questions, thought Lucy, and she really, really needed to be able to answer at least one question and not let her team down completely.

'Now for a little culture ladies and gents.' Jim was in his element as question master, and paused dramatically. 'Elgar's Pomp and Circumstance March number one, is better known as?'

'I know, I know!' She knew an answer, she couldn't believe it.

Everybody had turned round, Matt's chuckle rang across

the bar and Jim winked. 'The girl knows!' There was a brief outbreak of applause and she felt herself turning pink, but she didn't care, she couldn't stop smiling.

'I'll give her team a bonus mark if she can play chopsticks on the piano, here.'

She didn't want to, she hadn't touched the keys of a piano for more years than she cared to think about, but all of a sudden she didn't want to let her team down. And they were a team. She got up on unsteady feet, tried not to think about how it used to be, how she'd grown to love playing, how it had been snatched away.

Her fingers trembled, and the piano was badly in need of tuning, but she did it. She played, they applauded, and she took a bow before slipping back into her seat next to Charlie.

'You've done that a few times before.' His voice was soft in her ear.

'A long time ago.' Another life.

'You should play again, I bet you're good.'

'Flatterer!' She tried to make a joke of it, but she had been good. As a child she'd loved the feel of the keys below her fingertips, loved the melodies that echoed through their living room. Then the piano had gone. Another little piece of the jigsaw that she'd forgotten all about, that she'd purposefully pushed away. The piano had gone before they'd left, the same as her friends had. All the little fun things that had made up the picture of her life had been discarded one by one. Long before her and Mum had moved to the city.

'Hey, Lucy, do you know this one?' Sally's voice snapped her out of her thoughts.

She needed to talk to her mum later, this place had already brought back too many memories, too many loose ends that needed tying up and making sense of.

'Sorry, what was it? Oh, of course I know!'

There was a run of questions then linked to music, and Lucy started to enjoy herself. The time whizzed by, and before she knew it answer sheets were being swapped for marking, and although they'd not won, they'd not disgraced themselves.

The landlord rang the bell for last orders and as Sally turned her attention to Jamie, Lucy found herself alone with Charlie.

'I suppose I better get home.'

'I can walk you, if you'd like that is?'

'Sure, thanks. If you're sure...'

'It's on my way.' He smiled good-naturedly, then held the door open for her, and the waft of fresh air brought in the scent of the spring flowers that overflowed from the tubs either side of the doorway.

'Sorry the tour of the village didn't go to plan the other day.' His eyes were twinkling and he looked positively raffish – framed by the dark night sky, his hair mussed up, and dimples framing his mouth. 'I promise not to mention alpaca balls, or drag you into the church again...'

She stared, straight into those deep, dark eyes, and all she could think about was the kiss, the feel of his lips under hers, the sense of him that had drawn her in.

Still dark nights like this were made for kissing, for letting yourself get drawn towards a man with cool lips and capable hands, with only the moon (and a duck) as witness.

'Lovey, hey, hang on!' Lucy drew a sharp breath and stumbled back as Jane Smith bowled out of the pub, her hair awry, cheeks flushed. 'I forgot to give you this, just a little something to give you strength for tomorrow when the little buggers attack the maypole. My Sophie's had so much fun, says you've done a grand job teaching them to skip proper. She 'elped with these.'

She stared wide-mouthed as the woman shoved a box into her hands and then with a cheery wave disappeared back into the pub, shouting 'we'll talk about them sums another time' as she went.

Charlie chuckled. 'You okay?'

'Well yes, but she stopped me in the loos before to complain about my teaching, and I really didn't expect...' Stupid tears pricked at her eyes.

'Cake?'

She peeked into the box. 'Lots of them.' She opened the lid wider so that they could both look at the rows of iced cakes, complete with sweeties on some, and *thank-you*'s on others.

'They're a friendly bunch really, they just tend to say what they think. Bit different to your old place I bet?'

She pushed the lid down firmly, giving herself time to swallow the lump in her throat. 'Very.'

'Come on, let's walk and talk.' He put a hand out, and it seemed the most natural thing to slip her own into it. To fall into step with him, their arms swinging, her hand warm and secure in his much larger one. 'There's no escape in a place like this, you either let it draw you in and fall in love with it, or you hate it.'

'Too true! But none of the parents at Starbaston ever baked

me cakes.' In the city she could escape from contact of any kind, but that was the good bits as well as the bad.

As they walked, she glanced into the tidy gardens of the cottages that bordered the village green. 'None of the neighbours ever checked up on my garden either.'

'And they have here?'

'When I looked out of the window first thing, Jim was peering over the hedge. I felt like he was going to come marching up the path and tell me I'd ruined the roses. I mean I haven't got that much clue about gardening, I'm the girl that once carefully cultivated a patch of weeds.'

Charlie smiled. 'You're doing a brilliant job, I'm sure Annie will be pleased, you can't exactly destroy a garden. I'd say it's looking much better.'

'I suppose it's more that I feel I'm constantly being checked up on, watched. Sally even popped in to check up on the hen.'

'Not because she didn't trust you, I think she wanted a gossip. She's nice.'

She sighed. 'She's very nice.' In the city, nobody ever popped in on the off chance to share a bottle of wine. Nobody insisted she come down and join in the pub quiz. She didn't even know her neighbours, let alone where the local pub was. 'I'm just not used to it, I suppose.' It had been fun though, much better than the night in alone that she'd planned.

'I know what you mean. Even though I've been brought up here, it takes some getting used to again. You know that if you buy two steaks from the butcher, then go in the post-office next day they'll be asking who the romantic meal was with and whether you need to book the church.'

She laughed, trying to ignore the twinge of jealousy. 'So who was the lucky lady then?'

'Don't you start! It wasn't me buying steak, it was somebody I know.' He looked around, to check there was nobody eavesdropping, then dropped his voice to a conspiratorial whisper that made the hairs on her arms prickle. 'Don't you dare say a word, but it was Sally.'

'Sally?'

'She doesn't think I know.'

Lucy smiled. 'Poor Sally, she's mad about Jamie isn't she?'

'Young love.' There was a wry twist to his beautiful mouth. 'If one of them doesn't make a move soon then somebody in the village will do it for them. Seriously though, don't take the interference too much to heart, it means they like you.'

She looked at him doubtfully. 'I suppose at least it means they're interested. Jane Smith arguing about the way I do my sums has to be better than apathy I guess, and to be honest,' she sighed, 'I can see where she's coming from. I wasn't sold on the methods at first, and people don't like what they don't understand.'

'Nobody likes change.'

The hand that held hers had stiffened slightly, the corner of his mouth had tightened, and the words had such conviction that Lucy wondered just what it was that had happened to him. When he'd refused to come into school it had niggled her, it didn't seem to fit the person she was slowly getting to know. At first she'd thought he was just being awkward, or didn't like her, now she was sure he had to have another reason.

'Did you go to school here?'

'I did, probably sat at one of the desks in your classroom. I might even have scratched my name on the underside.'

The cheeky grin made her heart flutter in her chest. 'You'll have to show me.'

'I will.' His steps slowed. 'That field there,' he pointed, leaning in closer to her, 'was part of the strawberry farm when I was a kid. They did pick-your-own, and they also paid us kids to pick some to sell on the roadside stall. May Day marked the start of the season, and the smell of strawberries always takes me straight back to those days. We used to eat as many as we picked. Pay was terrible.' He laughed, a deep rumbling carefree laugh.

'It's tomatoes that remind me of being a kid. You know that fresh off-the-vine smell? All sweet and grassy, it makes me think of sunshine. Mum used to take me down to this little nursery and we'd fill a bag with tiny cherry tomatoes, and the old lady that owned the place used to pick out the ripest one she could find for me to eat.' She paused, she could almost smell that sweet fresh smell, her taste buds tingled as though expecting the burst of the fruit in her mouth. There *had* been good times. 'You enjoyed it when you lived here?'

'It was a good place to grow up.'

'So why move away?'

'Oh, there was a big wide world to explore, opportunities.'

He wasn't quite meeting her eye as he spoke. Which meant a woman. A relationship he didn't want to be tomorrow's juicy gossip.

'Same for you?' His tone was soft, he was looking straight

Zara Stoneley

into her eyes as they came to a halt outside her garden gate. He ran the back of his hand down her cheek, a soft caress she couldn't help but lean into.

'Not quite.' She swallowed, not sure if it was the memories, or being this close to him, that was causing the lump in her throat. 'I didn't have a choice.'

'But you do now.' His tone was soft, unexpectedly gentle. She did have. Nobody was pushing her, not even the demons.

'So do you.'

'My life's complicated.' He rubbed his thumb over her lips, but didn't make a move to kiss her. 'I don't think I have a choice yet, I don't know where I'll be this time next year, next month even. It's out of my hands.'

'We always have choice, have control, even when it doesn't seem like it.' The words came out before she even knew what she was saying. 'We can't always control where we are, what we do, but we can decide how we handle it, what we do next. Who we are. Nobody can take that away.'

'Maybe.' He leant closer then, and did what she hadn't expected at all. He kissed the tip of her nose, the slightest brush from warm lips that sent a shiver straight down her body to the pit of her stomach. 'Take care, Lucy. Good luck for tomorrow.'

Lucy instinctively put her fingers up to the spot he'd kissed as she watched him walk away. So that was a pretty firm hint to keep away. Even she could see the neon sign he was waving saying he didn't want to get involved. That he could be leaving even before she did.

Clutching the box of cakes to her she walked up the crazy

150

paving to the front door. This place was mad, crazy, wonderful. Tears burned at the back of her eyes as she fumbled for her keys, and then she saw it. Propped up in the tiny porch. A carrier bag.

Inside were a pair of shiny new garden shears, and a note. *Thought these might make the job easier, place looks grand. Jim x*

He hadn't been judging her, he'd been helping her.

She stumbled in, put the cakes and shears on the kitchen table and stared at them through the haze of tears.

Langtry Meadows was nothing like her warped, tarnished memory of village life. People were people, wherever they were. They cared, had hearts, needs, a desire to band together. To be stronger in a group, than working alone.

People wanted you to be part of a community – unless you decided not to let them. To shut them out. And in a city it was easy to shut everybody out, to put up barriers that nobody had the time or strength to chip away at. People battled away on their own because they felt they had no choice. She'd just told Charlie that nobody could take away who he was, and yet she'd let somebody do it to her. She just wasn't sure who.

'Oh Mum.' She sat down and buried her head in her hands. She was being dragged into this community whether she liked it or not, not being excluded. And she did like it. She knew that. The little things that she'd be so sure would niggle her, were fading into the background as the well-meaning villagers grew on her.

* * *

Lucy picked up her mobile phone, and dialled her mum's number before she had time to change her mind. It rang out, echoing emptily. With a start she noticed the time on the kitchen clock. She wasn't being fair, just because she'd decided she suddenly had a million questions, didn't mean her mother was there to answer them. She was probably fast asleep in bed. With a sigh she ended the call, put the phone on the table and wiped her eyes.

She was pushing her chair back, to get a glass of water, when it rang.

'Mum? I didn't wake you did I?'

'No.' Her voice said otherwise. 'What's wrong, what's happened, Lucy?'

'Er, nothing. Nothing's wrong.' She sat down again. 'Somebody gave me cakes, and garden shears.' A single hot tear ran down her cheek.

'That's nice dear.' There was a note of concern in her mother's voice as Lucy gave a loud sniff.

'Why did Dad sell the piano?' The words rushed out, before she could stop them.

She could sense her mother's hesitation.

'He didn't want me to do something I loved, did he?' She'd always thought that he didn't like the noise, that she played too loudly, and she'd begged him to change his mind. That she'd be quieter. He'd told her not to question his decisions, and sent her to her room. 'I really enjoyed playing that piano, I wanted to play it all the time.'

'I know.' The heavy sigh rippled over the airwaves. 'Your father liked,' she hesitated, 'to make the decisions.'

'To be in control.'

'To be in control. Yes.'

He'd liked to force her to practise, but as soon as he'd realised she *wanted* to do it, then he'd taken it away. 'He took everything away.' Her own words reverberated round the empty kitchen. He had. He'd taken everything away. Even her friends. That stillness, the quiet in the house hadn't been peace. It wasn't like the gentle, calm peace that had enveloped her and Charlie tonight as they'd walked home from the pub, it had been an undercurrent. Fear. Dread. Her mother had been holding her breath in anticipation of what he'd do next.

'Mum?'

'Yes, I'm still here.'

'Mum, did Dad leave us, or did we leave him?'

There was a deep, heartfelt sigh. 'It was complicated.' Her voice faltered. 'I did what I thought was best for you, I wanted you to be happy, Lucy.'

'I know.' She did. 'I wish you'd told me.'

'So do I. Maybe we need to have a little chat about this. You'll always be my little girl, Lucy. I didn't want to hurt—'

'I think I need to start growing up, Mum. Don't you?' She spoke softly, she didn't want to upset her mother, she didn't want to cause waves, but she needed to straighten out her memories. Then she could shut the door on them. Take control of her own life. 'I'll give you a ring next week?'

'Whatever you want, darling. Lucy, I am sorry—'

'Don't be sorry, Mum. You've nothing to be sorry for. Night.'

'Night, darling. Sleep well.'

Lucy put the phone gently down, and very calmly sat on

the kitchen chair staring out into the darkness. She didn't fully understand what had happened in the past, why her mother had made the decision, but she was beginning to wonder if their lives had actually been far different to how she remembered it, the reality she'd created in her head.

Chapter 8

'Good morning my dear.' Timothy Parry dodged around Sophie who was sitting cross-legged on the grass, making a neat pile of grass and daisies. Her skirt crumpled up around her chubby thighs. 'No Mischief?'

'Well they're being quite good so far,' Lucy couldn't quite cross her fingers at the same time as re-tying the ribbon in Daisy's hair, and with hairgrips in her mouth she knew the words were muffled but the puzzled look on Timothy's face still surprised her. 'It is early though, but at least the sun is shining.'

'Miss, Miss, my mam says you need to put sun cream all the way up my legs in case I fall over.'

'Sophie Smith,' Jill clapped her hands, 'your mam was given strict instructions to put the cream on before you got here. Now come and stand in the line like a good girl, we can see your knickers as well as your legs.'

'Miss?' Lucy put a clip through the ribbon to keep the bow in place and turned to find Ted studying her solemnly.

'Ted?'

'Sir doesn't mean naughty mischief.'

155

'Don't you?' She glanced from him to Timothy who was smiling benevolently, but not doing much to help as far as controlling the excited children went.

'No dear. I meant little Mischief.'

'Little?'

'Mischief the pony, Miss. Miss,' Daisy tugged her sleeve for attention, 'why can't my hamster come to the May Day if your pony can?'

Lucy did a quick check in Daisy's pockets to check that the hamster hadn't been smuggled in, then looked back at the headmaster.

'It's tradition.' He looked slightly disappointed, as though he'd expected her to know.

Oh God, she was beginning to hate that word. In fact she was beginning to get the same nervous twitch that Charlie had whenever anybody said 'Eric did'.

'I'll leave it with you, shall I?' He nodded, gave the children a quick once over. 'Back in a tick.'

'I'll go and get him for you, shall I love?' Jim, resplendent in bright red breeches, a white ruffled shirt, and jingling bells below his wrists materialised in front of her.

'You look, er...'

'Morris dancing, love.' He grinned, and waved a stick at her. 'You hang on to these for me and I'll get our Annie's little pony for you. Can't have a procession without Mischief, can we? He's been leading the way for years. Let's hope he hasn't got the runs like he did two years ago, eh? All this spring grass plays havoc with the little bugger's stomach.' He chuckled and Lucy felt like something was playing havoc in her own stomach. This wasn't butterflies, it was more like her insides had been replaced with a washing machine set to spin cycle.

She'd thought it was going so well, that she had it in hand. That none of the children were going to, accidentally or otherwise, strangle anybody with a ribbon, that sun cream had been applied to all, and that nobody had their skirt tucked in their knickers, or worms in their pockets. Now she had to cope with the prospect of a pony with an explosive bottom.

'Can I hold them, Miss? Jim, Jim, can I hold them?'

'No.' Lucy very firmly took the sticks and handed them to Liz, who was bustling about straightening collars and pulling up socks.

Twenty minutes later Mischief the Shetland pony, looking rather livelier, and a lot cleaner than normal arrived, clip-clopping his way over the cobbles of the village square. He looked around at the children, then lifted his tail.

Oh God, no. He couldn't. Not here. Not now.

He didn't. But she had never in her life heard any animal pass wind so loudly, and for so long. He looked through his large eyelashes at his audience to see if they appreciated his efforts.

The boys thought it was hilarious. The twins keeled over in a synchronised mock faint (why couldn't they skip simultaneously round the pole?), most of the girls covered their noses and mouths with tiny hands, and little Ted stared in awe. 'Cool. That's better than our cows do.'

Jim ignored it, pointing proudly at the clean and shiny coat. 'Looking smart, isn't he love? I gave him a quick once over. I mean,' he looked at her, wiggling his bushy eyebrows, but didn't seem to be judging, 'our Annie does normally give him a bath first thing in the morning, but I know you've not time for that, what with sorting the kiddies.'

'He is, erm, looking wonderful, thanks for brushing him.' It would be rude to talk through her hand, but she really didn't want to take it away from her nose and mouth. 'I didn't know he was in the procession though, or I would have given him a bath.' How the hell did one bath a pony? A ridiculous image of Mischief in the small claw-footed bath with a shower cap on jumped into her head. 'I am sorry, I don't want to let Annie down, if that's...'

'Oh don't you worry, love. All done now. Right, he's all yours, I've got to get my clogs on.'

She took the lead rope without thinking, then stared at it. She couldn't. She really couldn't look after a pony as well as all her little maypole dancers.

'Clogs?'

'We're leading the procession, love. Liven the crowd up a bit!' He winked, gave a brief nod and headed off at remarkable speed. Jim, she was discovering, had perfected the art of a quick exit when it suited him.

'Miss, Miss, my knickers are falling down.'

There was a tug on her sleeve and she looked down to see Daisy in front of her, pointing to a pair of polka dot pants pooled round her ankles like a fallen rainbow. ''Lastic gone.'

The elastic had indeed gone. She was just about to shout Jill and ask if she had any spares, when Mischief, realising her concentration had lapsed, made a bid for freedom and whisked the rope from her hand before she had a chance to react.

She'd never seen his little legs move so fast. In fact she'd never seen him move much at all. Since she'd arrived at Langtry Meadows, all he seemed to do was eat.

He headed off at a trot, head high, straight towards a float that carried the May Queen – and a carpet of fake grass. Realising his mistake, he veered away straight into the path of a startled Charlie – who caught the end of the rope as he passed and brought him to a neat halt, then looked around trying to work out where the pony had come from.

'Over here!' Lucy waved, and he glanced her way – a look of mild terror on his face as he took in the throng of children who were gathered around her. Straightening his shoulders he seemed to take a deep breath before heading her way, towing the pony behind him.

'You're the new vet, aren't you mister?' Ted studied him, unsmiling. 'My dad says all the new flungly stuff...'

'New-fangled,' corrected Lucy automatically.

'New flangly stuff you does isn't as good as,' he paused and frowned, 'experiments that Eric has in bucket-loads.' He looked at Lucy. 'Eric is the proper vet.'

'Experience.' Lucy put a hand on his shoulder. 'I'm sure Mr Davenport has lots of experience as well as new-fangled stuff, Ted.'

'My dad says Eric knows what's what.'

'I'm sure he does.' Lucy was surprised to hear Charlie speak. 'And as soon as he's better he'll be back. Until then it's me and my new-fangled magic I'm afraid.'

'Magic?' Ted's eyes opened wide, along with his mouth. 'Cor I never knew it was magic, do you have a wand like Harry Potter?'

'Ted Wright come over here and let me tuck that shirt in, you look more like Ron Weasley than Harry Potter.' Ted backed off towards Jill, his mouth wide open, never taking his eyes off Charlie.

Lucy stared at the pony and wondered exactly how she'd got herself in this position. In Birmingham the only animal she'd had to deal with was a fox that had trapped itself in the school wheelie bin, leaving the children convinced that there was a poltergeist, until the caretaker had opened the lid and it had shot out. 'You wouldn't mind hanging on to him, would you? It's just...' She waved a hand around at the children who were now getting far too hyper and jumping about excitedly in a way that did not bode well for a sedate skip around a maypole with coloured ribbons. They were also, egged on by Ted, waving imaginary wands at each other and shouting out random spells like 'expeli-pyjamas', and 'you're riddiklus'. Jill was stifling giggles and Charlie was looking totally bemused.

She frowned at him. 'This is partly your fault you know, so there is a price to pay.'

She suddenly realised that Timothy had wandered back and was swaying gently in a very un-headmasterly fashion. The beer fumes hit her as he collided gently against her then bounced back. She stared in shock at Jill who grinned, then put her hands on his shoulders, slowly spun him round and gave him a gentle push in the direction of the bench at the side of the square.

'It's...'

'Tradition?' Lucy knew she was rolling her eyes.

'Exactly. He just hates the chaos and lack of control. In school he's fine, but once the kids are let loose anything can happen. He's the first to the beer tent then pretends it is out of his hands.' Jill looked at Charlie who was still holding the pony. 'She's right, there is a price to pay.' She winked at Lucy. 'As our dear headmaster obviously can't take care of Mischief, and Annie isn't here, then I'm giving you responsibility for leading the way with that animal.'

She'd got her I'm-not-standing-any-nonsense voice on, which always worked with the children, but Lucy was shocked to see Charlie nod dumbly. The traces of a smile twitching at the corners of his mouth.

'We're going to be walking just in front of the float with the May Queen, behind the brass band. You lead the way with Mischief and the children follow on. Come on, I think it's time to line up. Billy stop trying to tie Poppy's plaits together.'

'Joe if you push that finger up your nose any further you'll make a hole in your brain and you'll be as daft as a brush like your father.' Lucy cringed as Liz's voice rang out clearly. She watched dumbfounded as the other woman walked over. 'Now we don't want that, do we?' Joe shrugged his shoulder, and examined the end of his finger.

'Er, Mrs Potts, I'm not sure you should say...'

Liz Potts studied her with beady eyes. 'Nonsense.' She turned her attentions back to the child. 'Good heavens, Joseph, get that finger wiped before your parents see you.' And she bustled off to check nobody else had fingers in orifices.

Lucy felt herself blush, and covered it with a grin and wave as Charlie looked over his shoulder at her and winked. He actually winked. And smiled. In a crinkle-your-eyes at the corner way. And his normal serious face and frown melted away so that she felt pleased in an almost childlike way. Which was ridiculous. She covered it up by moving the children into a tidier line, and backing Sam up from his position inches away from Mischief's tail. She wasn't worried about the pony kicking out, but she was worried about the effects the spring grass might have had on his tummy. Explosive diarrhoea was something she had absolutely no desire to experience.

At the far end of the square she could see Jim limbering up, clicking his heels together, jangling his bells and waving his sticks in the air. Behind the Morris dancers a horse drawn float, decked out in spring flowers rocked as the horse stamped with impatience.

Sally waved, then pointed at Charlie with an expression of mock shock on her face, then gave the thumbs up as the procession shifted and set off in fits and starts lurching its way through the village.

The whole village it seemed had turned out to watch as they made their way from the square down past the cricket ground and Taverner's Arms (where there was a particularly good, and noisy, turnout), around the green where a crowd were already assembled and the scary maypole loomed large, before passing the school and finally stepping onto the soft, green carpet of grass. The sun shone as the Morris Dancers entertained, and the children did her proud as they plaited the colourful ribbons. They skipped in and out, grins of pride and pleasure on their faces as their parents cheered them on – and the only hiccup was when Sophie stopped short and turned round to berate Joe, saying 'my mam says if you shove me in the back again, she'll give you a right sorting', before turning round and continuing with an angelic smile on her face. In her last school, letting the kids loose with long ribbons would have been inviting a manslaughter charge. But here it was different. Here it worked. In a fashion.

The crown bearer did burst into tears and rush off with the crown after being overcome by the pressure to perform, the ducks with their brood of ducklings timed their stroll from pond to pole perfectly just as the procession made its way to the makeshift throne next to the bandstand – causing a minor pile up and necessitating a re-start of the music. And there was a false start when the crown wobbled and had to be held in place by the village postmistress who crouched behind the May Queen while the photos were being taken. Lucy could swear you'd be able to see her fingers on the photographs. But it didn't matter. The imperfections were what made it all so perfect.

Lucy had loved the procession, but now that the children had been released and scampered with squeals towards their parents, she felt at a bit of a loss. She was surrounded by happy, smiling families. Friends. People who knew each other, belonged.

Jill and other staff from the school were in the centre of the green, cooing over the baby that Becky (the teacher she was covering for) was rocking in her arms. She felt a pang as she watched them, not because she wanted a baby, but because Becky belonged here. Her baby was already part of this large community that was wrapped over the countryside like a protective blanket. It felt like nothing bad could happen here. Nothing that they wouldn't pull together over and cope with.

'Can't beat village life on a beautiful day like this, can you?' Lucy looked up in surprise to see Charlie at her shoulder. He held out a plastic cup of lager. 'Hope you don't mind, I thought you looked like you needed a drink.'

'Thank you!' She did, but was surprised at the gesture. After last night she'd half expected him to retreat back into his taciturn vet persona, and only speak to her when she was clutching a poorly animal to her chest.

'I thought us outsiders should stick together.' Charlie raised his drink and it was as though he'd read her thoughts. It was strange though, as each day passed she was feeling more a part of the community, whereas he seemed intent on keeping a distance. It was almost as though he was determined to resist the pull of a village he'd obviously once loved.

'Whatever happened to...?' She suddenly realised that Mischief wasn't with him, and looked round wildly.

He chuckled, the sound sending a shiver down her back and making her feel awkward. 'I took him home for you. Safely locked up in his field shelter with some hay. I'll come and help you fence a starvation patch off one day next week if you like?'

'Starvation?' It didn't sound very vet-appropriate advice.

'It's for his own good. A small patch of grass he can eat

down.' My God that smile was cute, and his dark eyes were practically dancing. 'Talking of food, do you fancy risking a Taverner's burger? They've got a barbeque set up over there,' he pointed, 'on the edge of the green. Beef fresh from Wright's farm I'm told.'

'Not too fresh I hope.' She always said hello to Ed Wright's cows as she passed their field on the way to school each day, and the thought of them sliced up, fried and sandwiched between two slices of bread made her cringe slightly inside. They were so cute with their big brown eyes, and eyelashes to die for.

'Not ones you've petted.' He was grinning over his pint. 'These were long gone before you arrived in Langtry Meadows.'

She blushed. What was worse, talking to cows or being caught doing it? 'The kids seemed to like you.' She looked under her eyelashes at him. He'd seemed a bit twitchy when Jill had pressed him into service on pony-leading duties, but it had melted away during the afternoon. It wasn't that he'd been exactly awkward, like a lot of childless men were, more that he wanted to keep a distance despite himself. But when little Poppy had slipped her hand into his as they'd been watching the crowning ceremony he'd looked, as her mother would say, chuffed.

'You could just admit defeat gracefully and say you'll come and talk to them. I don't give up easily you know.'

'I noticed.' He chuckled, and took a swig of his drink.

'Charlie, Charles! Oh thank heavens I've found you.' Serena shouldered her way between them, knocking Lucy out of the way with her enormous tote bag which for once didn't have a dog in it. 'I've been searching everywhere.' Which Lucy thought was a bit melodramatic given the size of the village. 'The surgery was empty. Shut! I nearly died.'

'I've only shut it for the afternoon, I did run the normal surgery this morning, and we don't normally...' He was cut off, Serena waving a hand dismissively.

'It's my darling. It's Twinkle, she's hurt, injured. You have to come. I think she's broken her leg! Oh my goodness, it's so terrible,' she wiped away a tear and Lucy watched transfixed. Her makeup was as perfect as ever, whereas if she'd done that she would have had a smear of mascara down her cheek at the very least. 'I feel so guilty, oh it's terrible. You've got to come, now, straight away. I had to leave her on her own as she screamed, positively screamed when I tried to cuddle her, so I just couldn't put her in my bag. I was getting ready to come out, I mean look at the state of me, I'm only half-dressed.'

Lucy looked. She was immaculate. Her long hair as neat and shiny as was possible, her nails polished, her designer jeans (sparkling with diamantes from knee to ankle) as clean as if they'd just been delivered from the boutique, and her top with its plunging neckline showcasing a perfect tan.

'I sat down to put my shoes on, and she was there, on the chair. She has her own chair by the window, she never sits on this other one, but you know how her hormones have been. She probably wanted some motherly love, and what did I do? I sat on her!' She covered her perfect cupid bow red lips with a hand and cried out. 'My baby, oh my baby. What have I done? I sat on her!'

Charlie covered up the sigh that she was sure was about

to escape from his lips, and replaced his frustration with his normal professional demeanour.

'Don't worry, Miss Stevens, you get back home and keep an eye on her. I'll pop back to the surgery for a few things and be over as quickly as I can.' He shrugged apologetically at Lucy as Serena, after profusely thanking him and wrapping him in a hug, tottered off across the grass as fast as her high heels would allow. 'Sorry, duty calls.'

'You're a man in demand.' She tried to hide the unexpected rush of disappointment.

'I don't think I'll be long, she always exaggerates, but better to be safe than sorry, I can't...' He grinned in a sheepish way that brought a smile to her own face.

'It's fine, I understand. It's a twenty-four seven kind of job isn't it? Even worse than being a teacher.'

'Emergencies are part of it, I'm afraid.'

'Do you want me to have that?' She held a hand out for his glass and he handed it over. His fingertips brushed hers and without thinking she looked straight into his eyes. There was a weird moment when she was stuck for words, then she tore her gaze away and laughed nervously, suddenly awkward. Since when was Lucy Jacobs speechless? She glanced back up and his steady gaze was still fixed on her, and this time she didn't want to look away. The gentle lift of his mouth was almost mesmerising, and the moment was suddenly far more intimate than any kiss, any clinch, had ever been.

'I'll catch you later?' The words were soft, just for her.

She nodded and gulped away the lump in her throat. 'Er, yes sure.' The whole May Day experience had obviously taken more out of her than she'd realised. It had left her dazed and disorientated. Or something. And she could see now exactly why all the women in the village were queueing up at the surgery with totally healthy pets.

'And I'll think about what you said, about coming in.' Tiny lines of humour fanned out from the corners of his eyes.

Lucy stared at him, not quite sure she understood what he was saying. 'In?'

'To talk to the kids.'

'I'll hold you to that.'

He was studying her again, hesitating as though he was reluctant to go. She wanted him to stay, touch her fingers again and see what happened the second time.

'Good.' The word was soft, almost intimate, then he suddenly straightened up breaking the spell with a smile. 'But for heaven's sake don't tell Sal, I'll never live it down.'

Lucy watched Charlie head towards the surgery then stared into the empty glass, suddenly feeling lost without him.

It had been a perfect afternoon, the children had done their best, but now she had to admit, she did feel a bit like the outsider. The gooseberry. Which she was. Soon she'd be heading back to her neat and tidy house, thrown into the chaos of a busy school where she hardly had time to draw breath, let alone worry about whether she fitted in or not. Without the vet she was getting attached to in a way she knew she shouldn't.

'Lucy! Luce!' There was a squeal of delight then she was nearly knocked flying as somebody cannoned into her.

'Sally!' Sally, was somehow managing to have both arms wrapped round her in a bear hug, and was jumping up and down like an excited puppy at the same time so that they were both in danger of falling over. She grinned then let go.

'I've been looking all over for you.' Sally was wearing an ear-to-ear grin, pigtails flopping up and down as she bounced around like Tigger on speed in front of Lucy.

'Are you drunk?'

'Of course I'm drunk! You don't think I'd still be here listening to that bloody brass band if I wasn't do you?'

'Can you stop doing that,' Lucy hoped she didn't sound like a school teacher telling an infant off, but Sally didn't seem to care, 'you're making me feel dizzy.'

'Your kids were fucking amazing. You are amazing.' Sally kissed her on the cheek in a very un-Sally way. 'I think you should forget your sink-hole school and come and live here.'

'Sink-hole school?' Lucy tried not to laugh. 'Just how much have you had to drink?' She couldn't believe this was the ultra-professional, efficient veterinary nurse and receptionist. She looked younger, happier, un-leashed. Maybe that was what she needed herself, to be let out of school, let her hair down. Sally slipped her arm through Lucy's and span her round.

'Scrumpy, and this sangria stuff, and beer. Look.'

Lucy looked from a slightly abashed, but clearly merry Sally, over to the well-built James. He'd looked different in the dim light of the pub last night, but in daylight she could see he was a slightly softer-at-the-edges, sweeter, version of his brother. His eyes were twinkling, but were a deeper blue than

Matt's (not that she'd studied them that closely), the dirty-blond hair a shade or two closer to brown and not quite as neatly slicked back. But the washboard stomach, and muscled forearms were about the same.

'What are you lot plotting without me?' A warm hand on her shoulder cut Lucy's appraisal short, which was probably a good thing – she was always telling the kids it was rude to stare – and she had the opportunity to see just how much alike, and how dissimilar the brothers were when she turned to find Matt behind her.

'We're persuading Lucy to come for a drink at the Taverner's.'

'Are you? It's very kind but...' She had lesson plans to do, a garden to weed, job applications to complete.

The last unwelcome thought thudded into her mind. She'd already been here for nearly half of the agreed cover time, and she realised with a jolt that even if she was a bit of an outsider, she'd miss the place. But more than missing the place, she'd miss the people.

Oh God she was a confused mess; one minute she was planning her escape, the next she was realising that it might be harder to walk away from this place than she'd ever imagined. One random act of kindness from Charlie, followed by a near-flooring from Sally and she was getting all sentimental.

'It's Saturday, and it's a bank holiday weekend so I'm not letting you say no. And you can't leave me to handle Bill and Ben on my own.' Sally linked her arms through Lucy's, her mouth close to the other girl's ear. 'Please?'

Lucy saw Sally's gaze drift over in James' direction. She had a serious crush there, and Lucy wondered how long it had been going on. Probably from their school days.

'I can't do this without you.'

She smiled. Sally was nice, she'd gone out of her way to be helpful, and she'd smoothed the path with Charlie. She deserved a break with the sturdy farmer who looked more than alright. 'As long as you show me his whippets!'

Sally laughed, and she joined in. Then she leant forward and kissed her on the cheek. 'Thanks. I owe you one.'

Chapter 9

Lucy looked through the doorway of the Taverner's Arms in dismay. A three deep mass of burly locals stood between her and any hope of a drink. It looked like every single resident of Langtry Meadows over the legal age had the same idea.

Matt didn't hesitate; he eased his way into the crowd, Jamie right behind him.

Sally leaned against Lucy, and the loud conspiratorial whisper in her ear would have reached everybody if it hadn't been so noisy. 'Isn't he just so gorgeous?' She sighed, a heartfelt sigh.

'Matt?' Lucy couldn't resist. Then wished she hadn't when Sally's playful punch hit her arm.

'Jamie. Oh God, I've got to have him.' The words were slightly slurred, but the feeling in them came straight from her core. 'I thought the drink would help, you know, do it. But I'm not so sure now.' She wobbled a bit, and Lucy, giggling, grabbed her elbow. 'I've fancied him since we were at school. He's my hero.' She gave a heartfelt sigh that quivered at the end, and Lucy tried to keep a straight face. The girl really had it bad.

'He seems lovely. So you, er, you and Charlie, aren't?'

Sally giggled. 'Charlie!' It came out a bit loud and she clamped her hand over her mouth. 'Me and Charlie? Oh my God, no. He's lovely, but he never stops working, I mean, he's obsessed. Even worse than you!' Lucy decided she'd take that as a compliment rather than an insult. 'Whereas...' She stared after Jamie like a mooning calf.

So that put her straight on that one. 'He likes you too.'

'He just thinks I'm like an annoying kid sister that needs rescuing.'

'Maybe he did when you were five, but he wouldn't carry on doing it now if he didn't fancy you, would he?'

'You're sure?'

'Positive. He was watching your every move on quiz night.' Which might have been a slight exaggeration, but it wasn't far off the mark.

'After you told me about everything you've done, moving, job, everything – I told myself I had to do it. Now. Before I'm a wrinkly.'

'You've got plenty of time before you're a wrinkly.'

'Oh I do love you.' Sally slipped her arm round Lucy's waist.

'It's Jamie you should be telling that.'

'I know, but if he spurns me...'

'Spurns you?' Lucy tried not to laugh. 'Who says spurns in this day and age?'

'Books, films, everybody. If he *spurns* me,' she emphasised the word, 'Matt will never let me live it down. He'll take the piss.'

'He won't say no. But ignore Matt. I'll distract him.'

'You will? Oh I really, really do love you.' She moved in closer. 'I was hoping you'd say that though. But you won't let him snog you, will you? Miss Harrington said...'

What Miss Harrington said was lost.

'Let the dog see the rabbit, fellas.' Matt's voice boomed out, he was clapping backs and telling people to move their arses as he went, with Jamie not far behind. Lucy suddenly wondered what she was letting herself in for. Distract him? 'Spitting feathers here, and we've got a teacher who deserves a medal after getting your little buggers skipping around mostly in the right direction today.'

Lucy studied her feet as several pairs of eyes swivelled in her direction and there was a smattering of applause, along with a thumbs up from Jim who was standing in the snug with the other Morris dancers. 'Aye, and she even managed to persuade young Charlie to take part.' There were a few guffaws.

Sally had forgotten all about seduction and was staring wide-eyed. 'I saw him holding Mischief, but I didn't know you'd got him to do the procession.' She nudged her none too gently in the ribs. 'You are good girl. High five. Nobody had managed to get him out of that surgery to do anything. Timothy couldn't get him to the school, the vicar's wife hasn't managed to get him to agree to do the village show, and he won't even agree to be on the cricket team. So,' she lowered her voice which was a godsend, 'what's the secret, have you promised some private lessons?' Lucy felt herself go bright red.

'No! I didn't do anything so stop looking at me like that, it was Jill. Jill told him he had to help.'

'He's never done what anybody has told him before.'

'Stop it. He was just being helpful. You said yourself that he's nice.' She made a grab for the drink that Jamie was holding out to her, and buried her face in the glass hoping that the inquisition would stop. It wasn't that she'd done anything, so she had absolutely nothing to feel embarrassed about. He was just being supportive. He knew how it felt to be the odd one out. But thank God Sally hadn't arrived a few minutes earlier and caught her staring into the eyes of the man in question like some lovelorn teenager.

'He is nice.' Sally paused. 'In the surgery. He just never comes out.' She cocked her head to one side, 'I told you he's got a soft spot, he likes you!'

'Who likes who?' Matt squeezed his way in between the two girls.

'Charlie likes Lucy.'

'Oh, he does, does he? I don't blame him at all!'

'He helped her with Mischief, and,' Sally paused mischievously, 'they were in a huddle on the green.'

'No we weren't!' Hell, Sally had seen them. 'He was giving me advice about the pony, that's all.' She stared indignantly as all three of them grinned at her, and hoped she hadn't gone the colour she thought she had. Rosy red cheeks were so uncool. 'He said I need a starvation paddock, sounds cruel to me.'

'Oh no, it isn't cruel at all.' For a moment Sally slipped back into her professional mode. 'You don't want laminitis, do you?'

'Don't I?'

'No you don't.' Sally giggled. 'Well Mischief doesn't.' She slipped her hand through Matt's arm. 'You could go over and fence a bit off for Lucy, couldn't you?'

'Well,' Lucy paused doubtfully, 'Charlie did say he'd come and help do it.'

'Oh, he won't mind, and Matt's used to putting up electric fencing, aren't you? I mean, I'm not saying Charlie can't, but it'll only take Matt five minutes.'

'Yeah, won't take me long at all. I'll pop over first thing.'

'Well, I don't want to bother...' She'd quite been looking forward to a chat with Charlie. But he was probably only offering because he didn't want to see the pony suffer.

'No bother, babe.' Matt grinned at her.

'Babe?' She grinned back.

'He watches too many films, thinks he's cool.' Sally punched him on the arm playfully. 'Well, that's settled then. Anybody ready for another drink? Because I am!' She leaned in towards Lucy. 'One more then I can do it, I can tell him, I know I can. Just one more.'

Two drinks later Lucy had stopped trying to be invisible. Sally had more or less got Jamie cornered, not that he seemed to mind, and chatting to Matt was easy. He was good company.

It was rowdy in the pub and she soon found herself shouting to be heard, grinning in response to the flirty comments that he kept throwing her way. 'I wish my teachers at school had been like you.' He tapped the tip of her nose with a broad finger. 'There'd have been no running up the field to hide.'

She grinned up at him, feeling the blush that was spreading red-hot over her cheekbones. Then over his shoulder saw a disapproving glare.

Charlie. A look of fury on his face, until her gaze met his and the shutters came down.

It was like a black cloud had blocked out the sun.

What was it with the man? He was back to the grumpy vet who'd told her off in the car park, no trace of the guy who'd joked on the green such a short while ago.

Her and Charlie seemed to be playing some kind of weird ping-pong game of emotions and she didn't know the rules.

She'd thought they'd sorted out any differences. More than sorted them. He'd actually looked like he'd enjoyed the day, and that he was as disappointed as her that Serena had butted in.

And he'd even said he'd consider coming into school. Or was that just some throwaway comment that he now regretted? Why else would he be giving her that look again?

She must have really, totally imagined that weird moment on the green. Now, he was looking at her in much the same way he'd studied her hen, frowning. Which was a bit disconcerting.

'Charlie?' She edged her way over, past Matt who had been diverted by a barmaid who was fighting a losing battle to collect empties. 'Was Twinkle okay?'

'Fine.' Dry was the only way to describe the way he'd said that. 'Just a sprain. That woman is a pain in the arse at times.'

She knew her jaw had dropped at the unexpected words. Charlie was always professionalism itself. She'd never heard him criticise a client, and never heard him say anything at all unpleasant, or verging on an expletive.

'Sorry.' He swept his hair back with his hand. 'I need a drink. Looks like I'm lagging way behind eh? Sorry to intrude on your fun.'

'You're not...' But he'd turned away. She reached out, wanting to say something, to explain why she was with Matt. To ask what the matter was. Then there was a tap on her shoulder.

'Lucy dear. I need to have a serious word. It's rather urgent.'

Oh good heavens above. Did nobody get a moment's peace in this village? She looked at the headmaster with a frown.

He looked completely sober, the earlier drink had been to prepare him for the trial ahead. Insulate him from the mayhem.

'Oh, hi Timothy, I was just...'

'I really would appreciate a couple of moments of your time, if you don't mind?' He put a hand under her elbow, already steering her towards the door and he looked so serious a twinge of apprehension knotted deep down inside her. So much for her feeling that nothing bad would ever happen here. 'It's important, or I wouldn't disturb you. It's just,' he took a deep breath as he pushed the door of the pub open and daylight flooded in, momentarily dazzling her. 'I think they're going to close us down.'

'You will stay and help us save the school, won't you dear?' Timothy Parry looked completely sober, and very serious. He looked different without his normal tweed jacket, with leather elbow patches on, but still quite headmasterly as though being in school was his home, his whole life. 'I'm not asking for a lifetime commitment.' He patted her gently on the shoulder. 'Just a small slice of your life.'

It sounded simple when he said it like that. Undemanding. Which she was sure was exactly what he'd intended.

He led the way over the grass towards the duck pond, and

they sat down on the wooden bench, the remnants of the May Day celebrations scattered around them. The mallard she'd met on her first day here, well he looked like the same one, was rooting around their feet looking for scraps of bread for his family.

The late afternoon rays of sunshine sparkled on the surface of the pond. Across the way was the row of higgledy-piggledy cottages that she looked out on each day from her classroom window. The flowers were blossoming, rambling roses hesitated on the verge of showering the brick walls with a splurge of colour. She'd only been here for three weeks, but already there was so much that felt familiar. So much she'd miss.

The first tentative stirrings of summer were unfurling in the village, it was coming to life and as it changed so was something inside her. She might have felt the outsider as the Langtry Meadows villagers had celebrated earlier, but now, on this quiet bench she realised that the place was growing on her. People like Charlie were growing on her, the wonderful Sally, the welcoming Matt and his gentler brother Jamie.

A tiny bit of her was shouting out the truth – she was more at home here after such a short time than she'd ever felt in the place she'd been calling home for the last few years. At the end of the school day she didn't just walk away. In Langtry Meadows you became a part of the place whether you wanted to or not.

If she left at the end of the half term, she'd only get a glimpse of what Langtry Meadows looked like in the summer, a hint of the beauty that faded in the winter.

She slipped her shoes off, felt the cool grass beneath her toes and tried to work out how she felt. She had come here out of necessity, not through any desire to return to the type of place she'd been brought up in. There was no nostalgia attached to that. It had been a short term solution, to tide her over until a job closer to home came up. And she knew one would come up eventually. There was a high turnover at schools in the centre of a city, frazzled teachers who found they spent all their time dealing with difficult parents rather than their offspring. The constant battle to pull a school up from a slump with few resources and low morale.

It was impossible to imagine life any other way than the way she'd planned it.

It was impossible to imagine Langtry Meadows without its primary school though.

'We need fresh blood here Lucy, I'm getting old.'

She went to object, but he held a hand up.

'Now don't get me wrong. I'm in no hurry to retire, but youngsters like you bring in fresh ideas, a different way of looking at things. If we are going to be able to fight this, I need to demonstrate that we have a committed work force. That we're progressive, not some old-fashioned stuck-in-the-past relic.' He put a hand over her own which were clasped in her lap. 'You could really make a difference Lucy.'

She'd never made a difference to anything. She'd tried to make a difference to the way they lived when she was a teen-ager, tidy up after school when her mother was out. Send notes to her father telling him she'd be the perfect daughter if he came home. That she'd wash his car, help mow the lawn and never, ever complain. But he'd never replied. Life had gone on in the same way it always had.

The first time she'd ever felt valued was at Starbaston Primary School when she'd been praised by the Ofsted inspector, when she'd been promoted. And then those small achievements had been shot out of the water. She was back to nothing. Being nothing. Worthless. But determined to keep going.

'I suppose it was inevitable.' Timothy sighed. 'It is the nature of working in a village school these days my dear. Lots of small schools like ours are getting shut down, the numbers are just too low and the expenses too high, but if this school goes, then who knows what impact it will have on Langtry Meadows. We're in danger of being rationalised my dear. It's the thin end of the wedge, this is the first battle and there will be more. The multi-academy trust looms on the horizon. But,' he rubbed his hands together, 'that is in the future, my dear. Right now we have to concentrate on the immediate threat. Becky might well come back to school in due course, but I must admit I do have my doubts.'

Lucy knew what he meant. The children had crowded around to say hello to Becky, and she'd smiled a happy, welcoming smile, but the full, heartfelt look emerged only when she'd looked at her own child. You could almost feel the emotion pouring out of her. That look had briefly filled Lucy with an emptiness she'd never felt before. And then Charlie had appeared out of nowhere, bearing pints of lager. A man who had at least some understanding of how it felt to be on the edge of things.

'Now I wouldn't expect you to take on her position as deputy head my dear, but if you could commit until the summer holidays, I do feel it would make an enormous difference. It would help the other staff, give them hope. Not that they're not always tremendous and so supportive. But this will shake them.' He paused for a moment. 'This school has been here for a long time you know, I was a pupil myself many years ago.' He glanced over towards the old building. 'After I'd qualified I worked in London for a while, I had such grand ideas about changing the world.' His voice had drifted as his mind slipped back to the past. Then with an effort he returned to the present and fixed Lucy with the type of gaze she was sure always worked on difficult children. He was sincere. He was asking *her* to make the right decision. 'I left the city and came back here to nurse my ill mother, and I never left. Now,' a brisk no-nonsense edge crept in, 'you must do what is right for you, but please do consider staying. You have made a wonderful contribution already, but if you were on our "save the school" committee,' he raised his eyebrows, a flash of humour in his eyes, 'I do rather think you could make a lasting one. Now is that the time?' He stood up. 'Splendid performance today dear. See you on Tuesday morning.' And he ambled off as though he didn't have a care in the world.

She was being watched. She glanced over towards the pub, the unmistakable tall figure of Charlie was making his way over towards her.

'Room for one more?'

Lucy smiled and shuffled up. 'Seeing as it's you.' She'd hoped it would lighten the mood, but his smile was strained. 'You should have come over and chatted to us, in the pub.'

He shrugged. 'I didn't want to barge in, you looked...' His gaze caught hers for a second, then he glanced away, stared into the distance. 'He's a nice guy.'

'Sorry?'

'Matt.'

Lucy laughed self-consciously. 'He's a great guy.'

There was a strange hurumph sound.

'He's Sally's friend, not mine, but he was just trying to be helpful.'

'Sure.' He shrugged. 'Up close and very helpful.' It came out as a low mutter, but she heard every word.

'Very helpful.' She tried not to smile at the way Charlie's mouth tightened, then gave him a nudge with her elbow and leaned in a little closer. 'He's like that with everybody, you know he is.' Unlike some vet she could name, who was intent on keeping a polite distance from everybody. Including her. But that brush of his fingers, the way he'd held her gaze, looked at her as though he knew her inside and out had stirred her up more than any amount of flirtation with Matt could ever do.

'I do.' Charlie's mouth twisted ruefully, the rough edge to his voice making her want to hug him. Then he sighed, and his whole body relaxed a fraction. 'Sorry, I'm being grumpy. I'm a few pints behind everybody else.' He paused, then looked directly at her.

'Maybe we should go out for a drink some time?'

Her stomach flipped. 'Maybe we should.' She mustn't get ahead of herself. He was offering a friendly drink. The man who'd told her he'd be leaving soon, that he hadn't any choice, was just offering a glass of wine. That was all.

'If you'd like?'

'Oh yes, I'd like, I mean,' she took a steadying breath and looked him in the eye, 'that would be lovely.'

'Great. Tomorrow?'

'Tomorrow?' That was quick.

'Only if you...'

'No tomorrow sounds great. Great. Lovely.'

He looked down at his feet, probably wondering why lovely and great were suddenly the only words in a teachers vocabulary.

'Good.' He nodded, clasped his hands awkwardly together then glanced at her again. Their eyes met, and a boyish grin suddenly lit up his features. 'I've not asked anybody for a date since I was a student.'

Lucy grinned back, she couldn't help it. When he looked at her like that he was irresistible. Even if he'd be leaving soon, and the first date could be the last. But it was stupid to think like that. Since coming here she'd started to realise that it was time to take things as they came, let go a bit and enjoy things for what they were. Instead of interrogating them to death.

'Timothy looked serious.'

'Yeah, he's got,' she wasn't quite sure if this was supposed to be confidential or not, 'trouble at school.' She could at least tell Charlie she'd been asked to stay though. 'He's asked me to—' She never got to finish the sentence.

'So this is where you're hiding.'

They both swivelled round on the bench, and came face to face with a woman who'd walked across the grass behind the bench soundlessly, and was close enough to touch. A woman who was looking straight at Charlie with folded arms and a look of grim satisfaction.

'Run back to Mummy and Daddy, and little village life?' She snorted a laugh. 'All very quaint, isn't it? Even after the way you described it, I didn't expect anywhere quite so,' she wrinkled her nose, 'rural.'

Lucy looked from the woman to Charlie and back again, totally confused. Charlie looked like a bomb had been dropped on him, all the colour had been wiped from his face and his jaw was set, his lips a thin line.

'What the hell are you doing here?' The words were rough-edged.

'Well you wouldn't answer my calls so what was I supposed to do?'

'Leave a message?'

She ignored him. 'We,' Lucy was sure he flinched, 'would have got here earlier if we'd known about the dancing round the maypole.'

'We?' There was a note of panic in the single syllable. The woman gave a tight smile and looked straight at Lucy, then back to Charlie.

'You've not told your girlfriend...'

Lucy opened her mouth, not sure if she was about to deny being his girlfriend, or ask what he'd not told her.

'...that you've got a wife and daughter?'

'You're not my wife, Josie.'

'Well technically I think you'll find I still am, but anyway,' she waved a careless hand as Lucy tried to take the information in. This woman was his wife, he had a daughter? He was scared of kids, but he'd got a daughter? No, he wasn't scared of kids, he was … what was he? 'Oh, whatever. Your *daughter* wants to see you.'

Charlie glanced around wildly.

'Oh don't be ridiculous. You don't think I'd drag her round here while I tried to track you down, do you?' She shook her head in disbelief at what she considered his stupidity, shot a glare at Lucy then spinning on her heel shot a comment over her shoulder. 'I'll bring her down to your surgery in half an hour, if you can spare the time.' Her tone had a sarcastic edge that penetrated even the fuzz of Lucy's brain as she tried to compute this revelation. 'Don't keep her waiting, she's over excited and tired.'

Mischief was not in his field shelter when Lucy got back, feeling like she'd been run over by a herd of stampeding cattle. She groaned. This was all she needed.

He didn't take much finding though.

He was in the garden, his mouth full of apple blossom which was spilling out and looked like a slipped halo against his jet black coat. As he'd pulled at the twigs, more of the blossom had fallen, the pretty pink petals scattering across his broad back.

She sank down beside him, wrapped her arms round his neck and wanted to cry, but instead she laughed. Slightly hysterically. Charlie had a child. He had a wife. No wonder he'd said life was complicated. But why the hell hadn't he told her? Not that it was any of her business, and they weren't even going out or anything. But a child. How did you not mention a child?

He'd not wanted to come to school, he'd not wanted to get involved in village life, and she was pretty damned sure nobody here knew anything about his daughter. His secret. But why the hell did anybody want to keep that kind of secret? Her head hurt, and it wasn't from beer.

'Oh Mischief, what kind of idiot am I?'

He was being friendly, giving her an ally, and she'd kissed him. Been stupidly pleased when he'd chatted to her.

The pony nudged her hand, then blew gently out of his nostrils. She gulped down the blockage in her throat. 'He asked me on a date, but he's got a family Mischief.' She'd have never had him down as somebody who ran away. As a man who couldn't even love his own daughter.

But what did she know? She was the stupid idiot who'd gazed into his eyes, who'd thought they'd shared some kind of intimate moment. Who'd been ridiculously happy when he'd asked her out for a drink.

She ran her fingers through the pony's forelock then wearily got to her feet.

It was as she was securing the catch, that she spotted a pullover that had been slung over the gate. It had to be Charlie's. She picked it up, and without thinking held it close to her face. Oh God, she was turning into a loony, sniffing people's clothes. She dropped it. Oh pull yourself together, Lucy. It's a jumper. The poor man brought your pony back and you're throwing his clothes on the ground.

He'd asked her out.

He'd abandoned a child.

He'd never told her.

She shook her head, annoyed at herself. This was her over thinking things and being daft. There was bound to be a good explanation. And she liked him. Even if she'd misread all the signs. Even if he'd called it a date, but hadn't meant it.

She picked the jumper up again, ran her hand over the soft wool. What would Charlie say about the school? She'd wanted to tell him, chat about it. She'd thought he was an outsider, like she was. But now, all of a sudden, she felt like she didn't know him at all. She'd thought he wasn't exactly a hundred percent comfortable, or thinking about settling here forever because there were other more exciting places to go, not because he was running away from a family.

Chapter 10

Lucy stretched, then threaded her fingers through her hair and yawned. She didn't feel like she'd had a refreshing night's sleep. She felt like she'd spent the night chasing the children round the flaming maypole. That was something that would stay in her memory for quite some time.

She blinked in an attempt to clear her head, then snapped the kettle on and leaned against the sink, staring out of the window. It was another beautiful morning, the type that was hard to ignore. Whether she decided to stay until the end of the summer term, or go now, she really only had such a short time left in Langtry Meadows that she couldn't ignore a day like this. It deserved to be savoured. Even if the sensible side of her was saying she had school work to do, and her head was saying another nap would be nice.

Out of the corner of her eye she spotted the bag of stale bread crusts that she'd been saving for the ducks. Even after they'd gorged on the leftovers yesterday she was pretty sure bread would still be appreciated, and it gave her a reason for going out. A purpose.

The kettle clicked off, filling the kitchen with steam and

she scooped a generous spoonful of coffee into a mug and filled it with hot water. That was what had always been important in life, having a purpose. She'd always been certain of where she was heading, and now all of a sudden she wasn't. Which was why she hadn't slept.

Timothy wasn't asking for much, just a commitment for one more half term. So what was stopping her? She was fairly sure that Annie would be delighted to have her stay and look after the cottage. She could even put her house on the market for short-term let and stay here over the summer if she wanted. Have a holiday. It was years since she'd had a proper break and this could be the ideal opportunity.

Well, real life was stopping her for one thing. Keeping her career on track. Paying her mortgage. If she agreed to this, she was derailing her plan, and she'd never even thought for one moment about changing her goals. Not since the day she'd waved goodbye to high school and walked into university.

She'd been certain then of what she had to do, where she was heading – and it involved marching forwards, never looking back. Her future didn't lie in a quiet backwater, it lay in the places that weren't pretty. In the places where one wrong turn, one wrong friendship could change your life for the worse forever. It was in places where she could give kids confidence, help stop the bullying and the singling out of kids who were slightly different, it was about being in a place where she could make a difference. It was about making children feel wanted in a way she knew they needed to be.

Growing up in Stoneyvale, she'd never questioned that life

could be anything but good, and that friends wouldn't be there forever – until a year or so before they'd moved. In that last year she'd become the little girl that nobody wanted to be friends with. The one they barged past in the playground. If Amy was there it was okay, on the days she wasn't she stood alone. Watching. Flickering tentative smiles that were ignored. Hoping somebody would talk to her. Making daisy chain bracelets on her own.

It was just the same in her new school. Everybody hated her, she didn't belong. That was how it had felt back then. But an eight year old girl probably wasn't the most objective person in the world. She knew that now. Langtry Meadows wasn't Stoneyvale. She wasn't that frightened little girl any more.

When they'd moved everything had changed overnight. Even her mother. But when she'd moved up to high school one person, one teacher, had listened to her when her mother had been too busy with her own problems, with the upheaval of building a new home. One teacher had steered her away from the bullies, had given her the confidence to concentrate on her work, had understood teenage angst and how to explain that it wouldn't last for the rest of her life – even if it felt like that then. It had taken a while, but soon she had a plan, a future mapped out and then the horrible things didn't seem to matter quite so much. Corny as it had been, she'd decided she'd be that teacher. The one who listened. The one who made a difference.

But now she seemed to be on rocky ground, or more like sand that shifted underneath her feet. Nothing was how she'd thought it was. Yes, she did still want to be the teacher that made a difference – but even places like Langtry Meadows needed teachers like that. She was doubting her memories though, wondering if she'd got it all wrong. Wondering if the sour taste in her mouth about Stoneyvale, had been something she'd held on to for all the wrong reasons. Nothing was how she'd thought it was, not even Charlie.

She groaned. For the first time in years she wasn't sure what she really wanted.

With a sigh Lucy sat down at the kitchen table and opened up her laptop. Logging on she opened the email that had arrived on Friday (gosh was that only a couple of days ago?). It was from the recruitment agency. They were aware that her cover position would soon be at an end and were pleased to be able to inform her of a teaching vacancy closer to home. A cover position, with the possibility of it leading to a permanent post in a senior position in September. Did she want them to forward her details?

The perfect job. So why was she hesitating? She couldn't quite believe that she hadn't instantly banged off a reply shouting 'Yes!' But she hadn't.

So now she had a choice. All hers, and agonising. She could stay here, try and help rescue the school. Help not just one child, one class, but make a difference to the whole village. And risk losing the opportunity of a permanent position close to home.

Or she could go home. Take on a cover position that she was fairly confident would lead to a job in September. And she'd be back on track. Secure. Able to pay the mortgage. She could leave the whole nightmare of her redundancy behind and work towards a position on the school leadership team.

A no-brainer.

Lucy groaned and buried her head in her hands. She wasn't getting anywhere, just going round in circles. It was Sunday, so not a good day to progress anything, then tomorrow was a Bank Holiday but come Tuesday she would do something positive. Make a decision.

She picked up the bag of stale crusts and her keys. A walk and some fresh air would do her good. Then she'd come back and treat herself to a bacon sandwich.

'Good morning, my dear. Do you mind if I walk with you?'

Lucy smiled at the elderly, immaculately dressed woman who was standing by the garden gate outside the large house next to the church. She'd seen the woman a few times, walking a dog, watching the children as they played out during the school day. She'd been at her gate watching the start of the May Day procession, a pair of large sunglasses, flamboyant hat and colourful silk scarf had made it impossible to miss her.

Her silver-grey hair was scraped back into a neat bun, with one or two tiny tendrils that had escaped giving her an almost winsome look that was at odds with the rest of her appearance.

'Of course I don't.' Lucy had actually thought an early morning stroll, on her own with only the ducks to talk to, would have helped get her thoughts straight. But there again she'd spent the best part of the evening on her own and it hadn't helped. Although it was no wonder after the number of drinks she'd had. 'No dog with you this morning? She's not ill is she?'

'Oh no, not ill. Well only with a severe case of mummy-brain.' She tutted and shook her head as she pulled the gate firmly shut behind her. 'A darling dog, but since she's had the pups her hormones seem to have sent her doolally.'

'I've heard it can have that effect on women.' Lucy knew her tone was dry, but the lady laughed.

'I like you. I knew I would.' She chuckled again. 'I don't believe we've been introduced. I'm Elsie Harrington.' The old lady held out a hand and Lucy automatically took it. The woman didn't immediately let go. 'And you are Lucy, our new teacher.'

'I am. Well, I'm the cover teacher until Becky gets back to work.'

'If you say so dear.' She winked and released Lucy's hand, then waved her stick. 'Are you heading down to the green? A Sunday morning walk is good for the constitution. Not the same without Molly of course, but I'm sure you'll be just as good company.'

'Molly?'

'The dog dear, golden retriever. Loathe to leave her babies, she's being quite pathetic, just grins apologetically at me and flaps her tail as though it's all too much effort. Not at all like my old Rosie, she was a border collie. Mad as a hatter, didn't let motherhood get in her way at all.' The way she said it took the bite out of the words, and Lucy was sure she was devoted to her dog. 'Do you have a dog dear?'

'No, er I used to when I was a child, but I'm just looking after Annie's animals now.'

'You should get one. Damned good company they are, and people will always talk to you if you have one. That's why I got my Molly. Swore I wouldn't get another after Rosie went, but life just wasn't the same. If you have a dog you'll never be short of somebody to talk to, and I don't just mean talking to the animal,' she smiled, 'although you get more sense out of them than you get out of people sometimes. But look at young Charles' waiting room, full of women wanting a chat.' She chuckled, an unexpectedly dirty laugh. 'Can't climb trees though you know.'

'Charlie?' Lucy was startled, tree climbing was not something she'd imagined to find on Charlie's CV.

'Oh good heavens no. The dog. Molly. The collie used to climb trees, would be straight up there after the squirrels. Quick as you like. You should have seen the look on the squirrel's face first time she did it.' She hooked one hand through Lucy's arm, and leant on her walking stick on the other side. Though Lucy wondered if either prop was really needed. 'She was a feisty little thing was Rosie, kept me amused. But my Molly is far more sedate, suits me better now I'm old and doddery.'

'You're not—'

'Oh believe me I am my dear, I creak when I move. Damned old age. Molly has her mad moments, but she's much more suitable for an OAP like me. Lovely dogs they are, retrievers, had them when I was a girl. You can have one of the pups.'

'But I...'

'Annie won't mind.'

Annie might not, but how could she explain that she'd be

Zara Stoneley

going before they were even weaned? That her house wasn't really in the ideal spot for dog walking. That she didn't really want to get attached to an animal.

Despite her logical thoughts though, a pang of longing hit her. Sometimes it felt like leaving her old home, leaving the dog, had only been yesterday. She could remember curling up on her bed, desperate to wrap her arms round his warm body and bury her face in his fur. Smell the doggy comforting smell, feel him breathing steadily, keeping her safe, secure.

'You're a village girl, aren't you?' The old lady didn't wait for a response. 'A city girl wouldn't just slip into life here in the way you have. Take that young Serena,' she waved her stick flamboyantly, 'stands out a mile, and Felicity. Have you met Felicity dear?'

'I don't think—'

'Desperate to fit in, but she never will until she stops trying. Not that I'm saying there is anything wrong with them. This way dear, we have to say good morning to the ducks. But you are different. Much different. Now, I have to ask, have you considered Timothy's proposal?'

'Well, I...' Lucy had thought the discussion had been in confidence, but obviously nothing was in Langtry Meadows.

'We had a stroll and a chat yesterday while the Morris Men were doing their worst. There are some traditions that I'd be quite happy to see the back of, so noisy. All that jangling bells and leaping around like court jesters.' She tutted again. 'I've known Timothy since he was in short trousers, he can't keep a secret from me! You coming here was for a reason dear, the school needs you and I rather think you might need the school.'

198

Lucy didn't know whether to be cross or laugh, but Elsie Harrington didn't give her chance to do either. In fact, the way she jumped from one train of thought to another it was taking all her time to keep up, let alone contribute.

The elderly lady waved her over towards the bench, then easing herself down she patted the empty spot next to her.

'So dear, do you have a lot of friends where you are now? Is that your worry? Good friends will wait you know.'

'Friends?' Lucy paused. 'I keep in touch with my friends at college, but everybody is so busy.' And she'd been busiest of all, determined to leave with more than just qualifications. Teaching wasn't going to be just a job, like some of her friends had seen it, it was going to be her life. 'They work all over the country now so it's hard to keep in touch.'

'But you have new friends, where you live? Neighbours?'

She'd had colleagues rather than friends at Starbaston. Apart from Sarah of course. Sarah had been a good friend. But everybody had their own lives, all dispersed in different directions at the end of the school day. 'It's difficult, teaching is so full-on these days with all the lesson planning you need to do.' How did she explain it to Elsie, who had been brought up in another much slower time, with no Ofsted, or league tables?

Back in the day when teachers were trusted to teach.

She was up late every night in the week, and at the weekend by the time she'd tidied the house, all she wanted to do was flop down and watch a film, eat pizza and fall asleep before she'd finished either.

'You lead such busy lives these days, you youngsters.'

199

Her rapid promotion hadn't helped either. 'I was promoted as well and had to kind of keep a professional distance.'

'Ahh, you mean people were jealous? There are always those who will be passed over and blame the achievers, rather than seeing their own short comings.'

Some had been jealous, but it hadn't helped when the head had emphasised the need to keep a professional distance. Naively she'd gone against her natural instincts, taken his advice, and wished she hadn't. The staff needed to work as a team to overcome the massive problems. Like they seemed to do here, in Langtry Meadows.

She wriggled on the bench, feeling uncomfortable. Elsie Harrington was inadvertently painting her as a sad, work-obsessed, lonely singleton, which she wasn't at all. In fact, since she'd been in Langtry Meadows she'd spent more evenings out than she'd spent working. And she had, very briefly, had a date organised for tonight. Although she very much doubted that was going to happen now.

'I do go out sometimes, but we're all the same. Once I've been teaching longer I'll have things in place, it will be a lot easier.' Once I've stopped needing something to hide behind.

'So it isn't friends that you're bothered about missing. Something else.' She tapped her stick on the floor. 'Langtry Meadows is a pretty place isn't it dear? I feel so lucky to be part of it. Do you mind me asking about this village you were brought up in, and why you left?'

'Well, to be honest I can't remember that much about it. I was only eight when we moved, when my parents split up. I don't remember Stoneyvale being as pretty as Langtry though, it was bigger.'

'And you moved far away?'

'To the edge of a nearby town, it was all Mum could afford. Things weren't the same after that, the kids on the estate hated us, they said we were country bumpkins, and my old friends kind of drifted away.' She paused. 'Well, friend.' She wondered why she was telling an old lady this, she'd never really told anybody. But there again, had anybody asked? 'I didn't seem to fit with anybody anymore.' She gave a wry smile. 'I thought maybe Amy wasn't keen on visiting my new home, it was too rough.' She shrugged. 'Nobody wanted to know us, which kind of put me off village life a bit.' Major understatement. Except now she was starting to see it in a slightly different light.

'Children can be like that, terribly cruel and selfish. Especially girls. Thoughtless.' They could be. But she'd felt abandoned. 'And your mother, was she happy?'

Lucy was ashamed to realise that she'd always just assumed her mother was okay, she certainly always put a bright face on things, a positive spin.

'She was a bit manic, always rushing round.' Always working, saying she wanted life to be normal – but forgetting what normal had been like. 'She didn't have a moment to stop, talk.'

'It can affect you like that, loss.' Elsie's tone had softened, and Lucy wondered what she'd lost herself. But didn't like to ask. 'Children should be cocooned, and we try our best, but sometimes we can't come up with the perfect solution can we? We can be too busy aiming for the sky when we should be smelling the roses. A mother can lose sight of the very things she is trying to protect. But I'm sure she was trying to do the right thing.'

'Oh she did, she worked so hard.' Lucy had seen how her mother had worked to the point of cheery exhaustion to make sure they survived, but had never thought of her mother's loss. Losing her home, her friends, her husband.

'Maybe there was more to the move than you realised? Sometimes it's hard to explain to children, easier to leave things unsaid.' Her lips were pursed as though she was thinking about things that she wasn't voicing.

'Oh I knew she hadn't got any choice, it was all she could afford and we hadn't even got a car so it would have been difficult to stay in the village.'

'Or maybe she didn't want to, Lucy? If it had been a truly happy place for her, for all of you, I'm sure she would have found a way of staying. Mothers have rights if they have children.'

How come Elsie Harrington had managed to hit the nail on the head so cleanly? It was only in the last few days that she'd started to realise things hadn't been as straightforward as she'd assumed. That she'd started to question their family life, exactly who had walked away. And why. 'She was happier once we'd moved. More tired, but more relaxed. Isn't that strange?'

'Not really my dear. It rather sounds like it was your new home that was an unhappy place for you, but you blamed your previous friends, your old life, for not being there to support you. Whereas it sounds like for your mother it was the other way round. Not that I know anything, I'm just a silly old woman.'

'Oh you're not. But, honestly, I'm not complaining. I do love Mum, but you're right I hated where we lived, hated not fitting in, hated the fact she had to do so many jobs and had to be out all the time.' Oh hell, she felt so guilty now. She'd never actually stopped to think about it all from her mum's point of view.

'And you vowed that you'd be independent, it would never happen to you again? You would be in control.'

Lucy squirmed uncomfortably, and Elsie patted her knee with an arthritis gnarled hand.

'There is nothing wrong with wanting to be independent my dear, working hard, but from what Annie told me before she went off on her travels, you've maybe been working a little too hard?'

Lucy shrugged. 'Well not really, I mean I'm only just starting my career, I need to prove myself.' She needed a base, security, so that no matter who or what happened in the future she'd never have to be uprooted again. She'd vowed that she'd never have to watch *her* children lose everything. But maybe it hadn't been about money, about her father leaving, maybe sometimes life wasn't that simple.

'The governors at the school were very impressed with your credentials my dear, and for one so young. Remarkable.' She frowned at Lucy. 'One might say driven.' She waved at the ducks. 'You've brought bread?'

Lucy had forgotten all about the bread, all her thoughts

had been hijacked. She started to tear little pieces off and throw them.

'And you really don't have fond memories of village life?'

'Well I'm not really sure to be honest. I had a dog, friends, fun, but then all of a sudden I didn't. Everything had gone. I didn't belong there, or in my new home.'

Village life had always seemed a backwards step, she'd been determined to move on and working in a city gave her better prospects, opportunities that didn't exist here. Security. Or so she'd thought. She'd never stopped to think about the good bits of her childhood, until Langtry Meadows and its inhabitants had started to nudge the memories back to the front of her mind.

'But your new life is better.' Elsie patted her hand. 'Well done, dear. Good for you. The only problem is that we tend to have rather selective memories. Good and bad, don't we?' She sat back, and they watched as the ducklings circled at the edge of the pond. 'I suppose you are right though, village life is rarely "darling buds of May" perfect.'

'Sorry?'

'Well I've been here all my life my dear, and for the most part it has been good. But we haven't always had sunshine and fresh strawberries. In my childhood there were wars, unhappiness, and a good summer doesn't always help the heart recover from loss.' For a moment she looked faraway, sad, and then she snapped back to the present. 'I try to remember the good bits though my dear. The positive. It would be incredibly sad to let that get spoiled by the things you can't change, wouldn't it?'

'Well er, yes, I suppose so.' She screwed up her eyes and tried to remember. There were vague memories of happy times with her father, the whole family picnicking in the fields behind their home. But most of the good bits had been squashed down by the weight of bad memories around the time they'd moved. Elsie was right, it was sad. 'We were the broken family in the village though,' more than broken, they'd been on a downwards spiral that she was sure was something to do with her father, 'In the city, once I'd grown up I found out we were the same as everybody else. Everybody was struggling to sort their own problems, disguise the imperfections. We were happier, in the end.'

'So your mother did the right thing.' It was a statement, not a question. 'But you need to remember that however hard you look, you'll never find perfection, Lucy. Now,' she paused dramatically, waiting for Lucy to look at her, 'what on earth is happening with Charles? I hear that ex-wife of his was making a nuisance of herself.'

Lucy didn't know whether to laugh or cry, talk about nosey neighbours, this woman knew everything. She couldn't help herself, she blurted it out without pausing to think. 'She brought their daughter to see him.'

'Daughter?'

It was genuine surprise. The old lady pursed her lips. 'Ahh, I knew there must be something behind his return here, and his reluctance to talk. He was always an open book when he was younger. So sad. I am relying on you to look after him, my dear. Now, you must give my regards to your mother, and bring her round to see me if she visits. And you should talk to her, clear the cobwebs.'

'I know, she said she'd come for a chat.'

But it didn't change the fact that staying here could be such a bad career move. The school was under threat. Her CV would soon look like a minefield of bad decisions – redundancy in one post, followed by school closure at her next. Even she would be wary of employing somebody with that kind of record.

'It's always worth looking on the bright side. I'm a realist my dear, but where is life without optimism? Oh my, is that the time? Lovely to chat to you Lucy.' Elsie stood up and peered down. 'Langtry Meadows is such a delight in the summer, it would be such a shame for you to miss it. Just remember, our lives are never quite as neat and tidy as we plan, but where is the fun in that?' Her eyes seemed to be twinkling, and Lucy had a sudden desire to see what Elsie was like when she was younger.

'Has your life been tidy?'

'Oh no my dear, not at all. Total lack of control.' She chuckled. 'Although there were times I wished it had been. But hiding from things never helped, it didn't protect my heart. There are things in my life that I should have faced up to, but I've left them too long. Far too long.' She sounded almost wistful. 'It gets harder my dear to turn back the clock, there are right and wrong times to make choices.' She smoothed her skirt down briskly. 'Do pop in when you're passing, it would be lovely to have another chat. And if you do decide to leave, don't forget to come and say goodbye.'

Chapter 11

Charlie reluctantly flicked the surgery lights on, and opened the blinds, just as the door swung open and admitted a waft of perfume.

He hadn't felt he had any choice but to agree to check Twinkle over the day after the accident. In fact, it had seemed the only way to escape Serena's house. Rushing back over to the Taverner's Arms to celebrate his freedom with Lucy had been a mistake on his part though. By the time he'd got there she'd been giggling away in a corner, flanked by Sally and the Harwood brothers, which had made him feel grumpier than he had in a long time. And he wasn't sure why. He wanted to keep himself to himself didn't he? It had been his choice. Whereas she'd slotted in as comfortably as though she'd always been there. The pretty, ever-smiling school teacher without a care in the world.

And he was an idiot who'd already done an excellent job of cocking his life up. But he'd wanted to talk to her. And then off she'd trotted with the school headmaster in hot pursuit and he'd been left with a warm beer and an uncontrollable urge to run after them.

So he had. And then he'd somehow ended up doing the

one thing he hadn't expected at all. He'd asked her out.

He closed his eyes. He shouldn't have done that. It wasn't fair on either of them.

And then, just to prove what a mess his life really was, Josie had appeared.

He should stick to work. He could cope with that. He was good at it.

He gave the table an unnecessary wipe down and threw the consulting room door open.

'Miss Stevens.'

She was leaning on the reception counter. 'Oh, how many times do I have to tell you to call me Serena?' From the tote bag Twinkle gave a warning growl.

'Come through. If you'll just pop her on the table for me.' No way was he going to infringe on the animal's territory and put his hands in the bag.

'Come on my lickle Twinky-winky baby.' The dog carried on its grumbling as she lifted it out, little white teeth bared, its tiny nose wrinkled with annoyance. 'Aww, is your leggy peg still sore, babe?'

Charlie tried not to grimace.

'Now, you're not going to hurt her, are you?' She frowned at Charlie, switching from baby tones to gravelly seductress.

Not hurt her? He wasn't going to touch her if he could avoid it. Now was an ideal opportunity to persuade Serena that life in a tote bag wasn't an ideal existence. 'Well she's bearing weight on it. If you could pop her on the floor and walk her across the room for me.'

Twinkle positively skipped as she sensed her ordeal was

over and made a beeline for the door, she was slightly more reluctant when she was asked to walk back the other way.

'That looks fine.'

'You aren't going to examine her properly? Eric—'

'I don't want to stress her more than absolutely necessary. Eric explained to me how sensitive she is.'

'He did? He told you all about my little Twinkle? Oh, how sweet of him. Oh and he's right, of course.'

'Isn't he always?' Charlie nodded gravely, hoping his employee wouldn't mind the white lies. 'Now,' he was going to see how far he could play this one, 'I think he mentioned to you how important it is that she strengthens those legs, especially,' he coughed, he was going to have to say it, needs must, 'if she is going to have pups at some point.'

'Oh.' Serena looked at him blankly. 'They'll be tiny, and she can't carry them exactly. I thought about getting a bigger bag then the whole family could...'

'While she's pregnant?'

'Oh my, yes. I hadn't thought of that, silly me.' She lifted the little dog up in one hand, and patted her stomach. Twinkle snarled. Charlie wondered if she'd eat any offspring before they had chance to draw their first breaths.

'Well, er, it is something for the future, but nothing like preparing in advance.'

'But she does like her bag, don't you poppet?' Serena put the dog back in her bag. 'She looks so sweet in it, that's why I got such a small one.'

Charlie stared at the bag, speechless. He'd seen smaller suitcases.

'Small Chihuahua silly, not bag.' Serena giggled, and patted his arm flirtatiously and Charlie wondered which was more dangerous. Dog or owner.

'A short walk each day to strengthen that leg.' It was unprofessional, but he felt he had to do it. If she felt guilty she might actually follow advice. 'We don't want her losing the use of it, do we?'

Oh God he was really overstepping the mark now.

'Oh no,' Serena had her hand over her mouth, 'oh you don't think? Oh I'd never forgive myself.'

'A short walk,' he adopted his brisk, no-nonsense tone, 'every day. Walk her down to the green and let her socialise with the other dogs.'

'Other dogs?' Serena looked at him as though he was suggesting she tie a weight round the dog's midriff and throw it in the lake. 'Socialise?'

'Yes. Dogs need to socialise. You can have her on an extendable lead if you feel better, but she does need to run around. Every day.'

'Every day?'

'Every day.'

'Then you'll look at her again?'

'Yes Miss Stevens, ring Sally on Tuesday and make an appointment for the following week.'

'I will do, oh you're so understanding Charlie,' she glanced at his hands, 'I always feel we're in such strong, capable hands when we come here. Serena though, do call me Serena. Come on Twinkle.'

Charlie slumped back against the cupboards as the door

closed behind them, and wondered if it was too early to head to the Taverner's Arms. He groaned as the bell rang announcing another client – why, oh why hadn't he followed Serena and locked the door behind her?

'Hi.' It was Lucy. In jeans and pretty blouse, converse trainers on her feet, and her normally well-contained blonde hair tumbling over her shoulders. Her face was fresh and make-up free, her lips shining and her cheeks pink as though she'd been running in the fresh air.

Another why. Why, oh why had all that registered on his brain before he'd even thought to ask why she was here?

But he didn't really care why she was here, he was just ludicrously pleased to see her.

After she'd witnessed Josie's outburst on the green he'd expected her to come in all guns blazing, demanding explanations, or at the very least give him a wide berth. If somebody had done that to him, he'd have been off. Which might have been a sensible option for both of them. But he didn't want to be sensible. He was more pleased to see her than he'd ever admit. The fact that she was her normal easy-going self left him feeling like a kid who'd won the best prize on the tombola.

Except he'd cheated. He hadn't even bought a ticket.

He'd very nearly kissed her, he'd held her hand, they'd chatted, shared time and laughter. He'd asked her out for a drink. And he had no right. He'd not even had the guts to tell her why he had no plans to hang around, how he'd screwed up his life so royally.

But she was here. So maybe their date was still on. Or

maybe she'd come to tell him to stuff off. He wouldn't blame her. Or maybe if it was he should cancel it. Before this all got messier than it already was. He shouldn't have asked her out.

He hadn't a clue what the hell was going to happen next in his life.

'I didn't think you'd be open today.'

'I'm not.'

She gave him a quizzical look.

'Well, I mean I wouldn't be normally, but I promised Serena I'd give her dog a quick check over. Not that there was anything wrong with it, apart from a bad temper. That dog needs a good run and some rough and tumble.' He was rambling, she knew it.

She grinned, her hair swishing so that he caught a waft of something floral, and leant her forearms on the reception counter. 'Do you think people are like their animals?'

'Hmm.' He pondered. 'Well that little spoiled, demanding, pretty thing has some things in common with Serena. But,' he paused. 'You've got a pig, a fat pony, egg-bound chicken and stroppy goose, so what does that say?'

'I've got a split personality?' She laughed, an easy relaxed laugh that made him want to smile. 'But they aren't mine of course, I am purely the caretaker tending to their every needs.'

'And a good job you're doing of it.'

She blushed.

'Look, I'm sorry about yesterday,' he had to get it out, 'I owe you an explanation.' He didn't know exactly what he was going to say, he still hadn't worked it all out for himself.

'You probably do, but that's not why I came.'

'Oh.'

'Mischief was in the garden when I got back last night.'

'You're kidding!'

'I kid you not. He's a bit of an escape artist. Annie told me that he can undo the catch and I had to tie up the gate, but you weren't to know that. No problem, he'd only got as far as trying to strip the blossom off the tree. He was all pink.' She grinned. 'Anyway, I found this.' She held out his jumper. 'By the gate.'

'Oh thanks. I thought I'd probably left it in the pub, now you've ruined my excuse to go for a pint and check.' She put it on the counter. Paused. Giving him an opportunity to say something. To say why he'd not mentioned an ex-wife, a daughter. 'Coffee? Once I've locked the door so half the village don't come calling.'

'Well if you're sure you're not busy.'

She was giving him an out, the opportunity to dodge the issue.

'No, no, I can fix that gate for you as well, if you want?' What on earth was he saying? He hadn't had a day off for ages. Since the day his world had been turned upside down and he'd buried himself in work. And now he was offering to find free time. But the words just carried on pouring out on their own. Amazing the effect of a guilty conscience. The opportunity to put off the moment of truth. 'That pony is going to get even more determined to break out once we restrict his diet, and like I said yesterday I can help you put that electric fence up.' It was for the pony's good. That was all. She needed advice. Professional advice.

'Well Matt did say... but I'm not sure he really meant it. It would be great, if you're sure you aren't too busy?'

'I'm sure.' She'd be better off with Matt. Uncomplicated Matt. Except he didn't want her to be with Matt, he didn't want to watch her laughing at some other man's jokes.

'If you tell me how to do it, I can cope.'

'I'm sure you can, but I'd be glad to help. Really.' Really? 'One evening next week?' Ignoring the fact that he had a full appointment book.

'Sure then, thanks. I'll have a word with Jim and find out where the stuff is. I wanted some other help actually, some advice, well more of a sounding board. I met Elsie Harrington today, do you know her?'

'Oh yes, I know her. But she makes me call her Miss Harrington, I didn't even know she had a first name. She's lovely.' He headed through to the small kitchen area and was pleased she followed him.

'She wants me to have one of her pups.'

'Healthy lot, they'll make nice dogs if Molly is anything to go by.'

'I'm sure they will, but it's not that...'

'Oh?'

'It's just that everybody assumes I'm staying.'

'You're not?' He stopped short, his hand on the handle of the mug as it perched on the edge of the cupboard shelf.

'Well it's only a cover job, I'm only supposed to be here half a term.'

'Oh, I thought...' He wasn't sure exactly what he thought, but she seemed so at home. 'I assumed...' Even though she'd told him she'd taken a temporary position, it seemed that she was already a part of the village community. Here to stay.

'Everybody assumed.' She sat down and started to play with a tendril of her hair. 'It's almost like if they believe I'm staying, then I will.'

'And you don't want to?'

'Well I don't *not* exactly.'

He was confused now.

'It just wasn't in my plan, it was a stop-gap until I could find something closer to home.'

'Well surely Timothy Parry understands that?'

'I think he sent Elsie on a mission to change my mind.'

'It sounds funny somebody calling her Elsie, I think she'd give me one of her looks if I did it! Sorry, I am taking you seriously.'

'Yesterday evening, after I came out of the pub, he told me that the school is at risk of closure, and he doesn't think Becky will be back, and he asked if I could make my position more permanent. He thinks it will help persuade them that the staff are committed, that the village is.'

'Well, I suppose it makes sense. But if you've got another job to go to?'

'I haven't. Well I have.' She turned the mug round in her hands. 'There is another cover job nearer to home, and it could lead to a permanent job, maybe.'

'So, it's perfect. No decision to make.' Disappointment tugged at his gut. He'd miss her, although he probably wasn't going to be here much longer either so it would be selfish to try and persuade her to hang around. And he needed to keep life simple.

'But,' she drew a breath, 'I could make a difference here, and the job in Birmingham will still be there at the end of the school year, if it does materialise at all.'

'So stay here, until then. Sounds good to me.' And it did.

'But working in a village wasn't in my plan, and if it all goes wrong my CV will look worse than ever.'

'Why?'

'Made redundant at one place, followed by the next school closing down. I'll look jinxed.'

'True. Go for the other job.'

'But it would be selfish to go, if I can help.'

He chuckled. 'So you don't want my advice, you just want me to listen.'

She blushed. 'Sorry. I needed to talk it through, but you know how as soon as you start explaining something out loud, it starts to make sense?'

'I suppose so.' He wished his own problem was that simple to solve. 'You like it here, don't you?'

'Yep.'

'So stay, do it. Follow your instincts. A few months out of your life,' he shrugged, 'but maybe skip the puppy part.'

'I think I've got to stay.'

'It looks that way.'

'But no dog, definitely no dog. That is not in the plan.'

'Do you have a plan for everything?'

'More or less. A spreadsheet.' She grinned. 'Lots of spread-sheets. I even had one for moving here, what I needed to do each day. I put the electric fence down as a blue job.'

'A blue job?'

She looked slightly embarrassed. 'Well I've got pink jobs and blue ones.'

'Blue as in boy?'

'Blue as in bugger it.' She grinned, her dimples deepening. 'Blue means I need more muscle so,' she tipped her head on one side, 'I suppose you could help with that one. But most of it is pink.'

'I'm sure it is. Have you got one for today? A spreadsheet?'

'Nope. I was too drunk last night to care.'

'Then come for a walk with me? And a pint?' He held his breath, waiting for the rebuff. Waiting for her to say she should have never said yes when he'd asked the first time. He could see the hesitation in her eyes, she was right, he shouldn't be asking. 'Just a drink, friends, allies?'

'I suppose I could, but I do need to do some marking.'

He wanted her to say yes. 'It is a bank holiday weekend.'

'It is.'

'I tell you what, when we get back I'll feed your animals for you so you've got time to work.' He was doing it again. He had patients to check up on, a full day tomorrow and he'd just offered to add to his workload.

She grinned again, and for some reason he felt more positive than he had for a long time. 'Impossible to turn down an offer like that, Elsie would approve.'

'Bugger what Elsie would think.' He smiled back, he couldn't help himself.

'I'm sure she'll let us know, she doesn't miss much does she?'

'Nothing.'

'Charlie?'

'Yes.' He had a feeling he wasn't going to like this.

'She knows your ex-wife was here yesterday.' Josie couldn't have made her return more public if she'd tried. Turning up on the village green on May Day was better than taking out an advert in the local newspaper. Lucy's voice was soft, the tone inviting him to explain, but not demanding. 'Why haven't you told anyone?' It was his call. His opportunity to be open, explain. 'People get divorced all the time, Charlie.'

'It isn't just divorce.' That would have been a bad enough blow, but something he could have admitted to. Lucy's steady gaze was still on him. 'To be honest hardly anybody in the village has ever met Josie, I'm surprised Miss Harrington even knows who she is.' But they all would be talking, wondering who the mystery woman was. 'Look, I know what it looks like, but I haven't abandoned my daughter.' She was waiting. He struggled to find the words. 'When we split up Josie wouldn't let me see her.'

'But she can't—'

'Josie gets what Josie wants.'

'But why would she do that? It's not fair on you or your daughter.'

'I know.' They were getting to the crux of it now, and he suddenly realised he wanted to tell her. Tell Lucy the shameful secret he'd been determined to keep from the village, from his family. 'When she told me she was leaving me,' he took a deep, steadying breath and forced himself to look her straight in the eye, 'she said our daughter wasn't mine and she didn't want me to play any further part in her upbringing. She said it would be confusing.'

'Not yours? What do you mean, not yours?' She was frowning.

He'd had pretty much the same reaction himself. 'Apparently I wasn't the only man in Josie's life. Don't.' He held up a hand to stop Lucy asking more questions. It was still too raw. He couldn't talk about it in detail. Not yet. To find out she'd had an affair had been bad enough, but for her to throw their whole life, everything, into doubt...

There was a hint of a tremble in Lucy's voice. 'But on May Day she said...'

'Yeah, it seems she's changed her mind. Not about our divorce,' he added hastily, 'but she says I can see my daughter. Not that she let me yesterday – that was all just a ruse to get me to talk to her.'

'That's a bit...'

'Cruel?' He laughed, he couldn't help it. 'I wasn't very happy.' Which was the understatement of the century. He'd exploded with frustration when they'd got back and there was no sign of their daughter. When he'd realised what she was doing, Josie had just played the ice-queen. In all the time they'd been together, he'd never realised she could be like that. Strong-willed maybe, and a tiny bit ruthless. But not like this. 'If she can't get her way playing fair then she's more than happy to play dirty. It's too bloody complicated, Lucy. I'm sorry, I'm a mess, you should probably stay well away from me.'

'I think that's my decision to make.' She put a hand out so that the tips of her fingers rested against his. He wanted to take her hand in his, wrap those slender fingers in his own hand, feel her warmth. But he shouldn't. He couldn't. She pulled back, as though she knew. 'But she is going to let you see your daughter? You are going to?'

'I don't know right now. The worst thing would be to jump in without thinking it through properly and say yes. God knows I want to see her. But what if Josie then changes her mind again? I can't risk that. I need to check where I stand, but,' he paused, 'I'm going to see her at some point, I'm sure about that. She's my daughter.' He gritted his teeth. 'I don't care about the biology, she's my daughter. That's why,' he could feel a headache starting, the band tightening around his forehead, 'I've not said a thing to anybody here. Oh Christ, I hope Miss Harrington...'

'I don't think Elsie will say anything to anybody. But she can't be the only person to have noticed.'

'I know.' He groaned. 'It was quiet though, most people had gone home or were in the pub. That woman misses absolutely nothing though.'

'I like her, she's pretty amazing. I just hope that when I'm her age I still look like that, she's so stylish and on the ball. She's,' she paused, 'you know I think she's probably one of those rare people that is beautiful inside and out.'

'So are you.' That wasn't supposed to come out. They looked at each other and he had a sudden urge to brush her hair back, to kiss her. Properly. He had to. He leaned forward, just as she lifted her mug, looking flustered and embarrassed. The flush of pink along her cheekbones, her mussed up natural hair, made her look less teacher, more vulnerable and attractive, very attractive, woman. He sat back awkwardly. He was being ridiculous. This whole situation was ridiculous, he was making an idiot of himself.

She put the mug down, and this time when she put her hand out, it was to cover his.

He turned his own hand over slowly, instinctively threaded his fingers through hers, taking comfort from the surprising strength of her touch.

'You're pretty amazing yourself Charlie Davenport.'

He swallowed hard as he looked into her eyes, glad that he'd not spoiled things by doing what he'd really wanted to do. 'I wouldn't...'

'There's not many people would be able to cope with all this, and carry on as normal. You really love her, don't you?'

'I do. She's my daughter.'

'She's a very lucky little girl, I wish I'd had a father like you.'

'I'm only doing what any dad would...'

'No.' Her eyes were suspiciously bright, then he spotted the single tear on her cheek. He brushed it away with his thumb. 'Not any dad, Charlie. A good dad, a brilliant dad. An amazing dad.' She smiled and shook her head. 'You've just made me realise what a shit dad my father was.'

'Oh Lucy, what happened?' He gripped her fingers tighter, shocked by the uncontrollable need to find out, protect her, that shot through him.

'Nothing really.' She shook her head again. 'It's nothing, honest. He just wasn't the best. Just me being silly. Charlie, you've got to see her, you've got to make Josie let you.'

'I'm going to do my damnedest, believe me.' He watched the expressions flit across her face, and he wanted to press her, but something told him that now wasn't the right time.

'You don't have to come into school you know. I'm so sorry for pestering, for joking about it, I didn't realise...'

'It was my fault, how were you to know? Nobody did.'

'It is okay if you don't want to, honestly.'

'I want to, Lucy.' An awkward silence crept in between them. 'And the May Day procession was good, I enjoyed it.' He had, he'd surprised himself. 'I think it's time for me to stop running, isn't it?'

He released his grip on her fingers, pulled back, suddenly aware of the intensity between them. It wasn't good. It was everything he had to avoid.

Another few weeks then that would be it. Their lives would go off in different directions. Whatever happened with Josie, he probably wouldn't be here – under the watchful eye of the villagers. He'd be moving on, and she'd made the decision to stay. And if things went really badly, he might well be better buggering off to Australia and licking his wounds in peace.

If he kissed her now, if he started something, he didn't want it to be a fling that lasted a few weeks. Something in his gut told him he'd want more, much more. He looked into her eyes. It was better not to even touch.

Chapter 12

'Oh my God I need that. You're a life saver. Give!'

Jill laughed as she passed the mug of tea over to Lucy and perched on the edge of the desk to drink her own.

'I feel like I've already done a day's work and it's only first break.' Lucy watched the children playing hopscotch in the playground and took a welcome gulp of the drink.

'I'm really pleased you've said you'll stay, and I'm not just saying that so you don't keep me in late.' Jill grinned. 'What did Timothy do to persuade you? Send in the big guns?'

'He sent in Elsie Harrington!'

'Ah, you've met her. She's his secret weapon, creeps under your defences. Never trust little old ladies, they get devious in their old age and they don't care what anybody thinks.'

'She crept under mine.' Lucy looked at her classroom assistant over the rim of the mug. 'She caught me yesterday, then she was in there like an Exocet missile, straight to my vulnerable spots.'

'You do have some then?'

'Doesn't everybody?' She laughed self-consciously. Well she had been thinking she had rather less these days, Charlie

Davenport had tunnelled effortlessly through yesterday without even trying, despite the fact that there was an unexploded bomb – otherwise known as a daughter – between them. The way he'd been looking at her she hadn't known whether to dive across the table and find out if he kissed as well as she'd started to think he might, or if it would be better to dive for the door.

It must be his professional air, the stethoscope, the steady hands, the gorgeous caring eyes. Okay it was the gorgeous bit. He was all capable and strong, clever, but kind of sensitive and open. And grumpy and moody. That was the bit she should concentrate on. He'd made it more than clear that he had no interest in his adoring and unwelcome fan club. And she had no interest in gaining a boyfriend. And he'd be off to some far flung place soon, and she'd be off back to Birmingham. Which could be perfect; a fling. No a fling wasn't perfect. Particularly as he had an ex-wife and a daughter. She suppressed the sigh.

Jill had a raised eyebrow and was giving her a funny look. 'Are you alright? I was going to say you're always very together Lucy, I'm not criticising, but you do come across as a bit of a superwoman. A nice one of course.'

'Fine thanks. But Elsie peeled back my protective layers and reduced me to a mushy centre, I'm still feeling fragile.'

Jill put a hand over her mouth in mock disbelief. 'Wow, that's good even by her standards.'

'I'm kidding. I do like it here.'

'But not long term?'

'You haven't got a vacancy long term.'

'We will have if Becky doesn't come back.'

'I've got my house, and I do actually like working in the city schools, showing the kids that they can change their lives, do whatever they want.'

'They need that here too, Lucy. They don't all want to be farmers, life in a village can be hard and if this place is going to carry on and survive we need these kids to be high-flying commuters who have fab jobs but still want to come back here.'

'I suppose so. My early life was pretty sheltered, maybe a bit of independence sooner would have been good.'

'So,' Jill walked over to the window to join her, 'will your house be okay if it's empty for a while?'

'I got in touch with a letting agency, emailed them first thing and they got back to me and said they'd have no trouble at all renting it out short term, and I talked to Jim and he said Annie would love me to stay on for a bit, so it's all sorted. You've got to put up with me until the end of the school year.'

'Fab, I really am pleased. It's great to have somebody young to work with. I mean Becky was young too, but she was a bit set in her ways. You're brilliant because you can see things in a slightly different way, as well as being a fab teacher of course.'

Lucy tried not to wriggle. She'd never been that good at accepting compliments, something her mother had always told her off about. Just say thank you and smile, had been her advice. 'Er, thank you, I think.'

Jill laughed. 'It's true! I can't blame Timothy for sending in Elsie.'

'He's funny, Timothy, isn't he? He told me he'd always been here.'

'He has, you can just picture him in short trousers sat behind an old-fashioned desk can't you?' Jill giggled.

'Strangely enough I can. He seems to be a great Head though.'

'Oh, he is. He loves the place, the kids, and he's not at all old-fashioned in his thinking, even though he looks like he will be.'

'Is he married? I didn't see him with anybody at the May Day?' It was strange really, she knew he lived in the village. Jim had pointed out his house the day she'd come for her interview. Maybe he was like her, which was why she felt he was a kindred spirit and wanted to help him; independent, devoted to his job.

'Oh yes, he's got Mary. But she's more of a companion than a wife, we don't see much of her. I think she's in London at the moment.'

'Oh.' It sounded a bit strange. 'And no kids?'

Jill made a funny sound and when she turned back from the window looked embarrassed. 'No, he's not got kids. Plenty of cats though. Mary's away a lot, she always has been. But she's been there to support him at important meetings, shake the hands of governors and councillors if you get my drift?'

Lucy wasn't sure she did. What on earth was Jill rambling on about? 'I suppose lots of people used to marry more for companionship than love.'

'Convenience is more the word here I think.' There was a pregnant pause, as though Jill was expecting her to say something. 'Though they are very fond of each other, met at Oxford University I think.'

'Convenience?'

'Oh honestly Lucy,' she shook her head in exasperation, but was grinning, 'do I need to spell it out? I had you down as smart.'

Lucy frowned. Then gasped and gave a very inappropriate giggle as the truth dawned on her. 'He's gay?'

Jill rolled her eyes. 'Bull's eye. It might have been acceptable in private schools but it's never been the done thing to admit to homosexuality in villages like this, has it?'

'But people must suspect, I mean you...'

'Oh everybody knows now, of course they do. Some of them are total hypocrites, he just has to look what they term as respectable, fit the mould.'

'Couldn't he be open about it now though? I mean times have changed.'

'They have in the city, Lucy, but not so much in a small village, although we're getting there. But, to be honest, I'd guess it would be pretty hard for him now to, you know, come out, after he's lived this life for so long. I mean secrets get harder to talk about the longer you hide them, don't they?'

'Miss Harrington said much the same thing to me the other day.'

'Well we'd all like to know about the skeletons in her attic, I'm sure Elsie has a very colourful past, she looks like she was a bit naughty doesn't she?'

'A handful I'd say!' Lucy tidied the books on her desk as the bell rang out.

'Miss, Miss.' Poppy skipped through the doorway, her socks wrinkled around her skinny ankles, her red and white checked dress tucked in her knickers and effectively killed the conversation dead. 'Jill, Miss, look!'

Jill went to pull up her socks and got a scowl.

'Not that.'

'Stand still Poppy Brownlow.' She untucked the dress and straightened it.

'Honestly.' Poppy stood still, but gave a heavy sigh.

'Now, what did you want to tell us, Poppy?' The other children were milling round as they came into the classroom.

'Show.' She stabbed at her own forehead with a thin finger. 'I wanted to show, not tell.'

'Now that's beautiful Poppy, isn't it Miss Jacobs?' Jill had spotted the thin, and already wilting daisy chain.

'Very clever, we can show everybody later in show-and-tell shall we?'

Poppy reluctantly nodded and took her seat.

'Can I show everybody my bite Miss?' Joe looked up at the mention of show-and-tell. 'My dad says it must have been a big bugger to have left a mark like that, it's right at the top of my leg, want a look?'

'He's furtling up the leg of his shorts, Miss, tell him to get his hand out or he'll go blind.' Sophie had her hand up and was bouncing in her seat in her eagerness to be heard. 'My mam says boys go blind if they...'

'Everybody sit still. Bottoms on seats. We've got a big surprise for you later, but only if you're good.'

They sat still. Lucy avoided catching Jill's eye. She knew if she did she'd be lost, they'd be in stitches. Which would be so unprofessional.

'Mr Davenport is coming in to chat to you all this afternoon, and...'

'Miss, Miss, he's the new vet isn't he?' Ted was waving his hand in the air as he spoke.

'Hands up, lips sealed.' She gestured across her mouth. 'No talking until I say your name. Yes, Harry?'

'He made my hamster sleep.'

His bottom lip quivered and Lucy looked at Jill, she'd never known hamsters have sleep problems before. Jill made a subtle gesture of a cross.

'Oh dear Harry, that is sad.'

'It was sad. He'd gone all stiff by the time we got home and his feet were sticking up. My dad put him in a box and we buried him.'

'Miss, Miss.' Sophie was waving frantically, one hand over her mouth as though that excused the fact that she was speaking.

'Sophie?'

'My mam says if we get buried in cardboard boxes then the worms will eat our brains and we'll turn into zombies.' Lucy was beginning to dread the prospect of meeting Sophie's mam again at parents' evening.

'That's why it's better to be a cow, then you get made into beefburgers.' Ted folded his chubby arms across his stout body, his declaration briefly bringing the conversation to a halt. 'And beefburgers get put in the freezer and last forever.'

'No they don't, they get eaten.' Billy piped up, bouncing on his chair so much that it nearly toppled over.

'What do we say about chairs, Billy?'

'All four feet on the floor, Miss.'

'My hamster has gone to see all my other hamsters.' Harry had stopped looking like he was going to burst into tears, and spoke with the determination of one that knew, and had to spread the message.

'My goldfish went down the loo, is that where all goldfish go, Miss? I thought heaven was up in the sky, but goldfish can't fly, can they?'

'Elephants cry when their friends die. I saw that on the tele, and they've got teeny weeny eyes.' Billy circled his eyes with thumb and forefinger.

'Beefburgers go hard and meet all their beefburger friends.'

It was a long morning. Lucy abandoned her plans to talk about the May Day weekend and what they all did, and instead they painted a large rainbow and drew living, dead, real, and imaginary, pets – and a herd of weeping elephants. They talked about beginnings and endings, and new starts, they talked about grandparents and stillborn baby brothers, and they talked about the graveyard by the church in a surprisingly matter of fact way.

And Lucy had to admit she'd actually found the whole thing quite therapeutic, she'd finally felt that she'd given herself permission to grieve for the dog she'd lost (even though it hadn't, as far as she knew, died), for the life she'd had to leave. And now she was making a fresh start – not just one that involved running off to University, or burying herself in work.

Inside, deep down inside she gave herself permission to press the pause button, and all in a classroom surrounded by chattering open-minded children who questioned everything, but judged nothing.

Charlie probably knew exactly what he was doing when he'd said he wouldn't come in. She really hoped she wasn't going to be in trouble with him again after this. She'd rather like to see that cute grin of his again and hopefully the session wasn't going to be dominated by a big discussion about exactly what he'd done to Harry's hamster.

Chapter 13

'That was brilliant, thank you so much.' Lucy impulsively reached out and gave Charlie a hug, then realised what she'd done and took a hasty backwards step, tripping up over the piano stool. He caught her elbow with a surprisingly firm grip and for a moment they stared at each other.

Wow, she did love those incredibly warm eyes. She really had to stop doing this. Staring into Charlie Davenport's eyes was getting to be a bad habit. And a very disconcerting one. They were friends. Allies. That was all they could ever be. All he wanted.

She shuffled, suddenly self-conscious, and looked down at her feet. Then back up somewhere above the top of his head, then realising she was behaving like a six year old that had been caught stealing sweets from the cupboard she met his gaze. 'It er, wasn't as bad as you thought, I hope?'

'No. It was actually quite enjoyable, surprisingly enough.' There was a lovely fan of wrinkles at the corners of his eyes. Then he let go of her elbow and let his arm fall to his side.

Which was a bit of a shame as he really did have lovely, warm, strong hands. 'But I could do with a drink, how do they come up with all those questions?'

Oh heavens, she was sure that laugh that had come out had the kind of coquettish lift that would make her raise her eyebrows if anybody else did it. But he didn't seem to notice. And at least he was more relaxed than she was, and didn't seem at all embarrassed.

'Oh you should hear some of the stuff they came up with before you got here. Inquiring minds and all that, we could go grab a drink outside the pub if you wanted?' What was she doing? She hadn't meant to say that at all. It was only 4pm, he'd think she was an alcoholic, as well as another pushy woman. 'And, er, I'll ask Jill.'

'Sure.' Well that was alright then. 'Nice evening for it. This is what village life is all about, eh?'

'I'll tidy up here then get changed, then see you over there in a bit?'

'Sure. I better check in with Sal, make sure nothing has cropped up, but we've had a quiet day.'

'I have never, ever heard anybody suggest that the fallen off end of a gerbil's tail should be kept and buried along with it.' Charlie shook his head, but he was smiling. She could get addicted to seeing that smile.

'Well it does explain tailless cats.' Lucy said, trying to keep her face straight. 'Reincarnated gerbils come back as Manx cats, who'd have thought it?'

'Indeed. How do they come up with it?'

'They just say the first thing that comes into their heads. It isn't filtered.'

'It's going to take me a long time to get over little Ted's description of a breech calf.' Charlie shook his head. 'And as for the whole discussion on why farm dogs fart more than poodles.'

'You started that!'

'I did not! I just said that the things we enjoyed like chocolate, weren't necessarily the right things for a healthy pet to eat. Oh shit.'

Lucy glanced up to see Serena making their way over the green towards them, waving wildly to attract Charlie's attention.

'Bloody hell.' Jill sniggered, then tried to bury her nose in her glass. 'That dog of hers has actually got legs.'

'Charlie, Chas!'

'Chas?' Jill looked across at Charlie and then to Lucy, who fought to keep a straight face.

Charlie groaned, and Jill gave him a nudge in the ribs.

'Chas,' she laughed, 'oh Chas, darling what it is to be in demand. Never mind, you're safe stuck in between us two. Well as safe as you can be.'

'Chas, look at my Twinky-winky!'

Jill's eyes opened wider, 'That's what my little brother used to call his willy. She's not a transvestite is she? Cos she's got bloody good legs, check the Adam's apple and the ankles my hubby used to say.'

'I thought you said I was safe?' Charlie raised an eyebrow and looked from one girl to the other.

'It's all comparative.' Lucy nodded. 'Want me to get you another pint?'

'No way.' He put a hand on her knee, under the table. 'You're staying right where you are, so she can't get me.'

It felt nice, warm, and sent a very weird sensation straight up her thigh. Lucy wriggled. Then froze because that just amplified the sensation.

'Look Charlie.' Serena was getting closer, her heels slowly sinking into the grass. 'I've brought little Twinkle for a walk, look at her.'

'Oh God, you've got to save me from this woman.' Charlie muttered, his breath warm against her ear as he took his hand off Lucy's knee, and draped it over her shoulders. Which was marginally better, and marginally worse. Especially the bit where she could see his long fingers out of the corner of her eye. And feel the warmth of his side pressed against her body. And smell a wonderfully subtle aftershave that was nothing like the medical 'just out of the operating theatre' smell that always lingered in the surgery. 'Sorry, can we just pretend we're together? Sorry.'

'Er. Fine. Splendid.' She tried to resist the urge to lean in and press herself against his body, wishing it didn't feel quite as nice as it did. It was ages since she'd had the heavy comforting weight of an arm round her shoulders.

'She's walking. I've done exactly what you told me to.' Serena tottered to a halt and leaned in a bit closer so that they all got a view of her bright pink, lacy bra (shoes, bag, and bra? You really could take co-ordination too far thought Lucy).

'That's fantastic Miss Stevens. She looks very well. Walking…'

'Fantastically?' Jill's droll tone made something clench in Lucy's stomach. She must not laugh.

They all looked. Twinkle stooped down to wee, her beady eyes daring them to laugh. The liquid pooled on the stepping stone she'd stopped on, ran slowly down until the stream parted around Serena's pink tote bag and stopped short when it reached the toes of her pink shoes. 'Oh Twinkle.' She wailed, then scooped the dog up and put it in the bag. 'Oh how disgusting, she never wees in her bag, and now look, she's done it on the outside.'

'Aww, bless her she needed a little tinkle, didn't you Twinkle?' How Jill kept her voice even, Lucy didn't know. But it was too much.

Lucy could feel Charlie's body vibrating against hers as he fought the laughter, his fingers clenching spasmodically on her shoulder. And she knew without looking that Jill would be fighting a losing battle against the giggles.

'I'll get that drink.' She shot off the bench.

'So will I.' Jill shot off the other side, and together they made a dive for the doorway of the village pub, leaving Charlie to his fate.

'Oh my, she never usually does that much. Do you think it's the exercise, or,' they heard her pause theatrically, 'she's expecting?' Her voice drifted after them.

'I think she was just desperate Miss Stevens. We all get caught short at some time, don't we? Now if you'll just excuse me I need to see what Lucy ... splendid that she's recovered so well, great news, wonderful.'

Jill and Lucy swapped a look as they heard him struggling to get off the bench.

'Should we help him?'

'In.' His voice had a hint of desperation as he put a strong hand in the centre of Lucy's back and propelled her in through the door.

Matt, who was propping the bar up, grinned with delight as first Lucy, then Jill tumbled into the pub, giggling their heads off. He'd been getting a bit fed up with playing gooseberry to Jamie and Sally, he was used to being the main attraction.

'Well if it isn't my favourite teachers.' He beckoned them over. 'Sal said you wanted to inspect Jamie's whippets?'

'She did?' Jill looked over Lucy's shoulder.

'She did.'

'Well I...' She frowned at Sally, who smiled back and looked very comfortable in the corner with Jamie.

'I've been over and put that electric fence up for you, while you and wonder boy here were entertaining the kids. Reckon I deserve a kiss, don't you?' Matt winked and puckered up, his eyes half-closed, his arms open invitingly.

'You have?' Charlie and Lucy spoke in unison, and she felt a pang of guilt as his deep voice echoed in her ear.

'I have, popped in to see Sal and she persuaded me to do something useful.'

Sally laughed. 'Hope you didn't mind Lucy, but he was driving me nuts, it was the only way to get rid of him. I know you said there was no rush, but...'

'Well there wasn't, but thanks.' Lucy, with Jim's help, had unearthed the electric fencing, but she'd been reluctant to ask Charlie to do it. He had offered, but she already owed him for agreeing to talk to the school, and he'd given her advice about Mischief, and it was all beginning to feel like she was starting to rely on him. And she fancied him, more than she should. And she really did need to keep a distance (which she'd just failed miserably on – since when was thigh to thigh considered a distance?) before he realised and she looked a complete idiot. And he was busy, with lots on his mind. And, as Sal had pointed out, there were lots of people in the village who'd be more than happy to help out – so she'd not mentioned it again. So that was lots of 'ands'. But she hadn't thought Matt would turn up and do it.

And it just felt too *personal* with Charlie. Even more personal now he'd had his arm draped round her, and been so lovely chatting to the kids.

'I thought I was doing that.' Charlie's voice had an edge to it. A hurt edge. 'I did offer.'

Oh God, she'd upset him now.

'Well yes, but I thought you'd be too busy, and,' she was sounding pretty helpless and pathetic here. 'Sally asked Matt for me...'

'Always happy to help a damsel in distress.' He winked. She blushed.

She wasn't a damsel, or in distress, but it was sweet of him. And she wasn't exactly being grateful or gracious. 'Thanks, that's brilliant.' She could almost feel Charlie's scowl burning through her back.

'Brilliant.' His tone was dry. 'Good of you to help, Matt.'

Did that sound a bit territorial? Lucy glanced up at Charlie who was staring straight at Matt. 'Well, I better get off back to the surgery and check the animals over.'

239

Oh bugger. 'Thanks for today Charlie, it was fab, the kids loved it.'

He gave a tight smile. Banged his empty glass down on the bar and headed for the door.

So what had happened to sunshine Charlie? All of a sudden he was even grumpier than before. Maybe chatting to the kids had affected him more than he realised, and it was a delayed reaction. He obviously missed his daughter, and it sounded like there was a lot more hurt heading his way. She was trying so hard not to put more pressure on, add to his workload and worries, but it seemed she'd failed on that score.

'You don't need to check them Charlie, I've already...' Sally's words hung in the air. He'd gone.

'Well what's got into him?' Jill looked after him in surprise.

Sally raised an eyebrow, then nodded at Lucy. 'Lucy has.'

'What?' Lucy stared at her. 'I didn't do anything!' No way could Sally know about Josie, could she? Hell, if she did, that could mean everybody did, which had to be Charlie's worst nightmare.

'It's not you he's cross at, it's Matt.'

'What?'

'He's jealous.'

'Oh don't be ridiculous, we're just friends,' he'd made it quite clear before that he didn't want more, and with the complications of a child she could understand. 'We haven't even...' they hadn't even kissed. Well not properly. Which was good. A lucky escape.

'Oh, the silly sod'll get over it.' Matt held his glass up. 'Anybody for another drink?'

'I better pass. School tomorrow.' Normally she'd have started on her books as soon as the children had left. She sighed inwardly. So much for being friends. Maybe it was better if she just steered well clear of Charlie, better for both of them. Except it was pretty impossible to avoid anybody in this village.

'Me too.' Jill put her empty glass on the bar. 'I'll tell you what though, having you around certainly livens things up.' She grinned good-naturedly.

Lucy didn't know if that was good or bad. She'd never, ever been accused of livening anything up. She'd have to think about that one.

She leaned forward impulsively and kissed Matt on the cheek. Maybe not quite what he'd been after, but it would have to do. 'Thanks for sorting the fence for me.'

'You're welcome.' He grinned. 'I can always take it down so Sir Galahad can put it back up for you?'

'Don't you dare! He's probably got work on his mind, or something, I'm sure he wasn't bothered at all about doing my fence. It wasn't that at all.' It couldn't have been. Why on earth would Charlie be annoyed that Matt had saved him a job?

Chapter 14

Lucy couldn't believe how fast the weeks had whizzed by. If she hadn't agreed to extend her contract for another six weeks, and stay until the summer break, she'd already be thinking about saying goodbye to Langtry Meadows and the lovely children. Instead, it was the final week of the half term and she was getting ready for a week off and some serious gardening.

'Now then my dear,' the classroom door creaked open and all the children looked up at Liz Potts, who was looking more Mrs Tiggy-Winkle than ever in a pink and white summer dress with a full skirt, 'this is Miss Jacobs, hasn't she got a pretty classroom?'

She held out her chubby arms to encompass the room then looked down at the little girl who was doing her best to hide behind the secretary's generous hips. 'Miss Jacobs, this is Maisie who is here for a trial day.' Maisie peeped round, one hand clutching Liz's skirt, her big, brown eyes wide with trepidation, gorgeous auburn curls cascading round her face. 'Her mummy is in chatting to Mr Parry, but if you need her just shout.'

Lucy had seen Liz escorting a parent round the school earlier at her normal breakneck speed. There'd been a flash of glossy red hair, pale skin and floaty silk blouse before they'd disappeared.

Timothy had told her she'd be having a visitor for a couple of hours. It was a normal occurrence, although she was sure much more common in the city schools she was used to than in this village.

At her last school they'd had children coming and going all the time, traveller's children who stayed a few weeks then disappeared. They were used to change, to adapting, and hid any nerves with bravado. Then there were the ones who were used to their mother's, or father's, frequent change of partners. And kids who just seemed to have been born cocky and streetwise.

But for little Maisie she could see it was different. And she knew that feeling.

She'd told the children at registration that they were expecting a special visitor, that they should make her welcome and show her what a nice place the school was, but for some reason this ethereal child with her angelic features, cloud of hair and obvious fear clutched at her heart in a way she couldn't remember ever feeling.

The big wide eyes stared into hers and she saw a tiny bit of herself mirrored there. This little girl had the look she was sure she'd had. The uncertainty. The hope that things wouldn't be that bad. The fear of failure, of being unwelcome.

'Maisie, I am so glad to see you! You're just the person we need to help us make a very important decision.' She held out a hand, and Maisie, her thumb in her mouth reluctantly edged forward. Lucy crouched down so that she was on a level with the girl, she dropped her voice to a confidential tone. 'I hear you've got a very special dog and we really, really need to add one into our new pet display. You couldn't help us out could you?'

Maisie nodded eagerly, her eyes brightening, and Lucy heaved an inward sigh of relief. The little girl's mother had filled in all the advance information they'd asked for – which a lot of parents didn't – and it gave her something to work with, hints on how to make the little girl relax and feel at home. Make her eager to come back the next term and see her new friends again.

'Miss, Miss, can she sit next to me?' Rosie had one hand in the air and was dragging a small chair closer to her with the other. Lucy looked at her, and opened her mouth to speak, but Rosie beat her to it. 'I haven't got anything in my pockets, no frogs or nothing, honest Miss.'

'That's very kind Rosie.' Out of the corner of her eye she could see Jill grinning. 'Is that okay with you, Maisie? Rosie loves dogs, she loves all animals, big and small.' There was a splutter from Jill. 'Don't you, Rosie?'

Mid-afternoon break came round surprisingly quickly.

'They're very adaptable at that age aren't they?'

Lucy joined Jill at the classroom window, and watched Maisie happily skipping around the playground next to Rosie and Sophie. 'They are.' She hadn't been. But maybe it was all down to circumstance, luck, a million other things.

'Her mother said she's just got divorced, she said something about moving here so that Maisie would be near her father, he must live on that new estate. Some of the people out there don't really use the village shop, and if they haven't got family they don't come to any of the events on the green, so we just don't see them. Liz said that the move isn't definite yet, but she wanted to be sure that the school would be the right one.'

'Sounds complicated.' Lucy sighed, it always was complicated.

'At least the parents get on, it makes it so much easier for the kids if they can stay close.'

'True. I didn't see my dad after my parents split. Everything was strange and new, to be honest I felt like nobody loved me. Young children need to feel secure, wanted, and it doesn't take much to shatter the illusion.' And young children were so sensitive to the vibes around them, she knew that now. Happy parents made happy children, which was probably where it had all started going wrong for her at Stoneyvale. There had been a tension, something that she'd been too young to identify, but it had sown the first seeds of insecurity. Seeds that like weeds had flourished when she'd found herself in a new, strange environment. And it had taken her years to find her self-worth, find her own safe-place in the big, wide, world.

'It must have been tough.' Jill started to spread the paintings out on the window sill to dry. 'I can't imagine being dragged away from friends and the place you love. When I lost my husband it was the people here that saved me.'

Lucy stopped thinking about herself, she knew her eyes

had opened wide. Over the last few weeks Jill had given very little away about her private life, she'd just been a hard-working caring co-worker who always had a smile and good word for everybody.

'I'm so sorry, I didn't...'

'Oh don't be sorry, I don't tend to mention it.' Jill smiled reassuringly. 'It was a while ago, but working here, being involved in the village and all the bloody nosy busybodies saved me.' She stopped shuffling the paintings around. 'If I hadn't felt I belonged somewhere, that people cared, I would have drowned.'

'Oh Jill, I feel a complete fraud now. My problems were nothing like yours.'

'They were to you.' Jill patted her hand. 'You were young, children need to feel secure. I lost my husband, but I've got some good memories, and we knew it was coming. I had time to prepare.'

'You knew?'

'He'd been ill for a while, but he made sure I'd be okay, I'd be provided for. It takes time to heal, Lucy, but we find ways to cope. Time doesn't stop the hurt, you won't get over it, it doesn't make anything better, but it teaches you how to deal with the pain, how to cope and find a new slightly different way of living. We all need to be gentle on ourselves, I've learned that much. And we don't have to expect everything to be all okay again, because it will always be different. You lost your father and losing a parent as well as your home must have been terrible, it must have felt like the end of the world at times.'

'It did.' It had done. Her father had as good as died that day they moved. 'I suppose I felt totally rootless.' She picked up a handful of paintbrushes and took them over to the sink, watching the colour wash down the plughole. 'I felt alienated, I guess it coloured my view of the village. Left a nasty taste.'

'Even though it had been okay?'

Lucy rubbed at the remnants of sunshine yellow paint. 'Yep, it had been okay, once.' She nodded. 'I realise that now, but it had started going wrong before we moved, which is,' she'd not said this out loud before, she hadn't dared voice the feelings that had been gradually taking hold in her mind, 'maybe why we did move. At that age though all I could see was that my dad had abandoned me,' she paused, 'I always thought that it was Mum, that she hadn't liked it there.' Thinking back, her mother had never talked about the village as though she'd liked it there, she talked more about where she'd been brought up herself and what a wonderful life they'd have in the future. 'But now I'm starting to think that maybe it was more to do with my dad.'

Jill stopped what she was doing and put a hand on her arm. 'It's the experiences that make you who you are, stronger. If you'd never moved, would you be here now? Would you have been so determined to be a fantastic teacher? Would you be able to empathise with these kids the way you do?'

'Elsie Harrington said something like that. I wonder what her secret is? Who she lost?'

'I didn't know she'd lost anybody.' Jill frowned. 'She is a bit of a mystery though. Like you.'

'I'm not—'

'You keep things that bother you close though, don't you? When I watch you with the children I can see you really understand their issues, it's genuine, it makes you a special teacher Lucy. But you should let people help you, we're a good crowd really.'

'I know. You love it here, don't you?'

'I wouldn't be anywhere else. Now,' she took the brushes from Lucy's hand, 'there's the bell, let's get the little horrors cross-legged on the mat and do some show and tell. I don't know about you, but after clearing up all that paint I'm ready for the final bell.'

Lucy was ready for the final bell too when it rang. The sun was streaming into the school and she was dying to get home and sit out in the back garden with a glass of wine and the books she had for marking. Not that she was desperate to do the marking, but somehow sitting in the still slightly wild garden, with the sound of insects and birds, turned it into an almost pleasant activity.

She held a hand up and they all stilled and copied her. 'Is everybody ready to line up? Right what shall we do today?' She tilted her head and studied the children as though she was thinking. 'I know, hmm I know class 5 can do this, but it might be too difficult for us.'

'We're cleverer than class 5, Miss Jacobs.' Ted frowned at her, his face solemn.

'Okay, let's do shortest to tallest.'

At her last school getting her large class to form any kind of neat, quiet line had been a challenge in itself. More often than not, one or two would disappear under tables, some would dawdle round the display table reluctant to leave the safety of the classroom and return to parents who hadn't got time for them, and others would do their best to seek attention by disrupting the children that were behaving.

Here, the children were children, mischievous and at times frustrating, but just as they'd run in at the start of the day keen to be at school, they were also keen to get home as the bell rang to mark the end of the day.

As the school had a policy of allowing the youngest children out first, her class always had a short wait until it was their turn. So Lucy varied how she asked them to line up. It kept them occupied for a few minutes so that they weren't waiting and fidgeting for too long. Alphabetical order had caused the most chaos, with William insisting he was Billy (so that he could be near the front), Ted deciding he was Edward, and Sophie bursting into tears because she only had one name. Poppy had pointed out she could be Ophie if she wanted, which hadn't gone down at all well.

'Ted Wright, kneeling down does not mean you're the smallest.' Jill shook her head in disbelief. She held out a hand to Maisie. 'You can stand with me at the back Maisie, and see what we do and then we'll go and find mummy. How about that?' Maisie nodded her head vigorously, auburn curls bouncing.

By the time order was restored and they'd made their way out of the classroom and to the main entrance, the youngest children were already leaving, toddling on still-chubby legs, delight on their faces, as they made a bee-line for their parents.

Lucy leaned against the doorframe, the children in a neat line behind her, jostling and giggling with excitement, knowing it was their turn next.

Across from the school, the village green was bathed in soft May sunshine. Charlie, his veterinary bag in his hand, was chatting to Elsie Harrington. Molly at their feet.

It wasn't just Molly's pups, and the ducklings busying themselves at the pond edge, that had grown since she'd arrived here. Langtry Meadows had changed since she'd first driven into the village for her interview. April Fools' Day, she felt the smile tug at the corners of her mouth. She'd thought it had been foolish then, but like the leaves on the trees, something had unfurled inside of her, a different kind of promise had been made. It was as though Langtry Meadows had reminded her that another world existed outside the busy, city life she'd buried herself in.

Maybe she'd felt safer there, after all if you weren't noticed, weren't significant, if you had colleagues rather than friends, work rather than any kind of life where you interacted with other people, then you couldn't get hurt, could you? You couldn't be abandoned. She'd been invisible at Starbaston. She didn't even know her neighbours at home. But here in Langtry Meadows it was different. Nobody, nothing, went unnoticed.

Molly, the retriever, was creeping towards the ducks. The mallard flapped his wings in warning once, then settled down to watch the dog as she edged forward. Tiny steps.

That's what she was taking thought Lucy, tiny steps, but she hadn't any idea what the prize at the end was supposed to be.

'Is it our turn, Miss?'

'Can we go, Miss?'

The children craned their necks, trying to spot their parents as they all stood just outside the school door.

'Can I go, Miss? My mum's over there.' Ted pointed a chubby finger towards the far side of the playground, where Lucy spotted his mother waving wildly.

She grinned and waved back, it was impossible to miss the woman, who was as chubby as her son. As always she looked like she'd been in the middle of some farming activity when she'd realised it was time to pick her son up from school. Her wellingtons and overalls were mud-spattered (although from the wide berth the rest of the parents were giving her, Lucy guessed the brown stains weren't just mud), a collie dog at her feet.

'You can, Ted. See you tomorrow.'

'I've got cows to milk.' He declared self-importantly, then set off at a run, and Lucy waved at Mrs Wright, who gave a cheery wave back, before catching her sturdy son with a laugh as he cannoned into her.

Lucy smiled at Charlie, who had just turned away from Elsie, and clearly thought the wave had been aimed at him. He raised his bag, a broad smile on his face. He really was attractive when he smiled like that she thought. It lightened his serious features, and made him almost boyish.

She really couldn't fathom him at all though. He'd been wonderful when he'd finally agreed to come in and chat to the kids, he didn't talk down to them and was a real natural at explaining things in a way they'd understand – and responding to their random questions.

He'd actually looked quite relaxed by the time they'd finished and he'd been quite entertaining when he'd stopped for a drink with her and Jill, then half an hour later she'd been back in his bad books when he'd marched out of the pub.

Just like on May Day. When she'd been feeling a bit deflated, he'd been there. Somebody who understood. He'd helped her turn the corner, encouraged her to join in. Then he'd ended up being short with her after he'd got back from his visit to Serena. She sighed inwardly. What had got into the man?

Now though he actually looked happy to see her. And she was actually surprised how pleased she was to see him again, after a few days of not doing so. She'd been determined to give him a wide berth, the space he needed to sort out his own issues.

It had been nice to have a drink with him, but they'd both been on their best behaviour. Which was for the best. Getting involved with Charlie would be disastrous, he'd be leaving soon, and who knew what she'd be doing. And he had other responsibilities. But surely she was old enough, and grown up enough, to cope with being friends?

She grinned at him and waved back a little self-consciously.

Then he froze, his smile fixed and turning into a grimace. The colour drained from his face as though he'd seen a ghost. What the hell had she done now? All she'd done was wave back. She frowned, staring at him, then realised he wasn't looking at her. He was looking straight past her left ear. At Jill.

It didn't look like Jill had even noticed, she was busy talking to Maisie, who had found her tongue and was happily chattering away as the other children flew off in all directions across the playground. At least she was happy and settled.

Lucy sighed inwardly and glanced back. But Charlie wasn't where he had been. In fact, there was no sign of him. How could such a big man disappear like that?

'I'll take Maisie back into Mr Parry's office shall I?'

'Sure.' Lucy hardly heard Jill's words. After a wild glance round she spotted Charlie, he was marching down the road as though he had a herd of stampeding bullocks on his heels. This wasn't just him being Mr Grumpy. It was something altogether different.

'Her mother's in there. I don't know if you want to talk to her? Maisie's mum? Lucy?'

'Of course, yes, er sorry Jill.' It was weird. More than weird. He'd actually looked like he was running for his life.

'Hi, I'm Josie, Josie Atkinson-Smith.' Maisie's mother held out a hand. 'Sorry about the name being such a mouthful.' She had a warm smile, and the same ethereal delicate quality that her daughter had, emphasised by her pale skin. Josie though, unlike her daughter, had her curls tamed into a sleek bob of hair that gave her a more serious and sophisticated air. A quizzical frown settled across her previously smooth brow. 'Have we met? You look vaguely familiar.'

Lucy stared. She felt sick. The smile had thrown her for a moment, but there was no doubting it. This couldn't be happening. Mrs Atkinson-Smith couldn't be Josie.

Josie was Josie Davenport.

Maisie couldn't be, oh God she couldn't be Charlie's daughter. Except those gorgeous big brown eyes were just like his. Her hand flew to her mouth. How had she not realised? She had to be. Charlie hadn't been staring at Jill, he'd been staring at Maisie. His child.

'I, er...' What was she supposed to say? She stuck her hand out automatically. She had to say the right thing, the words that Timothy would expect. Why the hell hadn't Charlie told her that Maisie would be starting school? No, no from the look on his face, he couldn't have known, this was as much a surprise to him as it was to her. He'd panicked. Run off. 'Lovely to meet you. I must admit I was wondering how we're going to fit Maisie's full name in the register. If, of course, she comes.' But it meant Josie had made a decision, she wanted Charlie to be a part of his daughter's life. She wanted to live here. Jill had said so.

'Oh.' Realisation settled across Josie's features, which relaxed. 'I know, you were on the green with Charlie, weren't you?'

Lucy nodded, avoiding Timothy's eye. He was shooting her a questioning look, and had obviously not put two and two together. Although why would he? From the little Charlie had said, it seemed that Josie had never been a visitor here. She'd been part of his new life, not the Langtry Meadows one. Nobody knew. Yet.

'Well I must say, I'd love her to come here, she looks like she's had a great time.' Lucy felt her heart sink even lower, if that was possible. 'Mrs Potts let me peek into the classroom earlier and she looked so relaxed and happy.' How had she missed that? She could have rung Charlie, warned him. Been prepared. 'Thank you for that, Mr Parry told me you'd win her over.' She glanced over at Timothy Parry, who smiled back.

'Lucy is our secret weapon. Nobody can resist her charms.'

'Nobody?' Josie laughed, a tinkling light sound that was hard to resist. Then she gave Lucy a sideways glance that was more loaded than Lucy could have believed possible. 'I would love Maisie to come to the school, it's complicated though.' She paused. 'I need to check a few things out, sort some arrangements. Living arrangements.' This was getting worse by the second. Josie was back, and Josie it seemed was about to reclaim her husband's heart. What had Charlie said? *What Josie wants, Josie gets.* 'But I really do hope she can join you. I've filled all the forms in.' She gestured at the folder on Timothy's desk. 'I'm sure things will work out, although I might be wishing I had your powers of persuasion.' The smile was twisted as she looked at Lucy again. 'But don't worry about her name on the register, her dad's is much shorter.' The glance was a challenge, a statement of ownership. 'I've always kept my maiden name for business reasons, and even though I'm separated from Maisie's father it doesn't seem fair to saddle her with that mouthful.' The door opened and Maisie bounced in with Jill, her painting in her hand.

Josie jumped up from her seat and gave her daughter a hug. 'Are you going to say thank you?' She took Maisie's hand, and the little girl grinned.

'Thank you Miss Jacobs, thank you Jill.' She looked doubtfully at Timothy. 'Thank you Mr Parry.'

'You're very welcome, Maisie. Did you have fun?'

Maisie nodded her head, then glanced up at her mother. 'You promised we could go for posh cakes if I was good and didn't cry.'

'And we can. Thanks again everybody, it's a wonderful school. I wish I'd gone to one like this when I was Maisie's age!'

Maisie tugged at her hand. 'It's not like a school. It's not at all like the one I go to now. Did you know they've got chickens?' Her eyes opened wide and she stressed the last word so hard they all laughed. 'But I like my own school too you know, I don't really need a new one.'

'I know, darling.' Josie kissed the top of her head, and for a moment looked sad. 'I know.'

'Cake time?'

'Cake time!'

Lucy let Jill show them out of the school. She cast a last look round to double check that Charlie really had disappeared, then grabbing her cardigan, bag, and pile of books and waving goodbye to Jill she set off after him in the direction of the village square.

She had to talk to him, it was clear that nobody at the school had caught on, but they soon would. Or it might be better not to talk to him. He had Maisie to think about, and Josie.

She hesitated. It was none of her business. It would be better for Maisie if they could be a happy family again, if she kept well out of it. She slowed down as she realised her legs were actually trembling.

But he'd looked upset. He was upset. She felt ill. Despite all her best intentions she'd just realised – this wasn't just lust and a hard-to-control urge to kiss the man, she really cared for Charlie. She wanted to be there for him.

Josie had ripped their family apart, but was now trying to stick it back together and she had to help, whatever her personal feelings. Her mother hadn't been able to do it for her, but for Maisie it was different.

And she could help Charlie through this. Make a difference.

Picking up speed again she trotted over the cobbled village square, and was just about to turn down the lane that led to home, and the veterinary surgery, when a small figure caught her eye.

Elsie Harrington was waving. The last thing she needed right now was a gossip over the garden fence, but she couldn't exactly steam past and pretend she hadn't seen her.

'Lucy, Lucy!' Elsie Harrington, her normal even tone quavering, looked at her in relief.

'I'm sorry, I'm in a bit of a hu—'

'Oh thank goodness you're here.'

Lucy ground to a halt, suddenly noticing that the old ladies' top was askew, and her face creased with worry. 'Elsie, slow down, what on earth—'

'It's Molly, look.'

Lucy looked. The dog was stretched out on the garden path.

'We've just got back from our walk and she just wobbled, then fell over. I can't get her up.' Elsie looked distraught as she gently stroked the dog's head. 'I can't leave her, but nobody was about, I'm so relieved you came by.'

Molly looked from Elsie to Lucy, and gave a slow wag of her tail. Then as Lucy opened the gate, she struggled to lift her head. With an effort she struggled to her feet, then licked Lucy's hand.

'Oh good heavens, you've got the magic touch dear. I was so worried.'

Lucy smiled, she didn't want to rush off, but she really needed to talk to Charlie.

Molly sat down again. 'Oh Molly, you gave me such a fright.'

'I'll help you get her in the house, Elsie, make sure she's okay.' She resisted the urge to look at her watch as she dropped her books on the path and helped encourage the dog into the house.

'Do you think I need to call Charles? I'm probably making a fuss about nothing, but...'

'I'm popping in there now, Elsie. I'll get him to come down and set your mind at rest. But I'm sure she'll be okay, look at her, she's looking so much better already.'

'Oh I don't want to waste his time.'

'You won't be doing, and you know how much he likes to see you and Molly.' She smiled at Elsie reassuringly.

'Oh thank you dear, you're such a sensible girl. Now you get off to wherever you were rushing, Molly and I will be fine.'

Lucy gave the old lady a hug. She didn't know about being a sensible girl, but she did know that there was one issue Charlie clearly needed to get off his chest to somebody.

Maisie.

Chapter 15

Charlie sat down heavily on the chair in the back room of the surgery, and clasped his hands behind his neck. The skin was clammy, cold. His heart was pounding so hard his chest hurt and his ears were ringing. He closed his eyes, crouched over to try and ease the pain in his chest, rested his elbows on his knees and waited for the pounding to subside. Waited for his hands to stop trembling.

He could have been seeing things, an over-active imagination. But he hadn't. He knew he hadn't. The small girl framed in the doorway of Langtry Meadows Primary School was Maisie. His Maisie.

He might not have seen her for months, but he'd recognised her in an instant. And seeing her again had left him feeling wrecked.

He'd met Josie at the veterinary surgery on May Day to face a barrage of abuse – and no sign of the daughter he missed so badly. She'd shouted, then she'd cajoled, she'd made promises, then she'd lied. Then she'd said there was a chance he'd see Maisie again, that she'd move to Langtry Meadows. That they needed to do this together, that Maisie missed him. And then she'd gone.

Now this. Not exactly 'doing things together'.

He rubbed his eyes wearily. Why the hell hadn't Josie told him, given him some warning that she was taking Maisie to the school today? Instead of pulling a stunt like this. But that was her all over, proving she had control, playing him like it was some game. Not even caring if it impacted on Maisie, on the life he'd been trying to patch up. Was she just trying to force him into a corner, or was she honestly planning on moving here?

Whatever she was doing, she was going about it in the wrong way. He was sure about that.

He ran his fingers through his hair. She was trying to kill him.

Shit, he didn't even want to think about what Lucy's opinion of him was right now. From the way she'd smiled across at him it was clear that she still didn't know who Maisie was. Correction, hadn't known. She would now.

The thought of Lucy brought a whole new wave of discomfort. He liked her. Liked her far too much. Which was why he'd played along with the whole 'drink with a friend' thing, even though he would have liked it to mean a whole lot more. Why he'd been hanging around chatting to Elsie on the green, waiting to get a glimpse of her. See her smile. Why he'd insisted on helping her out, when Matt could have done the job in half the time, and had time on his hands.

He couldn't get involved with her, he'd been doing his damnedest to avoid it, but he did care what she thought. He didn't want her to think he was a complete bastard.

Somebody banged on the front door, then again, harder.

Right now it would be nice to have some peace and quiet, but it was obviously too much to hope for in this place. If he ignored it they'd be hammering on the back door in a minute.

With a sigh he stood up, feeling bone-tired, and headed to the front desk wishing that it was normal surgery hours and he had Sally there to head them off.

He looked up. It was her. Lucy. Smiling hesitantly, as though she wasn't sure of her welcome.

They stared through the glass. Into each other's eyes.

It would be easier to say he was busy, easier but more cowardly. But what he'd really like to do now was the one thing he'd been wanting to do since that day in the church. Hug her. The really hard bit would be to keep her at arm's distance. To pour his heart out, talk about all of this, and not give in to the impulse to hold her.

He couldn't do that to her. He unlocked the door.

'Are you okay?'

He'd expected her first question to be, why had he run away, and for a second he was thrown by the quiet words. All he could muster was a nod. Then a shrug. 'Not really.' Why start with another lie? He pushed the door open wider. 'You better come in.'

'Before I forget, can you go and see Elsie later? Molly collapsed.' She held up a hand as he moved towards his medical bag. 'She's fine, but I said I'd ask you to pop in and see her later.'

'I better...'

'In a minute, Charlie.' Her voice was soft. 'After we've talked. It can wait a few minutes, it's not an emergency.'

He hesitated, then locking the door led the way through to the staff room and sat down wearily.

'Lucy, I didn't know.' Her clear blue eyes were locked on to his. 'I was as shocked as you were.'

'You ran away, how could you run away? She's your daughter, Charlie, how could you do that? Abandon your own child?'

For a moment Charlie was shocked into silence at the look of raw emotion in her eyes, genuine hurt, and accusation. But the worst bit was the disappointment. He wanted to reach out, reassure her, but he knew he shouldn't. For both their sakes.

'I couldn't let her see me. You have to understand.' She glanced down, and he risked touching her, lifting her chin, so that she had to look into his eyes. Had to see how he felt, that he was being honest. 'Look, on the day Josie came here she hadn't got Maisie with her, like I told you. I've not seen Maisie for weeks.' An eternity. 'I would have given anything to have been able to run across the playground and wrap my arms around her. But that would have been wrong.' She was looking straight at him again now and he eased away, before he caved in and wrapped his arms round her. 'She might have thought I was back in her life, for good.' It would have suggested to her a future that he couldn't promise existed. 'It wasn't fair to let her see me, Lucy. That's why I ran. I've no idea what Josie has got planned, I can't see Maisie,' he gritted his teeth, 'until we agree what's happening. But believe me, turning my back on her felt like…' He couldn't put it into words, it had been a physical pain. A betrayal. 'I didn't want her to see me at school and think everything was going back to normal.'

'It isn't?'

'I don't know what normal is any more.' He paused. 'Lucy,' he stared into her eyes, willing her to understand, 'I don't know what it means if Josie brings Maisie here, even if I stay I can't...' he couldn't commit to anybody, he couldn't get to know Lucy better like he wanted to, he couldn't bury himself in his work. 'It could change everything.'

She nodded, slowly.

'But I know we're never going to go back to being a family, Lucy. I want Maisie to feel secure, I don't want her to have false hopes. I can't let her see me until I've talked to Josie properly, until we've got an agreement and I know where we all stand.'

'I can understand that.' The words croaked out of her dry throat.

'I love her, Lucy, I'd give anything to have her here with me, but I don't know.' He blinked his eyes. 'I just don't know, it's not even like I'd planned on staying here.' He gave a short laugh. 'Once Eric's fit I haven't even got a job.'

'But you could settle here? You could look for a job?'

'I'm not even sure I could get one round here.' But he was avoiding the issue, he knew that. He felt in limbo, again. How could he make a decision about anything? 'You don't fancy a drink do you?'

Lucy watched as he ran his fingers through his hair, and resisted the urge to reach out and smooth it down. She wanted to hug him, tell him they'd work it out. But she couldn't.

'Well, actually...' She did. She wasn't sure that talking could change anything between them, or help solve Charlie's problems, but she felt emotionally drained.

Charlie was heartbroken, he'd been struggling alone with the type of upheaval that would have floored many people. He wasn't a man who would abandon a child, he was the complete opposite of her father. A man who was determined to do the best for his daughter, even if she wasn't biologically his. Even if he had no idea what the future held.

She blinked and made a concerted effort to pull herself together. She had to support him, this man who she was sure had already stolen a tiny part of her heart. This man who could soon walk away from Langtry Meadows and take it with him. She had to be there for him, and for his daughter. To make sure that the little girl had a better childhood than she had, with no secrets, no lies.

'But what about Molly?'

He stood up. 'You could come with me? Then we could go straight to the pub, just for a quick one.'

'Actually, with all the stuff that's gone on today I completely forgot, it's the end of term tomorrow.' Maybe she'd go mad and have more than one drink. 'How could I forget that? The half term holiday starts tomorrow night!'

He grinned, a smile tinged with unhappiness that made something inside her quiver. It was wrong, all wrong, she had to stop letting him have that effect on her. 'You teachers, never at work. All these holidays.'

'You can stop that.' She punched him gently on the arm. 'I'll have you know I work damned hard, weekends, evenings, longer hours than most people do.' She paused. 'Well probably not as long hours as vets, but more than most normal people.'

'Are you saying I'm not normal?'

'Would I?' She grinned, she couldn't help herself. She couldn't stay cross with him, even if she knew she was heading towards heartache.

'Well, well, both of you are here!' Elsie opened her front door wider and gestured them in. 'Isn't this lovely.' She gave Lucy a knowing look, which she did her best to ignore. 'Well now, you can sit with the puppies dear, while Charles looks at Molly.'

Lucy headed across to the puppy pen, but watched Charlie as he put his case down and patted Molly. She liked watching him work. Well, she liked watching him full stop.

He caught her watching and winked, and she looked guiltily away, hoping Elsie hadn't seen.

Elsie though was more preoccupied with her dog. 'She will be okay?' There was the slightest tremble in her voice.

'I think she'll be fine. From what Lucy told me, I'm fairly sure I know what the problem is, but I will need to run tests to be one hundred per cent sure. Now let's just run over it again. When I saw you on the green earlier, you'd just come out for a walk?'

'We had yes, she's not been out much on her own she's been reluctant to leave the pups. But today she actually seemed to want a change, she was so excited and bouncy. I thought the pups were old enough, and I've always thought that if the dog's ready to get out then it's the right time, did I do the wrong thing?'

'No, no. They're well on the way to being weaned, aren't they?'

'They are, they eat for Britain, especially the podgy boy,' her features softened and some of the worry melted away, 'but maybe she's anxious. Stressed, it's the first time she's been out for a proper walk since she whelped.'

'She needed some time away from them. I'm sure she was more than happy to get away from them for a break, she wasn't in any particular hurry to get back home, was she?'

'Oh no, she'd been running round chasing birds as though she was a pup herself.' A faint smile skimmed her face, lifting the wrinkles for a moment. 'In fact, don't tell the village committee, but she was in the pond at one point swimming round and round in circles.'

Charlie patted Molly and she rolled over to have her tummy rubbed, then got to her feet, shook herself, and barked.

'She almost looks her normal self now.' Relief flooded Elsie's face. Molly wandered over to her mistress, rested her chin on Elsie's knee and stared up at her.

'Right, well I can't be sure at this stage, but I think there's a very good chance that it's what is known as exercise-induced collapse. It's common in these breeds, and dogs of Molly's age. It's warm and she's been running about. From what you've said she's had a mad half hour.'

'It won't happen again?'

'It's an inherited weakness, and so isn't going to go away. But if E.I.C. is the problem then she'll be back to normal now she's recovered, you're fine, aren't you Molly?' Molly pottered back over to him as he spoke and he fondled the dog's ears as she rubbed her head against his leg. She sniffed his shoes as though nothing had happened, then wandered back over to Elsie, put her head back in position on her knee and gazed at her with sorrowful chocolate eyes. 'It's more a case of keeping an eye on her, not letting her overdo things and making sure she doesn't get overheated or dehydrated. You're happy to bring her in tomorrow for me to run some tests?'

'Of course I am, but if you keep her in what about the puppies?'

'It won't be for long. The pups will be fine for a short while on their own.'

There could be nothing, Lucy told herself as she sat down on the floor, more adorable than a litter of golden retriever puppies. They clambered over her, tumbling and licking as they went, until one landed slap bang in the middle of her lap and gazed up with the type of adoration that nature had designed specifically for moments like this.

She'd been prepared to harden her heart, puppies were just puppies. But in that one moment, as it lifted its head and tried to lick her chin, Lucy was taken straight back to her childhood. She buried her face in its warm fluffy coat, breathing in the smell of warm puppy as it nuzzled her neck, leaned in closer so that she had no choice but to wrap her arms round it.

'Are you okay?'

Lucy looked up to see Charlie there, she hadn't realised he'd finished his examination of the dog and was watching her.

'Fine.' Her voice came out slightly strangled, and she realised that the pup's coat was damp, and so was her face. Bugger. She wiped her arm across her eyes. 'Fine, they're just so adorable.' Being buried under a mound of puppies had left her feeling all teary, although she was pretty sure that the earlier discussion with Charlie hadn't helped.

He didn't look convinced, his dark gaze never leaving her. 'Molly's fine.'

'Wonderful.' She wanted to look down, break the spell, but it seemed impossible.

'Splendid news.' They both jumped at the sound of Elsie's voice. 'Well you two youngsters can get off now. It's been quite a wearing day, all this commotion, I think I need a sit down and an early night if you don't mind.'

Lucy scrambled to her feet. Reluctantly putting the podgy puppy – that had scrambled its way straight to the centre of her heart – down.

'Ahh, you've met Roly-poly pudding have you? He's a naughty one, that one. You wouldn't think it would you? Looks like butter wouldn't melt. Right, right,' she made a shooing motion, 'off you both go, let an old lady have some peace and quiet.'

They were both ushered out, and Charlie held the gate open for Lucy, who hesitated awkwardly.

'I better go and do some lesson prep for tomorrow.' She couldn't face another it's-over-before-it's-begun talk. Not now, not the way she felt.

'I suppose I need to check on the cat that's in overnight.' They both spoke at the same time, then both stopped short.

Charlie pulled the gate to behind them. 'Or we could just go and grab that drink?'

The sun was shining down on them as they reached the Taverner's Arms, and Lucy let out a sigh of relief when she saw that the normal group of villagers were absent.

She loved chatting to Matt, Jamie and the others, but today she just needed to relax and unwind. To feel the evening sunshine on her face and not feel pressured to talk. And not inadvertently send Charlie into a bad mood and scurrying back to his surgery.

'It's the junior's outdoor cricket nets lovey, they're up on the ground behind the school.' The bar lady informed her, as she cleared the empties from the bench by the doorway of the pub.

'So, you've been here for a whole half term?' Charlie took a long swig of his beer, then set the pint down.

'Apart from one day.' She smiled. 'It's a bit weird really. When I first came here I'd got the days marked up on the calendar and I was,' she looked at him slightly guiltily, 'crossing them off with glee, but I'm quite pleased now that I'll be staying a bit longer.'

'You're not saying the place has grown on you?' He had a teasing, almost mischievous look on his face.

'I suppose so.'

'Miss Harrington reckoned that Timothy Parry always had it in mind you'd stay longer.' He chuckled, a deep, warm sound that came right from the centre of him, and she couldn't help but smile back. 'What? What have I done now to make you smile at me? That's what she said.'

'I think it's weird how she calls you Charles, and you call her Miss Harrington.'

'Ahh. I suppose she's from the generation where doctors used surnames.' He shrugged. 'I was a toddler when I first met her, so it was only good manners, and she's never asked me to call her Elsie, so it feels wrong to do it.'

'Sweet.'

'Are you taking the mickey?' He was dimpling at her in a way that was very nice and lightly unnerving.

'Not at all, Mr Davenport.'

'You like her, don't you?'

'Elsie? I certainly do, Langtry Meadows wouldn't be the same without her, would it?' Of all the people she'd met in the village, Elsie had to be the one that had made the most impact on her. Well, apart from the man she was sitting next to.

'You're probably right. She's a bit of a character, I'll give her that.'

'She's got rather a soft spot for you too hasn't she?'

He shrugged. 'So, you're here for the summer?'

She smiled. It had been a relief to finally make a decision. And she knew in her heart it was the right one, but it was bitter sweet. 'Well I'm here until the end of term, then I'll probably stay over the holidays, it seems a shame not to.' She had loved her old job, but she had fallen in love with the village, and she suspected, a certain man who would never be hers. 'What about you, now…?'

He stared into his glass. 'I hadn't planned to, no. But right now I don't know what's going to happen. To be honest I don't know whether I'm coming or going.' He paused. 'If there's any chance of me seeing Maisie, then obviously that changes everything.' He glanced up, met her gaze. 'I have to give her stability, make her feel secure.'

'So Josie didn't give you any clue that she was thinking about enrolling Maisie at the school?'

'Not a hint of it. She said we had to talk, that Maisie was missing me and maybe she'd made a mistake, which believe me is a big admission for Josie.'

'And she wanted you to see her?'

He studied his fingers. 'We were going to arrange for her to stay over some weekends, see how things went. That was it. Weekends. I never dreamt Josie would uproot them and come here, she hates villages like this. You saw her reaction on May Day. I thought I was seeing a ghost when I saw her holding Jill's hand. It doesn't make sense, none of it does.'

Lucy reached over, and put her hand over his shaking fingers.

'Did I do the right thing? Running away?'

'I don't know, Charlie. But you did it for the right reasons. You've no idea how badly not having my dad around hit me, but a lot of that was because I thought he'd abandoned me.'

'He left you?'

'No, I don't think he did. I think in my case there was a lot more to it than a break-up. Nobody abandoned me, and my mum did everything with my best interests at heart. If you're doing that then you're doing the right thing.'

'I'm not abandoning her.' His grip on her hand had tightened. 'Not unless I'm absolutely sure it's the best thing for her, whatever Josie thinks.'

'Even if she isn't yours?' She tried to keep her tone even, but she had to know.

'She's mine.' He said it with conviction. 'Even if there isn't a trace of my DNA there, she's still mine, Lucy.'

Hot tears pricked at the back of Lucy's eyes. She was trying to be matter of fact about this, but the realisation that Charlie was far more of a proper dad to Maisie, than her own had ever been to her had brought that hard lump back to her chest. Just as it had earlier, in the surgery.

'Good.' She tried to smile. She was glad, deep down. Glad that he was the man she'd thought he was, not some pale imitation. But sad. He had a little girl in his life, a child who would need every moment of his spare time to ensure she felt secure, safe, wanted. If it was true that Josie wasn't going to be in his life, it didn't leave room for their relationship to go anywhere.

'You looked happy today,' he peered up under dark eyelashes, changing the subject deliberately, almost daring her to hold his gaze and answer honestly. 'At Miss Harrington's. You looked at home, as though,' he paused, 'you belonged.'

She looked down. She couldn't help it. But she knew she'd gone scarlet, and knew that her fingers were trembling. She clutched the glass tighter to try and stop the feelings that were welling up.

'But you also looked upset.' He gave a wry grin. 'Not very good at reading emotions am I?'

'I'd say you're pretty spot on actually.'

He leaned in, and she knew it was because she was talking softly, not for any other reason at all. Even if she was finding his closeness more than a little disturbing. It was even more disturbing when he tucked the stray lock of hair behind her ear. Doubly so. Now he could see the expression on her face, and his gentle touch had made her stomach squirm in a very unsettling way – and she was sure it showed.

'At home and happy, but sad?' He chuckled, a low, vibrating sound that sent a tingle down her spine. She should pull back, but she couldn't. 'I'd say I'm rubbish.'

'They were happy tears.'

'Really?' He looked sceptical.

'The pups made me a bit broody.' Now he looked startled, and had definitely shot back in his seat. 'Not that way.' She laughed, suddenly freed from the intense scrutiny. 'I have absolutely no desire at all to have a baby yet. I had a dog once,' she shrugged, 'it just reminded me of happy times I suppose.'

'Ah. You said Miss Harrington wanted you to have one of the pups. Maybe it's a new strategy, wear you down. Send you in there alone, shower you with doggy goodness.'

'They are gorgeous. I guess it's dangerous to have got that close.' She laughed, but it sounded hollow. She could have hung on to that puppy forever, taken it home, promised to look after it. Something to hold, something to love of her own, that would never let her down.

'I daren't ask what you're thinking.' Charlie had somehow moved in closer again, his fingertips brushed over her cheek. She glanced up. Met that soft gaze head on, and when he dipped down she leaned in. Closed her eyes. Felt the gentlest, sweetest kiss as his lips covered hers.

'Sorry. I shouldn't have done that. I really shouldn't have done that.'

'It's, er...' Okay sounded a bit lame.

'I think it's probably time I checked up on that cat before this gets embarrassing. Thanks for the drink.'

'Right. Good, you're welcome, er Charlie?'

But he was already up off the bench and heading across the green, covering the ground easily with long strides.

Lucy stared after him, her fingers resting on her lips. That had felt and tasted so good. She swallowed hard. Too good.

Who'd have thought that the hardest part of living in Langtry Meadows would be trying not to fall head over heels in love with the village vet?

Chapter 16

A mass of bright colour tumbled across the narrow, winding footpath and Lucy stood, secateurs in hand, wondering where to start.

She'd promised herself that she'd spend as much time as she could during the half-term holiday out in the garden. It was rapidly spiralling out of control, but now she wasn't quite sure what to do. Glorious was the first word that sprung to mind, followed by abundant, and despite the fact that she normally liked everything tidy and under control, she appreciated this wild abandon. It seemed so wrong to chop any of the plants back, just to make them look neat.

She twisted from side to side, biting her lip, torn with indecision. She could cut some of the flowers and put them in vases in the cottage, and she could tie back some of the more sprawling plants. But then what?

'What a fantastic garden.'

Lucy jumped and spun round, nearly falling over. 'Mum! What are you doing here?'

'I thought it was about time I saw where my little girl was

hiding out.' She smiled. 'Have you got a little hug for your mum then?'

Lucy had more than a little hug. She dropped the secateurs, and the few flowers she'd snipped off, and wrapped her arms round her mother. It was true that she often hid out, but it wasn't because they had a poor relationship, but rather because it could be easier. Her mum would admonish her for working too hard, ask why she didn't go out with friends more, why she hadn't got a boyfriend. Why she hadn't even got a dog. And it was simpler to hide from it. She'd realised that since she'd moved to Langtry Meadows, since she'd realised how much she actually *liked* it here, and how much she'd miss the place when she left. And one person in particular. Even if they were now doing a spectacularly good job of avoiding each other. Stolen kisses seemed to have that effect on them.

'Fancy a cup of tea?'

'I'd love one, Lucy. Let's sit out here in the sunshine, it's beautiful. How on earth did you find a place like this? They must be paying you well in this new job!'

Lucy laughed. 'The place kind of found me, and they aren't even paying me masses, but as I'm house and pet sitting the rent is next to nothing.' She suddenly stopped. 'How did you get in without Gertie spotting you?'

Her mum grinned. 'I just said hello and she seemed quite happy, much more easy-going than some geese are. You probably don't remember, but the farm up the road from where we used to live had lots of them, the lady there told me they needed to know who was boss! Right, you put the kettle on dear, and leave the snippers with me. I'll do a bit of tidying,

I used to love pottering about in our old garden. It wasn't as big as this, but it was pretty and more than a little wild if you took your eyes off it for more than a day or two.'

'You look well, darling. I think losing your job might well have been the making of you.' Trish Jacobs put her cup of tea down and studied her daughter.

Lucy grimaced. 'I still have to find another permanent job.'

'You can't stay here? Oh that's a shame.'

'I've got the house and...'

'Well houses can be sold.'

'Mum!'

'Okay, okay, you know it's always your choice. But it is lovely here, and you do look well on it. Just look in the mirror, Lucy.' She lifted her cup again, and watched Lucy over the rim. 'It's different to the village we lived in when you were little. I don't suppose you really remember it.'

Lucy knew this was the opening, she could ignore the comment, the uneasy feeling in the pit of her stomach, they could move on. Or she could ask all the questions that had started to niggle at her, ask about the gaps in her background that she'd never thought existed until she'd come here. 'Not really, Mum. We never talked about it after we left, did we?'

Her mother ignored her. 'When I popped into the village shop to ask where your house was, they were lovely in there. Very friendly and helpful.'

'They are.'

'I suppose if things had been different between me and your dad then it might have been the same in Stoneyvale,' she pursed her mouth in the way she used to, just before she said *never you mind, now do as you're told*, 'but we just weren't compatible, love. We got married too quick, to prove people wrong, and then I stuck it out as long as I could. I really did Lucy.' Lucy didn't say anything. She'd always thought her mum had just walked away. And changed their lives forever. But she knew now that there was more to it than that.

'What was he like?' She could hear the tremble in her own voice. He'd just been a father to her, she'd accepted him at face value, trusted that he was the best dad he could be. Built all her beliefs about her childhood on a foundation that she was sure had never existed. Now she wasn't sure she wanted to hear the full truth, but she needed to.

'Your father? Well we were younger than you are now when we moved in together.' Trish took a biscuit and chewed it slowly, as though working out how much she should say.

'Mum,' Lucy waited until Trish looked up, looked into her eyes, 'you know we need to talk about this, we said we would last time we chatted on the phone.' She hated herself for this, pushing her mother into bringing back memories she'd obviously tried to bury in the past. 'I need to start growing up, Mum. I can't be that little girl you protect forever.'

'You are my little girl though, Lucy.' She blinked and Lucy had a sudden urge to say it didn't matter. Her mother never cried. Never.

'I did come here to sort it all out though, explain. I owe you an explanation.' The words were hesitant, brittle, as though they'd crumble if she interrupted them.

'You don't owe me anything, Mum, it's just I need to understand.' She was whispering, but she knew that her mother heard every word.

'I know love.' Trish sighed and looked away from Lucy, out over the garden, and when she spoke again her voice was stronger. The voice of the resilient, determined mum she'd grown up with. 'I've been selfish hiding everything from you, but it was easier for me to just pretend none of it ever existed. I met your dad when we were at University, everything was new and exciting.' Her voice was almost wistful. 'Life was one big adventure.' A sad smile settled across her features. 'He could boss me around a bit, but it didn't seem wrong, it was quite fun, quite nice having a masterful man instead of one of those dopey boys who kept asking what I wanted.' She put the biscuit down. 'When you were born, he wanted to move back to Stoneyvale. He'd been brought up there, he was part of the village and it sounded wonderful – a country cottage with the man I loved sounded like a dream come true.' She sighed. 'I jumped at the chance, I didn't even think about it. He said it was the ideal place to bring up children, and he could have been right,' she studied Lucy, 'in different circumstances.'

'Dad said you were a city girl, you didn't belong, he said we were both outsiders and nobody really liked us.'

'Oh he said it alright, Lucy, and if somebody tells you things enough times you can start to believe them. But it wasn't true.'

'But why?'

'He wanted to alienate us, love. He wanted us to rely on him.'

'That's what you meant on the phone the other day when you said it wasn't me, it was him?'

'What you said about the piano was true darling. He didn't want you to do the things you loved, which is why he got rid of it. It was only fun to him when he was in control, when he was *making* you play it.'

'He didn't want me to have friends, did he?'

'No, he didn't want you to have friends, he wanted,' she broke the biscuit into tiny pieces, 'he wanted you to only have him.' Trish looked her straight in the eye for a moment, then looked away, started shifting the biscuit pieces around into a pattern.

'And what about Amy? Why didn't Amy write to me, come and see me? How could he stop her?'

'That wasn't your father, Lucy. I'm to blame for that. She didn't get your letters. I'm sorry Luce, but when we moved I thought a clean break was better. I thought you'd make new friends faster if you weren't trying to stay in touch with the old ones.'

She put a hand over Lucy's, then pulled back. 'I never wanted to tell you this,' she pushed a strand of hair back from the side of Lucy's face, the tips of her fingers cool, 'but I do want to be honest with you. Amy didn't even know where we'd moved to. Nobody did. I couldn't tell them and I couldn't go back to take you to see them.' She frowned. 'They weren't ignoring you Lucy, don't ever think that.'

'You didn't want anybody to know where we were?'

'Lucy, look at me.' When she met her mother's gaze she was shocked at the raw emotion there. The pain. Ashamed she was causing it, that she was making her discuss this. 'No. I was scared.'

'Scared of what?' But even as she said it, she knew. She remembered that wary stillness, the look on her mother's face that she'd only realised recently had been fear. This time it was her that reached out, grabbed her mother's hand. 'You were scared of him, Dad. It was him that you didn't want to find us.'

'I was. I was scared for both of us, Lucy. I've made mistakes, lots of mistakes. I realise that now. I should have told you the truth before now, lies always cause problems. But at the time my head was spinning, it was all just too much and I just did the best I could for you. You were only young, but one thing that broke my heart was not being able to let you keep your dog.' Her eyes were damp as Lucy stared into them. 'I had to give him to a friend of mine. If I'd left Sandy with,' she paused, 'him, he would have killed your dog.' She squeezed Lucy's hand tighter. 'I know you were on your own, but he wouldn't even consider a brother or sister for you, Sandy was all we were allowed.'

'Allowed?'

'Yes, allowed.'

'But that's...'

'Ridiculous?' She nodded. 'But that's how it was Lucy, he laid down the law and heaven forbid if I tried to do anything different. The house had to be cleaned every day, he'd check out for dust, and meals had to be on the dot.' Lucy was surprised to see a wry smile playing on her lips.

She remembered now, the way her mother would constantly

check her watch. She'd be agitated, double checking that everything was in its place. She'd just thought of it as normal. Never questioned it.

'That's why you didn't tidy our new place.'

'It was my tiny act of defiance.'

'But why couldn't you have just said no?'

Trish Jacobs slowly turned, and all of a sudden she looked old to Lucy's eyes. Sad. Not the cheerful we-can-do-anything mother she'd always been. 'I could have never said no to your father, never. I should have told you, but the time never seemed right, and then it all seemed so long ago. Best forgotten.'

Where had she heard that before? Elsie Harrington had said something similar. 'I never realised. He was just Dad, I thought it was normal.'

'I know, love. I thought our marriage was just normal at first. But in a way I just wanted you to remember the good bits, not find all this out.' Trish stood up, and slowly followed the little path in amongst the flowers. Lucy followed, watching the petals fall from flowers as her mother brushed past them. Smelling the camomile crushed beneath her feet. 'It was fine at first, good, I loved him. Then he started setting down rules. It was funny at first, but then I realised he was serious. He was scaring me.' She stopped and turned round. 'I was petrified that he'd take it out on you, and he knew.'

'When he held me tight and said we didn't need you, he was just taunting you wasn't he?' An involuntary shiver ran down Lucy's spine as the full horror hit her. Her life could have been so different, so much worse, if her mum hadn't done what she had. It could have been her with the bruises, her always looking out, never having the opportunity to make friends. To change her life.

'Having you was the best thing that had ever happened to me, and that gave him power.' Trish's voice was little more than a whisper. 'I thought somebody in Stoneyvale would notice, that we weren't allowed out, that I walked into more doors than a blind man,' she took a deep inward breath, 'then I realised that they wouldn't help me. It wasn't that they didn't care, but they knew your dad, his family, they just couldn't see it, couldn't imagine somebody they knew doing that. People don't see what they don't think is possible. They believed the excuses not the truth, and he gradually, one snip of a thread at a time, cut off all our contact with everybody else.' She sighed, a long drawn out sound that made Lucy suddenly afraid. 'For a very brief time I thought I'd be better off dead, then I looked at you,' she swallowed, and when she spoke again her voice held a hint of the briskness Lucy was used to, 'and knew I couldn't do that.'

She reached out to grab her mother's hand. To hold on, make sure she'd never go. 'Oh God, Mum, no, no you should have never thought that.'

Trish smiled. 'I couldn't leave you, darling.'

'And he didn't leave us, and marry somebody else.' Lucy spoke slowly, the words slotting into place as she spoke. Completing the jumbled up jigsaw of her life.

'No, Lucy. He didn't leave us. We left him, I walked out, ran out, because I knew that one day he'd really hurt me, or worse that he'd turn on you. He always said he would if I told anybody. After your party, the last one you had, he said

285

that if I did it again he'd kill Sandy and make you watch, and that I'd know it was my fault. I'd made him do it.' She gulped. 'I never meant to tell you that,' she'd gone pale and Lucy instinctively moved even closer, put her arms round her mother, 'you shouldn't hear horrible things like that, but you need to know. I hated him Lucy.' She stared at her daughter. 'I would have killed him if he'd laid a finger on you, then what would you have left?' She rested her hands on Lucy's shoulders. 'When you were a baby he was nice, a generous father, but once you got a bit older you were just another bargaining tool, a way of making me do what he wanted.'

'He scared all my friends off, didn't he? It was him.'

'He liked to control who you mixed with, cancel play dates, respond to invites and say you couldn't make it. It was his game, he didn't want you to know, that way you'd cling to him not hate him. After your party when he'd lost his temper some of the parents decided not to have anything to do with us.'

'Heather's parents?'

'Oh yes, they didn't think about how cruel it was when they left you out. In their minds they were just sending him a message, but he didn't care.' She gave a short, bitter laugh that held an unexpected sadness. 'I couldn't stay after that, after hearing you crying your heart out and him complaining about the noise. He told me to shut you up or he would, and it was the last straw. That party was my trigger Lucy, I hung on like hell to the sheer anger that he'd upset you like that, and I packed, did everything in a whirlwind, as fast as I could before he came home. If he'd walked in that door before we left then I'd have never been able to escape the nightmare.'

'He never loved me, did he?' Charlie's words jumped into her head, his total dedication, his passion for a daughter who might not even be his.

'He loved you in his own way, but I don't think he loved anybody in the normal way. He would never have let anybody else harm a hair on your head, but he thought he was different. We were his, Lucy. Belongings. I'm not asking you to understand or forgive me, I know you hated it when we moved but I just tried to ignore it, pretend everything was alright, I didn't know what else to do. I wanted you to have a proper life, to be able to make your own decisions. Be independent. It wasn't alright, was it?' Trish shook her head. 'I was so busy trying to make a home for us that I didn't help you like I should have, I wasn't a good mother.'

'You were.' She had been, even if the chaotic life hadn't been what Lucy wanted. But she carried on as though Lucy hadn't spoken. 'You gave me everything, Mum.'

'I was scared, I had to go where he couldn't find us, that's why I cut you off from your friends. I had to disappear. Start again or he would follow us,' she gave a wry smile, 'he would have made us go back, he was very persuasive your father. People like that are. Clever.' She squeezed Lucy's shoulders, then let her hands drop to her sides and stood up straighter. She turned away, suddenly unsure of herself. 'Don't hate me, Lucy, please. I didn't mean to mislead you. It was just once I started...'

'I don't hate you, Mum.' Lucy put a hand out to stop her. 'I could never, ever hate you. You're the best mum anybody could hope for. I just wished I'd realised what you were going through, and I hadn't been such a selfish brat.'

'You were never a brat Lucy.' Trish smiled. 'You've always been the love of my life.'

Lucy flung her arms round her, buried her face like she had as a little girl.

'I'd have done anything for you sweetheart.' She wrapped her arms round her daughter.

'You did, you did everything, you were so brave.' She knew her words were muffled, but she didn't want to let go.

'I just did what any mother would.'

'Oh no.' Lucy thought of Josie who seemed to be playing games with her own beautiful daughter, of Charlie who was so much more of a father than hers had ever been, of Elsie who she was sure had let her own child go. 'You did far more than a lot of mums, if you hadn't have done what you did our lives, my life, would have been totally different.' For a moment she went cold. It didn't bear thinking about. And if her mother had given in to her pleas and let her get in touch with Amy, he would have found them. 'I'm so sorry I nagged at you, didn't make the best of things.'

'You were so young Lucy, children hate change, but you were brave. You made the most of it.' Trish slowly edged Lucy away, held her at arm's length and studied her face. 'Look at you now. You can't believe how proud I am of you.'

Lucy could feel the dampness on her face then, the tears she couldn't hold back. She flung herself back into her mother's arms, then swallowed the lump down. 'I'm proud of you too Mum.'

Chapter 17

Charlie stared at the cat and wondered if he was seeing things. If he was still drunk. If he was in fact still asleep. He hadn't been sleeping particularly well the last few nights.

Two images were haunting him the second he relaxed and closed his eyes. A young child from his past, and a woman who was very much from his present. But neither as far as he could see were ever going to be a part of his future.

The first he missed so much it left him clenching his fists, fighting the desire to curl into a ball and cry. The second he'd been avoiding.

Lucy.

Lucy who could soon be moving on, whatever Timothy Parry and Elsie Harrington had in mind.

But he'd kissed her.

Unintentionally.

Well, it had been intentional. It had definitely been intentional. You didn't kiss a woman like that by accident. But he hadn't intended to. He hadn't even known he was about to, until it was too late.

It had just been an impulsive gesture. She'd gazed at him,

looking slightly insecure, vulnerable, but totally lovable and kissing her had seemed the right thing to do. The natural thing. She'd just made him feel comfortable. Which he was far from feeling afterwards.

Years ago he'd probably have seen it as the ideal situation. Two ships passing in the night. Colliding in a village that wasn't home to either of them. Having undeniably hot and lustful sex, then moving on with their own lives. In opposite directions.

Shit, where had the 'hot and lustful' bit come from?

He felt himself break into a cold sweat, and tried to focus back on the animal that was glaring at him from his consultation table.

Charlie didn't know what had come over him. He'd asked Lucy out for a drink because he didn't really want time on his own to think, and he was being selfish – he just liked her company. And of course he'd owed her a full explanation. She understood, if anybody could help him make sense of his life, Lucy could. Not that it was fair to ask her.

'She just appeared like that for her breakfast this morning. Walking funny she was.' He blinked at the ginger cat, who stared back disapprovingly, so looked up at his client. 'I said to my Albert, there's something funny about that cat. He's not keen anyhow, and the cat isn't keen on him, so he couldn't catch her. I waited 'til he'd gone to deliver the post and I caught her, and here we are.'

Here we were indeed. Very firmly in the here and now, and not thinking about hot sex, or any of his other problems. 'So she's er, not very tame, Mrs Graham?' It looked fairly friendly, if a bit perplexed, but cats were like that. Especially cornered cats, he'd got the scratches and bites to prove it.

He'd actually likened Lucy (only in his mind of course) to a cornered cat, but she was more like a cute puppy. Adorable, loving, devoted to her cause... Cat. Concentrate on the cat.

'Oh it's not our cat, duck.'

'Sorry? Not your? But I thought...' He glanced at his computer screen.

'Well it thinks it's our cat. In our house all the time it is, but my Albert says we shouldn't have a cat. What do you think it is then?' She nodded a head towards the cat's middle, which was encased in a snugly fitting white tube. Like a corset.

Charlie had not had a good night's sleep and his powers of deduction appeared to have been shot to pieces. Seeing Maisie again had been an actual physical shock, kissing Lucy had left an image of her imprinted on his brain and affecting his bodily parts, and the time in between spent eating, drinking or staring at case notes that swam dizzyingly in front of his eyes had left him feeling like he'd been on a night march with a rucksack full of bricks.

He'd woken up this morning with a banging head, and the shakes. Looking at himself in the mirror had been a mistake, and he felt sorry for any clients.

'I'm not quite...'

'My Albert said to wedge it in his vice and leave the cat to wriggle its own way out. He said it had got itself into the fix so it could darn well get itself out. But that wouldn't be right now, would it? Poor thing.'

'No, it wouldn't be...'

There was a brief knock on the door, then it opened cautiously and Sally peeped round. Looking as full of life as she always did. 'Sorry Charlie,' she spotted the cat, and grinned, 'a cat flap would be a better idea, Mrs Graham.'

'What do you mean, duck?'

'You've got one of those window extractor fans in your kitchen haven't you? I've seen it when I've been round.'

'Well yes, but it's old and broken. It lets in a draft it does. I've told our Albert to get off his fat bottom and put a new pane of glass in. But...'

'I bet you the centre tube has gone missing,' she pointed at the tube round the middle of the cat. 'You go home and check. I've seen it before, cats like crawling through things. You've left the door shut so it's decided to climb through the window.'

Mrs Graham chuckled, a loud sound that built up like a tsunami and left her whole body trembling. 'Well I'll be damned, I reckon you're right from them cobwebs on it. Needs a good clean. Our Albert thought shutting the door on the cat would be enough. Would you credit it, little bugger.' She stroked the cat's head affectionately and it purred. 'You're not going to be outsmarted by a man, are you pet?'

Sally grinned at Charlie, who couldn't even summon the energy to respond. 'I'll take him through to the back where it's quiet, we'll need to make him drowsy so we can pull it off. I'll ring you later, okay Mrs Graham?' She opened the door, and gestured. Mrs Graham edged obediently over.

'She will be okay?'

'Of course she will, just come with me and sign the consent form then I'll give you a call as soon as she's ready to go home.' She ushered Mrs Graham through the door then looked back at Charlie. 'The cat will be okay but I'm not so sure about you. I'll make you a strong coffee, then I'm afraid you've got an emergency to go out to.'

'Oh God,' he rested his head in his hands, 'please don't tell me Serena's squashed that flaming dog again.'

'No.' She giggled. 'Lucy's lazy pig is acting, to put it in her own words, like he's had a night on the tiles.' She pulled the door half shut. 'A bit like you. Caffeine shot on the way.'

'Pig?'

'Pig. Pork-chop,' she grinned, looking alarmingly cheerful, 'that's his name not his state. I could always ask her to bring it in if you like?'

He wasn't taken in by the innocent tone. Lucy trying to control a pig in his waiting room was a crazy image too far in his muzzy head. 'Can't she call the vet up the road?' It wasn't that he didn't want to see her, it was the opposite. With each day that had passed he'd got more and more desperate to catch a glimpse of her. But what good would seeing her do? 'They're better with large animals.'

Not seeing each other was by far the most sensible solution. Then she could move on. She'd be much better off getting involved with a man like Matt Harwood, who was more than up for some mild flirtation to fill in his days, than a screwed up vet with a work addiction and a daughter.

'Charlie!' Sally tutted, as though she knew exactly what he was thinking. 'This is a very small pig. Honestly, anybody would think you were avoiding her.'

* * *

'Good afternoon.' Charlie stood there awkwardly, his case held between them like a protective barrier. 'Sally said you had a bit of an emergency.'

Lucy stared. She hadn't actually seen him since kiss-gate. 'Sorry, I wouldn't have called if I wasn't worried.' She'd actually been hoping for an over-the-phone diagnosis from Sally. 'I was going to come in, but you were busy, and Sal said...'

'It's fine.' His voice was mild, a hint of a smile at the corner of his mouth even if his eyes were a bit wary. 'It is my job.'

'Ahh yes, dealing with emergencies.' Okay, so this wasn't quite as embarrassing as she'd thought it might be. She'd honestly considered calling the vet in the next village. In fact, she'd looked up the number, and lifted up her phone to dial it. Then told herself she was being childish. Then double-checked on the pig to see if it really did look ill. And then after all her faffing about had decided it really did look like an emergency (unless she was prepared to message Annie and tell her that she now had a freezer full of sausages and bacon, but a pig-sized gap in the garden).

His mouth really was attractive, it tipped naturally at the corners (apart from when his lips were pursed which meant he was thinking, or cross with her) and his lips were just full enough but still masculine. Firm looking. Well they felt firm too, from the fleeting contact she'd had with them. Oh hell, she was going red. 'It is an emergency. Honestly.'

He was watching her intently, as though waiting for something.

'Or I wouldn't have...'

'Well do you think you should show me?'

Now she looked a complete numpty. Of course he was waiting. To see the patient.

Pork-Chop.

'It's Pork-Chop, the pig.'

'And,' he paused, 'what appears to be the matter with Pork-Chop?' His mouth twitched. 'How on earth could anybody call a pig that?'

She grinned. 'I'm beginning to think Annie has a quirky sense of humour. She's got all kind of weird things in the cottage, including a stuffed owl called Hoot. I had to turn it round, it was watching me.' He was watching her now, and it was a bit disconcerting. Better to stick to the matter in hand. 'He's er, acting a bit like he's drunk.'

'Drunk?'

'Drunk. Come on I'll show you. He's been all, well, trembly, and staggering about a bit.'

'Drinking?'

'Yes, it's like he's been drinking.' She stared. She'd already said that. 'But he's not actually drunk, I mean I'm not stupid I haven't been giving him...'

'I mean has he been drinking a lot?' He looked amused. 'Water as opposed to beer?'

'Oh, water.' Now he thought she was stupid, as well as a groupie. 'Well actually, yes, he has. I wondered if I'd not filled the trough up properly. But he's off his food, too.'

He really did have nice, long elegant fingers thought Lucy as Charlie ran his hands over the pig (she wondered what it would be like to have him run them over her?). He took his temperature (not as nice), checked his heart rate then straightened up. 'Has he been panting much?'

'Not much.'

Charlie ran his fingers through his hair, looking worried.

'He is going to be okay, isn't he?' Oh hell, how would she explain this to Annie?

'Fine.' Charlie snapped shut his case 'Sun stroke.'

Lucy stared. Sun stroke? She had a sudden image of the pig with a sunhat on as he pottered around the garden. She was losing her marbles. Maybe that was the heat as well. When she'd first arrived in Langtry Meadows, Liz Potts had reminded her of Mrs Tiggy-Winkle, and in a weird kind of reversal she was now seeing the pig in some kind of human form.

'Are you okay?' Charlie was frowning at her.

'Sure, sure. Er.'

'Well, heat stroke really to be more precise.' He leaned over and pushed open the window at the back of the pig shelter. 'He's come in here probably to get out of the sun, but there's no real air circulation. It's a bit like a sauna.'

'Oh crumbs, I've been frying him.'

He chuckled. 'Not quite. More like steaming.'

'I didn't even notice you could open that window, let alone think about doing it. I just thought it was open at this side, and...' She hadn't thought at all. Poor Pork-Chop.

'It was a good thing you spotted he was a bit distressed quickly.' He opened the pen. Stood right next to her, and she didn't know about the pig, but she was burning up. 'Pigs generate quite a lot of heat.' Like her then. 'And they aren't very good at regulating their temperature, they only sweat through their snouts.'

'Ah.' She wiped her sweaty palms down the back of her shorts, at least she hadn't got a drippy nose even if she was as pink as a pig.

'It's been warm for the time of the year, humid. We'll wash him down a bit, get some air circulating and he should be fine.' She could do with some air circulation herself. A fan. Luckily Charlie had hardly noticed her, he was looking at poor Pork-Chop.

'I'll get the hose pipe then, shall I?'

Washing a small grunting animal down should not be erotic, but crouching next to a hunk of male as she did it, and watching his capable hands reassuring the pig, was playing havoc with her mind, and her churning insides. Even if the vet in question did seem oblivious.

He wiped the back of his arm over his brow and grinned. 'It is a bit warm in here.'

'I've got some lemonade, fancy a glass? Or are you busy?' She was holding her breath, waiting for his answer, and it came out in a rush when he said yes. Along with a ridiculous grin. Why the hell was she so happy about him saying he'd stay for a quick drink?

The poor man was sweltering, and he was probably about to tell her that when he'd kissed her it had been by accident. Which was good. She hadn't got time for awkward moments with men. In a few weeks' time she'd be packing up and leaving the place.

The twinge in the pit of her stomach was unexpected, and

she sighed as she stood up, plastered a smile on her face and headed in to get the drinks.

'Oh.' He fumbled in his pocket as his phone rang. 'Better check that.'

'Another emergency?' Please don't be.

'Emergency or not, I'm still parched, so I'm having that drink with you.' He smiled reassuringly, as though she'd said the words out loud. Oh hell, she hadn't had she?

Lucy looked round, holding the two glasses of lemonade, and thought Charlie had actually done what he'd said he wouldn't. And dashed off. To avoid any discussions about 'the kiss' no doubt. Then she spotted him. Sat on the small bench that was half hidden by the old, gnarled apple tree, his head in his hands.

'Charlie?' He opened his eyes, looked through his fingers at her feet, then with a weary sigh he let his gaze drift up. She frowned down at him. He'd done it again, one minute happy and relaxed, and now looking like she'd done something terrible. Which apart from nearly cooking the pig, she hadn't. Well not recently. And not that he knew of.

He ran his fingers through his hair and slowly sat up straight.

'Do you mind if I sit down?'

'No, no, of course not, sorry.' He shuffled up a bit. Made some room.

She took a sip of her lemonade, sneaked a look at him under her eyelashes. He was staring at his hands, which were wrapped round his untouched drink. Fingers twitching ever so slightly, even though he'd got them so tight the colour had leached out of his skin.

'Charlie,' deep breath, 'is everything okay?'

'Fine.'

So that put her straight on that one. Even though he didn't look okay. He looked all uptight, like he had the day he'd fled from outside the school. Maybe a different approach. 'Do you mind if I ask you something?'

He gave a short laugh. 'What are you going to badger me about now?'

'Nothing. It's not work.' Another deep breath. 'Okay, tell me to mind my own business.'

'Is that going to work?' He had an eyebrow raised. 'Would you take the slightest bit of notice?'

She pulled back affronted, then relaxed again. 'You might be right. I don't tend to butt out easily.' But maybe if she'd persisted with her mum all those years ago, she would have got an explanation sooner. Understood. Realised that it wasn't all about her.

'Spill. I know having to see me again was a bit of an ordeal.' He made a bit of a harrumph noise and a glimmer of a smile appeared. 'But there's something else, isn't there? It's just,' no polite way of putting this, 'you look like you've seen a ghost.' He didn't immediately tell her to shut up, which was good. 'And it's just you looked like that the other day, when you scowled at me, well Jill, at school. The day Maisie...'

'As good as.' He put his hand over his mouth, pinched his nose between finger and thumb, and then exhaled. 'I feel like I've seen a ghost.'

Charlie wasn't okay. One phone call and his world had just been tipped upside down. Again. He felt a bit like a hamster, caught on the wheel, ploughing on blindly.

The warmth of Lucy's thigh against his was slightly comforting. 'Have you been called out?'

'What?'

'The phone call, when I went in to get a drink?'

He gave a short, snort of a laugh. 'I wish. That was Josie. She left a voicemail.'

'Oh.' She fell silent, studied her glass. 'Do you want to talk about it?'

She didn't even sound like she was that keen to hear, and his instinct was to say no. He'd said no to everybody. To his mother, father, to Eric, to Sally. But for some strange reason talking to Lucy was different. 'It's okay, I've unburdened myself enough on you. It's not fair, I...'

'Charlie!'

'It's complicated.'

'I know.' Her voice was soft. 'I thought we were friends?'

Friends. Yeah. That's what he'd said, but his body didn't seem to have bought into it. He'd kissed her, he'd told her the sob story of his life, and at the end of the summer they'd be going their separate ways. Never see each other again. What kind of friend did that make him?

'You've got problems of your own.'

'I'm fine. Believe me. I'm almost beginning to believe I might want to stay here longer.' She was smiling, encouraging.

This girl he'd only known a few short weeks, knew far more about his problems than anybody, and he knew she wouldn't judge. She'd be a good listener. But it didn't seem fair. But every time he tried to step back from her, he found himself drawn back. He couldn't help it. Couldn't help himself.

'I want to help.'

'Okay.' He took a gulp of the drink, let the ice cold liquid smooth his throat. 'When Josie told me she was pregnant I'd be lying if I said it was the best day of my life. We hadn't planned it, it was a bit of a shock, we were busy working, building the practice up. To be honest we hardly had time to share a meal, let alone make babies.' He laughed, never a truer word spoken in jest. 'But then when that tiny baby arrived she was perfect, I'd never loved anybody or anything like I loved that red-faced bundle. I brought her up, thought she was mine. She was born after we got married, so I guess the assumption was fair.' He fought to keep the anger under control.

'Totally.' Her word was soft, just filling the gap.

'Then she told me she'd had an affair and it all blew up.' His stomach churned as the day he'd tried to block out came rushing back.

It had more than blown up. What had started as simmering anger, a hint of distrust, had exploded into a battle of words, accusations.

'I thought it was something we could sort out, but how wrong can you be? She told me I was married to my job and what the hell was she supposed to do. She'd had an affair. Lots of them. I still didn't get it at first, until I said I'd never give up Maisie, then she told me. Maisie wasn't mine, she wanted a divorce, and she wanted me out of their lives. End of.' God, he'd been so stupid. How could he have been so wrong about everything? He'd loved her, loved them, and it had all just been some kind of twisted game – with him as the loser.

'Maisie was my daughter, I saw her enter the world, I'd fed her, changed her, sat with her at night when she woke up crying, rocked her back to sleep. I watched her take her first steps, heard her say her first word.' He could hear the break in his voice, felt Lucy slip her hand into his, but he couldn't stop talking now he'd started. 'I watched her pull at her first wobbly tooth, made her giggle with silly animal noises.' He'd kissed her knees better when she'd fallen over, watched the wonder that was his child as she slept at night.

'Oh, Charlie.' Lucy looked down at the floor. Then back up at him, before squeezing her hand in his.

He studied their clasped hands. He'd never thought he had that much love in him, until Maisie had come into his life. Then she'd been snatched away and it had taken every bit of willpower he had to get through the days that followed.

He'd always been a workaholic, but he'd taken it to a new level afterwards. He'd pushed himself until the words danced between his aching eyes, until he felt dizzy with fatigue. 'I came here to get away.' What else could you do when your lives had been so entwined? 'We had set up a veterinary practice between us, I had to get out.' He shrugged. 'But I don't know what the hell she's playing at now.' Just when he'd started to get a grip again. When he'd allowed himself to relax, to think that there was a way forward. A new, different life.

There was one easy solution, much as it would break his heart not to see his daughter, it was worse to see her messed around, used in whatever twisted way Josie had in mind. 'Don't let her come here.'

'Sorry?' Lucy looked startled.

'Tell her there are no places until September. I just need time.' He could be gone by then, or at least know that a court had ruled he'd always be in Maisie's life. Unlikely, but a straw he'd clung on to.

'It's not up to me Charlie, but we can't do that. You know we can't, the school needs as many children on the register as it can get. It's fighting for its life, Charlie.'

'So am I.' He had felt like he was, at first. But things had started to get better. Until now.

'It's not my choice. Timothy isn't going to turn anybody away.'

'I know, I know. Sorry, it was a stupid thing to say. I didn't mean it.' But Josie had meant it when she'd said she didn't want him in their lives. That he couldn't see Maisie, that it wouldn't be fair. She'd thrown that last bit in knowing it would be the decider. He'd want to be fair. However much it hurt him in the process.

'But you want to see Maisie, don't you?'

'Oh Christ yes.' More than anything. 'But you know why I bolted the other day.' He looked at Lucy. 'It would break my heart to hold her again then have to say goodbye.' It would kill him to have her in his arms again, than have Josie say it was all a big joke. He made an effort to pull himself together. It was either that, or crack. 'Anyhow, the phone call. Apparently

Josie had been round to the surgery looking for me when I was out on a call and Sal forgot to tell me.'

'Sal forgot?' Lucy gave him a look.

'Okay, I never read my messages. Anyhow, Josie says we need to talk.' He resisted the urge to roll his eyes.

'You do.'

'She was ringing to let me know about the school,' he gave a harsh laugh, 'bit bloody late now. She said she hoped I was going to be reasonable about it all. I've not seen Maisie for months. She'll either hate me—'

'I doubt—'

'I was there one day, gone the next. She'll either hate me or be completely confused.'

'She'll be pleased to see you.' Lucy dropped her voice. 'Whatever Josie has said to her, children are very forgiving at that age, and it's surprising how adaptable they can be if we don't burden them with all our baggage. You didn't abandon her, Charlie. You've got nothing to feel guilty about.'

'But she'll be devastated when I say goodbye again. And I haven't a clue what the fuck Josie has told her. For all I know she could have said I'm dead, or abandoned them, or...' No, he really hadn't a clue. What did a mother say to explain to a little girl that the man she's always called Daddy isn't? That she doesn't want them to meet again because it'll be 'confusing'.

'She could have told her that Daddy isn't actually Daddy for all I know, he's just a stand in and she's got a real, much better Daddy lined up. In fact, she might already have a new dad now. Maybe they're all heading here so we can be one big happy family.'

That didn't even bear thinking about. He'd loved Maisie as his own. She was his own as far as he was concerned. 'I do want to see her again, Lucy. It's not that I've run away. I've taken legal advice, but in the meantime I don't want her to see us screaming about who's done what. I just agreed we'd having a cooling down period, that she could take Maisie away and make a game of it, or whatever she wanted.' He paused. 'I don't want that little girl confused, I don't want her to feel that I don't want her. Whoever her biological father is.' He stood up, picked up the veterinary bag which was between his feet. 'I didn't intend seeing her again until I knew where I stood. Until I knew that I had a right to see her and it wasn't going to be a one off. Look, I better get back.'

'Charlie,' Lucy put a hand on his arm, 'you need to call Josie.'

'I know.'

'Soon.'

'Not right now. I need to simmer down, and I need a stiff drink.'

'I wasn't much older than Maisie when I lost my dad, Charlie,' he sank back down on the bench beside her, 'and it's taken until now for me to work out it wasn't my fault. That's a heck of a lot of wasted years. Think about it.'

'I've done nothing but think about it.' He felt exhausted.

'If you don't see Maisie again until it's all legal it could take, well I don't know, months, another year even?'

'That's what I'm frightened about.'

'A year's a long time for a little girl, Charlie.' She was so close to him now, her head leaning against his shoulder, and he automatically put his arm round her shoulder. She wrapped her arms round him, and it felt right. He didn't know the half of what had happened in her life, but he did know she understood. And he hoped they'd both be here long enough for him to find out more about her. 'Find out what Josie's told her, she's probably just said you're on holiday, or at work.'

'I'll call her.'

She looked up, just as he glanced down, and he couldn't help himself. This time he didn't stop at one tentative kiss, this time he kissed her lips a second time. Lingered until her lips parted, then they both pulled back at the same time. He cupped her face with one hand, closed his eyes so that he could really feel the softness of her skin.

'I really had better get off, I've got an afternoon surgery.'

She nodded, and this time didn't stop him as he stood up.

'Ring me,' she looked up, 'if the pig isn't any better.'

'Sure.'

'Or if you just want to ring me?' He tried a smile, even though the effort felt like it might crack his face. She gave one back and for some reason he felt a little bit better.

'How about I make you some supper later? Nothing fancy.'

'Sure.' He could see she was surprised that he'd said yes. 'As long as there's wine.'

'Sure. Buckets of it.'

Chapter 18

How exactly was she supposed to pitch this? Beans on toast in the kitchen? Pizza in front of the TV? It wasn't exactly a dinner date, well it wasn't a date at all. Well, he had kissed her. But then he'd run away. Then he'd kissed her again.

She could pretend that first kiss had been all him, that he'd taken her by surprise, that it was over before it began. But the kiss earlier, in the garden, was different. She'd responded, she'd wanted more, she'd reached out, wrapped her arms round him.

And it wasn't his fault, he had warned her his life was complicated, but she'd ignored it. Let her heart open up and let him in. But he was a father, a little girl's dad. Maisie needed him, and whatever the situation was with Josie, Lucy wasn't exactly mother material, or ready to be a mother, a substitute mother. Not that he was asking her to be. Maisie didn't need a mother, she had one. Oh God she was over thinking this. She covered her face with her hands. She'd asked him for supper. That was all.

But that kiss changed everything. That kiss had fed the ache in her heart, and she knew she was playing with fire. If she couldn't get her feelings under control then she really had to keep her distance or she'd be in serious trouble.

She looked out of the kitchen window to where Annie's large tabby cat was sunning itself by the apple tree. So much for sorting the garden out in her week off. Her mother's visit had led to a frenzy of hacking which had left her hot, sweaty and with a pile of clippings that needed disposing of.

Unfortunately they'd all been from the bottom of the garden, round the chicken coop, where nobody could find her. She'd needed some me-time. The chickens didn't really seem to appreciate her efforts that much and the garden still looked exactly the same from the cottage. Wild.

She sighed. Then just when she'd promised herself a proper day at it, Pork-Chop had thrown a wobbler. She'd never seen a pig pant before, or look like an old wheezy, drunken man about to keel over. But then she hadn't seen many pigs up-close before.

And then there was Charlie. Wonderful, clever, heartbroken Charlie.

This wasn't supposed to be an opportunity for them to finish what they'd started. She was here to offer support, booze and an ear. To help him work out a solution.

She took a handful of flowers out of the sink and stuck them roughly into a vase. When people did that on TV it looked artistic, her effort just looked like a bunch of flowers had been stuck into a vase.

Pizza would do. She'd got a freezer full. Cooking wasn't something she devoted a lot of time to, a once a fortnight trip to the nearest town and big supermarket meant she had enough ready meals in the fridge and freezer to keep her going during term time, and when she remembered she topped up on fruit and veg from the village shop.

During term time the most ambitious meal she tended to have was a baked potato with tuna and mayo, and a dash of sweet chilli sauce if she really was feeling adventurous.

Anyway, Charlie didn't look like the four course meal type, he was like her, on his own and a grab-and-go type of guy. Although maybe he thought she'd offer him something different, better? Arghh. She plonked the vase of flowers down in the middle of the pine table.

She was over thinking this. She was going to feed the cat, change her jeans (which she'd been wearing for gardening and pig washing), put a clean t-shirt on and open a bottle of wine. Then he'd be here, and she could offer him a choice of menu.

The cat, who had wandered in at the sound of a sachet of food being opened, looked at his bowl as though she was trying to poison him. 'Okay, I know it isn't the one eight out of ten cats prefer, but quite a few like it and it was all they had left in the village shop.' He stared. Inscrutable. 'I'd give you tuna, but I'm not even sure cats are allowed tuna. I mean, everybody says cats like milk, but then I read something that said they shouldn't have it.' He blinked. 'Cats can become lactose intolerant, did you know that?' He sat down, front feet tucked under so that he looked like he'd lost his legs. 'And they have diarrhoea, and I really don't want you to get a smelly bum like Mischief.' She pulled a face.

She needed a direct line to the vets, Jim had not been joking when he'd said it was handy having the surgery just up the road. 'So it's this food, or these biscuits?' She put both out and he sniffed at each bowl in turn, then sat down, stretched a back leg over his head and started to wash his bottom.

Lucy had never seen Charlie in a crisp white shirt before. Sleeves rolled up to show surprisingly strong, tanned forearms.

'I've brought you a present.' He held out a brown paper bag self-consciously, looking embarrassed.

'Oh, a present?' She took it gingerly.

'Aren't you going to look?'

'It's not alive?'

'Not exactly.' He looked at her bemused.

The smell hit her before she even had the bag open properly. Grassy, sweet, the smell of childhood summers, of juices dribbling down her chin, of her mother's laughing face. A smell good enough to make tears spring to her eyes.

'Sorry, I didn't...'

'Don't be sorry, they're perfect.' She sniffed. 'Nobody has ever brought me tomatoes before.'

He grinned with relief. 'I can quite honestly say I've never given them as a gift to anybody before.'

'You remembered.'

'Well I was called out to a smallholding on the edge of the village, I saw them and thought of you.'

He was making it worse, if she thought she could resist him before then she'd just found out it was going to be harder than ever. How could she not fall for a man who remembered the silly story she'd told him about fresh tomatoes, who knew that smell was one of the good memories from her childhood?

'And I brought wine just in case you were short.' He held out a bottle and she laughed.

'Another bottle is always welcome, but drink is one thing I never forget to buy. Cat food maybe, but drink never. Oh God, I sound like an alcoholic now, don't I?'

'A cat neglecting lush.' His eyes were twinkling as he followed her in and pushed the door shut. At least he looked a bit more cheerful now.

'Well I have got food, just not Tigger approved food.'

'Not wise to upset a cat, he'll be bringing mice in for you to demonstrate his superior hunting skills.'

'Great, that's all I need.'

'Pig okay?'

'Stop laughing at me. I've put all the animals on a spreadsheet.'

'Pink or blue?'

Oh no, he'd remembered her spreadsheets. 'Green or red depending on whether they're good to go or not. It isn't funny, this is my sanity at stake. How am I supposed to remember what they all eat, what to do if one of them looks constipated, another has got a runny bum and one is overheated and sweating down its snout?'

'You make animal ownership sound wonderful.' He really was laughing now, which was actually nice. 'Do you do everything by spreadsheet Miss Jacobs?'

'Not everything. In fact, not our supper. Just the animals. Four Seasons or Meat Feast?'

'Sorry? Is that a music choice?'

'I think you're getting confused with Meatloaf and The Four Tops, though I am of course far too young to remember either.'

'Of course. Me too, obviously. I blame our parents.'

'Pizza. I can offer a choice, no expense spared here.'

'Both. We need something to soak up the wine. I've not eaten all day.'

'I'll put the oven on then, and you can pour the wine. Funnily enough I've got a bottle already open.'

'Was she happy?'

Charlie's question came out of the blue, as he was finishing off the last slice of pizza and emptying the last of the wine from the bottle into their glasses.

But she knew who he was talking about. There was obviously only one person on his mind.

The words tripped out as though he couldn't stop them, as though they'd been there on the tip of his tongue since he'd arrived, and his voice had an edge to it that made her want to cry.

'She was.' She let herself move in closer, her voice softer as she thought about the sweet child that had reminded her a little of herself. 'She's a clever little girl, very bright.'

'She is.' He tugged at the foil on the neck of the bottle, slowly unravelling it.

'I'm really sorry I pestered you to come into school and talk to the kids.' It all made more sense now she'd seen just how cut up he was. How much losing his daughter meant to him. When she thought Charlie had been scared of coming in and chatting to her class, she'd teased him about it and carried on relentlessly. Oh God, she felt so guilty now.

Lucy took a sip from her glass. At least Charlie looked a

Summer with the Country Summer Vet

bit more his normal self than he had in the afternoon. He'd
tightened up the moment he mentioned Maisie, his jaw rigid,
shoulders tense, but at least he wasn't shaking like he had
been after the earlier phone call, and he wasn't as pale as the
day he'd seen her outside the school.

He just looked shattered now, and a little bit lost. She
wanted to throw her arms round him, tell him they'd sort it.
But she didn't. It would be false promises, and she knew all
about those.

'Well yep, it's all a bit raw, but I was being an idiot.' He
swirled the liquid round in his own glass and gave a wry
smile.

'No you weren't!'

'I didn't know if I was up to talking to a group of kids. I
know it's daft but I was worried I'd just be sitting there looking
at them and wondering what she was up to.'

'It's not daft. It's lovely, and natural.' Lucy cleared the plates
away and sat back down next to him. She wanted to sit closer,
exactly where she'd been before. But instead they had a polite
distance, and she wasn't quite sure if she should close it or
not.

'But anyhow, I'm glad you did use those infamous powers
of persuasion. I can't avoid kids for ever cos I'm feeling sorry
for myself, can I? And I enjoyed it, they're a bright lot.' He
sighed, brushed back the hair that had flopped on his brow.
'And I certainly can't now it seems. But,' he looked up, and
although his brown eyes were looking straight into hers, she
was sure he was thinking about somebody else. 'I don't get
it, I mean our break up was really nasty, but I never had Josie

down as evil. I don't get what she thinks she's playing at bringing Maisie here.' He shook his head and looked down into his glass. 'She loves Maisie, I can't see her doing anything to hurt her. But it seems I didn't know her at all did I?'

'She didn't seem nasty to me either.' She'd always thought she was a pretty good judge of character, and it was hard to picture Josie as somebody who'd do this type of thing. 'Actually, she did mention you, well not you by name. I mean, nobody else had a clue, but...'

'Oh?' He looked wary.

'Jill said that Josie had told her she wanted Maisie to be nearer her father.'

'But I'm not her father, am I?' He downed his wine and reached for the bottle again. 'I moved away so that she wouldn't have her life disrupted, so what the fuck is Josie doing bringing her here?'

'I don't know, Charlie.' She put a hand on his arm to catch his attention. 'But even if you're not her biological father, you are in every other way. What if Josie's changed her mind?'

'Oh no, she was pretty set that it wasn't me that had...' he paused as though he didn't know what to say next.

'She can't change that bit, nobody can, but she can change how it's handled.' This close she could almost feel the hurt rolling off him in waves, even if he was doing his best to close it off.

'It's too late for happy families, believe me that's not going to happen after what was said.'

'Maybe she's just going to move close enough so you can bring Maisie up between you?'

There was a haunted look in his brown eyes.

'Charlie, I never saw my dad again after my parents split and I would have done anything to have met up with him. I wrote him letters, begged him to see us. I know how it feels.'

He gave a heavy sigh. 'This is different, Lucy.'

'No, it bloody isn't.' She banged the fist that had been resting on his shoulder onto his chest in frustration, and he caught it in his own large hand. Closed his fingers around hers. 'There's a little girl out there, your daughter, and as far as she's concerned you're her dad.'

'If Josie's met somebody, or if she's with Maisie's real...' he faltered, 'I don't know if I can handle seeing that every day.'

'This isn't about you.'

'I know.' He ran his fingers through his hair. 'Christ, Lucy. I want to see her more than anything, God I've missed her every moment of every day, but I won't have her messed around not knowing where she stands. Surely that's worse? Surely she'd be better with them, and forget all about me?'

'She'll never forget you, Charlie Davenport. I can promise you that. She might love you, hate you, lash out at you, ignore you, but she will never ever forget you. Trust me.' She automatically squeezed his arm, willing him to believe her.

'I do.' He took a deep breath. 'Josie did try to ring me last week and I ignored it. And,' he swirled the wine in his glass, 'she tried to get hold of me at the surgery earlier on the day Maisie was in school. But of course I didn't know that then. I know, I know,' he held a hand up, 'I need to talk to her. I will. I promise. When I'm sober. Right, you said you'd got lots of drink, get the next bottle out.' He looked at her. 'I get her admitting that Maisie isn't mine, even though it hurts like hell, I get her wanting to own up. But why try and push me out of her life? Has she got the faintest idea what she did to me? She's an intelligent woman, Lucy. Smart.'

'Maybe she was ashamed, maybe she pushed you out before you had a chance to leave. She only put her name on the forms Charlie, no other guardian.'

He shook his head. 'Whatever her idea though, it's not fair. I won't be here much longer, I'm just a locum, here until Eric gets back, then who knows where I'll end up. If she really has had a change of heart and wants Maisie to see me, then this isn't going to work.'

'But you could stay?'

'I hadn't planned on it. I was thinking maybe a cattle station in Australia might suit me right now.'

Lucy stared at him. 'You're kidding!' She knew he'd mentioned moving on, knew that even though she was staying here longer, he might not. But, she'd thought he'd still be around, still be somewhere not too far away. Especially if he had Maisie to consider. The thought of him so far away, the other side of the world left her stomach feeling empty.

'Sure, joking.'

But even though she was a little bit drunk, she spotted the glimmer in his eye that said maybe he wasn't entirely.

'Lucy?' He was looking straight into her eyes and she realised with a start that she was practically in his lap. He'd not let go of the hand she'd banged on his chest, and her other was still clutching at his arm. 'That kiss.'

'It's fine, I...' she went to pull away but he didn't let go of her hand. If anything he pulled her closer. Against his warm body, his broad chest. Her side was pressed against his, his face was inches away. She swallowed.

'Earlier on I was going to apologise, say I didn't mean anything by it...'

'That's fine, I quite—'

'But I didn't say it, because it would have been a lie.'

'Oh.'

'It was a daft impulse at the time, but now I just want to try it again.'

'You do?'

'Just to see how it feels,' he tilted his head on one side. 'Would that be a problem?'

'No problem.' She was squeaking. Like a mouse. She cleared her throat. 'No problem.' He was going to kiss her. Then he was going to flee the country. Fine.

Her lips were still sounding the last syllable, parted in anticipation when his mouth covered hers. For a moment there was that polite gap between their bodies, then he shifted his hips round, threaded his fingers through her hair and pulled her hard against him. And she didn't care what was going to happen in the future.

Lucy was drowning; drowning in his taste, his smell, the feel of his strong body against hers. She was dimly aware of his thumb brushing against her jaw, of his other hand on her thigh, but all she wanted to do was press herself closer.

His tongue was exploring her mouth, skating over the edges of her teeth, and she caught her breath as his thumb rubbed over her nipple.

The warmth of his hand drifted down her body and it was her turn, to suck gently on his tongue until he groaned. A warm, deep sound that made her want more.

One finger strayed under the edge of her t-shirt and her stomach tensed, trembled in anticipation.

He paused, but she couldn't stop now. No way. This had been boiling up inside her since that May Day drink. She swung over astride his lap, ready to rip his shirt open, but she'd only managed to fumble the first button open when he stood up, sending them both to the floor in a tangle of arms and legs.

'I was going to say should I stop. But I guess...'

'No way.' Then he was peeling her t-shirt over her head as she managed to tug his shirt out of his jeans.

'You're bad. So bad.'

She wasn't sure if she was bad, he was bad, or what as he stumbled to his feet, kicked his shoes off and staggered about trying to get his legs out of his jeans. But it didn't matter.

'Miaow.' There was a loud indignant shout from the tabby cat as she flung Charlie's shirt triumphantly in the air, then it scarpered into the safety of the kitchen.

Lucy tilted her head. The early morning sun was edging its way into the room, a soft unobtrusive glow, a promise of something good.

Like the heavy arm across her body. She squinted at the man beside her. Now that had been something good. But should she have?

Except she had decided, the day after her mother had

visited, that from now on she was going to be completely open about everything. Absolutely everything. No covering up. No hiding stuff like her mum had done.

And admitting that she fancied the pants off Charlie (literally) had been unavoidable, especially once she'd realised he wasn't exactly immune to her.

She bit her lower lip, very aware of the fact that her legs were entwined with his, entangled. Dangerously entangled. She tried to tug one gently away, not wanting to disturb him, but her foot was going dead.

After her chat with her mum she'd seriously thought about giving in to her urges and having one of Elsie's puppies. Considered risking giving a little bit of her heart away, letting something more permanent into her life. But she was still considering. And that was just about having a puppy. That wasn't a *man*.

She squinted at the gorgeous, complicated man in question. He scared her.

So did the realisation that he'd got a daughter. She wasn't ready to be a step mum. Be responsible in that way.

Well it was just a pizza and a shag. He hadn't actually said, or even hinted he wanted more. And he'd be leaving Langtry Meadows soon. Maybe. Unless he stayed. Because of Maisie. And she stayed, because the school needed her.

Oh God, could she cope with the emotional upheaval? Falling into bed with somebody like Matt would have been fun, an adventure ... except she'd given up on the idea of just falling into a brief encounter years ago. If she really, really lusted after somebody it was because she really, really fancied them. It involved her heart, her mind, not just the hot, damp bit of body between her legs.

She was lying like this, slightly flattened in places (God he was solid), because she'd fallen hook, line and sinker for him. And that scared her.

He shifted. Opened one eye.

'You're thinking.'

She nodded.

'Dangerous.' He wrapped an arm round her shoulders and pulled her in tight against his chest, then sighed. 'Thinking can be a pain in the arse, can't it?' His words were muffled, his chin on her head.

He had bigger issues than what being in bed together meant. Being there to support and help him with the whole Maisie issue was one thing, no way could she abandon him and leave him to sort it on his own. If he wanted her, she was there. But that sounded bloody dangerous. Frightening.

'I've got a colt to castrate later, I suppose I better get up.'

Now what did she do? It was ages since she'd been in this position, and the last time she'd been younger, more confident about running around naked. Less wobbly all round. 'That sounds fun.' Fun? What had made her say fun?

'Not for the colt.' His tone was dry, amused.

'I'll let you use the bathroom first.' She was dying for a wee, but she could wait. She was pretty sure she could get dressed in the time it took him to go to the toilet. 'There's a clean towel by the bath.' She had a feeling her jeans were downstairs, abandoned somewhere between the sofa and the hallway.

'Great.' He threw the sheet back and she closed her eyes. Then opened them to peep as he headed stark naked out of the bedroom, nearly banging his head on the low beam as he went.

'I can rustle up toast and coffee if you fancy.' Once I've got my knickers on. He seemed to be doing a good job at keeping this casual, normal. The least she could do was join in.

Lucy paused as somebody rattled the door knocker. 'That'll be the milkman, I've not paid him for a while. Can't get used to the idea that somebody is actually leaving it on my doorstep. It's a bit like a tooth fairy.'

Charlie grinned. 'You're funny. Well go and do your fairy stuff and leave him some hard cash in return for his offerings!'

She stuck her tongue out, and dodged him as he went to grab her. 'Drink your coffee. You'll be late for your castration, whereas I, being on holiday, have all day.'

Lucy grabbed the money she'd left by the toaster and waltzed to the door, feeling more positive and at home since she'd arrived in Langtry Meadows. Having Charlie there was having a strange effect on her, making it feel almost like home.

Dangerous. But nice.

'Morning.' She flung the door open, then the words died on her lips.

'I was told I could find Charlie here.' It wasn't the milkman. It was worse. It was a slim woman, with glossy red hair, and pale china-doll face. Thin lipped. Josie. On her doorstep.

'Charlie.' It came out as little more than a whisper. But he was there behind her, as though he knew. Or maybe he'd just heard his ex's voice.

'Josie.' That one flat word held as much emotion as she'd ever heard.

'I've tried to call you, and you've ignored me.' Josie folded her arms and Lucy danced from foot to foot not sure if she should go. Although with Charlie slap bang up behind her, slipping away unnoticed wouldn't be an option. She'd have to crawl between his legs. 'Luckily somebody in the village told me where I'd find you.' Lucy tried not to let the groan out. Everybody in this place was so bloody accommodating. Or was it just her they were keeping tabs on?

Josie was looking them up and down and Lucy opened her mouth to object, but Charlie raised a warning hand and spoke first.

'I was going to call—'

'We need to talk. Now. I can't put this off any longer Charlie.'

It was Charlie's turn to fold his arms. 'Oh you're so right. We do need to talk. Maybe we needed to talk before you came waltzing over here with my,' he stopped himself, 'Maisie in tow.'

'Well, can we sit down like adults and talk now?'

'Give me one good reason.'

Josie sighed and her whole posture softened. She looked more like the woman that had brought Maisie into school. 'I've decided Maisie needs you in her life, but,' she gave Lucy a look, okay maybe she hadn't softened, 'you need to promise me that you're not going to complicate things by shagging her school teacher. Despite the fact that I have it on good authority,' she paused, 'that nobody can resist her charms.'

Chapter 19

'Making the most of the good weather, love?'

Lucy glanced up from her snipping and tying back duties, to see Jim pushing the garden gate open.

'I certainly am. Lovely isn't it?' She wiped her arm over her brow, trying not to smear soil down her relatively clean t-shirt.

'Everything in hand then? I told our Annie that you'd be the girl for the job.' He cast an eye over the garden. 'Looking tidier than when the old fool herself is here. You're a gem.'

Lucy wasn't sure she was a gem, but she was pleased that she'd passed the inspection. 'There was just one thing, actually.'

'Which is?'

'It's just all the garden rubbish, I wasn't quite sure if I was supposed to burn it? I can't fit it all in my bin or in my car to take to the tip.'

'Don't you worry about that, love. I can soon get that shifted for you. I've just been to see Miss Harrington, I do a bit of tidying there for her, and I can get your rubbish shifted the same time as hers.' He tapped the side of his nose. 'I know just the man for the job, and if he's doing what he should be he'll be on his way to her place now.' He started to root through his pockets and after a few minutes triumphantly waved his mobile phone in the air. 'Save me scampering back to her place if I use this, won't it?'

Lucy wasn't quite sure she could imagine Jim 'scampering' but she just smiled.

'Darned thing.' He jabbed at the keys with a stubby finger. 'Why do they make them so small and fiddly? It's one thing trying to see the darned numbers, and even worse trying to click on the buggers. These things were made for midgets. Ah, here we go.' He held it to his ear, and proceeded to bellow. 'It's Jim, Jim, yes can you come and collect some stuff from our Annie's when you're done there? Got the trailer haven't you lad? Splendid.' He took the mobile phone away from his ear, looked at it suspiciously for a moment, jabbed a button and dropped it back in a pocket. Rubbed his hands together. 'Right then, that's that sorted. Anything else I can help you with love while I'm here?'

'Brilliant. That's really kind. Do you want to come and see round the back, see the animals?'

'Not at all, not at all, I was just passing, not checking up on you.' He winked. 'Not that a girl like you needs keeping an eye on.' He took a hasty step back when Gertie popped her head round the corner of the house and Lucy laughed.

'She's fine.'

'She's the devil disguised in white she is.'

'Better than any guard dog.'

'Aye well, that's why our Annie keeps her I reckon. It's men she chases off, and our Annie always thinks there's something to be said for that.' He tutted. 'Silly fool.'

Lucy wasn't sure if he was talking about the goose or his sister.

'Ah, talking of old fools, I've just remembered.' He held up a finger. 'Timothy's sent out an email, emergency meeting first thing on Monday about the school's future.' He sucked air through his teeth. 'News isn't promising I'm afraid.'

Lucy stared at him. Meetings on the first day of term never sounded good. Why, when she'd started to feel so positive, did things have to go wrong? 'But I've just said I'll stay! They've not said they're closing it?'

'Not yet my love.' He sighed. 'Not my place to discuss it, but you will be able to get in early, won't you?'

'Of course I will.'

'Splendid.'

He stepped smartly through the gate, one eye still fixed on Gertie.

So what did they say about bad news coming in threes? Josie it seemed had killed any hope of her and Charlie ever progressing beyond a one night stand, and now just as she'd agreed to stay at Langtry Meadows longer, just as she was wondering whether maybe she should reconsider her life plan, it looked like she was going to be made redundant. Again. What on earth was going to go wrong next?

'You're looking serious. Think a hug will help?'

Despite his size, Matt, it seemed, could move pretty stealthily. Even Gertie hadn't had time to go into attack mode. He was standing a couple of yards from Lucy with a very welcome grin on his face.

'Well normally I'd say yes, but...' She waved her dirty hands in the air and then pointed down at her gardening clothes.

'The dirtier the better.' He winked and Lucy giggled. Then before she could stop him she was wrapped in a bear hug.

'What on earth are you doing here?' She was struggling to breath, but it was still nice.

'I came to move your garden rubbish, the trailer's parked just up the side, but I might just have to chuck you in it and take you home as well.'

'You wouldn't dare.' She chuckled and reached up to kiss his cheek. And before she could object he'd hitched one arm round her knees and had thrown her over his shoulder.

'Matt, stop it.' She was trying to thump his back, but was laughing so much there was no force in it at all. 'Matt, stop.' She was out of breath. 'You're such an idiot, but I do love you.'

There was a sharp intake of breath. And it wasn't Matt, (who was doing a fake stagger from side to side), and it wasn't Gertie who'd wandered off in disgust.

Even hanging upside down, she couldn't mistake who it was. Charlie. He had a face like thunder. Disaster number three. 'Seems that Josie was right about one thing.' He raised an eyebrow, his tone dry.

She hadn't heard that right had she? He couldn't have actually said *that*.

'Charlie, stop.' He was going to do it again, march off. 'Matt, put me down,' she pounded on his back, 'Charlie, stay right there.'

Matt didn't put her down, he wheeled round and gave

Charlie the thumbs up, so that she had to screw her body round to try and keep him in sight. He didn't stop, he was through the gate. He did pause though, and his voice was tighter than his rigid stance.

'I came to tell you what Josie had to say, and that it isn't up to her to lay down the rules, but I can see you're busy. My mistake.'

Shit. He was gone. Matt picked that moment to put her on her feet. 'Did I cock up?'

'No, Matt, it's not you.' She sighed. After that conversation with her mother she'd made a pact with herself, never to tell the smallest of white lies these days. 'Well it is a bit.'

'Ignore the daft bugger, he'll come round. Tell you what I'll take Archie in later and tell him the poor little thing has got a complex and wants a hair transplant. That'll give him something to think about.'

'You're potty. He'll tell you to piss off.'

'He can't.' Matt looked hurt. 'He has to be professional at all times once he's got his little green tunic on. I also want him to come and look at my lesbian cows, spend far too much time humping each other they do.'

Lucy smiled despite herself.

'I'll ask him for advice on how to seduce the most beautiful woman in Langtry Meadows.'

Lucy felt herself going red. 'Don't you dare!' She better cover herself here. 'Whoever she is. He's worried, he's got a lot on his mind.' She daren't say any more, she suspected that Charlie very much liked to keep his private and personal life just that.

'Oh Lucy, Lucy, Lucy, I really have lost you to that big oaf haven't I? You've broken my heart, destroyed my life.' He crossed his arms over his chest and swayed from side to side.

She thumped him. 'Stop right there, Matt.'

'Well until the Taverner's opens you have, then a couple of pints might put me right.' He winked. 'Right, well if you're going to be boring, where's this rubbish you want shifting?'

Charlie opened his eyes and stared at the bright green toe nails. Dainty, pretty feet with nice slim ankles.

He stood up and grabbed a cloth.

'You can't just ignore me you know.'

'I'm not ignoring you, Lucy.'

'Yes you are! You're tidying up round me as though I'm not here.'

'I have to tidy up.' As she was standing between him and the consulting table he walked round her, then started to wipe it down. 'Is there something wrong with one of your animals?'

'No there isn't. You know that isn't why I'm here.'

'I don't know anything.' He sprayed the table with more than enough disinfectant to kill any army of bugs. It had been a shock seeing Josie, and after fighting with her over his rights to see whoever he wanted, whenever he wanted, he'd felt like he'd been run over by a lorry. He'd called her a hypocrite, and every ounce of hurt flooded back through his body like a physical pain, and then they'd spent a tense hour talking about Maisie.

His instinct when she'd gone had been to rush over to Lucy. Explain. Tell her it didn't change anything between them. But 'anything' it seemed was 'nothing'. It couldn't be a bloody coincidence that every other time she saw him she was practically in the arms of the very footloose and fancy-free Matt Harwood. This time there had been no practically. They'd been in the type of clinch that normally came before (or after) a session like the one he'd just shared with her.

He couldn't take much more. He wasn't prepared to. He was being kicked from pillar to post and it hurt.

'Well you'll be better off with Matt anyway.'

Lucy blinked, shocked into silence for a millisecond. 'What's that supposed to mean?'

'Well he's always hanging round for you, I've even caught him waiting at the school gate.'

'He's not waiting for me you idiot.'

'Oh no? Well he's not looking out for Mrs Potts, is he?'

Lucy sighed. 'He's got a thing about Jill.'

'Rubbish.'

'That's what I thought at first, but he has. He's got a way of always being around when she is. It took me ages to notice, but once I did I couldn't not. If she doesn't catch on soon I'm going to turn into a Langtry Meadows interfering old bag and tell her.'

'Oh. So telling him you love him is part of a master plan?' His tone was dry, and she shook her head and smiled.

'Charlie, it wasn't how it looked. Why do you always jump to conclusions?'

She was spot on there, he did jump when it came to her. The tightening of his gut every time he saw her joking with Matt was physical, not logical. Which scared him. Which was another reason for steering clear. 'I can't do this Lucy.' He dropped the cloth and leaned on the small sink, resting his head against the wall, then slowly straightened. She obviously didn't feel the same way about him as he did about her. But it was probably a good thing, because sorting out his family – what had been his family – had to take priority. 'Josie agrees that it's a good thing for Maisie to see me, but...'

'But she doesn't want Maisie to see her dad shagging his way round the village? Seems reasonable.'

'It's not just that, if I thought...' What was the point in saying what was in his head? That if he thought for one minute that he and Lucy could be an item, more than the odd 'I can't resist you' clinch then it wouldn't matter? 'I need to keep this simple.' For his own sake as well as Maisie's.

'I can help you.' Her voice was soft and she was looking at him with a steady gaze. She swallowed and he watched her throat constrict. 'If you'll let me. We can work through this together. Honest, I understand. And what happened,' she shrugged her shoulders, 'it could happen to anybody after a couple of bottles of wine.'

'That's not fair.' That hurt. It hadn't been the wine, even though following through on his desires probably hadn't been the smartest route to take. 'Lucy, if things were different I...'

'But they aren't. It matters to you seeing Maisie again and trying to sort this.'

'In court I probably wouldn't stand a chance of getting any rights if she's not mine. This way...'

'This way's the right way, Charlie. I get that. The important person is Maisie, not you and not me.'

'I did tell Josie she couldn't lay down the rules.' He had

done, but in his heart he'd known that getting involved with Lucy, getting involved with anybody right now, would be madness. Maisie already had enough changes on her plate, and so did he. He needed a clear head for this.

He really didn't know what had got into him the other night. When had he last felt like that? Probably as a student, when he'd been out on a pub crawl. For seven years they'd worked hard and played hard, and it was always the smart, pretty girls that he'd been drawn to. Lethal. Like Lucy. Like Josie. You'd have thought he'd have learned his lesson.

'I'll help you.'

That probably wouldn't help with his clear head.

'Charlie, she's going to be in my class, you can't help but see me and nor can Josie. So let's be adult about this,' a sad smile played on her lips as she echoed Josie's words. 'Forget what happened and we can help your daughter together. Please?'

Chapter 20

Lucy stifled the yawn. The first day back at school, even after only a week off, was always hard. Getting in even earlier than normal for an emergency meeting made it even more difficult. And when you'd spent the night checking your watch, in between dreams about a dark haired vet shunning you like you thought your father had, then snogging you like you were the best thing he'd ever tasted, then even the *thought* of a day at work with a group of lively children was a killer.

She looked round hastily, hoping nobody could read her mind. But they were all looking at Timothy Parry.

'Right, good news first, we have a new child on the roll from this term.' He looked at Lucy. 'I've had confirmation that young Maisie will be joining us, which is always good news, keeping the numbers up.' He shuffled his papers about. 'Now as you can see, Jim,' he nodded at Jim who was sitting next to Lucy, 'has been kind enough to come along so that he can pass any comments on to the governors. As you all know, we had a respite until the end of the school year, but it very much looks like we've won the battle but not the war. We have a choice,' he peered over his glasses at them all, one at a time, 'to admit defeat and give up, or,' he paused so that the words sank in, really the man should have been an actor thought Lucy. 'We can up our fight and prepare to give this everything we have got.'

Lucy couldn't concentrate on Timothy's words. All she'd heard was that Maisie was now officially on the school roll. So, that was that confirmed. Josie obviously knew that Lucy posed absolutely no threat at all to her happy family, and had brought Maisie in to school. Which meant she was confident that she had a future here. With Charlie. No doubt she'd be persuading Charlie to return to the fold (if she hadn't already), which was good. Yes, good. Keeping a family together was excellent.

She swallowed. Even if for one brief period of time she'd thought that ... well she wasn't going to think any more. Not about the way his lips on hers brought her out in goose bumps, or the way her heart had bumped down into the bottom of her stomach when he'd seen her with Matt and jumped to the wrong conclusion. She still wasn't sure he believed there was nothing going on, but what did it matter now anyway?

Except it did matter to her. Deep down. Maybe she should have said so louder. After all she had told herself that from now on she was going to be upfront and open about *every-thing*. No confusion, no misunderstandings. But then maybe it didn't count when all you wanted to do was throw yourself at a man who had far more important things on his mind anyway. And hadn't *actually* wanted to devour you, had just been a bit drunk and in need of a good shag.

'Ahh takes me back to the last time the school was under

attack.' She jumped guiltily at the whisper in her ear, realising she'd missed most of Timothy's speech. It was Jim. She turned to him wondering if an explanation would follow, and he winked. 'You ask Miss Harrington! The wily old codger had a plan then, should have been a general. There's no stopping this man when he's got the bit between his teeth, he'll use any kind of dirty tactic.'

Timothy was looking at them, and Lucy felt herself go beetroot red, even though it wasn't actually her that was whispering. 'Well I think that wraps it up. It would have been nice to have known we were off the danger list, but I'm sure that we are more than capable of going into battle and winning this one.' There was a small round of applause, which Lucy joined in with. 'We have this half-term to prove ourselves, so let's end this academic year on a high that is hard to ignore, and come up with an action plan for September. That is if I can count on your support?' There was a general nodding of heads. 'Splendid. I knew I could rely on my wonderful staff. Believe me I am so proud to be part of this school. Now, to battle!' He cleared his throat as the staff started to stand up and push chairs back. 'Could I have a quick word, Lucy, before you head off to the classroom? I'm sure Jill will make sure everything is shipshape.'

More like a ship's captain than general maybe. 'Of course.' Oh hell, what kind of dirty tactic had he got planned for her now?

'I know what I'm about to say is a big ask for you.' He steepled his fingers together and balanced his chin on them. The head at Starbaston had done much the same, but her instinctive response then had been very different.

At Starbaston, David Lawson had seen her as expendable. A number. An expensive salary. He had been looking at her like he'd look at an exhibit in a cold, dusty museum. Or a statistic on a spreadsheet. But to Timothy Parry she knew (fingers crossed) that she wasn't just a number; she was a member of his team. 'I do realise that despite being such an outstanding teacher you've had a rough ride lately, and the job security you, well we all, crave has been elusive. I'm being unfair, selfish, but I really would appreciate it if you'd consider staying on at Langtry Meadows. I have the backing of all the governors here, and of course every member of staff. I can't promise you'll have a job in twelve months' time, but I'll do my damnedest to make sure we all have. I'm sorry,' he smiled, a slightly sad smile, 'I'm not being that clear, I'm offering you a job in my roundabout way. A permanent position. Well, if we're honest, a terrible, insecure, job in a small village school with very terrible promotion prospects. All I can offer is our people, kind supportive people who love you and admire your work. I can't raise your salary, promise a pay rise, or say you won't be made redundant again in the not so distant future. Not a very good offer is it?' He held up a hand to stop her, just as she was about to speak. 'It looks better if we have committed staff, and I would, we all would, value your input and experience. I'm well aware that you've worked in a far more difficult environment and have no doubt learned valuable lessons in staff motivation and turning situations round. It's a terrible offer, but I really would appreciate you giving it a little thought.'

'I don't need to.' She swallowed hard, not sure if she was going to regret these words for the rest of her life. 'I don't need to give it thought.'

Timothy Parry sat more upright, and straightened his bow tie. 'Not even the rest of today?' For the first time there was a note of defeat in his voice.

'I'll stay.' He frowned. 'I want to accept your job offer. Thank you.'

'Really?' The frown turned to a beam, lifting his features. A big smile that lit up his whole face, and seemed to lighten the invisible weight on his shoulders. 'Goodness gracious me.' Then he held out a hand. 'Welcome to the team Lucy. I can't say you won't regret it, but...'

'I won't regret it.' She took the large, warm hand in hers. Whatever happened she wouldn't, couldn't, regret helping Timothy Parry and his school out. 'If I can help save the school then I want to. We're not going to fail, Timothy.' And it wasn't just Timothy she was doing it for. She was doing it to save village life as they knew it, for everybody who lived in Langtry Meadows, life would alter for ever if the school closed.

'That,' his eyes were positively sparkling, 'is exactly what I was hoping to hear.'

She took a deep breath and put her shoulders back. It was time to move on with her life, to make some decisions that came from the heart – that meant something. What her mother had explained didn't really change anything – except deep down inside her. She'd realised over the half-term holiday that it was in her power to decide where she belonged, she knew that now. And right now she wanted to belong here. She wanted to stay – whatever her spreadsheets were telling her.

She might not be able to win the battle for Charlie's heart. But she wanted to be responsible, to stay and help him. Because after all, didn't she understand? And she could help the village that had already gone a long way towards showing her how her life could be. Once she'd opened her eyes and let it.

Out of the corner of her eye Lucy saw the cross-legged Maisie slowly keel over. She knew exactly how she felt. However, she had to do 'show and tell' followed by a story before she could go home. Then she had books to mark, a lesson plan to prepare and emails to write before she could collapse on her own bed.

She raised an eyebrow in Jill's direction, and with a grin Jill stepped in and quietly gathered the little girl up, and took her over to a pile of comfy cushions in the corner of the room by the overflowing bookcase.

At least it was nearly the end of what had seemed like a very long day.

'Can I pick the story, Miss?' Daisy had stuck her hand so high in the air she was at serious risk to keeling over as well.

'You always pick girl books, I want one about real stuff like Batman.' One of the Hargreave twins (she had no idea which) folded his arms and pulled a face.

'That isn't real stuff, is it, Miss? My mam says it's a load of twaddle.'

Lucy twisted her mouth, to stop herself laughing. Out of the corner of her eye she could see Jill's shoulders shaking.

'We'll do show and tell first, and then I think we'll let Maisie pick the story shall we, once she's had a little rest?'

'Do you want to see my newt, Miss?'

She stared at Ted, who was sitting cross-legged near the back, fumbling about between his legs.

'He's called Bob.'

She glanced at Jill, who had decided to do some totally unnecessary tidying up but was obviously still trying not to laugh. 'I found him when we was pond-dipping.'

'Were.' She corrected automatically, wondering if this needed stopping now.

Ted lifted a jar up triumphantly in the air and the water sloshed alarmingly, nearly swishing Bob out of the jar and onto his head. 'I call him Bob cos my dad is always saying Bob's your uncle.'

'Right.' She drew the word out to give her chance to gather her thoughts.

'But my uncle is called Mike.' He poked a podgy finger into the jar.

Lucy glanced to Jill for inspiration, or assistance, but her assistant was too busy trying to keep a straight face to offer anything but a shrug, which came from shaking shoulders.

'Now Ted, what are we supposed to do with everything we catch when we go pond-dipping?' At Starbaston the nearest the kids had got to pond-dipping was jumping in the puddles, it was potholes not ponds that had featured there. Spending an hour or so in the part of the schools grounds that was known as the 'nature reserve' had left her with a smile on her face, after she'd got over the panic of a child falling in face first and her having to explain how one of her charges had drowned.

'Put 'em back in, Miss.'

'And why do we do that?'

Daisy stuck her hand in the air. 'Cos that's where they live.'

'But Bob doesn't live there.' Ted had a sullen look on his face. 'He comes from my uncle's.' He dropped his voice to a whisper, a loud whisper that even Lucy could hear across the classroom. 'But don't tell anybody, cos it's a secret.'

'It isn't a secret, my mam said—'

'Well I think it's his home now, wherever he came from.' Jill expertly whisked the jar out of the chubby grasp. 'We don't want him falling out and dying, do we?'

'Like them worms you had, my mam said it's dirty to put worms in your pockets.'

'It's not.' The angry response from Ted sounded very much like 'snot'.

'Right.' Lucy clapped her hands briskly. 'Sophie, sit down. Hand in the air if you want to say anything. I think it's time for a story, don't you?'

As the children shuffled round into a circle, she took the opportunity to sidle up to Jill. 'What is it about newts?'

'You mean you haven't heard about newt-gate yet?'

She raised an eyebrow. 'Should I have done?'

'The last time the school was under threat?'

'Well actually, Jim did mention...'

'Ask Elsie Harrington. You should have seen your face when he asked if you wanted to see his newt!'

* * *

Lucy had realised, after the first week at Langtry Meadows that she needed a rucksack if she wanted to avoid looking like the hunchback of Notre Dame by the end of term. It was quite a novelty living within walking distance of work, but meant that she could no longer just fling all her school work, and laptop, onto the back seat of the car.

What with all her animal duties, the walk to school carrying a load of books, and her gardening she'd certainly got fitter in the two months or so since she'd arrived. Even if all the glasses of wine and lager that she'd drunk with Sally, and the pizzas seemed to have settled around her middle. Maybe she needed to start jogging. She'd always preferred a session at the gym in the past, but that was when straying on foot off her estate was inviting physical assault, or at the very least the kind of verbal assault which would have soon had her bolting back towards the safety of her front door.

'You look very jovial this evening my dear.'

Elsie Harrington was standing at her garden gate, looking as elegant as ever. Molly was at her side, wagging her tail, and the puppies were spilling over the borders flattening the flowers as they played.

'I am.' She smiled. 'They look a bit of a handful.'

'Wonderful as the little treasures are, I can assure you that Molly and I will be quite relieved when life gets back to normal. Do you have time to humour a lonely old lady and share a pot of tea?'

The weight of the rucksack dragged down on Lucy's shoulders. 'Of course, that would be lovely.' What on earth had happened to her work ethic? She'd be working past midnight at this rate.

'I hear a small celebration is in order.' Elsie smiled broadly, mischief spread across her features.

Lucy shook her head. 'How on earth?' She tried to look annoyed, but she couldn't stop the fizz of pleasure. Who was she to complain that she was actually being talked about? 'And I hear,' she swung the rucksack from her shoulders as she followed Elsie into the cottage, 'that you can tell me all about newt-gate.'

'Ahh.' Elsie laughed. 'When young Timothy gets a notion there is no stopping him.' She filled up the kettle, and Lucy waited for her to switch it on. 'The Parish Council think that they solved the problem, but without Timothy and his obsessive search for facts we could have lost part of the village to development. Not that I'm against progress, but there is a time and place my dear. Sugar, milk?'

Lucy nodded.

'Villages do need new blood, we all know that, but they were all set to develop on the land behind the school.'

'Really? Where the chickens are?'

'Oh yes, the chickens, that lovely little vegetable patch and the dipping pond would have all disappeared. Rather sad, don't you think? Much better to build on the other side of the village, which they were eventually persuaded to do. The main problem,' she patted Molly's head and sneaked her a biscuit, 'was that the land there was owned by somebody quite influential. A major landowner who knew just which strings to pull, a nimby they call them, don't they? Quite ridiculous, the man doesn't even live in the village.'

'But why newt-gate?'

'Ah yes, Timothy very luckily discovered that there were newts in the pond.'

'Newts?'

'Yes, newts.'

She sighed at what Lucy knew was the blank expression on her face.

'They might not be much to look at, but they're rare and very valuable.' Her eyes twinkled. 'Rapidly declining numbers, and where would we be without our newts?'

'Indeed.' Until this afternoon, Lucy hadn't even known what a newt looked like. In fact, she still wasn't very sure as she'd only seen the poor thing at a distance as it was being sloshed around. They were a bit frog-like weren't they?

'Great crested newts are protected by law. Now,' Elsie paused, 'you might know young Ted Wright – he of the worms in pockets?'

Lucy nodded.

'Well that poor boy has been known to get a little confused. He may well tell you that the newts came from his Uncle Michael's pond, and not to tell anybody, but those of course were different newts altogether.' She gave Lucy a stern look, and waggled a finger for emphasis. 'There are of course quite a few newts in the ponds round here, despite their rarity. For some reason they're quite prolific. Easy to get confused.'

'I can imagine.' Lucy tried to cover her smile up by taking a sip of the too-hot tea. 'He did actually produce one this afternoon, and said something about his uncle. But it would be er, wrong, probably illegal to move one, on purpose.'

'It would.'

'I expect there are so many scattered around the area because you're so careful not to destroy their habitats.'

'Exactly. The point is though that Timothy went to great lengths,' she paused and Lucy was sure there was a twinkle in her eye, 'to protect that patch of land for the school, and I'm sure he will be equally determined to win the battle to keep the school.'

'Through fair means or foul?'

'I couldn't possibly comment, but I'm delighted to hear he has persuaded you to stay and help. Another biscuit, dear?'

'Did Jim have a role in saving the land as well then?'

'Oh yes, Jim is on the Parish Council as well as being a governor, he has a foot in both camps as it were.' She smiled to herself. 'He's very determined in his own way, a credit to the place.'

Which Lucy thought was a bit of a strange thing to say. 'He's been very kind to me since I came, and it was him that told me about the newts, in a roundabout way.'

'Ah, he did, did he?' She chuckled. 'Quite the mischief maker, and has his finger in every pie.'

'A bit like somebody else I know.' Lucy didn't quite like to overstep the mark, but she'd have said exactly the same about Elsie.

'There's nothing wrong with having your finger on the pulse. Timothy and Jim were quite fixated with that pond though, like a lot of little boys. Look, be a dear and pass me that photograph.'

Lucy looked over to where she was pointing and picked up the black and white photograph of a group of young boys in short trousers gathered around what had to be the dipping pond.

'That is Jim, and that,' she stabbed the photograph, 'is posh George. He's in the next village now, a councillor, always was a bossy boy, liked to meddle.' Lucy had to smile at the disapproving look on her face. 'And there is little Annie, podgy even back then.' She sighed. 'It has quite a history our little pond, and of course the school. Now you see over there,' she pointed at an album, 'I've got photographs going back years, there's May Day of course, and the wonderful summer picnics. Everybody is in them, and some of those children have done very well for themselves, quite influential they are now. You might want to borrow it dear.'

Lucy wasn't exactly sure when she'd have time to look into the history of the school, but it seemed rude to say no. 'Thank you.'

'Now, my dear, am I right in assuming you will be here all summer then? Or will you be spending your break back in your own house?'

'Well I had thought it was a bit of a shame to go back.' Lucy sighed, one of the best bits about agreeing to stay until September was that she'd get to spend her summer in the lovely village, pottering about the garden, looking after the animals. 'If Annie will let me.'

'Oh Annie will be delighted, believe me.'

'I thought I'd try and get a long-term tenant in my house, the agent said she didn't think there'd be any problem at all in renting it out.' *'Desirable property, sought after location, however long you require'* were the terms she'd used. And a year was all she required. Tops. In a year's time she was sure they'd know if the school had been saved or she was out of a job. Again. But either way, she was sure she wouldn't regret doing this. It was her new start, a conscious decision not something she'd been forced to do. It was the first step in trying to wipe out all those insecurities that had lurked in the back of her mind for far too long.

'Splendid. Then I can ask you a favour. I need somebody to look after Molly for me for a week or so while I'm away, and she's very fond of you. I know I can trust you not to spoil her and she's stayed with Annie before. She likes it there.'

Now how did she say no to that? Except she didn't really want to. Molly was no trouble, and it wasn't like she was in her own home with its cream carpets and spotless cushions. Annie's cottage was lived in, very lived in, by animals as well as people.

'But what about the puppies?'

'They will be off soon, dear. All growing up. I've got homes for all of them, but one. I'm sure you can fit him in as well.'

'Er.'

'That's wonderful.' Lucy was pretty sure the word 'yes' hadn't come out of her mouth at any point. 'You have taken a weight off my mind. Actually, in a week's time I'm off to my sister's in London for a couple of days, dear. You could take them then as a trial to see how you get on. It's her birthday and we see so little of each other these days.' She gave a heavy sigh. 'And who knows how many more years we have left.'

Lucy thought she was pushing it now.

'It's only for a few days, and Sally is always happy to help out as well if you're busy at school. I've spoken to Timothy.'

Lucy raised an eyebrow. There was no stopping this pair she decided, and she was very suspicious of Jim too now. He seemed to have steered her right in Elsie's direction, and the red-herring that was in fact a newt.

'He is more than happy for you to take Molly in to school if you wish, all the children love her.'

'I'm sure they do.'

'She'll be quiet as a mouse under the desk, you won't know she's there. Although that podgy puppy might be a different matter.' She frowned briefly, then patted Lucy on the knee. 'But I know you will sort it. You're very sensible, capable. I won't keep you then dear, if you're busy.'

Lucy put her empty cup down on the tray and picked up her rucksack, wondering just how she'd been persuaded to take on a permanent, but not so permanent job, plus the job of dog-minder all in one afternoon.

'And Jim will keep an eye on my house, he's a great help like that, so you've no need to worry about it.'

It had never occurred to Lucy to be worried about the house as well.

'Elsie, can I ask you something, something personal?'

'I'd love to be able to say ask anything, my dear. Isn't that what I'm supposed to say? But old ladies like me have secrets that are so far in the past that they're long forgotten, and that's the best way.'

She'd said something like that before – about things she'd left too long, about the right and wrong time to make choices. 'Are you happy, Elsie?'

'Most of the time, my dear.'

'Do you have any regrets about the way your life has gone?'

Elsie paused and looked her straight in the eye. 'Oh yes,' her voice was soft, that faraway tone she'd had when they'd first met and chatted by the pond. It seemed years ago now.

'Who did you lose?'

'A child my dear. A child. Which is why you have to make sure that young man of yours—'

'He's not my—'

'Don't let him do anything he will regret.'

'You *can* change things, Elsie. Sometimes you need to dig up the past, that's what my mum did for me, and she didn't want to.'

'Your lovely mother did it for closure my dear. With me it would be opening up a can of worms, altering somebody else's life, and I'm not sure that would be fair. Now,' her tone was brisk again, 'I thought you had work to do young lady? You can show yourself out, I'm sure.'

Lucy shook her head as she pulled the gate shut behind her. She'd get to the bottom of this. Elsie and Timothy might consider themselves experts at unearthing every secret the village had, but she could be just as determined when she got her teeth into something. She really did want to get to the bottom of Elsie's sadness – she seemed so capable at helping everybody else, it just didn't seem fair that some incident in the past was still coming back to haunt her. Because Lucy was pretty sure that the mystery child was constantly in the back of the old lady's mind.

'So,' there was a chuckle in her ear and she jumped guiltily, 'you all up to date on the old newt situation then?' Jim fell into step with her, looking very pleased with himself.

'You're a devious man.' In fact, he might be as good a person to start her inquiries with, he seemed quite close to Elsie. 'Sending me off like that, you knew I'd be too nosey to ignore it!'

He grinned. Then sobered up. 'She might come across as sprightly as ever my dear, but she's getting older.' He shook his head, and Lucy was struck again by the similarities between the pair. All the time they spent together had obviously rubbed off. It was a shame Elsie's elegance and good dress sense couldn't rub off on *her*, she'd give anything to look like that when she was eighty, or even now. 'I reckon she gets a little bit lonely, like we all do, so I try my best to pop in and help her out. She's glad of a chat though.'

'I know. I was kidding, it's very kind of you and I know she appreciates it.'

'You can't be out and out kind though, she's a proud lady. Have to be a bit sneaky, devious like you said, and not give her any choice. I just tell her I do the garden so that we get a chance to regain that Best Village trophy.' He winked. 'She's quite fond of you, love. I reckon you could get away with bossing her about a bit.'

'Did you know she'd asked me to look after Molly?'

'Oh aye, and I also know she asked you to have a pup and you declined.' His grin broadened into a toothy smile. 'She's a very determined one, Elsie is. Kind but determined.'

'Hmm.' Lucy pulled a wry smile. 'She said much the same about you and Timothy Parry.'

Chapter 21

Lucy put a hand out to open her front gate and was astonished to see she had a visitor. A tall, dark, ruggedly handsome kind of visitor. With steady hands and a steadier heart. The type of man you could have ideas about, if you were really stupid.

The type of man who had a maybe-ex and a child.

After a week of very successfully avoiding each other (which really was a miracle in this village), he was here. In the flesh. The very attractive flesh.

Making light of it was the only way out. If whatever spark they had (well she had) had to be quashed she wanted to be a good friend. Well she wanted to at least know she'd tried. 'Whatever it is, the answer is no.'

Charlie was standing awkwardly on her doorstep, looking like a guilty dog that had stolen your steak out of the fridge but really did want you to forgive him. He looked up, startled.

'So far today I've been persuaded to rewrite my life plan.'

'Ouch, that must have been painful for you.' He grimaced in sympathy. 'I know how attached you are to that. How many new spreadsheets will be involved?'

'Very painful. I might need therapy. And I seem to have agreed to set up a doggie hotel.'

He raised an eyebrow, and Lucy realised she'd now run out of pleasantries (she just wasn't good at small talk) and really didn't know what to say. She was just shuffling about outside her home, looking at him, and he was looking back.

She started to search through her bag for the key; it was easier than meeting those deep brown eyes. 'I wasn't expecting...' To ever see you on the doorstep again. Ever.

She'd only be seeing him when she took an animal into the surgery, or bumped into him in the village, or talked to him about Maisie. But not here. That had been the plan.

He looked worried.

'Is there something wrong with Maisie? She did seem fine at school today, I wouldn't worry about her falling asleep.'

'Not that I know of.' A small frown creased his brow, fine lines between his eyebrows. 'She fell asleep at school?'

'Lots of kids her age do that. And I mean she was tired with all the excitement, and having to travel so far and...'

'Oh. Fine.' Awkward pause. Did she fill it in, or wait? Wait. Definitely wait. He stuck one hand in his pocket, ruffled the fingers of his other through his hair. Which wasn't fair as it made him look far too huggable. Her best option would be to run off, but he was standing between her and her own front door. 'I just wanted you to be the first to know, our, er arrangements have changed a bit and...'

Running off would have been a better option.

He was going to tell her he was moving back in with Josie. Or, more likely that Josie was moving in with him. Except he lived in the small flat adjoining the surgery didn't he? The one that was really for nurses, in case they had a dog in overnight.

It had surprised her to find out that apparently cats were fine being left overnight, but legally dogs weren't. Since when had it been right to discriminate?

'I would have thought it would be a bit cramped for you all to be in your flat.' She shouldn't have said that. It was unfair. But it had just spilled out before she could stop it. 'Not that it's any of my business. Fine, I mean, great, er.'

He sighed and looked slightly perplexed. An injured, as well as innocent, dog.

'It would be. That flat is hardly big enough for one, believe me.'

'So?' So what was he telling her here? That they'd bought a place together in the village? Josie had filled all the forms in with an out-of-village address, which was where little Maisie had told them she still lived. *I've got a new school but an old house, does that mean I get to keep all my old friends and have new friends?* She'd asked when Lucy had managed to wake her up. And it had been like a heart-stopping thump to her chest. How on earth could she do anything but support Charlie in looking after this little girl? *I had to get up very, very early today. We had toast in the car. That's why I fell asleep.*

She fought the urge to rush past Charlie, bury her head in schoolwork and leave him to whatever his issues with his new life were. 'You'd better come in.' She hadn't meant to say that. 'But I do have a lot of work to do.' She swung the rucksack off her shoulders pointedly.

'Sure. I won't keep you.' He sounded put out, and didn't move from the doorstep. 'I just wanted you to know...'

'Okay. So where are Josie and Maisie living? Has she bought a place?' It hurt to say the words, but the more times she said them the easier it would get. A bit like a blister when you kept giving it a gentle prod to see if it was getting more bearable. The pain would wear off. That was a known fact, wasn't it? Or it would burst out, like a blister, and be even more of a mess. Take even longer to heal.

'That's what I wanted to talk to you about. It isn't that simple.'

No it wouldn't be, would it? Nor was the fact that she'd just agreed to stay on in Langtry Meadows and watch Charlie and Josie make up in front of her eyes. They'd hold hands at parents' evenings, stand together as Maisie danced round the maypole next spring. She'd look at those broad shoulders as he swung Maisie up on them, and remember what it had been like to rest her head on them.

She was mad. It had been one night. Not even a full night. They'd not even had breakfast. Josie had put paid to that. Who could enjoy bacon and eggs when you'd just had that kind of interruption?

'And anyway,' she frowned at him as a thought struck her, 'is this really fair on Maisie? You're just a locum, like me,' like I *was*, she'd come back to that later, 'you said you'd be moving on soon. Australia?' She hadn't forgotten Australia, and that look in his eye when he'd said it. Before he'd kissed her, and tangled her feet up in his and...

'I know.' His hand was working overtime so that bits of his hair were stuck up and her hand was twitching to smooth them down. 'I've er, well Eric asked if I'd support him for a bit once he was back on his feet. He reckons he'll have trouble handling the full job at first and it could be months before he was back to full strength. I told Josie I'd probably be around for the next twelve months, but beyond that...'

'Great.' Impossible to be enthusiastic. 'So you can all—'

'Josie said she might rent a place in the village, so we can share custody.' He paused. 'Don't look at me like that! It's for her and Maisie, but she wanted to be sure I was happy with it—'

'And not sleeping with her teacher or any other village slapper.'

'Lucy! Look, I told her I'd see who I wanted, but I know how to be a responsible father without her telling me. I mean, what does she think I am?' He sounded very frustrated now, and his hair was suffering.

'You'll be bald if you carry on.' Lucy couldn't help the smile, even if this was about to turn into a crap day.

'What? Oh. Yeah.' He shoved his hand in his pocket. 'Will you let me finish? This is hard enough ... she wanted to be sure I'd be happy with seeing Maisie again.'

'And of course you would.'

'I would.' His voice dropped to little more than a whisper, a cracked whisper. 'I'd give anything to see her again.'

'But why didn't Josie just ask you to go back there, to where you used to live? Why all the uprooting?'

'I did ask that. She said she couldn't manage the practice on her own. She's sold up and is looking for something more meaningful to do with her life.'

'Meaningful? Like looking after orphan puppies? Rescuing homeless kittens? Sorry, that sounds mean.'

'Like rescues,' he gave a wry smile, 'supporting things like that. I don't know, I really don't care. But,' he took a deep breath, 'I said it was good if they were here, that I'd see who I wanted. She gave up the right to tell me what I could do with my life when she walked out, and that I'd be here at least another 12 months, but she really had to give Maisie stability not just move around.'

'And?'

'She just said thank you.'

'Thank you?'

'Yep. And went.' He narrowed his eyes. 'With the old Josie I wouldn't have questioned it, but I just wonder if she's got an agenda.'

'Hasn't everybody? Sorry, that came out wrong, I've had a long day.'

'We're not getting back together, Lucy.' His voice was soft, and he was looking at her in that earnest, disturbing way. 'Me and Josie were never really right, I couldn't let go of work, she couldn't let go of the need to party. She's got restless feet, she needs to be doing something, thinking about new things all the time, whereas I,' he did that cute, lost smile thing, 'I'm just a boring old vet who is quite happy doing what I do.'

'I wouldn't say you were boring.' Their gazes locked and she wished she hadn't said that.

'No?'

'No.' She swallowed. She'd never classify their night together as boring, in fact that bit where they'd nearly shot off the bed had opened her eyes to a whole new experience. 'You, er, you're very good with the animals, and their, er owners, and at the May Day you...'

'I think you better stop there. You're making me sound even worse.' But his eyes had a hint of that light in them that she loved.

'So, Maisie's been enrolled...' Better to get back to the reason he was here.

'She has.' Lucy wished he'd stop looking at her in that intent way. 'I know you won't be her teacher forever but...'

'Well, I've got some news of my own actually.'

He stared back at her.

'The change to my life-plan bit, I've been offered a permanent position at the school.'

'Oh.' A mass of conflicting expressions flitted across his face. 'And, you...?'

'I accepted it.'

'But I thought you didn't like it here. I thought there was a risk the school would close and...'

Okay so he'd been only too keen to see the back of her. But she wasn't going. She wasn't going to make it easy for him, or for the people who wanted to see the school shut down for good.

'I know. But I've decided I do like it here, and I think our school,' she realised as the words came out that she'd called it 'our school', it was hers now, not just the village's, 'is as good, better than a lot round here. Maybe one day there will be a big academy and they'll all change, but until then I think we should fight to keep the school open.'

'Good.'

'Good?' Had she heard him right?

'Good for you. I'm pleased.'

'Oh.' She frowned. 'You're pleased?'

'Why shouldn't I be pleased?' He was frowning too now.

'Well I thought you'd be glad to see the back of me, I mean Josie doesn't exactly like...'

'I told you, I don't give a damn what Josie does and doesn't like, and I haven't a clue why you think I'd want to see the back of you.'

'Well Josie said...'

'Lucy, stop talking about Josie, I can't let Josie run my life anymore.'

'But that's why you left ... I mean you wouldn't even talk to me. You said—'

'I didn't not talk to you.'

'Oh yes you did.'

'That was because you were snogging Matt bloody Harwood.'

'I was not.' Okay, she had a feeling she'd stamped her foot then. 'I was hugging Matt bloody Harwood, not snogging. There is a difference.'

'Not from where I'm standing.'

'Well move then.'

'This is getting stupid.'

'Charlie, he hugged me partly because I was upset about what Jim had said.'

'Jim?'

'About the school being in danger of closure still.'

'And the other bit of partly?'

'Well that was your fault of course.' He stared at her uncomprehendingly. 'Josie? Your ex? Arriving while I was still half asleep after...'

He grinned.

'And I looked a mess.' She stared back, cross that he thought it was funny.

'You looked gorgeous.'

'Oh yeah, so gorgeous you high tailed it off to have a chat with her, then wouldn't even listen to me.'

'I'd come back to talk to you, and found you in a clinch. A man has the right to be jealous now and again.'

Had he just said jealous? Didn't jealous mean he hadn't entirely had it down as a drunken shag, no strings attached?

'Oh Lucy.' The sigh seemed to come straight from his heart and headed straight for hers. Then he closed the distance between them, and tentatively leaned forward, arms out, as though he wasn't sure he should be doing whatever he was doing. 'Oh sod it.' The arms came round her, wrapping her up in a warm, secure blanket, pulling her in close against a chest that felt like home. His breath was warm against her neck, his words soft in her ear. 'Oh Lucy, what are we going to do?' The touch of his hand, stroking her hair gently sent a tingle down her spine. This was bad.

'Going inside might be an idea, you never know where Elsie might have her spies.'

He kicked the door shut behind them, held her tight, his chin on her head.

'I needed to hold you. Talk to you. You're not going to put me on the naughty step, are you?'

'You said something funny!' Lucy tried to look shocked, but instead giggled. Charlie normally just did serious, deep, sincere ... oh God this wasn't good. She wriggled free under the pretext of another laugh. 'Pizza and wine?' It was safer to keep it this way. She had to help him work out things with Maisie. With Josie. She couldn't let herself just crumble. And anyway, crumbling was pretty pathetic for an independent woman.

He didn't comment about her pulling away. 'Is that all you ever eat, pizza?'

'Or chips. Or both. Take it or leave it?' She might be good at nurturing minds, but as far as feeding the body went...

'Pizza sounds fine, but, look I don't want you to take this the wrong way, but...'

'Maybe not as much wine?' He nodded. 'I understand, Charlie. Honest.'

'I know.' He kissed her. It was gentle, it was sweet, it brought tears to her eyes and made her insides tremble in a way that hadn't even happened when they'd been in bed together. 'Shit. I didn't mean for that to happen. It isn't fair on either of us. Maybe I should go.'

'Stay.' She put a hand on his arm. 'I'll get fat if I eat the whole pizza. Stay, on humanitarian grounds.'

Lucy sat up in bed, feeling slightly wobbly. Luckily, Charlie had drunk most of the wine last night, but all they'd had to eat was a shared pizza. She'd be regretting this in a couple of hours' time when her class was bouncing about full of life. She groaned and put her hands over her eyes. And after school when she was trying to catch up on the work she'd not done yesterday evening. She'd never, ever not done her work.

There was something not ringing true about the whole Charlie and his ex-situation though. He was genuinely hurt, distraught; she'd never seen so many emotions playing across somebody's face. So she believed what he'd told her. But what kind of woman dragged a young child from her friends, her home, on the off chance that her ex would be happy to see them?

Josie had seemed nice, warm. Sensible. Not like some evil, cheating wife who couldn't care less about her child. Well warm until she'd discovered the pair of them in a post-coital warm fuzz. She felt herself go all hot and bothered just at the thought.

She pulled her knees up to her chest.

Charlie had said it was over between them. But maybe Josie still hoped they'd get back together. Maybe in the heat of the moment Josie had pushed Charlie away, but realised now that it wasn't the right thing to do. Otherwise it seemed a bit extreme, a bit stalker-ish, to move to Langtry Meadows.

She sighed and rolled out of bed, too many maybe's were making her head bang. What did she know?

It did seem a bit extreme for Charlie to hide himself in the outback too, although it looked like now Maisie was back in his life, he'd abandoned that idea. Although that was more or less what she'd been doing. Except her outback had been concrete.

This time though she wasn't running away. Neither of them were.

Chapter 22

'Miss Jacobs?' Lucy looked at Josie warily. She really could do without being accosted in the playground right now. She'd actually told Jill that she'd do the meeting and greeting, and Jill could prepare the classroom. It had seemed a good idea at the time, to get some fresh air. Now all she wanted was a strong cup of coffee and a lie down though.

How could the woman even know she'd shared a pizza with Charlie and they'd got drunk again together? She felt like blurting out, '*It was only a kiss, no sex involved. No nakedness.*' But she didn't. She smiled.

'Hi. How can I help?'

'I want to apologise.'

That stopped her in her tracks. 'Oh, er, there's no need.'

'No really, I was so rude to you the other day, and it's really none of my business what Charlie does.'

Lucy had instinctively liked Josie when she'd first come into school with Maisie, and this seemed more like the woman she'd thought she was. Despite the way her stomach was churning, and her emotions were taking a hammering, she had to tell the truth. 'But your daughter is your business and

363

you need to do the best for her.' Her mum had done the best she could for her child, she'd turned her whole life upside down, been prepared to leave a cosy life so that her daughter could be safe, could be happy.

'I know things aren't always what they seem.' She'd taken the words right out of Lucy's mouth. 'I just overreacted,' she held up a hand, 'I know I did. I'd been trying to track Charlie down for days, because I really needed to talk to him before I made a decision about the school. He wouldn't answer the phone, or return calls. You know what men can be like at the best of times, but after what I'd said to him...' She smiled apologetically. 'So I was already in a pretty ratty mood when I decided to go on a hunt.' She smiled. 'Then when I saw you semi-dressed I saw red, I wanted to lash out at somebody and just thought that he was too busy shagging to even be concerned about his own daughter.'

'His own daughter?' Lucy kept her voice soft, not wanting to inflame the situation.

Josie had the good grace to look embarrassed. 'He told you?' Lucy nodded. 'I know I've fucked up, but Maisie thinks of him as her dad, and I do too. I just lost it when we had that massive argument, and once the words were out I couldn't get them back. It was easier not to talk about it, just to go the whole hog and call it a day. But it's important for me to know I'm doing the right thing now for both of them.'

'Good. You've got a lovely daughter, whatever you're doing it's working fine for her. She does though,' she paused, not wanting to add to Josie's worries, but needing to be honest, 'seem a bit over tired. The school change and everything is bound to be affecting her, but the early mornings ... it's a very long day for her.'

'I know.' Josie sighed. 'I know. I had a, well, there was an issue with the place I was going to rent, but I think it's all in hand now. It's very short term, I promise you. She does seem alright?'

Lucy nodded. 'We're keeping an eye on her, you'll be the first to know if I've got any concerns at all.'

'Thank you.' Josie rested her hand briefly on Lucy's arm, then withdrew as though she wasn't sure if she should have really done it. 'We've got a lot to sort out.' She shrugged again. 'Look, I know you're busy. I just wanted to say sorry. I'm not a bad woman.'

'I'm sure you're not.' And she was being honest. Josie seemed nice, not the nasty woman that she could be painted as if you just took her actions in black and white. That was the trouble wasn't it? Seeing the simple, biased picture and not the whole.

She'd been oblivious to the whole picture when she was young. She'd just seen a lonely lost girl who didn't belong, rather than the abusive husband and father that had turned the safe, happy place into a no-go zone. Not that she'd known that. Who ever knew what was behind the heartbreak, what guilt people carried?

'Are you alright?' Josie touched her arm lightly again, and brought Lucy back out of her gloomy thoughts.

'Sorry yes, I'm fine.'

'It's no excuse, but I needed to get away for both our sakes. At first I wanted to get through to him, startle him out of the way he was. Then I realised it was never going to work.

Charlie was just married to his job, we didn't have anything really. We'd grown apart, or maybe we just both grew up into different people. But I didn't want to tear my family apart, I didn't mean to hurt him or Maisie. I just,' she looked briefly into Lucy's eyes, then away. 'I used the fact that I'd had an affair, that Maisie probably wasn't his, as a way of lashing out at him. Then I felt so fucking guilty at breaking up what everybody thought was my perfect family. I felt so guilty I'd done it in the first place. It was a mad fling after we'd been married for a couple of years, we'd been invited to a big do and he'd pulled out at the last minute because of a crisis at work and I was furious, I went on my own, got drunk. Shit, I am so sorry at spewing all this out. You must just look like a good listener, or a good person … Maisie won't stop talking about her wonderful teacher.'

'It's, er, fine.' Lucy didn't really want to hear all about the ins and outs of Charlie and Josie's marriage, it felt disloyal, but Josie was so upset. She must have torn herself apart over the guilt of the affair which had had to come out into the open some time. Then she'd done a runner before the recriminations came. She probably was here trying to apologise, trying to slowly make it up to Charlie … if she could. And Lucy was going to have to watch her. And try and forget just how good it had been to have Charlie's arms around her, to hear his steady heart beating at a rate that mingled with hers, to look into those gorgeous eyes, that serious, intent face.

'I'm sure you're doing absolutely the best you can for Maisie, and that's what matters now, isn't it?' Her voice sounded tight even to her own ears.

'I hope I am. Charlie will be picking Maisie up tonight, is that okay? Do I need to fill out a form or anything?'

'No, no form filling needed, I'll make a note of it.'

'Great, and,' Josie paused, 'thanks, Miss Jacobs.'

'Lucy.'

'Thank you, Lucy. And forget what I said, you know the other day, you've been great for Charlie. You will look after him for me, won't you? He's a lovely guy, just not the right one for me.'

That was a strange thing to say. 'Well, it's not really, we're not...' She drew a breath. 'It wasn't really how it looked when you came round that day.'

'Really?' Josie smiled, and then she turned round and walked away. And Lucy wasn't quite sure what had happened.

The rapping on the window made her turn round. Jill was there holding up a net in one hand, with a questioning look on her face. Lucy nodded and smiled, walking back into school. Pond-dipping it was, and this time she'd have a proper look at what a newt looked like.

'Miss?' Maisie slipped her hand into Lucy's and looked shyly up.

She really was the most beautiful child. She squeezed, and Lucy felt like she was squeezing her heart. If she had to give up Charlie for anybody, then this little girl was the best ever reason.

'Yes, Maisie?'

'My dad's picking me up today. I'm having a sleepover.'

'Really?' She knew there was a quake in her voice, but she

was pleased for Charlie – and his daughter. This was progress. She would have given anything when she was eight to have been able to say the same words. Except now she knew that was something that would never have happened. Which hurt in its own way.

Yes, now she thought about it, her mum always had seemed happier when her dad hadn't been around. But she'd been too busy doing her own stuff, growing up, to really notice, and just been cross when she'd been sent to her room so that the 'adults could talk in private'.

He'd been a silent menace. She realised that now. Lucy sensed that the external bruises had been such a tiny part of it, it was the psychological threats, the fear, the awful anticipation that something terrible would happen that had been the really bad part. Her mother had been lucky enough to have had a good friend to talk to about it. A friend who had taken her seriously, recognised the warning signs for what they were. Helped her find a way out.

Her mother had told her about just one incident, once when he'd threatened to drown her, and practically carried out the threat. She'd skated over the details, but Lucy had heard the fear that still lingered in her voice. That one event had set the wheels in motion, had convinced her to confide in somebody, and then that disastrous party had made her realise she couldn't wait any longer. Nothing was going to change. She had to be brave. She had to change their lives. A shiver ran down Lucy's spine, a tug on her hand bringing her back from the brink of the nightmare.

'My mum said she'll come over later with my stuff. I saw

him yesterday and I'm going to stay there for ages.' She smiled, a wonderful full, happy smile. Lucy wasn't sure it was for ages, but that was up to Charlie or Josie to correct.

'That's nice, Maisie. I'm sure you'll have lots of fun. Now, isn't that daddy over there?'

Charlie was hesitating by the entrance to the school playground, his hair tousled, his arms held awkwardly. Maisie spotted him, gave a squeal of delight and dashed over.

He smiled. The biggest, happiest smile Lucy had ever seen. The heat of tears filled her eyes and she tried to blink them away. But she couldn't.

Charlie caught Maisie, swung her up in the air and she giggled. Then he kissed her, glanced over the top of her head at Lucy and mouthed 'thank you'.

'So what are you going to do?'

'Sorry?' Lucy turned her head to look at Jill, who had sneaked up behind her.

'About super vet?'

'I said I'd help, if he needed it. But he looks just fine.'

'No nookie?'

'Jill!'

'Although I suppose it could be tricky with company.'

'That was a one off.' She tried to sound definite.

'Oh yeah?'

Okay, maybe she hadn't succeeded. 'He's got more than enough on his plate, and the last thing we want to do is confuse Maisie.'

'Maisie is as bright as a button from what I've seen, I'm sure she'd cope.'

Lucy decided it was best to ignore that one, and carry on regardless. 'I expect she'll be spending a few weekends with him, I'm not quite sure what the arrangements are yet. But it is none of my, our, business.'

Jill grinned, ignoring Lucy's attempt to kill the conversation. 'Weekends? That's not what a little bird told me. Come on, let's get cleared up, I've got an episode of Emmerdale calling me.'

'You go ahead, Jill; I want to catch Timothy before I head home.'

'I've had an idea.' Lucy sat down in the chair next to Timothy Parry's desk, still wondering which little birds had been chattering to Jill.

'About?'

'Newt-gate.'

The headmaster raised an eyebrow.

'Well not exactly about newt-gate, but it got me thinking about how to make sure our school isn't top of the list for closure.' After Charlie had told her he'd scratched his initials on one of the school desks, her and Jill had spent an amusing lunch hour looking at the old desks and been caught in the act by Jim. 'Jim was telling me about all the past pupils who'd done very well for themselves.' He'd actually been pointing out the names under the lids of the old-fashioned desks they'd found in the store room. 'One of them was the Right Honourable George Cambourne.' Which had rung a bell, and had her rifling through the photograph album that Elsie had been quite insistent she borrow.

'Ah yes, Georgie, but I don't quite understand...'

'He's on the county council?'

'He is indeed. Lives not that far away, inherited a very nice place.'

'Elsie leant me a photograph album, and she showed me a class photograph with Jim and George, at the big summer picnic.'

'This one?' Timothy picked up one of the many photographs that were scattered along the bookshelves.

'That exact one. I think we need to resurrect the summer picnic on the green.'

'We do?'

'We do.' She said it quite firmly. 'And we need to invite all the people that are now influential. As Elsie pointed out, quite a few of the children that used to attend our little school have done pretty well for themselves.'

'Ah.'

'Elsie suggested a trip down memory lane, she said there was a lot of nostalgia about our pond. I thought that maybe if we resurrected one or two of our old customs and invited some of the past attendees to come and celebrate, and also see all the wonderful improvements we've made?'

'And if some of those people are the decision makers...? I knew you were the girl for the job, Lucy. You're brilliant!'

Chapter 23

Charlie looked from the dog, to the puppy, to Sally and then his daughter, and wondered when life had got so complicated.

Molly pushed her wet nose into his hand, then sat on his foot.

'Tell me again why we've got Miss Harrington's brood here?'

Sally stroked the head of the puppy that was trying to escape from the pen and smiled. 'We're taking them both round to Lucy's.'

He didn't miss the 'we' bit. 'And is Lucy expecting them?' He hadn't got over the last time he'd seen her with the pups, crying silently into the fur of one of them. In fact it could well be the same one that Maisie was now looking longingly at. He'd wanted to wrap his arms round her and make up for all her years she'd felt lonely and unwanted.

It was a bad habit, holding her, kissing her. Which is why he'd tried to steer clear, until he had a better idea of the direction his life was taking. He didn't want to mess up her life, or Maisie's.

'Oh yes, Lucy is expecting them.'

'Oh isn't it cute, Daddy. Can we have this one?'

'It is gorgeous Maisie, puppies always are. All babies are, it's nature's way of stopping their mummies eating them.'

Maisie giggled. 'Mummy said I'm good enough to eat.'

'Well you're very lucky she hasn't actually done it then.'

'So we can have one?'

'No we can't. You've already got a dog.'

'Miss Harrington has got lots. Some people have more than one.'

'True, but all the other puppies have gone to new homes and this one will soon as well, so then she'll be back to just having Molly.'

'Oh.' Maisie frowned. 'But you haven't got one.'

'Not at the moment.'

Sally raised an eyebrow, which he did his best to ignore.

'Here, Maisie, will you look after him for a moment for me?' Maisie nodded, her auburn curls bobbing, and Sally steered Charlie out of the room.

She'd obviously had far too much practice at herding wayward animals he decided, as she shut the door firmly.

'When are you going to tell her, Charlie?'

'We're telling her next week, together.'

'I don't mean Maisie.'

He'd known she'd not meant Maisie, but that was the easier question to answer.

'When the time is right.'

'Charlie!'

He started tidying up the consulting room, moving boxes of tablets round, to avoid facing Sally.

'It isn't fair on Lucy.' She put a hand out and stopped him in his tracks.

'What isn't?'

'She thinks that you and Josie are getting back together.'

'Don't be daft, she knows we're not. I've told her.'

'You might have told her, but that's not what she's seeing is it? As far as she's concerned Josie is moving back here, Maisie is here, all happy families eventually. That's why she's been keeping her distance.'

'Nonsense.'

'Charlie.' She stood between him and the table, her arms folded. 'She's not doing her best to help you and Maisie just because she's her teacher, you know.'

'Sally, it's none of your business, but I've actually hardly seen her this week.' He sighed. He'd not seen Lucy since the pizza night, when he'd very nearly forgotten all his good intentions, and he'd spent every day since hoping he'd spot her somewhere. He'd begun to feel a right idiot, peering up the road, slowing down as he passed her house, lingering outside the school on his way to home visits in a way that might have got him arrested anywhere else.

But he hadn't done the simple thing and knocked on her door or called her. He knew that he had to sort his life out first. It wasn't fair on Lucy to pretend that he was in any kind of position for a new relationship. And he didn't want a fling. She deserved more than that.

But he'd missed her more than he could ever have believed possible. Her smile, the bounce of her hair as she walked, her scent ... it was driving him nuts. It was even distracting him from his work, he'd turned up at the wrong farm yesterday and very nearly started to inseminate a herd of already pregnant cows – much to the farmer's amusement.

'Well I've seen her,' Sally wasn't going to give up. It was a quality of hers that was very useful in work related matters, and a pain in the neck when it came to discussing his personal life. Which he didn't want to do. 'And she's no happier than you are. You need to talk.'

Charlie scowled. 'You know what? You're getting worse than Elsie Harrington!'

'You look happy.'

'I am.' Lucy looked up from her position on the floor, arms full of puppy. She was. She actually felt more settled and positive about the future than she had for years. Apart from the tiny, very unsettling issue of the man in her garden.

'I'm really glad you said you'd stay. I like having you round.' Sally smiled.

Lucy looked back at the girl she'd got quite fond of. 'You know what? The feeling's mutual. How's it going with Jamie then?'

'Good.' Sally blushed. That was a new one. 'That was down to you.'

'It wasn't.'

'It was. If you hadn't been there backing me up on May Day I would never have dared push my luck.'

'Even after you'd drunk that much?' Lucy grinned. 'You must have had one hell of a hangover, mine was bad enough and I was pints behind you.'

'Even then.' She sighed. 'He is cute, I mean this might sound so bad, but I think I might be in love.'

'It's not so bad.' Lucy was pleased for her. It was hard having a crush on somebody from a distance. Excruciatingly painful when they didn't want you. But Sally and Jamie were meant to be, she was sure of it.

'You're going to end up keeping him, aren't you?' Sally grinned, trying to deflect her from saying more, and nodded at the puppy that had curled up on Lucy's lap.

'I never said...'

'You don't need to! And you want to keep somebody else, don't you?' She gazed out of the window, and Lucy scrambled to her feet and walked over, the puppy still in her arms.

Maisie was running around the garden squealing, with Charlie chasing her, and Molly the retriever running round in circles barking.

She wasn't going to answer that. She wasn't even going to think about it. It was better to talk about something else. 'I wish I could sort things for Elsie. She's sad; I'd like her to have a happy ever after too.'

'Everybody can't.' Sally patted the puppy. 'And she wouldn't be the person she is, if things had happened differently. I suppose things happen for a reason. Maybe one day she'll let somebody in on her secret.'

'She's getting old though. I'm sure it would help her to do it, but she says she doesn't want to upset things.'

'Maybe you should send your mum round, you know they might have common ground.'

'Maybe.' Lucy paused. 'Yeah you might have a good point,

and I'm sure she'll be over again to keep tabs on me and make sure I'm eating properly.'

There was a squeal from the garden, and they both looked up to see Charlie swinging his daughter through the air.

'Do you think we better go out there and warn him about health and safety?'

Lucy laughed. 'I don't know about that, but I suppose I better take the lemonade out that I promised.' She paused. 'Or rather you promised.'

Sally gave an innocent shrug of her shoulders. 'I just thought it was daft us all rushing off.'

'Mm, I bet you did. Come on, grab those biscuits.'

Lucy hesitated for a moment in the doorway, not really wanting to intrude on Charlie and Maisie, then felt Sally nudge her in the back. She opened her mouth to shout them over just as Molly barked out a warning.

There was a brown flash and Lucy tried to shout Charlie to grab Molly, or the loose dog, the last thing she wanted was a dog fight on her hands. But she didn't have time. With a yelp, the ball of brown fur charged past Maisie, dodged underneath Molly, and threw itself at Charlie's feet, collapsing in a squirming, squeaking heap, wriggling its bottom in the air.

Charlie laughed, bent slightly and it jumped. Straight into his arms. 'Oh, Roo.'

The little dog squirmed frantically. Licking Charlie's chin, his mouth, trying to wriggle its way higher so that it could nuzzle under his hair, all the time yelping and wuffling as though it couldn't believe what was happening.

Charlie was laughing, a broad grin on his face as he fought

to hold the wriggling dog still, and Lucy couldn't help but smile herself.

Eventually the dog calmed down, resting in his arms, occasionally throwing its head up as though to check it really was him, before licking his chin.

'Daddy, Daddy.' It was Maisie now who was leaping about. 'It's Roo, it's Roo.'

Lucy and Sally looked at each other, then over at Josie who had appeared round the side of the house. She didn't even glance their way, just gave a thumbs up at Charlie and disappeared.

'Well.' Sally put the drinks down on the table.

'Well.' Lucy didn't know what else to say.

Maisie wrestled the little dog from her dad's grasp and headed over to Lucy. 'This is Roo, he's named after the one that's friends with Pooh bear. You know? The one in Winnie the Pooh? I named him myself. I wanted to call him Pooh actually, but Mummy and Daddy said he was more like Roo cos he bounces so much.'

Lucy nodded. 'Roo is a perfect name, he's very bouncy.' She glanced up at Charlie, who had an apologetic grin on his face and his hand in his hair. 'I didn't know you had a dog.' It had seemed strange that he hadn't, but she'd assumed he was like her, not really wanting to get attached.

'No, er. We couldn't talk could we? I mean if you don't mind staying here Sal with Maisie, while me and Lucy take Roo for a walk?'

'No probs. Hey, Maisie, how about some lemonade?'

* * *

Charlie never said a word as they walked down the lane, he waited until they sat down on the small bench by the pond. The little dog jumped on his knee.

'He's cute.'

'He is, you can't believe how much I've missed the little terror. When Josie and I split, she said it wouldn't be fair on Maisie to take her dog away.' He launched into his speech as though he'd been preparing it all the way there. 'I know she had a point, but it was kind of the last straw. She'd taken everything.'

Lucy stroked the little dog, fondled the soft ears and tried to ignore the lump in her throat. She could understand. Perfectly. 'It's hard isn't it?'

'Yep.'

'So the dog, Roo, is staying with you when Maisie comes to visit?'

'Something like that.' He risked a glance in her direction, and looked a mix of sheepish and worried. 'What are your thoughts on one parent families?'

'Well, er.' She hadn't expected that change in direction. 'Mine was fine, I mean it's always nice for kids to have both their parents, but it doesn't always work that way.' Was this his way of telling her he definitely wasn't going to make it up with Josie? 'I mean, it's far more important that they're brought up in a happy and secure home and feel wanted. I'm sure Josie is doing a great job, and you'll be seeing Maisie as well, so it won't be any different really to if you were like a dad that worked away. And lots of people do that these days. Well, providing you don't bugger off to Australia, now that would be awkward.'

380

'Lucy, stop.'

She stopped.

'I'm not buggering off to Australia. I mean it wasn't a completely offhand comment, I did seriously think about it at first. I'd dreamt about it as a kid, so kind of thought why not? But I do actually quite like it here, it's fun having a mixed practice and being right in the middle of the down to earth stuff.'

'Like depriving alpacas of their balls?'

'Exactly, and,' he paused, 'if there was any chance of seeing my daughter then I wasn't going to go anywhere.' He paused. Put the dog on the floor. 'And she is my daughter, whatever the biology.'

'She is. But, well I was thinking...'

'Go on, spit it out.'

'You could have a DNA test if you wanted, you know, to be sure?'

'It did cross my mind, when Josie first told me, but I don't think I want to do it, Lucy. It's not important, is it? I mean, what are a few strands of DNA, being a father isn't about biology, is it?' He grinned self-consciously. 'It's more about coping with projectile vomiting, feeling your stomach scrunch up when you hear Dada for the first time, letting go of the back of the bicycle seat and watching her whizz along on her own.'

Lucy smiled. 'I'm not so sure about the vomiting bit, but I know what you mean. And you're right.'

'It's got a bit more complicated though.'

She was lost now, it had seemed pretty complicated before. Maybe Josie was going to move a lover in as well. Except

Charlie looked pretty chilled and happy on the whole, just a bit edgy.

'I need to tell you something. I wanted to before, but then I wanted to be sure, but now she's brought Roo.'

This was getting stranger by the second. What on earth did the dog have to do with anything?

'You know I told you that Josie wanted to do something more meaningful?'

'The fostering puppies thing?'

'She's going abroad, she wants to go and help out in places where animals really are suffering.'

'Oh.'

'She asked me the other day if Maisie could come and live with me for a while, six months initially, maybe more. Not immediately of course, we're going to build up to it. I guess that was her game plan all along, she just hadn't known what my reaction would be, and she wanted to be sure Maisie would be happy at school here. We had a long chat, tried to put some sticky plaster over the broken bridges.'

'Oh.' She'd been turned monosyllabic. 'Ah.' A thought had occurred, and broadened her vocabulary slightly. 'That's why she said she wasn't renting here? Why she'd been bringing Maisie over from home?' Why she'd asked Lucy to look after Charlie for her.

'Yep.'

'And why she brought the dog?'

'Yep.'

'Does Sally already know? Is that why you all arrived en masse?'

'I reckon so, though I honestly haven't told anybody. Not a word. Really. And Sally kind of ushered us all over.'

'She's getting as bad as Elsie. And.' She frowned. 'You can't keep anything quiet in this place. I'm the last person to know!'

'Well, that wasn't intentional, I mean you're the first person I've told, and I definitely didn't tell Miss Harrington, though she gave me a far too knowing look this morning. I thought for a minute she was going to hug me.'

Lucy laughed, despite all the conflicting thoughts that were at war in her head. 'She's lovely, though how she gets to know absolutely everything is incredible.' She watched the dog potter round at the edge of the pond, then jump back alarmed when the duck quacked at him. 'It's just a shame she doesn't let anybody know anything about her.'

'Meaning?'

'I really would like to sort things for Elsie, she's sad. She's got some kind of secret that really bothers her, but she says it's too late to put things right – whatever that means. There she is keeping an eye on everybody else, but who's doing the same for her? Sally suggested I get Mum to talk to her.'

'Well you could, but you can't push it if she doesn't want you to. Maybe she can't alter things, she's being sensible.'

'Sensible isn't always right though is it?' Sometimes you just had to jump into the unknown, take a risk. Although she was starting to wonder if she was over doing that side of things.

'Lucy, I asked what you thought about one parent families, because I was kind of hoping you might stick around and help this one out?'

'Oh.' She hadn't expected that. 'Do you really want me involved? You've got a busy summer ahead, Maisie to think about, work.'

'And you've got a lazy one, just pottering about like you teachers do.'

'Cheeky. Actually I've got a big summer reunion picnic to organise on the green.' It was surprising how keen everybody had been to help, once Timothy and Jim had spread the word, and the Right Honourable George had been the first person to officially accept his invitation as guest of honour. Things were looking up for the school, even if her own future still looked a bit dodgy.

'But you'll have done that before the end of term?'

'Well, yes.'

'So I thought maybe you could stop me going crazy. Lucy, this is a big thing for me, I don't want to cock it up.'

'You won't.' She put her hand over his. 'You'll muddle through.'

'I'd like you to be there to help, if you...'

'Really?' He was telling her that this wasn't complicated because of Josie, because his ex was still on the scene. He was telling her he was a parent. He was telling her he liked her. He was telling her that they had a chance of making this work. Maybe.

'Really.'

'I'd like that.' She could cope with that.

'So would Maisie, but mostly so would I. And you can protect me from Serena.' He nodded over the green to where Serena was standing, dressed up to the nines as normal.

'Ah, your fan club could get upset if I'm around more.'

'Good.' He looked straight into her eyes, and a little shiver ran through her body. 'Have you ever thought about the benefits of old fashioned courtship?'

'Chaperones and no sex?'

'I didn't mean that, I meant just taking it slow, getting to know each other, you know, seeing how it goes.'

'That sounds nice.' She leaned over and kissed his cheek, her cheeks flushing as she did so. But she didn't care. 'I wonder who that is with Serena? Maybe you don't need protecting, and this is under false pretences.'

There was a man with her, broad set. The couple were heading their way. Serena wobbling on her heels, clinging on to his arm.

'Chas, Chas.' She waved wildly.

'We're the only people here, and she has to do that?' Lucy hissed in Charlie's ear and he grinned, then put his hand on her knee. Which was rather nice, and slightly disturbing. It was sending all kinds of mixed messages to her body and brain.

Serena came to an unsteady halt in front of them. 'This is Charles, the vet I was telling you about.' She ignored Lucy, and simpered up at the man.

He looked, Lucy decided, rich. It wasn't just the expensive looking watch on his wrist, it was the confident air, the leather shoes. He almost smelled of money, if that was possible.

'So it's your fault I'm having to throw all masculinity out of the window is it?' He threw a playful punch at Charlie, then laughed. 'Better when she was carrying the bloody thing.'

Lucy looked down. Twinkle was at his feet. 'The things you bloody do for love, eh?'

Serena giggled, but looked happier than Lucy had ever seen her. 'This is my Thomas. We've decided to get together again, haven't we, darling?' She fluttered her eyelashes.

'We have.' He gave Charlie a warning look. 'Sorry, mate. Best man wins and all that.'

'Oh yes, yes. Best man...' Lucy could feel Charlie's body shaking slightly, as though he was stifling a laugh, which made it harder for her to keep her own in.

'We better be off, hadn't we, honey? I just wanted you to meet Charlie, he's been so good with Twinkle, haven't you? So good with his hands.'

Thomas frowned, Charlie gave an uncertain grin and Lucy kept her eyes on Roo, gritting her teeth to keep the smile off her face.

They watched the couple walk off across the green. 'Phew, that should cut down on the number of visits she makes to my surgery.'

'So you don't need me then?' Lucy glanced up and they shared a smile.

'I need you. I do, Lucy.' His grin slipped. 'I know I'm not perfect, and I know it's going to be tricky with all the changes. For a start I'm going to have to find somewhere bigger to stay, move out of the surgery, and I have to make sure Maisie feels secure, important. So I'm not a very good bet, really.'

'You wouldn't be a good bet if you weren't determined to look after her, Charlie.' She stood up, then held out a hand to him. He took it in his own much larger, capable hands and stood. He was inches away, close enough to kiss. 'Seeing how it goes sounds perfect.' Then she leant in, she couldn't help herself, and kissed him.

A Note from the Author

Dear Reader,

Thank you so much for picking up this copy of *Summer with the Country Village Vet*, I hope you enjoy your visit to Langtry Meadows with Lucy and Charlie!

This book has been waiting to be written for a long time. I've always loved animals (I dreamed of being a vet and following in the footsteps of James Herriot), and you may have noticed that all my books feature at least one four-legged friend. But when I started writing, one quote kept springing to mind:

'Never work with children or animals' *W. C Fields*

I can quite understand the sentiments behind these words! Both can be unpredictable, scene-stealing, mischievous, temperamental – and never quite do what we expect (or sometimes want), but don't we love them for it? They enrich our lives and touch our hearts. Young children and animals don't judge; they give unconditional love, they forgive, teach respect, acceptance, and loyalty. They look to us to do the right thing, to take care of them – and can sometimes give us optimism, and a reason to keep going.

In short, they give us hope – and a few tears of laughter and sadness along the way as well. Which I hope this story also does.

Happy reading!

Zara x

Acknowledgements

Big thanks to the HarperImpulse team for your enthusiasm and skill in bringing this story to life, especially to the amazing Charlotte Ledger, the incredible Emily Ruston, and unsung hero Samantha Gale. I feel tremendously lucky to be able to work with all of you.

Thanks to my agent, Amanda Preston, for your advice and support, and your enthusiasm for my country vet and the village of Langtry Meadows.

These acknowledgements wouldn't be complete without mentioning veterinary surgeon Mike Venables, who encouraged my aspirations and introduced me to the world of veterinary science – and cows!

And lastly, love and thanks to my family for your never-ending support (and supplies of coffee, cake and cava).